... ...emic is young British writer and teach... from Gr... Manchester. During his teaching care...r he dev...ped an interest in kukri blade fighting and martial ar... ...n general. Although an expert in chainsaw combat, Andy Remic prefers writing, hacking computer systems and the powerful adrenaline of motocross. WARHEAD is his third novel.

Find out more about Andy Remic at www.andyremic.com and register at www.orbitbooks.co.uk for the free monthly newsletter and to read about other Orbit authors.

By Andy Remic

SPIRAL
QUAKE
WARHEAD

WARHEAD

ANDY REMIC

orbit

www.orbitbooks.co.uk

ORBIT

First published in Great Britain in October 2005 by Orbit

The author gratefully acknowledges permission
to quote from the following:

My Country
Words and Music by Justin Sullivan and Stuart Morrow
© 1985 Attack Attack Music Ltd
Intersong Music Ltd, London W6 8BS
Reproduced by permission of International Music Publications Ltd
All Rights Reserved

A CIP catalogue record for this book
is available from the British Library

ISBN 1 84149 174 8

Typeset in Plantin by M Rules
Printed and bound in Great Britain by
Clays Ltd, St Ives plc

Orbit
An imprint of
Time Warner Book Group UK
Brettenham House
Lancaster Place
London WC2E 7EN

www.orbitbooks.co.uk

DEDICATION

This one is for the Tioda Boys, Paul Rem and Darren Ralph – for a childhood filled with laughter, (bad!) music and an eternity of happy memories which can never be taken away. And yes, our songs *will* last for ever!

```
  641
  110
  160
   89
  172
  119
   62
  118
   64
  119
3 9 2
─────
17 4 6
1896
```

ACKNOWLEDGEMENTS

Nothing is created in a vacuum, and as always I would like to thank my loving wife Sonia, my little boy BIG JOE, my family and friends, and everybody who has made this work possible. I salute you all!

CONTENTS

PART TWO: DEUS EX MACHINA

WARHEAD

PROLOGUE

THE SCOURGE OF WAR

It began with a contract.

A building contract worth 939 *billion* US dollars.

The sleek black Manta screamed through the heavens at over a thousand klicks an hour, armoured engine ports hissing and thumping, exhausts vibrating with metal torture. Carter gave a nasty sideways glance towards Mongrel as the sun broke in a sudden explosion over the distant horizon, its rays sparkling through the tinted cockpit and radiating fingers of violet iridescence over the serrated steel-blade skyline that defined New York City.

'ETA one minute,' growled Mongrel as tracer started to streak and flash from the urban landscape below; heavy-calibre rounds smashed up from anti-aircraft guns and localised groups of small-arms fire. Thunder seemed to rumble in the distance. Explosive purple flashes flickered, lighting the underside of the fist-bunched clouds in a surreal display. 'I've got SAMs coming in; get your shit together, Carter.'

'Let's do it.' Carter hit the cockpit release, which folded neatly back on tiny hydraulic sighs. Wind thumped in, making the small fighter rock violently; Carter stood, gloved hands grasping alloy rings riveted into the fighter's flanks as Mongrel banked the aircraft and Carter felt suddenly – weightless. His eyes widened and his breath was ripped away in a ragged gasp as Manhattan rushed beneath him. The Sentinel Corporation tower block raced towards him. Tracer streaked all around, coloured bursts tossed carelessly into the dawn sky on high-explosive projectiles.

'*Da vai!*' screamed Mongrel, but Carter was already leaping. The fighter roared over him and was instantly gone – and the wind cracked him in the face like a brick. He dived, and the Sentinel tower block sped towards him.

Carter armed the Spiral Parasite, felt it buzz beneath his gloved fingers as the world spun crazily around him . . . and fired: it rocketed into the lip of the concrete roof, tiny alloy teeth chewing to burrow deep. Carter was jerked violently and abruptly, swinging in a huge arc on an umbilical cord of two-millimetre TitaniumIII cable. His speed carried him forward and around with the stepped world of Manhattan flashing below him as a tiny buzz screeched like an insect in his earpiece. His dive decelerated as the Parasite hummed in his fist, and his downward trajectory slowed as his boots thumped against the vertical dark glass wall of the Sentinel Corporation's New York HQ.

Carter grunted, all wind knocked from him. He glanced quickly around. The tower block fell away beneath him for a hundred storeys. Far below, NYC was a toy town, with hundreds of tower blocks staggering away in huge stepping stones. Carter's M24 carbine was slung

4

tight against his back, his battered Browning 9mm HiPower holstered on his hip, and he grinned.

'Knock, knock.'

Kicking himself backwards, he swung for a moment, aimed and threw a tiny HPG, which connected with the black glass fifteen metres to his left, with the dial set to CFE – concentrated funnel explosion – it was designed to create a rapid entry point for Carter. He averted his gaze, and there came a sharp *crack*. Carter walked himself across the vertical wall, buffeted by the wind, nostrils wrinkling involuntarily at the cold chemical stink from the pressure grenade's explosive – and blinked in astonishment.

The explosive had failed to penetrate the Sentinel tower block – and failed even to shatter the glass. Which was unusual: an HPG could eat a ten-metre hole in twelve-inch armour plate.

'Son of a *bitch*.'

Bullets ricocheted with howls and sparks to Carter's right and he flinched, feeling suddenly extremely vulnerable.

Carter looked around frantically, hanging on his tiny spider's thread. Gritting his teeth, he began to climb as Mongrel banked the Manta far above, and the tiny matt black fighter went into a steep dive, its heavy machine guns thundering.

Carter kept climbing.

Reflected in the dark glass of the tower block, the world seemed on fire behind him. More Spiral fighters tore through the glittering heavens, tanks rumbled through the streets far below, crushing cars under heavy steel tracks, and Spiral soldiers fought Nex killers across the insanely ordered grid of streets and buildings that was modern New York City.

Carter focused on staying alive. The Parasite buzzed beneath his gloves and he carried on walking his way up the skyscraper, boot soles squealing in protest. Within a few minutes he reached the roof, leapt onto the galvanised flat roof rim and turned, inhaling deeply and looking down into the Valley of the Shadow of Death.

Bullets spun up towards him, tracer rounds trailing streamers of fire past his gaze. Carter dropped to a crouch and turned. The roof spread out before him on a gentle incline that rose to a tapered point – on which flashed the steady pulse of a bright white light as a warning to air traffic. The roof panels were formed from corrugated alloy, undulating away and criss-crossed by galvanised grey walkways with handrails for the use of servicing personnel. Huge extraction fans stood in grille-masked steel enclosures, and smoke poured from a narrow silver chimney beside a scattering of high-tech satellite dishes.

Carter's boots pounded heavily as he made a charge for the black-alloy lattice-work doorway—

Which burst open, three masked Nex spilling out onto the concourse. The butt of Carter's Browning thumped against the palm of his hand as his bullets tore the face from the lead Nex and crushed the chest of the second, leaving it on its knees.

The third Nex had disappeared.

Carter changed mags, his back against the ridged alloy columns of a satellite dish's support struts. His head snapped right, then left, eyes narrowing, tongue moistening dry lips. His breathing calmed and his boot found purchase against the Sentinel skyscraper's rooftop as the Nex with the caved-in chest coughed and vomited a stream of blood and mucus into a large puddle to one side.

'*You want me to do it?*' came the cool voice of Kade.

'I don't need your help, *brother.*'

'*Yes, but I need you . . . Come on, don't be such a spoilsport, let me kill them − I will take them all! It's months since I imbibed the copper stench of blood. An age since I rolled from dreams of pumping bullets into unprotected faces, watching soft, rotting fish-flesh part and the handsome, neatly carved flush of crimson spurting from a perfectly pulped brain . . .*'

Carter rolled, his Browning describing an arc that ended with a—

Bullet. The Nex tried to flip, but was a nanosecond too slow; the bullet entered high in its throat, slightly to one side but still destroying the larynx. The Nex sat down slowly, hands pressed against the heavy flow of spurting blood, eyes swivelling up to stare at Carter. He strode forward, cautious gaze scanning left and right. Above, Mongrel's Manta screamed and accelerated with a burst of stinking aviation exhaust. Carter looked down at the Nex, gazing into the soft glow of the copper eyes − fixed on him in anger, and hatred, and loathing. His steps left imprints in the Nex's blood. He rubbed at his mouth with the back of his gloved hand and clamped a boot on the Nex's MP38 sub-machine gun.

He aimed the Browning.

Carter thought briefly of Natasha. Natasha, the mother of his baby boy; Natasha, lying cold and dead in a grave over two thousand miles away, flowers withering against the simple black marble cross bearing no inscription. Carter's teeth bared in a grimace that displayed his burning need for revenge.

The bullet smashed through the Nex's nose, spattering its brains across the damp roof from the back of its shattered skull; the body flopped limp.

Carter should have felt better. Should have felt *avenged*. But he didn't.

'*We need to get this thing done*,' said Kade.

Carter looked deep within himself; looked into the glossy black emotionless eyes of Kade set in a face that was his own, only seen through a much darker mirror. 'Yes.'

With a blink Carter spiralled back into reality.

Took a deep breath.

And headed for the stairs . . . and Durell beyond.

The Spiral mainframe had decoded the signals thirty-five minutes earlier. All units had been scrambled – not *available* units, but *all* units. The call had gone out – Code Silver. They had received the coordinates of Durell's exact location in New York.

Carter crouched in the darkness on the stairs, the only light a stroboscope of spinning red, flickering on-off, on-off, on-off. He moved forward, boots smooth against the alloy and eyes scanning for sensors. His ECube rattled in his pocket, digitally disabling a hundred different detection sequences. And yet – Carter knew. Knew that *they* knew he was there.

Carter grinned a malicious grin and hefted his trusty, battered Browning 9mm, his loyal and steadfast friend – the one thing in his life which had never – *ever* – let him down.

Carter moved down the stairs – expecting a fight, and wondering where the hell the rest of the Spiral squads had got to; Carter was merely one among many. And yet now he felt suddenly alone . . .

He reached a door. Behind it he could hear voices.

Bracing himself, he lifted his leg and delivered a kick which thumped open the steel portal, revealing . . .

Antarctica

16 kilometres south, Mount Erebus Base Camp

Sunlight gleamed against slick ice. Corrugated waves rolled off across an endless plain leading to distant mountains.

Metal gleamed under the witch-light of a cold and frosty Antarctic day. A snub nose emerged, followed by a smooth tapered cone edged with four delicate fins. Ice fell away, tumbling to the frozen plain as the missile rose on powerful hydraulics. Motors whirred and engines ignited, fire flowering out against the ice and briefly scorching it black before it melted. There came a roar and the missile suddenly leapt into the sky like a fish escaping the jaws of sudden death snapping at it beneath the surface of a still lake. It powered away on twin jets of glowing purple into the cold vast bleak sky.

The ice continued to crack, revealing subsurface black alloy blocks: missile batteries, containing M1270-k launchers, advanced 2ti radar and tiny elegant Engagement Control Stations.

Another missile nose appeared. Then off to one side of the broken web came another, and they were joined by still more, until the whole plain of ice seemed to be covered with the tapered, eerily ascending bulks of TitaniumIII warheads – and their gleaming single-stage rockets.

Within seconds the air was filled with sleek, ice-streaming bodies as two hundred glistening missiles, each the size of a PAC-5, arced up into the big blue like a spreading plague, engines thundering as the glinting machines rapidly accelerated and dispersed – each one targeting a specific destination.

And then it was done and it could never be *un*done.

Namibia, Africa

Global Army [GA5] camp, 35 kilometres west of the Kalahari Desert

The missile carrying the 5000-kiloton warhead flashed from the sky's fathomless blue vaults. A thousand metres above the huge structure of the combined Global Army HQ, on the plains of south-western Africa where 2,000,000 amassed troops of all nationalities were camped, along with enough military hardware to conquer any land mass on Earth – the HighJ explosives detonated, creating a massive shock wave which propelled plutonium-239 shrapnel fragments into a sphere. They struck pellets of beryllium and polonium at the sphere's core, which in turn started the basic initial fission reaction accelerating quickly to create supercritical mass – and causing the trigger-bomb to explode . . .

This initial explosion took 560-*billionths* of a second.

The warhead's cylinder casing was cast from uranium-238. Within this tamper squatted the fuel for the explosion – lithium deuteride, and a hollow rod of plutonium-239. As the implosion fission device exploded, this trigger released lethal X-rays which heated the interior of the bomb and the tamper, causing the uranium-238 to expand and burn away forcing pressure towards the lithium deuteride; these compression shock waves initiated fission within the plutonium rod which in turn ejected radiation, heat and neutrons, the neutrons impacting with the fuel to create tritium. As a result, deuterium-deuterium and tritium-deuterium fusion reactions began producing excesses of heat, radiation and neutrons – and the neutrons from this first fusion induced fission in the uranium-238 pieces from the tamper. Fission of tamper and shield occurred, producing yet more radiation and heat, and causing the nuclear warhead to

explode.

The fission reaction took another fifty-billionths of a second.

The Global Army – its soldiers, tanks, helicopters, fighter jets, jeeps, trucks, weapons, artillery, ammunition, tents, support staff – was immediately and utterly vaporised.

What detritus remained on the outskirts of the blast after the initial ignition was fused into a sea of molten glass. The world merged with the desert sands in a bright white blinding of insanity and death.

Moscow, Russia

Red Square: Spiral and RFSS HQ

Rekalavich reached the entrance to the Sp_bunker in the narrow back alleyway. He stood, chest heaving, stars of exhaustion dancing in front of his eyes as he fought to halt himself from retching. And then, by some unbidden instinct, his eyes lifted, squinting into the darkened sky.

Something, the tiniest of sounds, intruded on his thoughts as a glint appeared in the sky.

Realisation kicked him viciously in the heart and he stumbled backwards, tripping and tumbling and bouncing down the long narrow stone staircase, falling and slamming his way down and down, deep beneath the ground as outside—

Outside, a white flash ignited the sky.

An 800 k.p.h. blast wave screamed outwards, exerted pressure smashing everything within its roaring path and pulverising all that it met above the ground for twenty kilometres. At the hypocentre of the thermonuclear explosion, the rising and expanding fireball reached 480 million degrees Fahrenheit and vaporised the collapsing Cathedral of Vasily the Blessed. The initial blast destroyed Red Square, the Spiral and RFSS HQ and all buildings and life instantly within a six-kilometre radius.

The sky became illuminated by a surreal, blue-green tint. A writhing column of fire and dust and smoke climbed steadily into the sky, four kilometres wide at its base and curving majestically upwards; colours flickered and danced within the mammoth tower, grey at the base, amber at the heart and pure white capping the rising column until suddenly it sprouted a huge mushroom cap which surged up and out, driving the column upwards.

Thunder seemed to be churning the ground and there was a roar of awesome destruction, wrought by the hand of man.

New York, USA

Sentinel5 Tower, The Sentinel Corporation

'Ah, Mr Carter. I'd like to say "I've been expecting you", but that would be *so* clichéd.'

Carter uncoiled, eyes scanning left and right, Browning held high against his chest. The entire top floor of the Sentinel Corporation's New York HQ was a single high-ceilinged room – filled end to end with a dazzling array of high-tech next-gen equipment. Radar and guidance systems, military servers, with wall-sized banks of glittering lights, mammoth, free-standing plasma displays sporting spinning maps of cities, countries, continents; distant squatting banks of military simulators, gleaming and silver on silent resting hydraulics. On steel benches sat prototype engines, glittering machines of incredible complexity, and a small black platter on which nestled a tiny, inoffensive-looking frost-hazed black cube.

Durell, with his hood thrown back to reveal the terrible deformities of his twisted face, smiled with a twisting and a *crackling* of flesh, and stared at Carter with slitted copper eyes. In one deformed claw he held a tiny silver disc which he squeezed – and there came a hiss of superheated air as Carter was suddenly surrounded by a haze, a gentle green glow . . . He was caught in some kind of force field, a cube of pulsating energy which ensnared him from all sides. Carter started firing, Browning slapping against the palm of his hand as he dropped to one knee. But the bullets were caught in the haze of the field, spinning gently as Durell turned his back on Carter and moved towards a long alloy panel.

Slowly, Carter uncurled and glanced quickly around, a bad taste nestling in his mouth as he watched the still-spinning bullets *melt* and drip slowly to the floor. What would it do to a human body? he thought.

'You are just in time,' said Durell, pressing a small black button. To Carter's left, the QIV Quantech Edition military processor began to hum. Durell laughed. 'In fact, this is a *perfection* of timing. Especially for you, Mr Carter. Especially for our oldest adversary – and, dare I say, *friend*? You will be here, at the beginning, at the end, you will witness our triumph – you will witness *my* triumph.'

13

Durell's head had lowered, his voice dropping to little more than a whisper, eyes fixed like bayonets on Carter's expression.

'What are you *doing*?' hissed Carter, filled with horror, submerged in bile.

Screens, previously black squares of obsidian, flared into colourful life along one wall. Cities sprang into view, aerial views displayed in real time from locations across the globe. Durell moved towards the window and looked down over Manhattan. It was bathed beneath him in early-morning sunlight. Durell gave a deep sigh.

Carter's frowning gaze was dragged to his left, to the glittering images on the screens: to the images of twisting, speeding missiles.

Carter changed the magazine in his Browning and moved slowly forward, towards the walls of his hazy prison. He reached out with the tip of the Browning, and almost had his arm torn from its socket as the field wrenched the gun from his hand – and slowly melted it. Carter watched as liquid metal ran down the inside of the ethereal green glow and pooled near his feet.

'I hope Spiral have a good life-insurance policy,' said Durell softly. Carter's eyes lifted to see—

To see a tiny glitter against the blue sky, a fleeting needle of mercury. And then there came a flash of such brightness, such *intensity* that even through the heavily shielded windows of the Sentinel Corporation skyscraper Carter flinched, dropped to his knees and knelt there, arms hanging loose, useless, mouth open and incredulous eyes filled with sudden tears.

'No,' Carter croaked.

Durell turned. 'But yes,' he whispered, as a wall of fire smashed across New York, powered screaming towards them – and left a rising cloud of pulped and pulverised debris, atomised and crushed and pulled into the all-consuming mushroom cloud.

Carter knelt, eyes dark and hollow and fixed disbelievingly on the furnace of devastation. Durell turned, slitted copper eyes watching him closely, and Carter thought:

We are going to die.

We are going to fucking die.

Kade was silent in his brain, observing as the blast wave hit the Sentinel5 tower from which they watched in trepidation. Carter's stare was dragged back to the screens and he saw missiles flashing through the glittering blue atmosphere of the planet called Earth.

The tower shook. Shuddered. Rocked.

Outside, the world before them was excluded; covered by a death veil; drowned by a sea of ash and fire.

'You are quite safe,' came Durell's soothing voice. 'These towers were built specifically for this day.'

'To survive a nuclear blast?' spat Carter.

'Yes – only a nominal yield, but yes. After all, nothing without such a design brief would be able to survive *that . . .*' The screen flickered as satellite scanners kicked in and Carter looked down on a desert. His stomach churned as he saw the fused and glowing glass, the edges of a crystallised wasteland, the charred half-corpses of an army lingering at its edges. And he saw that the Global Army, the mammoth united worldwide conglomeration of the soldiers and weapons of all nations formed to combat the Nex and Durell had been utterly – totally – destroyed.

Carter vomited onto the smooth stone floor as the building around him shook with thunder and below him millions of people died in the raging fireball.

There came a *fizz*.

The force field surrounding Carter disintegrated and

15

Durell motioned to two Nex warriors carrying Austrian Steyr TMP 9mm sub-machine guns. They moved forward on well-balanced heels, clad in simple body-hugging grey uniforms, their faces pale and white, eyes copper and burning. They approached Carter. One reached down with a gloved hand and Carter's face snapped up, lips covered with spittle and vomit. The long black knife in his fist slammed into the Nex's eye. The dark steel thrust hard and deep into the brain beyond. Blood spattered against Carter, pumping out over his fist, and he had the Steyr TMP in his grasp even as the Nex began to fall, the sub-machine gun's strap caught across its shoulder. Carter squeezed the trigger and a swarm of bullets ate into the second Nex, drilling a slick, bloody groove up its chest and caving in its throat. It flipped to the ground, fingers clawing at the metal in its flesh. It screamed long and shrill.

Carter rose to his feet, face covered in speckles of blood, eyes wide and wild and filled not just with anger and hatred but also with a terrible emptiness.

What good? What good now?

You are just *too late* my friend . . .

Durell turned, mouth opening to show deformed teeth within the circular void of his black mouth. His tongue was like a tiny fish. And he was smiling in *victory*.

Carter wanted to speak.

But he did not. Could not.

There were simply no words.

Outside, the conflagration caused by the thermonuclear explosion continued to roar.

Carter closed his eyes, and pulled the trigger.

*

16

SIU Transcript

CLASSIFIED NK54/nuke277/SPECIAL INVESTIGATIONS UNIT
ECube transmission excerpt
Date: November 2XXX

On 5 November 2XXX two hundred nuclear warheads with varying yields struck strategic military and civilian targets within the space of 35 minutes. Targets included heavily militarised cities such as London, Paris, New York, Tokyo, plus a variety of vast armies and stockpiles of military hardware.

The destruction was on a vast scale. The loss of human life runs into billions.

During the emergency, World Agencies were crippled. They were unable to do anything about these targeted strikes; all fail-safes failed, anti-nuke satellites swam blindly in near-space orbits, ground silos refused to operate: all were under the seemingly omniscient control of the QIV cubic processor. This fully sentient machine finally delivered its threatened promises.

Shortly after the staggered nuclear strikes, a further wave of long-range missile warheads was delivered; this time they did not contain bombs but advanced chemical agents named Half-life Accelerators. These chemicals were scattered over strike zones, and over the following months quickly reduced dangerous radiation levels to a moderate and effectively survivable level.

The self-proclaimed perpetrator of these nuclear attacks was the former Spiral agent named Durell.

World governments have been assimilated and are run with pro-Nex staffing; centres of control, trade and finance [CTF] have been shifted to the many Sentinel Corporation towers which adorn most major world cities. From these Sentinel towers Durell now rules his empire.

More to follow>>

SIU Transcript

CLASSIFIED SG54/nuke976/SPECIAL INVESTIGATIONS UNIT
ECube transmission excerpt
Date: December 2XXX

SpiralGRID/GRID network update:

All major Spiral installations have been destroyed.

All Spiral HQs have been destroyed.

Personnel numbers have been reduced by 75%

and Spiral are operating on a skeleton structure.

All Spiral core mainframes have been destroyed.

Sub-system mainframes remain operational.

Secondary controllers remain operational.

SpiralGRID has been activated and is now live; it is fully on-line.

With the SpiralGRID active, covert operations are being allowed on an accelerating and growing scale. This is being closely monitored. It is suspected that Spiral contains several spies who have leaked critical data, thus allowing such an incredible and devastating attack.

[Note: SpiralGRID is PlanZ. The last line in defence. The final safeguard that nobody ever dreamed would have to be used: a vast network of underground tunnels controlled by the sub-system mainframes; this is what keeps Spiral operational. This is Spiral's hiding place. This is Spiral's last resort and its final hope. Let us pray it does not become its tomb.]

Durell and the Nex are aware of the GRID's existence. They seek to wipe out Spiral once and for all.

We must hope the enemy never discovers its secrets. That is why the rooting out of traitors is KEY PRIORITY.

The current media propaganda for HATE is intensifying; Durell's empire is seeking to rewrite history, offering the people of the world a fictionalised past. Durell proposes - via FactAds - that HATE was a US-military-created biological weapon - unleashed in the wake of the nuclear dominance, which he claims were nothing more than acts of gross incompetence by world governments.

It has been rumoured than an 'antidote', an anti-HATE agent known provisionally as EDEN is being designed alongside HATE and could be used to free humanity from their current thrall. This is an unsubstantiated rumour, but nevertheless contains a high probability factor - when analysing the manner in which Durell first nuked cities, and then used Half-life Accelerators to reduce radiation levels in order to achieve his desired long-term effects.

Priority codes:

873267865098634876487 3648

897635879643897689764 3534

879689634897654378965 8734

890709876987653223234 3223

a] GRID protection

b] Spy termination

c] EDEN confirmation

More to follow>>

[FIVE YEARS PASS]

ADVERTISING FEATURE

The TV-ProjU sparkled into life with a digital buzz of humming phosphorescence. Images spun and leapt, dissolving and then reanimating into the mercury logo of HIVE Media Productions . . .

Scene slowly pans [ground-level shot]: a wide-shot pan of crumbling, devastated cities, buildings half-collapsed and swaying eerily in a bleak holocaust wind; the roads lie cratered, strewn with blocks of concrete and twisted, rusting steel wires.

Scene morphs: into the city perimeter, where huge coils of raze-wire protect a wilderness of green, lush, verdant grasslands beyond. Trees stand swaying in the breeze and grass rolls down to salmon-rich streams. Guards stand to attention, monitoring the checkpoints, the black-masked Nex and gas-mask-protected JT8s inscrutable behind their individualised protection – and nodding knowingly. These are the Guardians of HATE – and the final barrier between a habitable urban landscape and the biological wilderness of No Man's Land beyond . . .

[sombre deep male voice]
– Do you remember a time when you could walk hand in hand with your children through the long grass, the swaying shrubs, the sighing trees?
– Do you remember a time when you could breathe the purity of nature?
– But then came the incompetent military devastation of HATE – a biological weapon spawned from the loins of an incompetent military bureaucracy, ejaculated from the army science labs like alien semen to poison billions of square miles of organic

*landscape – **Trapping YOU** – in towns and cities – unable to commute, unable to enjoy the God-given countryside, unable to sample your FREEDOM.*

Scene slowly dissolves [into]: a sterile laboratory environment filled with serious-looking men and Nex scientists, working together like brothers, wiggling test tubes, poring over charts, nodding in grim satisfaction at yet another wonderful and incredible breakthrough . . .

– Well, all this can change . . . here at HIVE Labs we are close to a CURE, close to an ANTIDOTE to the terrible bio-weapon known as HATE. We have invented an almost magical chemical called EDEN, a substance which will obliterate this HATEful disease, this cancer of the green world . . . EDEN will bring love, and peace, and most of all . . . freedom!

Scene morphs [from HIVE Labs to-]: grass, swaying at toe-level, sounds of giggling children, brown, black and white feet running towards the camera as we pull back, showing children of *all* nationalities skipping and running through the grass, breathing the once-polluted HATE air. They stop at a convenient picnic table under a spreading oak tree. Mum and dad (an inter-racial marriage; mum with knowing smile, dad with chirping laptop) hand out cream-cheese sandwiches and strawberry ice cream.

– You WILL walk free through the world once more! You WILL help the rebirth of a new EDEN!!! DONATE TODAY! HIVE LABS NEEDS YOUR SUPPORT!! . . . To make the world a greener place. Your unborn babies deserve a cleaner, HATE-free future!
don't be filled with HATE . . . learn to live in a new EDEN!!

SCENE DISSOLVES TO SILVER

PART ONE

COVENANT

no rights were ever given to us by
the **grace of god**
no **rights** were ever given by some
united nations clause
no rights were ever given by some
nice guy at the top
our rights they were bought by all
the **blood**
and all the **tears** of all our
grandmothers, grandfathers
before . . .

> My Country
> New Model Army

CHAPTER 1

SACRIFICE

Carter sat staring at the Mediterranean. The sky was black, strewn with a scatter of uncut diamonds. The sea crashed rhythmically against the rough jagged rocks.

Beneath him, the patio was hard and cool, and his hand dropped, fingers tracing the delicate contours of honeycombed terracotta as his free hand lifted the bottle of Lagavulin to his lips. He took a long, burning sip. The whisky warmed his belly, and Carter smiled, eyes fixed impassively on the distant sea.

Too much shit, he thought.

Too many years, and too many deaths.

What the hell have we done to our world?

Just what the hell have we created?

He turned at an insignificant sound, a battered Browning 9mm appearing in his fist. Samson padded close, the chocolate Labrador rubbing his velvet nose against Carter's ribs and looking up with soft brown eyes. Carter placed the Browning on the patio and rubbed at Samson's grey-peppered muzzle.

'Getting old, buddy,' he said and Samson gave a little whine, tilting his head in contemplation. Carter rubbed at the dog's ears as a cool breeze blew in from the sea – making him shiver. 'And I'm not really sure who I'm talking about . . . you or me? Both of us, I think, my friend.' He chuckled softly, releasing a long pent-up sigh and feeling nostalgia stab sharply at his drifting memories.

In the distance, fireworks suddenly erupted. A silver shower, sparkling briefly and illuminating the rolling waves. They disappeared, and another shower ignited, sparkles of red and blue and green. Carter caught the retort of the explosive: crackles peppered the distance and concussive bangs made Carter shiver.

What the hell have they got to celebrate? The world's a mess. A living nightmare.

Carter crawled to his feet, sliding the second-hand Browning into the cargo pocket of his knife-cut combat shorts, and lifted the Lagavulin to his lips. He took another sip – just a small one this time. He didn't allow the alcohol to run freely any more; not like it had when Natasha died. Whisky had flowed like a river, then, into his shattered, welcoming remains.

No, he limited the alcohol fiercely now – had to, with his boy to look after.

Carter's steel gaze swept the area before his small house, built on a lonely section of deserted coast on the island of Cyprus. The landscape rolled down from a heavy copse of citrus trees to the rocky seafront and a small stretch of splintered, sandy causeway. In the distance more fireworks showered from the yacht. Carter shaded his eyes and could make out the flashing silhouette of the sleek white craft. He weighed the whisky bottle thoughtfully, and wondered at the foolishness of the partying people on the boat: in the current climate of war, terrorism and post-Nex domination, *fireworks* were the last thing a man needed. Not unless he wanted a quick return-hail of bullets and a black-clad Nex squad banging on his cabin door.

Ducking inside, Carter padded in bare feet along the tiled marble floors and deposited the whisky bottle on the kitchen worktop. Gritting his teeth stubbornly, he moved like a ghost through the darkness with Samson close behind, halting at the door to the bedroom. He stopped, head tilted, listening. Within, he could hear soft breathing.

Carter pushed open the door, allowing a little moon-light to spill tentatively into the room. He moved forward and stopped by the low bed, gazing down at the pale circle of Joe's face, serene in sleep, eyes closed, lips pursed, chest rising and falling in a steady rhythm.

Carter knelt and placed a hand against the warmth of his son's skin. He felt tears well gently, pressure building within his chest, but he pushed them back and smiled instead. For this boy sleeping below him was the only reason Carter still lived, the one thing that had kept him sane; his son was why Carter had not taken his own life.

I am scared of dying now, he realised. Not because of pain, anguish, suffering. Not because of bullets or knives. Carter didn't care a damn for pain – he had survived enough, lived through enough to understand that. But he now felt a pervasive fear of death – because if he died, then he would never see his son grow up; he would never witness those first moments of which there were so many, moments which would flood his heart with gold and make life in the bomb-tangled mash of the modern world under heavy Nex law and the stranglehold of HATE . . . well, make it *worthwhile*.

Carter kissed his son on the forehead, picturing the

young face with its broad cheeky grin and sparkling bright excited eyes from earlier that day; a face which held the ghost of Natasha.

Natasha.

Her face swam at the forefront of his mind. He could feel her lips brush his neck. He could taste her sweet honey. He could smell the autumn breeze of her musk.

All gone, he thought. All dead and gone.

Carter drank. The powerful flavour caressed his lips, burned his throat and warmed him from oesophagus to belly. His head swam a little and as sleep claimed him, tiny flickers of a twisted, deformed face haunted his slowly sinking conscience. Carter curled into a ball then, wound himself into an embryo and Samson put his big grizzled head on Carter's feet and together they dropped tumbling into a deep well of sleep where Durell waited, where a savage history waited. Carter flowed unwillingly back to the Syndicate HQ in New York and stood there, could still feel the cold trigger of the Steyr under his merciless finger and oblivion blowing a Harmattan in his soul.

Bullets sprayed from the gun, pounding at Durell's merged insect flesh as the gathered Nex turned automatic weaponry towards him and bullets hissed and spat past Carter's face. The Spiral agent turned, leaping a low alloy bench and racing for the door. Bullets chewed alloy in his wake, hot shavings stinging his skin, and he slammed into the stairwell and pounded up the stairs.

Outside, New York had been obliterated and a hot wind blew. Carter had stood on top of the world surveying the destruction of a nuclear warhead; the destruction of Man.

Jets roared, and Mongrel's Manta howled into view and a cable hissed through the brittle baked air; Carter's gloves had caught this umbilical, this lifeline, and as Nex spilled out onto the roof behind him with fire-spitting guns Mongrel had pulled Carter's bleak-eyed hollow carcass to safety . . .

All gone.

All dead and gone.

Carter stirred uneasily in his sleep. Outside the fireworks gradually died, the yacht glided across the inky black waters and was lost in the swallowing maw of the darkness.

Carter kick-started the 699cc KTM in a burst of LVA fumes. The motor roared harshly for a moment and then fell to a rough fast idle. He revved the bike hard, grinning for a moment like a child with a new toy.

Joe was staying in a nearby local village, a modest gathering of five white-walled houses surrounding an ancient, crumbling stone well; his nanny was a tiny, twisted old lady named Mrs Fickle. Mrs Fickle was a widow, small in stature but gnarled and powerful – like a stunted old oak. In a heavily lined face sat sparkling blue eyes, a vivid contrast to the surrounding results of decades of dermatological abuse by the sun. Carter trusted her wholly with his son. With his life. Not just because of her squat iron strength which had surprised many a larger man, and not just because of her mule-like stubbornness; but because of her unquestionable ability with a double-barrelled sawn-off shotgun. Like the one she kept under her bed. And the one behind the settee. And the one mounted above the fireplace.

Mrs Fickle was Spiral. Retired.

Carter gently eased the bike across the ground, which was still damp from the previous night's drifting light rainfall; he wheel-spun the powerful machine up the rise, out onto the rough dirt and the broken tarmac track beyond.

33

He cruised through the cool air, bike rumbling and shocks pounding beneath him as he rode over ruts and rocks.

Cyprus, Carter's new port of exile, had suffered somewhat during Durell's rise to world domination. It had been attacked – during the height of the Nex onslaught – mainly because it boasted a number of British troops and a harbour filled with British Royal Navy warcraft. But the island had taken no nuclear or biological strikes, being reckoned a low-priority target despite the ships and soldiers stationed there.

However, the town of Paphos on the coast did have a Nex garrison, housed in a smaller version of a Sentinel Corporation tower, and as a result Nex patrols roamed the island, sometimes together with the savage JT8s, police murder squads. They were continually searching for anti-Nex military personnel, REB Squads or Spiral sympathisers – although the quiet island of Cyprus gave the Nex little cause for concern.

Carter rode with the utmost care, constantly on the lookout for the black FukTruks and 4x4 vehicles favoured by the Nex and JT8s. His mission was to scout the Nex, keep track of their patrols and monitor them for any changes to patterns; and he regularly called to check on his friends, Ed the Sniper, old Tomas and Mary, and, of course, the indomitable Mrs Fickle. All supplied him with Spiral goodies that no ex-Spiral operative could do without . . . ammunition, updated ECube codes and complex HPG internals.

He rode for an hour, and with the sun hiding behind heavy bunched fists of cloud, Carter felt chilled. Keeping off the main roads, and away from any obvious Nex waypoints, Carter's bike growled its way through heavy woodland and rolling rocky hills near to Tomas and

Mary's farm; he rode until he reached an off-road vantage point where he parked up the bike beneath the spreading branches of an olive tree. Dismounting, Carter moved to the edge of the skyline and lay flat, easing himself up until he was looking down over the distant slopes which fell away to the small town of Paphos and the heavily built-up district by the harbour. The Nex Sentinel Tower stood apart, in a hundred-metre concrete square, its flanks a mixture of cool white and glass which Carter knew from personal experience was not only TNT- or HighJ-protected, but could also withstand the effects of a low-yield nuclear blast. On the *outside*, at least; an interesting engineering brief, he mused, still picturing the leaked Spiral plans in his mind. Carter was a DemolSquad member – a demolition expert. And he could see the flaws in the blueprints he had pored over one evening at Ed's small cottage.

Carter initiated his digital scope and peered down its barrel. The Sentinel tower sprang into focus and Carter stepped the range back, allowing his gaze to fall on the doors of the building. As usual, the portals were flanked by eight heavily armed Nex. Carter watched as a truck drew near, engine huge and belching, to disgorge another Nex squad who entered the building through smoothly sliding electric doors.

Carter watched the Nex for a while. Several JT8s appeared, roaring off in a 4x4. Carter timed the exit and entry of patrols and watched for anything out of the ordinary, any individuals he might recognise, any activity that he found out of character. After all, the Nex were creatures of habit. They had the predictability of insects; of machines.

He watched for an hour as the sun emerged from behind towering white clouds and the temperature began to rise. He was just about to withdraw and call it a day, when something – a commotion – caught his attention. He moved the scope's sight to the nearby harbour-side. Five Nex had surrounded two people – a man and a woman. One of the Nex struck out, its Steyr TMP sub-machine gun butt smashing into the man's head and dropping him instantly. The woman was kicked to the ground and the five Nex set about the couple, pounding them into bloody heaps as a group of JT8s arrived with huge black shaggy dogs on TitaniumIII leashes. The beasts, drooling and straining to reach the two civilians lying broken by the white harbour walls, heaved so hard against their leashes that even the heavily muscled JT8s struggled to restrain them.

He swept the scope from side to side. No crowds had gathered – because to gather in a crowd was to incite further suspicion. People hurried by, heads down, eyes averted, just hoping to hell that they would not become involved.

The whole incident left a sour taste in Carter's mouth. He withdrew with care and moved towards the shade of the olive trees. As he approached the KTM, something slid into his soul, like a bad injection of heroin. His head tilted. Over towards the farm of Tomas and Mary, he heard the powerful rumble of a distant FukTruck engine.

Carter moved on up the slope. As he reached the top of the gentle ridge he dropped to a crouch so as not to reveal his position against the skyline; then he angled to the left between a small copse of olive trees and stopped. Again, his head tilted. He could hear the shrill young voices of two girls. Children. He could not hear what they said, only identify the panic in their hysterical tone.

Feeling cold inside, Carter crested the rise and crawled between low scrub bushes. The landscape fell away ahead of him, rolling down into cultivated fields before climbing again to distant conifer forests. A stream ran glittering from the far slopes of a steep hill, and below, nestling in the valley, sat the sprawling farm that he had visited on many occasions. The main building – old and white and fallen into disrepair – was a long low farmhouse with white walls, grey in places where painted rendering had dropped away. The roof was red-tiled, but with several broken tiles gaping rudely; many had been replaced with grey mismatches.

Beside the old white farmhouse was a more modern addition: a big three-storey brick house – obviously destined to become the replacement dwelling, joined directly to the old farmhouse and still without a roof or even joists. Holes squatted where window frames had yet to be fixed, and the doorways were shadowed rectangles of rough-edged brick. Carter could still see marks on the ground where footings had been laid, and the project was far from complete.

To one side of the white farmhouse stood several small wooden buildings with thatched roofs and open fronts – one was a wood store filled with hunks of axe-chopped timber. And to the far right there was a large barn with double wooden doors. Outside, hung against the wall, was an old worn leather saddle; Carter knew this building was used as a stable, but he had never been inside.

A winding dirt track led through scattered trees and fields, climbing a rise to meet with the front of the farmhouse. An old bicycle was propped against the wall, its deflated tyres dusty as they rested on an ancient wooden porch beside two pairs of battered boots.

All this information was absorbed in a sweeping glance, but Carter's mouth went dry as his gaze locked on the large black Mercedes 8x8 which sat outside the farmhouse.

Three Nex stood levelling Steyr sub-machine guns at the heads of the five subdued people. Tomas was an old man. His lined and ancient face was filled with fear. Mary was kneeling, physically shaking, beside her husband, hair a neat grey bun, her arms wrapped around the smallest of the three little girls, Alice, Georgina and Freya stood in flower-painted dresses, weeping.

The Nex were ignoring the family; they were talking among themselves, and then turned their attention to Tomas. Carter's eyes focused on the back of the FukTruk. How many in there? It could hold perhaps fifty Nex . . .

Too many, he thought.

Carter started to crawl forward through the scrub. Much of the Nex conversation was lost to him because of the distance. All he managed to pick out was, 'Where are they?' and the old man's reply, '. . . don't have answers to your questions.' Gestures were made, and the old woman climbed wearily to her feet and was escorted by one of the Nex towards the stable . . . leaving two Nex alone with old Tomas.

Bad, thought Carter sombrely.

There came another exchange, angrier this time, and the butt of a Steyr TMP smashed into Tomas's skull. He toppled sideways, blood spraying from a jagged head wound, to lie stunned in the dirt in front of his home – as Carter increased his pace.

So you want to play rough? he hissed inwardly. Well, we can play rough if you like. We can play *real* nasty.

The two Nex spoke together for a moment. Then they both started to kick the old man, boots smashing into his face and body. They quickly tired of the game and, hefting their guns, followed their comrade and the old woman and crying children into the stable.

'*Come on. You going to be the Big Man?*' Kade mocked.

'*You going in to give them a taste of your bullets? What are you waiting for – a personal invitation? Go on, Butcher, do the right thing, my boy, you know those children deserve a better future . . .*'

'For a change, Kade, I agree with you.' Carter's voice was low, his tone deadly as his boots trod the long grass. He moved silently from tree to tree, his gaze swimming between the approaching barn and the sinister black Mercedes truck. The Nex did not reappear.

'*Yeah? Well, I'm bored, Carter, bored of this fucking life, bored of this fucking world. Come on, let's do the right thing . . . let me out to play so we can see some precious fucking blood flow.*'

Carter withdrew his battered matt-black Browning 9mm HiPower. He stared hard at the squat weapon – his trusted companion. And grimly, moving with as much speed as he dared, Carter approached the farmhouse.

The Merc's engine was still clicking loudly as it cooled, and Carter crouched beside the vehicle. In the dusty road, Tomas was groaning softly and trying feebly to wipe pools of blood from his face.

Carter, the Browning gripped in his fist, crawled to the old man, keeping his stare locked on the buckled timber walls and warped doors of the ancient stable-barn. Up close now, he could make out the ravaged face of Tomas – lined by the passage of time and the Cypriot sun. Anger flared in Carter's breast.

When Tomas saw Carter, his rheumy old eyes widened. 'Thank God . . .' he began, but Carter shushed him into silence.

'The Nex have taken Mary and the girls into the stable,' said Carter softly. 'Tell me the layout inside.'

The old man shook his head slowly. 'You have great

39

honour, coming like this to help,' he spoke softly, his voice heavily accented, 'and I thank you for that, Carter – I really do. But they will kill us all. They will kill *you*, as well.'

Carter stared at the old man's wrinkled face, seeing the resolve that had finally been betrayed by the weakness of age.

Something clicked inside Carter. He smiled.

'What would you have done? In your Spiral days?'

The old man smiled back. They both knew the answer.

'Do you still have the Skoda?'

'It's behind the house.'

'And there are three Nex?'

Between the coughing and wheezing, the bright-eyed old man managed, 'Three, yes, that I have seen. There are no others in the back of the truck.'

'Tell me about the layout inside,' said Carter again, pulling free an HPG and turning the timer dial with tiny metallic clicks. 'I'm going to bring the girls out.'

The stable housed six horses. There were six large stalls against the back wall, and the right-hand side of the stable housed a workshop for the working of wood; the old man had been a great carpenter in his day.

Behind the barn at ground level, amidst a clump of low bushes, there was the mouth of a narrow tunnel, a sluice exhaust for when the stables were hosed down and swept out. It was beside this square-section portal that Carter now crouched, staring down through a galvanised grid into the deep pit which contained a slurry of ancient horse-manure in a deep grey slop.

'Great. Just fucking *great*.'

Carter climbed into the narrow confines of the sluice pipe, wrinkling his nose at the stench of years of accumulated excrement; immediately a thick slime coated his hands and knees, the back of his head and his shoulders. He pushed himself along the narrow tunnel, which travelled for perhaps fifteen feet on a gentle incline before taking a sharp upward turn. Carter eased round the bend, sliding a little and fighting for a grip. Then he pressed his face up against the grille recessed into the floor of the actual stable building – and listened.

He could hear the Nex. One was pacing, one was toying with his TMP (Tactical Machine Pistol) – Carter could hear the rub of leather on alloy – and the girls were still sobbing into their grandmother's protective embrace. There was also another sound – the clacking of heavy hooves on the concrete floor, the occasional whinny of the nervous, skittish geldings.

Carter realised there was no talking between the old woman and the Nex; and this worried him. The time for talking was done . . . which could only mean the time for slaughter was about to begin. He checked his watch. Fifteen seconds.

Carter tried not to breathe, so bad was the stench in the narrow pipe.

The sounds of the stamping horses secmed to increase. They were extremely nervous, one pawing at the concrete surface and making a curious whinnying growl like nothing Carter had ever heard before.

Carter's mind took on an ethereal calm.

Five seconds, four, three . . .

Carter sensed rather than heard the ignition click of the HPG planted on the underside of the beautiful gloss-black Mercedes 8x8 FukTruk. There came a concussive *crack* followed by a scream of fire, a rush of igniting LVA, a screech of twisting, wrenching steel panels and chassis and then the sudden *boom* of detonation as the Merc was kicked up into the air, spinning slowly in a bubble of gas and fire, then stomping back against the earth as colourful streamers of fire and smoke billowed.

Carter heard the Nex run outside. Slowly, he eased up the grid and peered into the stable. It was gloomy after the bright sunlight outside, but Carter had had time for his eyes to adjust. He was positioned in the far corner of the barn, by the workshop – which was divided from the main compartment of the stable by a low, three-foot-high wall made of wooden beams and rough-cut timber panelling – a waist-high divide. The stable stalls were to his right, set against the back wall of the barn and leading across dusty concrete to large double doors whose buckled antique timbers allowed streamers of sunlight to illuminate dancing motes of dust. Beside the end stall by the doors stood a single Nex guarding the woman and girls. The Nex was staring towards the door, presumably sniffing after its comrades who had gone to investigate the explosion.

Carter rose to a crouch, using the wall of the horse's stall beside him as cover, and crept forward towards the sparkling shafts of sunlight illuminating the matted straw and dung-covered floor. His Browning was pressed against his cheek. His breathing had descended into a spiral of concentration as—

The Nex whirled towards him, copper eyes wide, focusing, its Steyr TMP smashing up as Carter's Browning bucked in his fist and three bullets sped towards the Nex's face; the first bullet skimmed its ear as it started to turn, the second one missed and embedded itself in a wooden beam with a loud *thunk* – but the third hit the Nex's lower jaw side on, ripping it – and the bottom part of the Nex's face – completely free.

The TMP in the Nex's gloved hands was yammering,

bullets cutting a furrow across the floor towards Carter. He rolled to the left, then leapt for the workshop and the low wall and a promise of sanctuary beyond.

He dived over, bullets slamming into the wood behind him, and collided hard with a wide wooden bench. Footsteps slapped concrete, sprinting towards his cover, and shots continued to blast from the Steyr TMP's smoking barrel – punching holes through the wooden panel to explode around Carter in a sudden hail of metal death. Carter hissed, rolling around as several flattened bullets skimmed his face and shoulders, and he started to fire back through the panel, allowing even more tiny dancing shafts of sunlight to spill through. Beyond, booted feet left the ground and settled lightly on the rail. Carter found himself looking up into a face dragged kicking and screaming from the depths of a horror movie. The Nex, its entire lower jaw missing, tongue lolling for five flapping inches from its root and dangling against torn streamers of skin and muscle, glared down at Carter in a copper-glowing insanity of pain and hatred. Its visage was a platter of destruction, a gaping maw of ruin. Carter, stunned for a moment by this apparition, stared up into the face.

The Nex could not speak. It had no lips or mouth. Only the tongue remained, dangling, smeared with blood and tiny, embedded shards of shattered bone.

The Nex leapt as three more of Carter's bullets whirred past it. A fist cannoned into Carter's face, a second blow crunched against his nose and his Browning skittered across the floor. Carter aimed a powerful punch of his own but his fist whirred through the air where the Nex's lower face had been; a right hook connecting with nothing but the swaying and now useless tongue.

Carter's knee came up and the Nex grunted from deep

in its belly. Then Carter rolled and hammered a blow to the Nex's head; they spun apart, leaping up among the wide wooden benches, the lathe and circular saw, the three large upright drills and the industrial sanding machine. The Nex reached for a magazine for its emptied TMP, but Carter delivered a front kick which sent the magazine sailing through the air to clatter under a bench. They squared off for a moment, and Carter nodded as the Nex raised its fist.

'I think you're going to have some trouble with the ladies from this point on,' he snarled through a string of blood and saliva, his freshly broken nose slamming sledgehammers of pain into his face and brain.

The Nex's eyes widened, tongue swinging with violent slaps against its blood-speckled throat.

'But then, hey, I'm pretty sure you always had trouble anyway – with that unholy Nex stink.'

The Nex leapt, and Carter swayed right, pounding three blows into the Nex's head as it sailed past. It rolled, came up with awesome speed – and attacked, throwing an incredible array of punches that forced Carter back under the powerful onslaught. The Nex's kick cannoned into Carter's chest, slamming him backwards into the wall – and a bank of switches which operated the workshop's machinery. Unexpectedly, the machines sprang into life, lathe spinning, drills turning, and an unhealthy vibrating whine coming from the awesome circular saw. This machine's blade accelerated like it was turbocharged and Carter's gaze snapped left, taking in the uncovered sweep of the eighteen-inch toothed metal disc.

Carter glanced back – into a left hook, which spun him towards the screaming circular blade, his hands lashing out to halt his fall with his nose a mere inch from the whirling scream of discoloured steel. Carter's teeth gritted tight in a vicious snarl and he powered around, right elbow pounding the Nex's temple, left fist slashing thin air over the Nex's head as it ducked and then lunged forward. Its arms grappled with Carter as they locked together for a moment, stumbling back against the saw's bench.

They held one another tight. Then Carter's fists lifted and he pounded the Nex's head three times, but the Nex was stronger than Carter – it forced him slowly backwards, twisting him towards the whirling saw blade.

Carter was face to mangled face with the Nex. He leant back as the creature's tongue dangled forward towards him, disengaging from bruised skin with a *schluck* sound and dripping its purple blood onto his flesh. Carter growled something incomprehensible, muscles screaming, body straining against the iron power of the Nex and he could almost feel the insect-human hybrid *smiling*. Its copper-eyed stare bore into him with a focus so intense that it seemed to burn his soul with bitter vitriol. Inch by slow, painful inch Carter was forced towards the spinning, whining blade. He could feel its breeze caress his hair. Steel teeth swept past his gaze. His muscles were bulging, cramping, and the insect stench invaded his nostrils, making him want to gag . . . he was forced closer and closer, and he threw a few more ineffectual punches which the Nex absorbed. Panic consumed him. His hands scrabbled out to the right, brushing wildly against the wall, over glass paper and sanding blocks, and onto the rack of mounted – chisels.

Carter's hand curled around a handle, and slammed the edged tool into the Nex's neck. Blood spurted out, drenching him in an instant as the Nex released its grip. Carter felt himself choking, suddenly aware that his supply of air had been restricted, and he looked on with cold fury as the Nex's hand curled around the handle of the chisel and tried to pull the tempered blade free.

'You just won't fucking *die*, will you?' snarled Carter. Then he lurched forward, grabbing the Nex and performing a judo shoulder throw; the Nex sailed through the air, slamming down onto the circular-saw bench – and the saw's blade. There came a high-pitched *shhrrn* of blade slicing flesh and spinal column, and the Nex seemed to dance, lying face up with the blade protruding from its sternum, jiggling uncontrollably, legs kicking as blood spewed down through holes in the bench to spread out in a wide pool beneath, where it was soaked up by shavings.

Carter took a deep breath, staring mesmerised at the spinning circular blade tipped with tiny globes of crimson – which suddenly spat sparks as bullets struck it and spun off in flattened trajectories. Carter hit the ground hard and searched frantically for his Browning. Grasping the gun's worn butt, he changed magazines and edged towards the bullet-holed wooden partition. Two more, he thought. Just two more . . . I hope they die easier than the first son of a bitch.

He crept sideways and peered through one of the bullet holes. The woman and children had moved back into one of the horse's stalls where they huddled beside a quivering gelding, its nostrils flared, its flanks vibrating in fear.

The two Nex were there, 9mm Steyr sub-machine guns pointing in his direction. They started to move slowly forwards, spreading out – and Carter shuffled backwards towards the wall hung with a hundred woodworking implements. And there, near the floor, a stack of spare blades for the circular saw . . . Carter pulled three of them free of their greased wrappers and returned to the partition. He stood suddenly, and threw the discs, spinning, in quick succession. The first Nex dodged left, right

46

and left with ease – as Carter's Browning barked and a single shot took it between the eyes. It dropped to its knees and remained there for several seconds, its copper-eyed gaze locked on Carter's narrowed stare. Then it fell face-down in the dirt.

Where had the other one gone?

Carter eased himself to the doorway and peered out. Behind him machinery was rattling and spinning, the lathe whining its 10,000 r.p.m. rotary song.

'*It'll be with the woman and the children, like the true fucking coward it is,*' came Kade's dark whisper. '*Come on, Carter, let me have a go – I've been a good boy recently, I promise I won't do anything naughty. I'll do everything that you tell me. Honest.*'

'Yeah, right.'

Carter crept forward, out into the realm of No Man's Land, the muzzle of the Browning weaving slowly from left to right and back, tracing invisible trajectories in a figure of eight covering both the stalls which housed the horses and the stable entrance, one of the doors of which was now slightly ajar.

Away from the churning of workshop machinery, Carter could hear the sobbing of the young girls once more. He had been right in his assumption; they were in the end stall. And the chance that the Nex was with them? Using them as cover? Perfect. It would have four hostages if it needed them to escape . . .

Fucking terrorists, thought Carter.

Always willing to sacrifice the innocent.

He reached the stable doors and glanced quickly outside. The Mercedes was still burning, smoke pluming up into the bright sky. Carter turned towards the first stall where a huge black gelding quivered, eyes wide and nostrils flared. Then something smashed into his back, arms

47

wrapping around him, sending him and his assailant stumbling sideways to crash through the stall door where they rolled past the prancing hooves of the huge nineteen-hand thoroughbred.

Carter powered a punch into the Nex's mashed face, then rolled to the right as the horse – which had reared up at their sudden intrusion – brought its hooves savagely down to strike sparks from the concrete.

'Shit!' He rolled again as the prancing rear hooves came close to caving in his head, stood and turned – straight into a Nex roundhouse kick that smashed his chest and hammered him back against the thick wooden wall. Carter ducked a blow and sent a right straight into the Nex's nose, then a left hook, left straight and left uppercut which sent the Nex spinning down to the ground.

The horse was turning in panic and crashed into Carter, its huge bulk crushing him for a moment, then sending him sprawling to the floor where he rolled between its striking hooves – as the Nex dragged free its Steyr TMP and unleashed a stream of bullets directly into the animal's glossy black frame—

The horse screamed.

Carter's jaw dropped. Never had he heard such an unholy, pain-filled, haunting sound; and the mighty beast reared as bullets punched holes of blood-fountain gore up its sweat-gleaming flanks. Its head was thrown back, mane shaking, huge teeth grinding as a hoof crashed out, catching the Nex a massive blow to the side of the head.

The Nex went down hard. An instant later the stomping sounds of iron-shod hooves rang out as the horse crushed the Nex's head into a purple pulp of butcher's-meat slop.

The horse staggered against the wall of the stall, which

creaked alarmingly in protest under the weight of the mighty animal. Then, slowly, its front legs buckled, followed by its rear ones. It thumped onto its side and lay, blood oozing from the fifteen or so holes in its chest and belly, eyes rolling. It wheezed softly as its ability to breathe slowly faded.

Carter slowly pushed himself away from the wall. He moved forward, knelt on one knee and slowly stroked the horse's velvet muzzle. It made a tiny nuzzling sound and Carter shuffled around, placed the Browning's muzzle to the back of its head and, with his eyes closed, ended the animal's life.

After the sound of the shot, the world seemed suddenly, desolately, silent.

Carter climbed wearily to his feet, adrenalin still pumping, and left the stall. He turned, through the dancing motes of dust, and moved to the end stall where Mary crouched, trying to protect her grandchildren with the bulk of her own body.

'It's OK,' Carter croaked. 'The Nex are dead. You can come out.'

'Carter? Carter . . . what are you doing here? Oh thank you, thank you! Have you seen Tomas? Is he all right? Is he still alive?' The old woman's voice was powerful, and Carter witnessed a hardness in her eyes. These are tough people, he thought: the Nex had underestimated both their tenacity and their pride.

'Tomas is alive. I sent him behind the house when I blew up the Nex's truck.' Carter crouched, and one of the little girls glanced tearfully at him. 'You OK there, little flower?'

She buried her face back in her grandmother's skirts.

'Follow me,' said Carter, rising to stand in acute agony – the horse had cracked several of his ribs when it had crushed him against the wall of the stable stall – and he looked along the length of the stable, which in the last few minutes had turned into a charnel house. He led the way to the doors – and the warmth of sunlight and freedom beyond. He dragged the portal open a little more with a scraping of old timbers, then stepped out into the sunshine with the old grey-haired woman and tear-stained children trailing behind his aching battered shell—

Two sub-machine guns were pointed at Carter's head – one from either side of the stable doorway, both in the gloved hands of copper-eyed Nex soldiers. Carter glanced, very slowly, from left to right.

'*There were five Nex,*' said Kade smugly.

'Yeah, thanks for that, Kade. Big *fucking* help you were with that one.'

'*Let me sort this out, Carter. You know I can take them. You know I can burn their skulls and piss on their graves. This is just a walk in the park for me. As dangerous as feeding the quacking ducks.*'

'Kade – you can just drop dead.'

'*Hey, Carter, maybe we both will – just look at that!*'

From behind the smoking ruins of the Mercedes 8x8 came an enormously muscled figure on all fours – like a huge stocky cat, moving with a heavy feline grace, long claws gouging the dirt road, heavy triangular head swaying from left to right. Its skin was the glossy black of insect chitin, with spiralled patterns of skin blending with silver armour down its flanks. It stalked forward in arrogance, slitted copper eyes focusing on Carter – and it made the Spiral man's breath catch in his throat and his skin go suddenly cold. He felt the two Nex to either side take a step back.

'*Sleeper Nex,*' came Kade's soft whisper, laced with just a hint of joy. With the thrill of *battle*. '*You have* no *chance with that, my friend. Last time, it was just luck . . . but this time?'*

The Sleeper Nex halted, claws flexing, and a long string of drool dripped from its thick twisted fangs. Its head tilted a little then, observing Carter with the slow appreciation that all predators reserve for their prey. But what horrified him most was that there was a *recognition* in that narrowed stare.

The Sleeper Nex *knew* Carter . . .

And then it spoke, sending spider crawls of horror rippling down Carter's spine. How can it speak? his mind screamed at him. Just how the *fuck* can that monstrosity *speak?*

'Mr Carter,' came the low sibilant whisper.

It blinked, slowly, lazily. Saliva, a thick mixture of black and grey, continued to drip from its jaws, drooling to the ground where it formed twin puddles.

'You have evaded us for too long. Now your time has finally come.'

Spiral Mainframe
Data log#12327 [amended]

CLASSIFIED SADT/5345/SPECIAL INVESTIGATIONS UNIT
DATA REQUEST 324#12327

Durell

All existing files concerning Durell were
destroyed (by the man himself) prior to his
betrayal of Spiral.

It is known that he was heavily involved in
the Nx5 Project early on in his career. He

worked with Gol and Count Feuchter. It is known that he carried on with this work illegally after Spiral withdrew funding and closed down the Nex operations.

It is believed that Durell was the instigator in creating the Spiral mobile, an anti-Spiral warship designed to overthrow world powers and take control of the world's military and financial institutions via the all-powerful QuanTech Edition 3 processor. He was later responsible for global terrorism using a QuakeHub linked to the deadly QIV processor, again in further attempts at world domination by the use of terrible, continent-hammering quakes – which he could target at will.

Durell is the most dangerous individual ever encountered by Spiral. His knowledge and lust for power are insatiable. He is considered extremely dangerous and ranks No 1 on Spiral's terrorist hit list. There is intel regarding some form of ancient 'Nex DemolSquad', although no Spiral records have ever referred to such a creation – nor can anybody envisage why such a deviant squad would arise.

Keyword SEARCH>> NEX, SAD, SPIRAL_sadt, DURELL, FEUCHTER, SPIRAL_mobile, QIII, QIV, QuakeHub

// Also see military texts *SPIRAL* and *QUAKE*.

CHAPTER 2

EMPIRE OF HATE

let us () out
make () us free
we see you () we see you
we see the traitor ()
() traitor of our breed

The light was dying over the New York skyline – or
what remained of it. The one building which still
stood perfectly erect, at the centre of Manhattan, was the
Sentinel Corporation's New York HQ.

Durell stood within the enfolding glass embrace of one
of the upper floors, computers glinting dully behind him,
their lights reflecting on the high-sheen oak of the thirty-
foot lacquered desk surrounded by soft leather chairs. He
stood beside the smoked privacy glass, one clawed black
hand lifted and pressed against the TitaniumGL lami-
nates.

Durell smiled within the folds of his dark hood.

Light aircraft swept above him, thundering through
the skies and spraying out another fine mist of chemical

Half-Life Accelerators over the still devastated but gradually renewing world below him. Whilst most areas of New York had been made safe in terms of radiation levels upwards of a year ago, there were still pockets of dangerous radioactivity that necessitated regular and constant sweeps.

Durell looked down as the spray fell and disappeared.

Distantly, people moved like tiny insects through the streets. Fires burned in pockets among the devastation. Whilst most of the roads had been cleared of debris and many structures had been rebuilt, there was still an amazing amount of post-blast destruction. The Nex patrolled with an iron fist, closely backed by the JT8 police squads – Justice Troops, once the police and military of the Old World before the Nex Agency had taken global control. Now retrained and rearmed, paid a handsome wage, and given the best in city-living accommodation, they were the human untouchables. The Mercs. The modern face of law and order.

Gunshots flickered distantly, although Durell could not hear their blasts from his luxury office. The JT8s swarmed forward against a blockade, overrunning it. Fire flared. There was a tiny green glow of detonation, and more ragged shooting from unleashed automatic weaponry.

Turning his back, Durell moved towards the long wooden desk and seated himself at its head. He ran a deformed claw hand along the fine lacquered wood, tracing patterns of dark grain, delighting in the flawless smooth surface.

A steel door at the far end of the chamber opened and a Nex stepped onto the plush carpet, dragging a half-naked, battered, raze-wire-bound captive.

The Nex was of no great stature; she wore a tight

body-hugging black uniform and soft black boots. She had an AK52 slung over one shoulder and her face was unmasked; copper eyes glowed brightly in a beautifully pale and oval face. The hair was cut short near the scalp, leaving a tight black forest of spikes, but the lack of hair only accentuated the cold beauty of the high cheekbones and unblemished skin.

She prodded the man, who stumbled forward and fell to his knees for a moment. He was breathing heavily, and blood had dried on his face. He lifted his steel-grey gaze and fixed it on Durell, then snarled something incomprehensible and surged upwards. He lurched to a halt in front of Durell – with the female Nex's sub-machine gun poking viciously into his back.

He smiled, a low spiteful smile laced with traces of blood. 'So you've finally chosen to see me. You've finally found your balls, Durell, you twisted piece of rat-shit.'

'Welcome to my simple home, Mr Haven.' Durell spoke softly. Without emotion. He pushed back the hood of his heavy robe and smiled his own curious twisted smile. 'I am sorry for your pain – truly I am.'

'Fuck you.'

'Tut, tut. Your anger is misplaced, my little *Spiral* friend. I never gave the order to beat you into a senseless pulp; you may thank the JT8s for that honour – and let us be honest with one another: the Justice Troops are a product of *your* world, not mine.'

Haven seemed to sag a little then; Durell saw the raze-wire digging into his wrists and the blood rolling down over his hands, dripping to the carpet. Durell motioned to the female Nex warrior who reached forward. There was an electronic *blip* and the raze-wire retreated into itself and dropped to the carpet.

Haven looked up, rubbing at his deeply lacerated flesh

55

and flexing his fingers slowly, allowing life to flood back into his crippled near-blue hands. He took a step forward, but felt the prod of the gun in his back once more. He laughed then, a bitter laugh of cynicism and despair. 'You going to kill me then, Durell? You *know* I don't have the information you want. I just don't have it – and no amount of torture can make me talk.' His tone was mocking, and despite his obvious pain and hopeless predicament there was a glint of victory shining in his cold hard eyes.

Durell sighed, shaking his head. 'We will scan you for brain tattoos. It will be very painful.'

'Scan me, fucker. I don't have the access codes to the SpiralGRID – as you will shortly discover. Now *I* have a question for *you* . . .' Their eyes met and for a long moment there was a tense silence. The female Nex retreated a little, as if sensing that she wasn't needed.

'Please feel free to ask.' Durell turned and moved once more towards the darkened glass. He stared down over the devastation of Manhattan – and over the distant chaos of rubble across the East River, in Queens and Brooklyn. He stared at the destruction he had commissioned, the sea of rubble he had wrought.

'What happened?' Haven's voice was softer now, gentler. There was a thick slur of sentiment; of nostalgia. Durell turned and saw that Haven's head was tilted slightly, eyes bright as if the man was holding back tears. 'What *happened* to you? We used to be friends.'

'Nothing happened, Haven – except the world became more corrupt, Spiral passed over more and more abominations. The politicians and the generals said the right words, earned their promotions and elections by clever words, by slick marketing and money games and underhand tactics. But when the world fell into decline they never did what was necessary; they complained and moaned, whined and stalled and found an eternity of feeble excuses. And yes – I have wrought a terrible destruction – but nothing so terrible that it cannot be rebuilt, cannot be reborn, cannot be *improved*.'

'Improved? You call the Nex an *improvement*? You truly are insane, Durell. I always used to joke back in the NexSquad days that you drank your fill from the mercury fountain – but fuck me if you weren't bathing in a toxic lake instead.'

'You misunderstand my intentions,' crooned Durell, his gaze locked on New York. Once more he witnessed the flashes of shotgun blasts. The city below him was a turmoil of anarchy, a maelstrom of human struggle. A battleground for Nex and Spiral, REBS and JT8s.

A high-pitched shrill alerted Durell, who moved smoothly – with only a few tiny crackles from beneath his robe – and pressed a sleek alloy button. A huge black screen shimmered into life to reveal the face of a Nex, haughty-looking, with narrow copper eyes and short black bristling hair.

'Yes, Mace?'

'Sir, the QIV processor has completed the compilation. We have mapped the new definitions for the HATE zones and managed to control further creeping by spraying anti-HATE borders delivered by chopper. It can no longer infiltrate the cities.'

'Good. So are we –' Durell chuckled lightly, as if amused by the word '– *safe*, for the moment?'

'It is controlled,' said Mace simply.

'Good work. Well done.'

'What shall we do with the recent prisoners? The ones who unknowingly wandered into Half-Zones?'

'They broke the Five Laws of Contamination.'

'They did not intend a non-compliance, sir. It was an act based purely on ignorance.'

'You suggest I should release them?'

'I suggest nothing, sir. I am merely stating the facts. There are loyal JT8s and Nex who were out of their jurisdiction because of the nature of the HATE biological weapon; it shifts on the wind and was able to infiltrate edges of the cities, using plant spores as organic carriers. Although the Nex and JT8s were not confined to their Lanes, they had unwittingly entered KillZones and I feel that—'

'Kill them.'

'Yes, sir. Out.' Mace signed off and the screen went a terrible matt black; it reflected Durell's contemplative expression for a moment before he turned and settled his gaze on Haven. Then he glanced over to the slim female Nex who stood, stoic and impassive, her sub-machine gun pointing down at the plush carpet.

'Did we run the preliminary checks on Viktor Haven here?'

'Yes,' said the female Nex softly, her voice gentle and sexless.

'And we found nothing?'

'He is clean, although his ECube does condemn him as a Spiral terrorist purely by association.'

'I know that,' whispered Durell. 'Any fool can read his Spiral Agency loyalties in his stance. But what does he truly know about the GRID? What does he know of EDEN? And what does he know about the Dreadnought constructions?'

Durell caught the glint in Haven's eye.

'So you *do* contain some knowledge. Take him to Mace for . . . *questioning*.' The Nex moved forward and placed a hand on Haven's shoulder.

58

'And Alexis?'

'Yes?' she purred tenderly, her copper-eyed gaze meeting Durell's.

'Come back quickly. I have another *task* for you.'

Durell sat in the darkness, curled on the settee and staring down over New York City. A few fires still burned from the riots earlier that day – but the disturbances had been crushed mercilessly by the JT police squads and Nex Assault Teams. Over five hundred people had died on the streets – and for what?

To wave their pathetic banners opposing the NEP. Voicing their petty concerns – in direct violation of Durell's order. Orders highlighted and constantly transmitted on the entire range of vid channels, making it clear that opposition to the Nex Enhancement Programme was prohibited.

'Democracy,' he hissed. It had a lot to answer for, he thought.

Mace arrived, sliding into the darkness to stand in front of Durell. He looked agitated – an emotion that Durell rarely saw flickering across the fish-white face of his oldest and most loyal subject.

'Durell, I have a question. A question based on, shall we say, an unreliable source.' Durell nodded for Mace to continue, and the compact Nex's finger lifted to rest gently against his narrow lips before he went on. 'There is talk. Of a warhead – a super-weapon designed and built by Spiral when it ruled and stagnated in its decadent prime. Have you heard of this weapon?'

Durell tilted his head gently. 'Where did you hear of this?'

'From the lips of a dying REB. I persuaded her to release her knowledge before she . . . unfortunately, my skills are not what they were – old age is creeping slowly into my limbs, and as a result I could not keep her at the brink of life with the steady hand I once possessed.'

Durell smiled. And nodded.

'So it is true?' persisted Mace.

'Worse than true, my friend. Spiral created a weapon so devastating that if they were to initiate it against us, we would do well to survive the onslaught. Our Empire would be toppled. It is our only weakness.' Durell's voice had dropped to a low croon, his copper eyes glinting in the darkness.

'Surely one warhead could not possibly pose such a threat? We have more than fifty armies. We have nuclear-blast-proof Sentinel Towers in nearly every city of the world. And even without Nex forces we now control the JT8s. Even as we speak, they forget their lives under the old rule. Soon we will be all they remember. The Old World will not only have died – it will have been extinguished. We have rewritten the past, Durell – cast it into shadows.'

'The Warhead is not simply a warhead; it is Evolution Class. An EC Warhead is a *machine*, a prototype of the next generation of intelligent, self-sufficient, *sentient* weapons systems.'

'Sentient?'

Durell's eyes sparkled with the reflections of distant fires. A lone machine gun rattled. 'The Evolution Warhead was a project locked in a development cycle from the same era as the QII and then QIII processors – it followed similar design pathways and used many modules from some of the same programmers who applied their skills to the QIII and, later, QIV systems. I did not think the project was ever completed – because, by its very nature, its design specifications seemed almost impossible. A wet dream of the weapon designers and the military generals.'

'Tell me more,' said Mace, with a barely suppressed shiver.

'The Evolution Warhead was supposed to be a warhead that could have unlimited targets. Once released, it would be completely self-sufficient. It had battery cells that would last a century. It could increase and decrease its own mass and size by accumulation and dissemination of its structural polymorphing chassis. It could reduce its own size and act as a stealth missile, infiltrating anything down to a room-size target by using a discrete global positioning system – not a standard military GPS, but from *its own individual* mainframe. It could – on paper – distil elements from the air, the ground, the sea – and increase its own capacity for speed and destruction. Its chassis was a Shift Unit – it could change shape and purpose and construct its own detonation units, its own independent missiles from *within itself*, like a metal insect giving birth to a progeny of war and destruction. And it was sentient – it had a brain modelled on our previous Quantell technology. It could, ultimately, construct intelligent procedures. It could think for itself.'

'But it was never created?'

'No, I thought the project abandoned. Because . . .'

'Yes?'

Durell turned, his dark copper eyes glittering. 'Because to create a weapon which could assimilate its own miniature but equally devastating nuclear missiles and rain them down like fire on a million chosen targets if so required; to create a machine so incredibly lethal to mankind that it was, in effect, a machine gun that would fire nuclear bombs – with the ability to destroy and destroy and destroy and never, ever stop; to create a weapon with unlimited capacity for detonation . . . well, that would show the perverse nature of man, would it not? To build something *guaranteed* to wipe out the entire planet if it was deemed necessary?'

'Our Sentinel Towers – they are resistant to nuclear blasts.'

'The Evolution Warhead, once programmed, would analyse its target; it would detect our fail-safes, shed its skin like a serpent, infiltrate the tower and detonate from within. Let me ask you: would one of our Sentinel Towers survive a nuclear explosion that went off *inside*?'

'They are only braced for impact from outside. But then, this is not a problem – because this warhead does not exist . . . yes?'

'If it does not exist, why are the REBS talking about it?'

'Propaganda? A boost to the morale of a dying unit? Every religion needs its Holy Grail.'

'And what if the Holy Grail really did exist?'

'The power for immortality?'

'Immortality and *immortal destruction*.'

'I'll get some people on it,' whispered Mace.

'Use the best,' said Durell, returning to gaze out over New York. He surveyed the rubble, the destruction. 'I don't like nasty surprises. And I don't want to find the Evolution Class Warhead knocking on our back door with my name at the forefront of its digital mind.'

An hour later, the trouble outside had ceased and New York was finally calm.

A door opened on silent hinges, allowing a tiny triangle of yellow light to spill onto the thick carpet. A figure stepped in, and Durell's slitted copper eyes narrowed for a moment as he recognised the silhouette of Alexis.

I need this, he thought.

She closed the door behind her and moved forward, bare feet padding across the carpet. In the gloom Durell could see she still wore her tight body-hugging black uniform. Her copper eyes moved, focused, came to rest on Durell's impassive face.

Durell studied her pale oval face as, without a sound, Alexis peeled off her tight uniform and stood with legs slightly apart, arms limp by her sides, fingers flexing slowly as if in anticipation of battle. He noted the hint of moisture on her pastel lips, and the short panting breaths – gentle, almost unheard, but hinting at her deep and desperate *need*.

Durell's gaze dropped, past Alexis's lifted chin and to the pale skin of her throat, and the small but perfectly rounded breasts. Then lower, his stare moving over her flat stomach and to the black glistening scales which began at the top of her vagina where her pubis gave way to armoured scaling which spiralled and scattered down across her groin and inner thighs. It tightened again into armoured panels which ran in twin glistening strips down the back of her legs to end in sharp points of insect chitin just above her heels.

Durell's appreciative gaze lifted, following the trail of tiny armoured scales, most black but several glistening with oil-slick rainbow hues. The smell of Alexis's Nex flesh prickled his nostrils, her scent mingling with his own and forming a natural perfumed bond as Durell finally moved and rose from the settee.

Behind the two, the city glittered. Fire erupted occasionally. A large CityScreen atop a skyscraper flickered with images of LVA, then modern KT weapons, then the NEP in an attempt at enticing normal, everyday people into the joyous union of becoming . . . Nex.

The ultimate warrior.

The ultimate soldier.

Protectors of freedom.

Upholders of truth and law and order . . .

You know it makes sense . . .

'You wanted me, sir?' breathed Alexis, her voice soft, husky, her eyes dipping a little as Durell's dark armoured claw came up to cup her chin. Her eyes lifted to meet his stare and he marked the strength there: the incredible, awesome physical power which she held tightly in check.

Alexis: Durell's finest Nex assassin, Durell's most awesome general in this bright new world.

'Yes,' he said, his deformed face smiling softly, pallets of chitinous armour sliding across his cheeks under glowing slitted copper eyes. He moved forward a little, felt her body lift towards his – as if offering herself in eager anticipation. 'And I think you need me as much as I need you.' It was not a question.

'It has been a while,' she soothed, stepping in close as her arms slid neatly inside his heavy rustling robes, moving over the contours of his armoured flanks and to the soft, supple human skin of his back. He tensed for a moment – as he always did – and then slowly relaxed as her long fingers soothed patterns of tenderness across his skin. Durell's head dropped, and Alexis's tongue flickered out, tracing a trail across the hard scales of his deformed face and then sliding into the small round hole of his mouth. Their tongues entwined and danced, hers a moist writhing muscle reminiscent of the human from which she was joined, his a black triangulated stump riddled with thick black hairs that prickled like sharp wires. Their tongues mated, Durell's hairs tickling Alexis's mucous surface roughly and drawing tiny pin-pricks of blood.

Durell shrugged and his robes fell back, leaving him

naked. He moved, stooping with crackles of his armoured spine to lift Alexis so that her feet left the carpet, their mouths still joined in a tender lover's caress, her taut breasts brushing against his cool slick armour, erect nipples leaving wet oozing trails of grey mammary milk against the protective chemical gel that coated Durell's armour like a liquid exoskeleton veil.

Alexis groaned, a deep low animal sound, and pressed herself into Durell. He turned, bearing her down to the settee, armoured forearms leaving grooves in the leather as his claws came up and ran gently through her short black spiked hair. Alexis's legs opened, spirals of protective armour scattering from her cunt to reveal a dark honeyed opening, glistening with pink and blood red and corkscrew trails of bright green as her legs came up and over Durell's hips. Jagged ridges of plate-chitin poked into Alexis's calves and as Durell kissed her once more, his tiny triangular tongue darting into her mouth and leaving trails of acid, her long white fingers danced down his chest and across his flat, powerfully muscled abdomen and to the flat area between his legs. She gently prised apart the armoured shields and pushed her fingers inside him, into the pocket of thick gel, feeling his slick penis suddenly flex in her hands, tiny rippling spikes driving like needles into her flesh and drawing blood in twenty different places. She felt the injection of hormones from him, felt his pulsating penis suddenly swell and burst free of his shell and she gazed down lovingly at the throbbing black and purple shaft between her blood-trickling hands. Her head snapped up then, tongue darting to moisten her lips as her breath came in short, eager gasps, copper eyes glistening as one of her hands reached behind him and pulled Durell towards her lust.

Durell entered her hard, and she screamed a high-pitched

scream, back arching as her hands clawed at his armour. The spikes rippling across his huge pulsing penis dragged ragged bloody grooves through her vagina; their blood and hormones mixed, and her muscles suddenly constricted in a hugely powerful grip around him – trapping him there, held within bars of sex, locked in place by a need to fuck like a fly caught behind the teeth of a flytrap.

His clawed hands dropped, leaving delicate tentative trails across her quivering oozing breasts, down her flanks and under her buttocks. He inched himself further, pushing hard, enjoying the pain as her clamped muscles fought him . . . and then, slowly, they began their insect fuck. They moved with a gentle painful rhythm; pinned onto and into one another, fastened and gripped and locked, injected with stabs of pain and needles of lust. They kissed hard and fast and then slow and gentle, slipping from the settee with soft *thumps* to the thick carpet on platters of their own slick blood and discharged sexual effluvia which oozed from skin pores as their Nex stink enveloped one another. They panted, gazing into one another's copper eyes, mouths only an inch apart as Durell's spine crackled softly in rhythm and his claws stripped narrow thin lines of flesh from her flanks, from her breasts, from her tensed and heaving buttocks . . .

Locked together, their pace slowed until their writhing, flexing thrusts came at maybe one a minute. They were panting still as they both rose to a slow, grinding, indomitable climax and Alexis began to come first, her mouth opening wide as she emitted a high ululating insect shrill which filled and reverberated around the room. Durell gave one huge and final heave as his twitching penis started to pump, accompanied by a *cracking* sound like the breaking of trampled cockroach shells. They clung together, rolling on the carpet while far below them, in the

darkness of NYC, a thousand patrolling Nex soldiers murdered innocent people in breach of the strict curfew laws.

Durell was cold. He dragged his robes around his shoulders and stared down at the sleeping face of Alexis, her
copper eyes closed for the moment, her breasts rising and
falling in a slow and steady rhythm. He shifted slightly,
and Alexis murmured, rolling away from him on the
carpet.

Almost human, thought Durell. She is almost
human . . . He gazed down at his clawed hand, at the black
shimmering armour, at the twisted appendages that had
once been his fingers. They still worked – only not like
human fingers, their movements accompanied by clicks
and strange, alien reverse-joint contortions.

And he pictured his own face.

A monstrosity, a deformed chimeric blend of man and
insect. And yet he believed – *truly* believed – that the Nex
was indeed a superior life form, a genetic extension of
man, a physical and mental and chemical evolvement—

But the irony was complete. Durell had been one of the
first Nex; and whilst he was superior in terms of strength,
speed, agility and mental capacity to the mere human he
had once been, he was trapped and bound in this
deformed shell.

Tears rolled softly down Durell's armoured cheeks as
he stared at Alexis's white-skinned, pale, powerful body;
and the sun rose slowly over New York and came seeping
into the Sentinel Tower.

With the dawn came violence.

Viktor Haven, now heavily beaten, his face distorted
with a broken cheekbone, cowered in the corner of his cell
with his hands and feet bound tight with raze-wire.

The cell was large, spacious and bright: a white floor, white walls, a steel ceiling sporting bright halogen-III illumination. A low pallet bed stood in a corner and on it Haven lay crushed, curled into himself in a world of personal agony.

The cell's door slid open and Durell moved in, sweeping forward to stand over the curled shape of Haven. He waited patiently for recognition, until Haven slowly lifted his head and stared at Durell through blood-bloated eyes.

'What do you want?'

Durell smiled, and made a low clicking noise. Through the open doorway squeezed a broad stocky figure that moved on all fours, like a cat. Its head was triangular, armoured and tufted with thick strands of fur, and its eyes were a deep iridescent copper. It opened its maw to reveal thick ropes of saliva as it heaved itself into the cell and moved slowly forward, claws clacking against the white floor.

Haven suddenly tried to scramble backwards, eyes widening. 'No,' he said, his back pressing against the white wall. 'No, wait . . .'

Durell turned, moving towards the doorway and leaving the Sleeper Nex standing, its heavy muscles quivering like coiled steel under tension, staring at Haven with a cold and intelligent malevolence.

'Wait, man, you can't leave me to *this* . . .'

The Sleeper Nex growled softly, its triangular head swaying. It took a step forward, the heavy pads of its feet placed with precision and its head dipping a little towards Haven.

'I can help you, help you with the GRID . . .'

But Durell had turned to leave.

Haven tried to swallow. But his fear denied him the solace of saliva.

The Sleeper Nex moved forward to a series of screams. As Durell closed the door wet cubed chunks of flesh slapped suddenly against the walls, and the snapping and cracking of bones made him take a deep breath and stare down at the small dull ECube gripped in his curled clawed hands.

'Yes, Mace?' he said softly.

'We've got your Spiral mole on the q-line. Seems happy enough to supply us with all the info we need on the GRID – he is keen not just to see Spiral die, but to witness the breed pulped into extinction. I think somebody must have upset him.'

'Is this mole ready to meet?'

'Yes. Claims to have the coordinates for where we can obtain the SpiralGRID map – and thus put an end to their covert global attacks.'

'Good,' said Durell softly, as in the room behind him the Sleeper Nex shook the bloody rag doll of Viktor Haven's corpse. 'Because I want those Spiral fuckers exterminated. Permanently.'

**Spiral Mainframe
Data log#12874 [amended]**

CLASSIFIED SADt/6778/SPECIAL INVESTIGATIONS UNIT
Data Request 324#12874

Nex

The Nex Project Nx5

Nicknamed 'Necros' or 'Nex', the Nx5 Project was pioneered in the 1950s as a response to the Cold War games of the USA and Russia.

The design brief was simple – create a creature that was a blend of insect and human capable of withstanding chemical, biological and nuclear toxins. Using an ancient machine originally discovered by the Nazis, called The Avelach, Skein Blending allowed genetic strands to be spiralled together – woven into an artificial or enhanced creature. When the human was kept dominant then the resulting hybrid had many of the powerful characteristics of an insect – a much-increased strength, agility and speed. An increased pain threshold. A resistance to chemical, biological and radioactive poisons with an incredibly enhanced immune system. Improved thought processes. Some grew external and internal armour to protect organs and bones, and all became incredibly lethal killing machines without remorse. The perfect soldier with an ability to repair itself. Some would say, the perfect *human*.

Spiral withdrew funding following bad media coverage, several laboratory catastrophes and a growing concern over the morality of the programme.

The Nex, under the deviant control of Durell and his minions, spawned several different variations. A by-product of experimentation was the ScorpNex, or Nx6, but due to serious complications and chemical algorithms, Durell and his scientists found it extremely hard to replicate.

And finally (or originally) came the Sleeper Nex. All info on this creature is highly CLASSIFIED.

After destruction of the QuakeHub, the machine known as The Avelach – which was used in deviant conversions of human to Nex warrior – was taken to a safe storage depot by The Priest, the acting head of SpiralTac. However, it is known that Durell had made many pirate copies of this technologically advanced hardware, and so Spiral cannot rule out continued future production of Nex soldiers.

Keyword SEARCH>> NEX, SAD, SPIRAL_sadt, DURELL, FEUCHTER, QIII, Q1V, Avelach, Spiral_NX, Nx5, Nx6, Sleeper Nex, PureBreed

// Also see military texts *SPIRAL* and *QUAKE*.

CHAPTER 3

BAD GIG

Carter felt his body relax as the sun sent its rays cascading across the house and fields around him. To either side stood a Nex with a sub-machine gun pointing at his head; behind, the rising wail of the children as they caught sight of the *monster* out in the sun – and in front of him, tensed and expectant on the dirt road, stood the Sleeper Nex . . . one of Durell's greatest hunters. Greatest *killers*.

What had The Priest said that night Natasha had died? Back in London, after facing one of these terrible creatures? In his deep and melodious voice he had told Carter how the Sleeper Nex were *old*, a template for the actual Nex soldiers Spiral even now battled – they were a genetic master from which the Nex had evolved. The Priest had told Carter that if the Sleepers so much as scented you, they had your essence; they would never let you escape. They would pursue you to the ends of the Earth and *eat your soul*.

Carter shivered . . .

'Mr Carter. You have evaded us for too long. Now

your time has finally come,' came the low and sibilant whisper; the voice of a snake slithering through the grass; the voice of a creature beyond the true understanding of mortal man.

To one side of the dirt road lay a small shed stacked high with logs – used for keeping the farmhouse fires and stove burning through the winter months. From among these stacks of roughly chopped timber came Tomas, craggy face coated with drying blood, aged hands bearing a double-barrelled shotgun which he levelled at the two Nex – and Carter.

Carter tensed. Then his elbow shot out to the right as he launched himself sideways, connecting with the Nex's nose in a spurt of blood. The gun's barrels blasted out deadly twin sprays of shot picking up the second Nex and spreading it messily across the stable wall – in several pieces. Carter rolled, coming around fast as he took the Steyr TMP from the stunned second Nex's gloved hands, placed the muzzle against the hybrid's lips and pulled the trigger.

Bullets shattered bone. Smoke poured from the Nex's nostrils as Carter placed his boot on its twitching dead chest and lifted the gun, spinning to level the Steyr at the Sleeper Nex – which had not moved during the sudden vicious exchange.

Abruptly, silence reigned.

Tomas was fumbling with the shotgun. He had cracked open the weapon and was struggling to insert new shells, his fingers trembling. Carter's eyes narrowed. The Steyr TMP yammered in his hands as the Sleeper Nex back-flipped away, rolled and swiped with a massive armoured paw at Tomas, picking him up with a neck-breaking *crack* and hurling him into the wood store. The old man bounced like a rag doll, arms and legs flailing, slamming onto the floor with blood pouring from his battered face – and by the way he moved, his head lolling, Carter could see that he was quite obviously dead . . .

A stream of TMP bullets had followed the Sleeper Nex, each and every one failing to meet its target. Then the gun's firing pin clicked on an empty chamber and Carter dropped the weapon with a clatter to the dirt road. He levelled his Browning, gripping it in both hands.

The Sleeper Nex was swaying slightly, its slitted copper eyes locked on Carter.

'We have your scent,' it hissed, head tilting to one side. Claws slid out further from its huge armoured paws. 'We *all* have your scent, fucker; even if you evade me, even if you kill me, others will hunt you; others will find you.'

Carter swallowed, and fired off a shot.

The Sleeper Nex rolled with incredible speed; the bullet cut a narrow line across the surface of its black chitinous armour, but did not penetrate. The two combatants started to circle, with a good ten feet of space separating them. Carter stooped, pulling free a long black knife from his boot, and with Browning and knife held out in front of him they faced off – turning slowly, warily – two hunters, each with an insane concentration of purpose.

'Why me?' asked Carter softly.

'Durell wants you . . . Durell will *find* you.'

They had moved now, so that the Sleeper Nex had its back to the stable doors; its heavy muscles coiling under its plate armour were huge, powerful, thrumming with the tensioned promise of violence.

Carter swallowed softly . . . and knew. *Understood.* He did not know if he was physically capable of killing such a creature in one-on-one combat. He had no benefit of surprise. No back-up. No comrades with machine guns . . .

74

Out here, without Spiral, Carter was alone.

And the feeling hit him hard.

The Sleeper Nex growled and ducked a little, as if readying itself to attack. Carter braced himself for the onslaught as Kade emerged, taunting in the back of his mind, offering promises of dark salvation.

Carter's trigger finger tightened.

As the stable doors scraped against the floor, the Sleeper Nex half turned and Carter began to shoot, his Browning spitting fire. The doors burst open, spewing forth a cataract of charging, panicked horses that reared and jostled as they galloped over the creature in their path. Rearing and stomping and smashing iron-shod hooves as they screamed and whinnied in panic, they eventually veered off, heading away into fresh air and freedom, escaping the stench of Nex and death.

Carter suddenly froze, realising that he had dropped to a crouch as the horses stampeded around him and his Browning emptied. Slowly, warily, keeping his stare fixed on the prostrate figure of the battered Sleeper Nex, he changed magazines.

The thing's eyes flickered open. Copper eyes narrowed to slits.

Its front legs gathered beneath it and it heaved, muscles rolling. Then it gave a tiny chittering noise before slumping down once more. Carter uncoiled his own body and squinted at where the clear liquid oozed from cracked plates of armour across the Sleeper Nex's back.

Carter moved forward and looked down at the creature. He noted that three of his bullets had struck home, and this, combined with the steel hooves of the horses, had disabled the beast. He also noted that the horses' kicks had broken the Sleeper Nex's spine.

'You win this one, little man,' came the sibilant hiss.

The head tilted, causing the Sleeper Nex great pain, and it surveyed Carter more carefully as he pulled free an HPG and turned the dial. A blue glow bathed his hand like ice-mist, and he smiled down at the creature.

'Funny how things work out, my diseased little afterbirth.' Carter dropped the HPG beside the Sleeper Nex and said, 'I'll see you in hell.' He strode around its broken body, away through the doors and into the gloomy interior of the stable.

Outside, there was a concussive *boom*, followed by rattling sounds as shards of Nex armour peppered the exterior of the stable's walls. Carter looked over to where Mary stood beside the opened doors to the stalls – holding a Steyr TMP in her gnarled hands.

'You need to get away from here,' said Carter. 'It's a very dangerous place, and will become more so when the Nex discover what has happened.'

'I will take the Skoda. Go to my daughter up in the Troodos Mountains. The Nex do not know she is there.' She looked him in the eyes then. 'You are a very brave man, Carter. The only way evil triumphs is when good men stand by and do nothing . . . that was an option for you this day.' Her hand dropped to ruffle the hair of her grandchildren. 'Thankfully, you chose to help us and we will be eternally grateful.'

'I . . . am sorry, about Tomas.'

The old woman sighed, and it burned Carter to see tears on her cheeks. 'He was a good man. A good husband . . . like you, a good man standing up for what he believed in.' She reached forward, surprising Carter, and kissed him gently on the cheek.

'I am not a good man,' whispered Carter.

'You have risked your life. You have saved us. That is enough. God and his angels will be the judge of your worth.'

Carter helped the woman and her grandchildren to the Skoda, and lifted the body of Tomas, laying it gently across the back seat. The Skoda, trailing blue smoke, disappeared in a cloud of dust up the hill. Carter threw a glance at the bent and buckled Mercedes, and the corpses littering the ground – including the mangled carcass of the dead Sleeper Nex.

The world stank of death.

I thought I had left all this behind, he thought.

I thought the days of oblivion and destruction had vanished . . .

'*Not vanished. Just hidden. You know they will never leave you,*' snarled Kade from the dark side of Carter's soul. '*You know you are entwined with death, from the moment you were born to the moment you fucking die . . . programmed, like the most efficient of computer-generated killers . . .*'

Carter walked up the dirt track, heading back for his bike and the calming mental sanctuary of his young son.

'I thought those days were gone for me. I thought that life was finally over.'

'*Never, Carter. Never.*'

Carter was stripped to the waist, his old combat shorts stained and tattered above tanned legs and scuffed army boots. Sweat gleamed across his well-muscled and heavily scarred torso as he sawed at the thick plank of rough-cut timber, the teeth of the blade slicing neatly through the grain and filling the air with a scent of resin.

The sun sat, a copper pan nailed to the sky as the engine sound reached Carter and he ceased his work, straightening and wiping a layer of sweat from his face. His gaze moved from the broken fence he was trying to repair to the giggling distant form of Joseph running barefoot across the rocks with Samson bounding behind him to the rear slope at the back of the house from where the sounds of a badly maintained engine intruded.

The battered black KTM spluttered into view, knobbled tyres churning sand and pulling to a halt on dipping, leaking shocks. Carter shaded his eyes as the old man climbed free, one leg stiff and nursed by a protective hand, and then limped through the sand and up the three steps to the stone-laid path which wound down to the patio overlooking the sea.

'Sounds like your plugs are in need of some TLC,' said Carter.

'If I wanted your opinion, boy, I'd ask for it.'

The shaven-headed old man approached, fearsome and savage-looking. Suddenly his face broke into a beaming smile as his gnarled hand thrust out. Carter returned his grip – surprisingly strong, for the other man was well into his sixties.

'How's life, Ed?'

'I've felt better. My bloody leg is giving me real grief.'

'That bullet still eating you?'

'Aye.'

'You could always see a doctor.'

Ed looked sideways at Carter. 'A *Nex* surgeon? I'd rather have my manhood chewed off by a shark. Anyway, lad, you going to offer an old soldier a beer – or what?'

Carter grinned, and motioned to the nearby table and bench seats. Ed limped towards a seat, steely blue eyes staring off to where Joseph ran through the surf. Carter retrieved two beers, tossing one to Ed who caught the can neatly in one fist. On one set of army-tattooed knuckles was the word TUFF, complemented on the other hand by CUNT. Carter's gaze drifted, reading the self-inflicted army script. On the back of one hand it said, '*Too young to die*' whilst the other read, '*Too tough to kill*'. Both slogans were smudged and blurred with age, and both wrists had the word ELVIS LIVES inscribed on them.

'How's the boy doing?'

'Well,' said Carter, sipping his beer. His guts were still churning from the previous night's whisky and he acknowledged that beer was probably the last thing he needed. 'He's a little monster, mind, always getting into mischief. Poisoned my fish the other day—'

'How did he do that?' asked Ed.

'Dumped in a tin of sausage and beans, and a pound of butter. When I asked him what he'd been doing, he said he was giving them breakfast. Killed the whole damned tank!'

'Aww. But he only had their best interests at heart!'

'Yeah, not quite the way I saw it when I lost my entire stock. Anyway, listen, Ed, the Nex came sniffing around here last week. Masked and heavily armed. They are going to impose registrations on the island. Left me forms to fill in, the paper-pushing bastards.'

'From assassins to fucking civil servants.' Ed nodded, grinning maliciously. 'Pieces of shit, the lot of 'em. We could always hire a yacht; sail off to sea, avoid the fucking paperwork that way.'

'Well, that's always an option. Although listening to the engine on your bike, I don't think I'd entrust my life to any mechanical skills you might claim to possess. You fixed your boat yet?'

'No.'

'Thought not.'

They paused, and Samson's bark drifted over to them as Ed cracked his tattooed knuckles and turned his glittering eyes on Carter. Ed's face was worn, creased with age, battered by too many battles and a war that would never end. An ex-pat, he had already been living on

Cyprus when Durell had conquered the world – when, with the aid of the QIV military processor, he had decimated the Global Army and a huge number of cities with tactical nuclear strikes. When Carter had arrived, a fugitive, in exile as the Nex searched out and murdered those survivors from the Spiral army that they could find, Carter had shunned the company. And in the five years he had lived (*hid*, whispered Kade with mocking laughter) on the island, one of the few men he had allowed through his mask of suspicion, hatred, frustration and horror, had been Ed. Formerly King's Regiment, serving in Northern Ireland, Africa, Germany, Egypt, Hong Kong and finally China, this ex-sergeant had retired to Cyprus looking for peace and tranquillity. A retirement from battle. An end to war and death.

Then the Nex had arrived. And brought their own version of hell with them . . .

'Have you heard from them recently?' asked Eddie.

Carter stared hard. He sipped at his beer, then shook his head. 'Spiral? No.'

'Not even Nicky?'

Carter grinned nastily. 'Straight to the point, eh? No beating around the bush for you, you old donkey.'

'No point, lad. Bushes are like GPS systems – only for pussies. So then? You had no contact at all with Spiral, or any of its operatives?'

'Nicky called. Maybe two months ago. Why the sudden interest? Is something going down that I need to be told about? *Should* I be expecting a visit?'

Ed reclined and watched Joseph and Samson down by the edge of the sea. Waves were rolling gently over the rocks and Joe seemed to have found something which he was inspecting closely.

'He safe down there? On his own like that?'

'He's safe, Ed. Come on, spill.'

'The Nex caught somebody. A Spiral terrorist, so-called. It was plastered all over the news last night – I thought you might have seen it.'

'Who was it?'

Ed's eyes met Carter's stony gaze. 'A big black guy. Been at the forefront of Spiral activity since Durell's big push five years ago. He's a friend of yours. Man by the name of Justus.'

Carter said nothing. He turned his head slightly, gaze fixed on his son splashing in a rock pool and poking at something with what looked like a stick.

'He was a good friend, yes?'

Carter nodded, sighing. 'Yeah. The best a man could have.'

'It is a great shame,' said Ed sombrely. 'Your companions are being picked off one by one. Durell and the Nex are compromising the SpiralGRID. Soon, Spiral will have nowhere left to run – or hide. There will be nothing left for them.'

'I'm no longer part of Spiral,' said Carter softly, standing and moving to the rail where he grasped the sturdy timber with both hands, gazing out over the gently rolling sea. A breeze ruffled his short brown hair, soothing his skin, making him shudder slightly as within the dark recesses of his brain a million dark and twisted images flickered a nightmare reel of murder.

'It's not my problem any more,' he said.

Carter slept badly again that night after a shower and some calming cuddles from his now dozing, gently breathing child.

Once Joe had been put to bed, Carter tossed and turned, sleeping fitfully; haunted. He had a dream. In the dream Natasha appeared to him, her naked body grey and withered, her eyes empty black holes which expressed despair and an eternity of suffering and horror. Carter awoke at dawn, groggy and with his head pounding. Pulling on shorts and battered trainers, and checking quickly on his son, he jogged down to the rocky beach with Samson leaping around his feet. He pounded along the wet sand, leaping shallow pools and narrow crevasses sea-worn from the dark jagged rock.

He put down six miles at an intense pace which left Samson trailing miserably behind him, head down, tongue out, eyes pleading for his master to halt.

Reaching home, he found Joseph sitting on the porch, eating cereal. Carter pounded up to the wooden boards and stood, hands on hips, face red from exertion, allowing his body to calm as Samson slunk off to bury his head in his wide ceramic water bowl.

'You OK, lad?'

Joe nodded, munching. 'Nicky called on the telephone. She said she was coming.'

Carter silently cursed, and moved inside to shower and change quickly. He returned wearing knife-cut combat shorts, boots and a tattered Che Guevara T-shirt and stood, leaning against the porch and giving in to his craving – much to Joe's frowning disapproval. He lit a cigarette, and stared out over the sea, eyes searching for the Manta. Eventually he spotted it, glinting darkly, sleek and mean as it sliced through distant drifting clouds. The tiny matt-black fighter banked sharply, jets rotating smoothly to allow it a neat vertical landing a hundred metres away from the house.

The cockpit canopy slid to one side and Nicky stood, stretching, and waved at Carter with a beaming smile.

He gave a short wave back, finishing his cigarette only

to light another immediately. Nicky climbed down from the Manta, shouldered her pack and jogged towards him over the black, volcanic-like rocks, jumping nimbly from one outcrop to another.

Joe ran across the porch as Nicky came close, and she scooped him up in a big bear hug, throwing him into the air. He giggled, rubbing his face in her hair, against her neck, and she slapped at his bottom. 'How's my favourite little man doing?'

'I'm being a good boy.'

'Have you stopped daddy smoking yet?'

Joe frowned. '*Nobody* can stop daddy smoking. You should know that.'

Nicky, protesting at Joseph's recent weight gain, put the young boy down. There followed a few minutes of small talk. But all the while Carter was watching her eyes – and he could read something there. A word which taunted him with the initial letter M. M for Mission.

Finally, Joseph ran down to the beach with a yapping Samson. Carter and Nicky sat on oppose sides of the table, Nicky's pack between them on the rough-cut pine boards as Carter poured two cups of coffee from a jug. Nicky took her coffee black, whilst Carter added cream and three sugars to his.

'You'll get fat.'

'I am fat. Now, what do you want?'

Nicky pouted. 'What makes you think I want anything?'

'I can read it in your eyes. And I've got a horrible feeling it's not something I'm going to like.'

Nicky nodded, accepting a cigarette from Carter, and then a light from his Zippo. She allowed her smiling mask – a mask held in place for the benefit of the young boy – to drop.

'We have a problem.'

'We?'

'Spiral.'

'Yeah, but I'm not Spiral any more.'

'You'll always be Spiral, Carter. In your heart. In your soul.'

'Not true,' he said, looking away, gaze drifting to where Joseph played beside the rolling surf. The sea boomed behind him. 'I have different priorities in my life.'

'Such as?'

'Survival.'

'You think Durell's domination of the world is conducive to your survival? You're living in a dream world, Carter. Durell has filled the cities with Nex and JT8 murder squads. He's nuked the hell out of us, then dumped HATE over every damned patch of non-urban landscape the world over – or so he would have us believe via his HIVE Media system of shite – and all to hem in the people like prisoners in the largest concrete prisoner-of-war camps ever devised. If it wasn't for the Spiral labs churning out anti-HATE drugs there would be no way we could operate outside the cities – and that's why Durell needs us seriously *dead*.'

Carter shrugged. 'I played my part, Nicky. I risked my life, countless times. But it was no good – Durell was too strong, too resourceful, too powerful. As you've just described.'

'What is this shit?' Nicky frowned, her pretty face twisting in anger. 'This isn't the Carter I know! This isn't the man who stood by his friends, stood by the people who had fought alongside him . . . this isn't the *soldier* who I know and love!'

Carter shrugged once more, then lit another cigarette. Nicky reached out, took it from his fingers and allowed herself a deep drag. She sipped at her black coffee, frowning to herself at some internal dialogue; then she visibly calmed and looked up suddenly, her gaze meeting Carter's cool and calculating stare.

'You don't know what I want you to do.'

'I don't care.'

'You do care.'

'All right, I do care, but Joseph is my priority. I said I wouldn't leave him, and I won't fucking leave him. You understand me? You know what I've been through, you know what happened to Natasha—'

'Yeah, and you think you're the only one to suffer a casualty of war? Don't hit me with that fucking arrogant selfish standpoint, Carter. You lost Natasha, I lost Jam. It's a cruel fucking world we live in, I know, but sometimes we have to make sacrifices and they both died doing what needed to be done – doing what they were paid to do but, more importantly, doing what they knew to be right.'

'I'm not interested in sacrifices. Those days are over for me.' The lie tasted bad, even as it left Carter's lips. He knew the words were not true. He knew he was . . . *better* than that. Because the day mankind no longer made sacrifices . . . well, that was the day the Nex deserved to win.

'Spiral are in trouble.'

'I don't want to know.'

'Spiral are in a world of shit, Carter. Durell's New World Order has forced us underground – they're calling us fucking *terrorists*, for Christ's sake. The Nex Agencies are just too powerful now, too dominant. We are fighting a battle we cannot win and the real bitch is that we *know* we cannot win it.'

Carter sighed, sipping his coffee. Samson's barks drifted over to him, followed by his son's giggles. He felt his heart flutter then – and a sudden vortex of darkness clamped his mind.

He looked into Nicky's eyes.

For long moments, an intimacy of understanding passed between them.

'Go on,' he said softly, finally.

'We are compromised. The only thing that keeps us in the game is the SpiralGRID: the network which allows us to wage a *terrorist* war from below the streets, pop up, slam a war factory, disappear into the GRID again. Well, we recently discovered that we've got a traitor – a piece of shit who is going to compromise the SpiralGRID in its entirety. He's one of Spiral's top men, one of our few generals who have the SpiralGRID brain-tattooed. He has been detected by covert tracking, digitally recorded sending coded messages to the Nex Agency; they were hacked by accident, by one of our sub-system programmers. This man has set up a rendezvous with the Nex Agency: he plans to allow them to laser the details from the surface of his brain – that's the only way to access the information. He will compromise the GRID. He will betray Spiral – he will betray the last chance humanity has to overthrow Durell.'

'His name?'

'Jahlsen.'

'And you want me to—'

'Kill him. Blow the bastard to Kingdom Come.'

'Ahh.'

Carter rose and moved to the steps where he stood, hands in his pockets, staring out over the sea. Waves crashed against the rocks in a turmoil of white foam.

'What about Joseph?'

'I would look after him. Me. Probably the only person in the world you still trust. Or . . . Mrs Fickle. You sometimes have her look after the boy, don't you?'

86

Carter shook his head, turning to stare at Nicky. 'I'm retired, Nicky. This is not my fight any more. This is no longer my fucking *gig*.'

'This has *always* been your fight, Carter. You know it, and I know it. Now, I'll not bullshit you. This is a tough fucking takedown – CitySide London, halfway through the nuked zone, crawling with Nex and JT8s. You can go in alone, or with a squad – whatever you prefer. But we need you, Carter – we need you to do what you do best.'

'Kill?'

'Yeah, Carter. Kill.'

'I don't know.'

'Come on, Carter, we *need* you. Believe me, there were many who didn't want me to ask for your help; they think you're fucked, brain-fried, heavy on the whisky and burned out. But I *know* you can do this – and there's not many I believe can. Without this assassination Spiral will be crushed – all of us will be captured, tortured, murdered. The Priest, Roxi, Mongrel, Simmo . . . me.'

'You'll have to give me time to think about it,' said Carter softly.

Nicky stood, and dropped a silver ECube onto the table. She smiled at him then, and took a deep breath. 'If you choose not to do this, then I understand. Truly, mate, I really do understand.' She glanced to where the boy was splashing in the waves. Samson's excited barking echoed along the beach.

'Give me a few hours.'

Nicky nodded, long, elegant lashes blinking at him. 'A few hours,' she agreed.

Daylight was fading.

The soft hiss and surge of the surf taunted Carter through the half-gloom. He sat on the steps leading to his porch with a bottle of beer in one hand, cigarette in the other. Samson sat by his side, broad chocolate head on Carter's lap, snoring, one eye opening occasionally to give his owner a baleful glare.

The glow of the cigarette brightened as Carter inhaled, then dimmed to a dull glow. Footsteps padded across the porch and Ed dropped to the planks beside Carter, handing the ex-Spiral op a fresh beer.

'You OK?'

'Never better.' Carter smiled weakly.

Both men watched the sea for a while, lost in thought, then Carter glanced sideways at Ed and studied the man's ravaged visage. In his sixties, Eddie was a veteran: an old soldier, burned out by the army and a hundred battles – and by visions of his dead friends which haunted his nightmares. Heavily tattooed, head still shaved and boots still polished, he was the wisest, sanest influence Carter had encountered in many years.

'What are you going to do?' asked Ed softly.

'What would you do?'

'Not my decision to make, laddie. It's a tough call, that's for sure. I know you believe you're well out of the loop now, retired, ex-Spiral and all that – but what's in your mind? What's in your *heart*?'

Carter said nothing. His stare locked on the sea, mouth a grim thin line.

'They were your friends, yes?'

'Yeah.'

'They are still your friends?'

'Of course. Until we die.'

'Then ask yourself this question – can you stand by while they are betrayed? Are you going to watch Durell's media circus parade your friends like freaks across the TV screens, watch as they are slowly tortured on the box?

Murdered on fucking Pay-For-View? Slaughtered like lambs?'

Carter worked his bottle into the sand, then fished out the silver alloy ECube. It glinted dully in the rays of the fast-falling sun. He toyed with it briefly.

'I'll come with you, if you like.'

Carter met Ed's gaze. 'Why would you do that?'

'Back-up? Mate, I am a fucking mean shot with a Barrett. Can't say I'll charge into the action – a gammy leg, you understand – but any Nex sneaking up behind you is *guaranteed* a .338mm round up the arse.'

Carter sighed – seemed to deflate. He stroked Samson's velvet ears and looked out to the sea once more, then activated the ECube. It glittered with blue digits. He smoothed a pattern across the surface and there came a tiny blip.

Carter flicked his cigarette end towards the sea; it landed on the rocks, glowing briefly before dying.

'You made a decision?'

Carter thought about his friends, thought about the many battles he had waged against the Nex – and against Durell – as a Spiral operative. He thought about Jam, about Natasha, thought about his son, Joseph. And, finally, he pictured the dead eyes of Tomas – an old man just caught in the wrong place at the wrong time.

'I'll do it,' he whispered, and closed his eyes against the rays of the setting sun.

AN INTERLUDE:

PROLOGUE TO
THE CHAINSTATIONS

The Cobra-S lifted on a cold cushion of LVA fumes as it left behind a desolate, barren landscape. A cold wind was blowing, scattering the fine exhaust fumes as the Cobra-S lifted its nose and climbed steadily into a cold blue sky trailing streamers of broken cloud.

Behind lay the distant devastated skeleton of New York.

Ahead lay the eighth Dreadnought.

It had begun as a cooperative project between NASA, the RFST and CRSA upon the discovery of a technology which would simplify and ease the myriad problems of construction in space – in terms of scale, materials and finance. The new technology was a machine grandly entitled a Gravity Displacer. No larger than a football, it could specify digital global parameters and neutralise gravity, in effect creating a specific area which contained zero gravity for the duration of a construction. Normal gravity would persist in and around the building zone itself – but the actual structure would, in effect, be weightless. Like a ten-million-tonne helium balloon.

In this manner, the first of the Dreadnought construction blocks had been fashioned. People gathered on the ground beneath in their tens of thousands to gawp open-mouthed at this eighth wonder of the world – hanging solid and immovable and matt black against the glowing backdrop of the sky.

The size of a seventy-five-storey tower block which had been flipped onto its side, the BCB construct hung solid and cold, a skyscraper slab painted against the heavens, suspended by the digital precision of a GD in its own parameter fields of weightlessness.

Helicopters and fast Manta Shuttles ferried personnel and building materials, news crews and ASP workers to and from the suspended building block as work on it was, over a period of months, completed. News programmes ran features in solid rotation, along with advertisements for *ChainStations – a New World For a New Tomorrow,* and *LVA – the Fuel For a New Space Age.*

Just as interest started to wane, and the crowds of techno-tourists drifted apart, the first freight tug using its own tiny onboard GD was put into service. The long, vaguely doughnut-shaped vehicle had hooked up to the BCB construct and, with flashes of silver and violet across the darkened evening sky, the Gravity Displacer fashioned a tunnel through which the freight tug towed the enormous building block – up past the Earth's atmospheric influences and out into the dark expanses of space.

With this first ChainStation building block in place and actively operational, the Accelerated Space Programme had thrown massive funding into the project, buoyed by success and public support – especially in the wake of the HATE outbreak which, in effect, imprisoned the majority of the world's population in the cities, those desolate half-destroyed concrete wildernesses.

Six months after the initial success of the first BCB construct, another six units had been tugged down their Anti-G tunnels and into the darkness of space, looking down upon the glowing sun-bright orb which had spawned them.

Now the ASP was actively developing another ninety-four BCB units globally. They would, within three to six months, join their cousins circling the Earth to create the first-ever ChainStation: a promise of escape for those tortured souls who were sick of the ever-present threat of HATE and toxic disintegration . . . a promise of a New Future, a New World.

The Cobra-S accelerated silently towards Dreadnought8, which hung immobile and strangely silent in the cold gloom of the dawn. Rain was falling gently around the sleek craft as it banked, the huge black tower block half enshrouded in thick drifting clouds that filled the craft's scanners which issued mid-prox warnings with low-level bleat sirens.

The Cobra-S pulled alongside the huge black construct so that it was cruising a parallel course and the pilot glanced out to his right – through the fine mist – and thought he saw a slight resonance.

The BCB vibrating; so delicately and so quickly that it was hard to see as more than a barely visible vibration. But it was there, evidence of the GD field which held this ten-million-tonne block of space station in temporary stasis.

The Cobra-S slowed and then turned, hovering with tiny hisses of cold matrix exhaust. In the blank black surface of the BCB a huge portal slid into itself, fine spirals of metal rotating to reveal a circular hollow punctuating the zero-gravity field. The Cobra-S slid into the opening and the slivers of alloy closed neatly behind it, leaving nothing but a fine mist and a grey, upwards-falling rain.

*

There came a huge crash as the freight tug engaged with the BCB construct; engines screamed and the TitaniumIV thread-chains went from slack to taut as the tug shunted sideways, taking its position.

Computers hummed, altering Gravity Displacement coordinates, and then, slowly, the tug started to pull the mammoth Dreadnought across the sky.

Below, thousands of people turned aside from their daily chores. They watched in awe as the tower block lying on its side, impossibly huge, at first crawled and then accelerated away into the distance. It gained altitude in a broad upsweeping arc until it was climbing vertically – until the freight tug finally released its chains as great swinging slack pendulums and the GD motors whined down as the BCB construct was shunted into a precise orbit around the Earth.

The tug's work was far from over. Several miles away, seven Dreadnoughts had already been linked – by floating, undulating ChainLink Corridors, so that seven Dreadnoughts formed huge tower-block couplings in the ChainStation set-up as a whole. Even now, lights flickered across the vast expanses of these primary test modules – and plans were being finalised in boardrooms and laboratories for the newly planned NG Units: BCBs a hundred times larger than the skyscraper construct units currently being tested. A billion diagnostic tests were run through, with checks and counter-checks.

This proto-chain was the first stepping stone to the ChainStation as a real entity. A new synthetic world. It was the first toddler footstep of an unsteady mankind – or, at least, *Nex*kind – towards the conquest of the solar system and the stars far beyond.

ADVERTISING FEATURE

The TV-ProjU sparkled into life with a digital buzz of humming phosphorescence. Images spun and leapt, dissolving and then reanimating into the mercury logo of HIVE Media Productions . . .

[deep male voice]
– A normal working weekday, with normal everyday people travelling to their places of business, of fun, of productivity.

Scene pans slowly to: an ordinary city street. Normal people are striding on their way to work when suddenly a deafening crack echoes across the world and the street shakes—

Audio:
– A backdrop of echoes and a metallic rumbling reminiscent of a devastating earthquake.

[deep male voice]
Beneath this world, beneath this normality lurks a danger so terrible that it could rip apart the very fabric of our whole universe . . .

Scene zooms quickly to: a man's face, which suddenly explodes into ravioli-like sachets of flesh rushing out towards the camera, shooting past the lens in a shower of liquid meat – and as we zoom through the fine mist of blood and slowly spinning brain globules, the everyday city scene has been turned into a vision of HELL. Bodies lie battered and broken; men, women and children sprawl on the pavement and the roadway, limbs missing, trailing streaks of gore to the slick layer of blood which coats everything in a shining new gloss.

Audio:
- *Screams echo.*
- *Women weep for children.*
- *Children sob for parents.*
- *And a terrible final silence descends.*

Screen fades to black; TEXT [scrolling L > R/ silver lettering FONT LUCIDA SANS]: SPIRAL are a group of rogue soldiers working throughout the world to bring down your New World Government – the very World Government which saved **YOU** from the biological horrors of the HATE biological virus and the accidentally detonated military nuclear warheads. SPIRAL kill indiscriminately in their war of terror. **EVERYBODY** out there has the potential to discover a SPIRAL agent . . . **EVERYBODY** out there has a duty to their fellow men, women and children – a duty to wipe this **FILTH** from the planet. Do the **RIGHT** thing, call the **NEX AGENCY NOW!** on 0999 999 999 or text/cube your information. All information is treated in the strictest confidence.

Audio:
- *Soft violin music; a haunting and harrowing solo, lilting and gentle.*
- *DON'T BE AFRAID – PROTECT YOUR CHILDREN AND OUR MODERN WORLD . . . HELP THE NEX ANTI-SPIRAL UNITS TO HELP YOU – HELP THE NEX TO RIGHT THIS TERRIBLE DOWNWARD SPIRAL OF WRONG.*

SCENE DISSOLVES TO SILVER

CHAPTER 4

ASSASSINATION

The low sleek alloy Manta skimmed over the churning waves, spray spitting up over the cockpit, the speed filling Carter with exhilaration and a sense of freedom.

As dawn broke the Manta banked right, heading north. Carter's euphoria gave way to a sense of foreboding. Nicky had smiled and nodded, filling him with the reassurances he needed; she had taken Joseph in her arms, his head snuggling to her chest as he fell instantly into a deep sleep. She had smiled, as if to say, 'There, you see?' Carter had reluctantly thrown his pack into the black craft and used the recessed steps to mount up into the cockpit – closely followed by Ed in his worn old GPs.

'Now, you look after my little boy,' Carter had called down.

'Just get out of here and save your friends . . . Jesus, if you can't trust Joseph with me, then you can't trust him with anybody!'

Carter nodded, closed the cockpit canopy, and within a minute was airborne and screaming low over the Med.

Now, heading inland and with the weather turning

bleaker and wilder by the minute, Carter thought back to that conversation and his own deep-rooted suspicions born from the loss of love: the loss of his Natasha, Joseph's mother.

'You OK?' came Ed's gravelled voice from the co-pilot's seat behind.

'Yeah. Just worried about my boy.'

'He'll do fine, Carter. It's yourself you should be worried about. This is no easy gig.'

'Yeah, London fucking gangland with a wanted face like mine. All I need. Maybe I should paint my arse orange and stand on top of Big Ben! I'm sure that would present a less obvious target.'

They swept low over rain-drenched forests and rolling fields through the gloomy autumn ice-light. Below, nothing moved – no man, woman or child could be seen, no cars on the roads, no pedestrians standing on pavements and staring up as the Manta cruised past.

Occasionally they spotted – on the radar or ECscans columns of armoured vehicles; Nex-led convoys of tanks and FukTruks, usually ferrying infantry across the countryside that had become a desolate wilderness.

HATE had seen to that.

A wonder of military, biological and chemical design, the HATE virus – when released over non-urban areas – would spread to the concrete outskirts of major towns and cities, killing all in its path. In effect, it would force populations into heavily built-up conurbations – herding humans (and certain types of animal) into areas where they could be either easily policed or easily exterminated.

HATE, invented by a team of American, British, Russian, Japanese and German military scientists, had ironically been used by Durell against the very people whom it had been developed to protect.

Spiral operatives maintained their freedom of movement through this poisoned world by the use of Spiral-developed anti-HATE drugs. But as with any drug that altered an organism's responses, there were side effects. And this resistance to Durell's grand scheme gave the Nex an even greater need to exterminate the seemingly perpetual thorn in their side: Spiral.

Carter lowered the Manta on a whine of engines, and then skimmed the top of a huge, sprawling, rain-drenched pine forest, sweeping up over a massive hillside and banking past an old stone Bavarian castle mounted on a narrow rocky outcropping.

Carter's mind started to settle itself, readying for the confrontation he knew was to come. He breathed deeply, watching the rolling forests undulating beneath him. They crossed a river swollen by heavy rainfall . . . then flew low over a deserted German village, the desolate streets empty except for a few rusting, overturned cars. Occasionally Carter caught a glimpse of skeletons squatting in corners, huddled in wet torn clothing, bones picked clean by scavengers. Carter shivered in the confines of the Manta's cockpit.

A ghost town, he thought.

HATE did its job well . . .

'*Yeah, but never well enough,*' came Kade's bitter words.

'Why don't you just fuck off and die?'

Kade chuckled, a bone-rattling sound filled with lead and toxins. '*Never in your lifetime* compadre – *Brother, Father, Son and Holy fucking Ghost. We are together. Merged and bonded into One. For now and for all eternity . . . or until we crumble into dust. Amen.*'

Carter's dark, sombre eyes stared steadily ahead through the gloom. He severed the connection.

★

Carter landed on the outskirts of London, in a park beside a river. The distant skyline was a ravaged silhouette of broken buildings; the relics of the nuclear blast five years earlier.

A SmutCar – an old rusting black Range Rover which had had the roof cut free with a Stihlsaw and sported folded, jagged edges – was waiting patiently for the two men; just as Nicky had promised. Carter landed the Manta and climbed free of its warmth and into the chilly London air. Ed followed, shouldering the soft case containing his Russian Dragunov SVD sniper rifle with its PSO-1 telescopic sight, and carrying an M27 carbine in his tattooed hands. His face was set, blue eyes focused on the job that had to be done.

Carter moved warily to the Range Rover, checking inside and out – mainly for bombs. He palmed the key and slid it into the ignition as Ed scanned the area. The powerful Perkins 7.2 diesel fired after a few spins of the starter, and black fumes belched from the triple exhaust pipes. Carter slid into the damp rain-slick seat and fixed his eyes on the distant remains of the capital. Even from this distance he could make out the war-torn features; the crumbling, bombarded, bullet-riddled buildings.

'We're clear,' said Ed softly, climbing in beside Carter. 'Too much chance of contracting HATE out here – looks like the people have defined their own borders.'

'It's still classed as a KillZone,' said Carter. 'If the fucking Nex see us they'll open fire without question.'

'Yeah, but if they see your face, mate, they'll open fire anyway. You're a wanted man.'

'Good point. You fill me with supreme confidence.'

'That's why I'm here.' Ed grinned, slapping Carter on the back.

Carter nudged the old tiptronic into first and stomped

the accelerator pedal. The Range Rover wheel-spun across loose stones, bit tarmac and shot down past the edges of the tree-lined park with its black wrought-iron fences. They disappeared into the narrow, shadowed confines of a deserted huddle of Victorian terraced buildings.

They drove slowly through a light fall of rain threatening to become snow, tyres crunching rubble, eyes watching warily the people who moved along the pavements.

They cruised past several groups of JT8s, black-clad and wearing alloy and plastic gas-masks. Occasionally, their heads kept low, the two men rumbled past a squad of Nex – but the authorities seemed uninterested in this old SmutCar with its two anonymous-looking occupants.

The atmosphere in London was bad; it was wrong.

Something nasty was going down.

'Roadblock,' said Ed softly.

'I see it.'

They slowed, caught in a crawling queue of traffic moving towards Covent Garden. The rain turned to snow and swirled in the gently moaning wind. The quality of the light seemed to become subdued.

'Shall we ditch the car?'

'We're too close to them now; they've probably tagged us,' said Carter softly. 'We'll have to chance it.'

They moved on, closer and closer to the checkpoint. Carter pulled his collar up as snow settled across his shoulders and head and into the Range Rover's damp interior. He allowed the snow to build, disguising the colour of his hair. As they reached the checkpoint – a temporary construction fashioned from sandbags and concrete-filled oil drums, and protected by two GAU 19/A Gatling-type three-barrelled machine guns that fired .50 Browning cartridges and were capable of putting down two thousand rounds per minute – the Nex waved the Range Rover through with only a cursory glance at the occupants.

Still Carter felt tense; the Browning dug into his hip as if reminding him of their mutual agreement – a blood-brother agreement written in the splattered souls of innumerable victims.

Carter eased the Range Rover forward, past the intimidating GAUs. They turned right at the earliest opportunity, down a narrow side street which had once been home to some of London's finest West End restaurants but was now an avenue of dereliction. Carter killed the engine and both he and Ed clambered out, shouldering their packs. Carter checked up and down the gloomy street, looking back at shattered restaurant fronts and the bullet-riddled stonework around gaping doorways. He discreetly checked the ECube given to him by Nicky, then orientated himself. He killed the tiny machine, looked into Ed's eyes, and said, 'This way.'

They walked along the buckled pavements for five minutes, passing groups of people huddled in the snow or hurrying with heads down and dark-circled eyes shadowed by their fear. Stopping outside a deserted building Carter and Ed quickly stepped into the cold and draughty interior.

The building's windows had long ago disintegrated, and the interior sported nothing more than rotting carpets. The walls were pockmarked with the signs of old battle. One wall sported a long jagged crack running from ceiling to floor.

'Is this place condemned?' Ed asked.

'I would hope so,' said Carter softly, his Browning in his fist as he moved forward past a disused buckled lift and towards a wide sweep of marble stairs. 'Somebody sure shot the shit out of this place.'

The stairs were incomplete, with sections of marble facing missing to reveal gaps and blocks of supporting stone beneath. Carter trod warily up the snow-slippery steps.

He moved slowly and with care, eyes scanning continually. After four storeys of climbing the two men finally came to a series of narrow galvanised steps rising steeply to the roof.

The wind snapped at their exposed skin like a terrier, and snow settled across them in a diagonal fall. They moved carefully to the large stone blocks at the edge of the building, crouched, and peered over at the spread of the city around them. To their left rose a slick dome of green copper and the large white clock face – bullet-pocked like the victim of some awful skin disease.

Traffic moved in blocks below, held up by various checkpoints. Some people gathered on the streets, but this was lessening with the severity of the weather now that the snowstorm had increased in intensity. Carter's sharp eyes picked up plenty of Nex – a more heavy concentration of them than he would have liked.

'There's a lot of them down there, boy,' Ed muttered.

'Yeah. And that's why you're going to stay up here. Watch my back.'

'Which is the target building?'

Carter nodded over the low stone lip to a grey-walled block with small square windows laid out in perfect symmetry. The building was a huge rectangle, with streets on all four sides – an island amidst the chaos of rising and falling rooftops. 'I think it used to be a bank headquarters at one point – but the old financial institution is long dead, and it's used as housing now— He checked the

ECube. 'By my calculations, our target is top floor, four along – in that room there.' Carter pointed, and Ed pulled free the separate components of his Dragunov SVD and slowly, lovingly – despite the snow and the biting chill – fitted the weapon together.

'You want me to take him out from here?'

Carter shook his head. 'No – if you miss, we'll never find him. He'll disappear like a rabbit into a warren with five ferrets on its arse. I'll go in on foot.'

Ed grinned.

'What is it?'

The older man gestured at the snow-filled expanse. 'You going to slide across?' Carter gazed out at the numerous swaying cables which linked the two buildings, dropping in curves between the two structures and gleaming with a slick snow peppering.

'*What*? No, fuck that, I'm going to use the stairs.'

'And there was me thinking you were the perfect action hero!'

'Action hero?' snorted Carter. 'In this world, my friend, there is no such thing.'

And then he was gone, swallowed by the darkness.

Carter spent a full hour scouting the building that contained the target. He circled it three times, from different angles, making sure he was unobserved and approaching from different directions every time. He had kept his head low, stuck to the shadows, and used the natural cover of the falling snow to allow him to get closer than he could ever have managed on a clear day.

'*I love it when we're alone together,*' said Kade happily.

Carter had cursed Kade's return. Stagnant for many months, his dark brother had resurfaced once more at the promise of a fight.

'I wish I was alone *for ever.*'

'*You don't mean that, Carter. I know that deep down in your soul, you love me. I know that we are brothers; that we are integral, entwined – lovers, if you like.*'

'Love? Between us? Don't make me fucking laugh. I thought you were useful once – but you disproved *that* when we faced off Jam in Austria. Not much use then, were you?' Kade remained silent. 'What's the matter, Kade? Cat got your tongue, you pile of shit?'

Carter grinned to himself, eyes scanning the building for the fifth time. As far as he could surmise, and judging by the number of people entering and leaving the large housing block of grey stone, the place was pretty much crammed to the rafters. Which made a covert assassination all the more difficult. And to make matters worse, Nex *and* JT8 patrols passed the building in a regular pattern – sometimes within four minutes of each other.

Slowly, Carter screwed a silencer onto the Browning and checked the magazine one final time. He stowed the weapon in its holster against the small of his back. He had recently stashed his M24 carbine and pack just inside the doorway of a disused building a street away from the target – his escape route if things went well. About his person he carried an array of weapons, from his trusty Browning to a selection of grenades, including HPG silent chemical explosives, a hidden thread of MercG – a liquid-metal thread activated by mind augmentations, a high-tech processor-controlled garrotte so thin that it could be concealed as a thread and so deadly that it could cut through concrete or steel – and a long black dagger concealed in his boot. His last resort.

Carter moved from the narrow, snow-filled alley, gaze scanning swiftly from left to right, slid into the building, and disappeared.

The snow continued its diagonal descent. Shadows slid along the wall of the building in silence, their small boots making no sound. The figures were clad in body-hugging grey uniforms and balaclavas; they carried 9mm TMPs and their copper eyes communicated with one another in silence as they weaved through the heavy snowfall and merged with the building's silent open doorway . . . scant seconds after Carter's passing.

Within the blink of an eye, the Nex were gone.

Carter paused, turning himself into the building. Noises assaulted his ears from all levels – voices, shouts, music, the blaring rattle of TVs, the stomp of footsteps. Carter held his Browning concealed at his side and moved towards the stairs, eyes narrowed, continually searching for any signs of something out of place.

The ECube had given him a room number, along with a digital representation of the building's layout; he had memorised these details, along with viable escape routes over the rooftops, through drains and back alleyways, if things happened to turn bad.

He ignored the polished steel of the lift, and padded up the first flight of wide stairs towards the rear of the building. The first landing stank of piss – whether human or animal, Carter could not tell – and the lighting was extremely poor.

On to the second flight, where the smell of piss was stronger and the yellow-flowered velour wallpaper hung in wide strips trailing to the rotting threadbare carpets. Huge stains painted patterns on the plaster beneath, which in turn sported hairline fractures and a pervading stench of damp.

What a place, thought Carter. What a *shit-hole*.

He moved up, past the deserted third floor and to the

fourth. He stood on the landing, breathing deeply, feeling himself finally calm. Now he was in an almost robotic state of mind in which all that mattered was his objective, his *mission*.

The assassination.

Carter moved slowly along the corridor, boots silent on the thick damp carpet. All his senses were screaming at him as he stopped beside the door of Jahlsen's – the Spiral man's – room. He listened, head tilted slightly to one side, then removed his ECube and activated its sensors.

The ECube reported nothing.

No trackers, prox sensors, EC alerts – *nothing*.

And yet, this man was Spiral. An operative. And active in one of the most dangerous cities in the world . . . Carter frowned, extended the Browning in front of him and, making sure that his body was well to one side of the doorway, gave a rapid triple knock.

Nothing.

No sounds, no footsteps, nothing.

'Interesting.' Carter placed the ECube against the door and stroked in a magnify instruction. The ECube relayed sounds of a TV set burbling – ironically, with an advertisement warning viewers against so-called Spiral terrorists. He initiated an organics scan – which revealed one human.

Carter knocked again.

No reply.

Maybe Jahlsen was asleep? Or drunk?

'*Or dead*,' mused Kade.

Carter took a step back, lifted a boot, and hammered a front kick against the door which splintered it from its lock and smashed it back against the wall. Carter leapt to one side and waited, then slid into the room and closed the door behind him.

Rubbish was strewn everywhere, a mass of pizza boxes, bottles, cartons, tissues, the waste of human deterioration scattered across the stained floor and torn settee. Carter scanned quickly, then moved on through, checking each room in turn until he reached the bedroom.

Jahlsen was kneeling, wearing only a pair of boxer shorts, on a filthy bed. The room was dark, illuminated just by the TV set which sent strobes of imagery across Jahlsen's seemingly blank eyes. Carter glanced to one side, where a tinfoil tube revealed its grey powder contents. Several spent matches lay beside it.

Carter moved slowly in front of the man, blocking out the TV and sending his own silhouette stretching across the far wall. The stink of GodSmack still filled the room, twitching at Carter's nostrils and making him want to gag.

Carter shook his head. Shit.

This is wrong, he thought.

The whole situation is *wrong*.

He lifted the Browning and sighted on Jahlsen's forehead.

Why is he here?

Carter allowed his breath to escape.

Jahlsen's eyes snapped open. He blinked rapidly.

'No,' he croaked.

Carter froze. Jahlsen was in the grasp of a GodSmack high. He shouldn't be able to speak. Jesus, to have been able to *vomit* in such a condition would have been a miracle . . .

'You picked the wrong side,' said Carter softly, eyes fixed on the grey-haired man, on his strong face, his well-toned body: the body of an athlete, a soldier. Not an *addict*.

'*Kill him*,' hissed Kade.

'Carter, *no*!'

107

Jahlsen seemed to be struggling to break free of the grip of the drug. He swayed precariously on the bed, its springs creaking, and his hands flexed into claws. Veins stood out across his neck, chest and forearms; he swallowed rapidly, gulping the precious stinking air around him like a drowning man.

'You . . . have . . . got . . . it . . . wrong . . .' he gasped, claws grasping at the stained bed sheets and head dropping.

Nicky's words beat a tattoo in Carter's brain: *he is one of Durell's; he will condemn Spiral, condemn us all to death; he carries the plans for the SpiralGRID . . .*

Carter's expression hardened.

He took a deep breath . . .

And pulled the Browning's trigger.

A single bullet leapt from the barrel. It slammed into Jahlsen's forehead, lifting his chin up into the air and exiting from the back of his skull, in a spray of blood and brains to bury itself in the plaster of the wall. He crumpled backwards and rolled slowly from the bed.

There came a moment of total stillness. Carter felt something, some part of his soul, die a little; as he did with every death.

A tiny blip sounded.

Carter's head turned to the right, his eyes focusing on the small black ECube standing on a bedside cabinet amid glasses of water and liquor, tissues and bottles of pills. A tiny red light flashed on and off.

'*Not good,*' hissed Kade, the voice a dark rattle of bones in the back of Carter's spinning mind.

The TV suddenly hummed. The images died, leaving the room momentarily in darkness – and then the screen sparkled back into life. Images spun and leapt, dissolving and then reanimating into the mercury logo of HIVE Media Productions.

'What the . . .' Carter muttered, confused.

The logo spun into nothingness, to be replaced by a hooded figure. Slowly, the figure threw back his hood and Carter looked into a slightly pale and deformed face; looked into the narrowed and slitted copper eyes of Durell. The ex-Spiral traitor who had brought the world to its knees with his control of earthquakes, his Nex soldiers and his New World Order.

'Mr Carter,' came the soft, melodious voice. Carter took a hurried step back. He hefted his Browning, his eyes scanning the room as Durell smiled from the TV screen.

'You want something, fucker, or is this just a social call?'

'Well done. You have performed a great service for us. You have delivered to us the SpiralGRID.'

'No.' Carter shook his head. 'I have killed the man who would have betrayed the SpiralGRID to you. I assume that's why you've got this fucking room bugged?'

'On the contrary.' Durell smiled. 'Jahlsen was a Spiral man through and through. He was top-dog, T-level; had the SpiralGRID hard-tattooed on his brain. When you killed him, the ECube blipped the SpiralGRID back to the sub-system mainframes – and it was en route that my clever little QIV processor plucked the GRID from the global digital map before it could reach its safe haven. You have delivered me the greatest weapon I could ever use against Spiral . . . and you killed one of Spiral's finest at the same time. Congratulations, Carter. You have finally joined our side.'

'Fuck you, Durell, this isn't true . . .'

'Carter.' Durell smiled a broad smile. 'You have *betrayed Spiral*.'

The TV screen died. Ed's voice suddenly hissed on a wave of static in Carter's ear.

'We got company.'

'Nex?'

'Aye, lad. Lots of them . . . get on the roof before they pin you down in there; the snow stopped me taking pot-shots at them on the ground – bastards slid through like ghosts – but if you can lead them up onto the roof I've got a much clearer view . . .'

'Roger that.'

Carter turned, catching sight of Jahlsen's slumped body on the floor. His blood had stained his old clothing and soaked into the scattered, soiled bed sheets. His eyes had rolled up into his head showing nothing more than the whites, criss-crossed with tiny blood vessels.

Carter shook his head. 'I don't believe it. Son of a bitch.'

He turned, sprinted for the door and darted out into the corridor – where a Steyr TMP opened up, bullets eating a line from the wall behind Carter and chewing wood in long splinters from the frame of the door. Carter threw himself flat, his Browning thumping in his fist as 9mm bullets caught the Nex in the arm and shoulder, punching it backwards from the landing doorway . . .

Carter rolled with a thump against the wall, and came around on one knee with the Browning raised. The Nex reappeared, blood slick against its tight grey uniform, copper eyes moving to fix on Carter's position as it aimed the Steyr TMP—

Carter steadied his own aim.

Two bullets took the Nex in the forehead, exploding the top of its skull up and out in a gruesome shower of bone shards and brain tissue. Carter was already moving, pulling the pin from an HPG and launching it behind him, towards the dark mouth of the stairwell . . .

He ran, heard the hiss and concussive *whoosh* of HighJ explosive; purple fire raced along the corridor singeing Carter's trousers as he threw himself to the right through a doorway, toppling over an upturned chair and sprawling as a whirlwind of flames rushed past behind him . . .

The muted roar suddenly died away, and the conflagration was sucked back.

Leaving silence.

Carter stumbled across the room in darkness, and sensed rather than saw another human in the room.

'Paddy?' came a young lad's whining voice. 'Is that you? Did you get the photos of the bridge?'

Carter ignored the voice, reaching the window and delivering a front-kick which shattered the glass. The alloy frame swung outwards, lock broken and dangling free.

'Hey,' came the sleepy voice again, 'who are *you*? You're not Paddy. Where's Paddy? What have you done with Paddy? Have you got Paddy's photographs?'

Carter leapt up onto the rim, feeling glass shards bite into his gloves, and peered out into the snow. It was a long drop to a hard distant ground.

There was a small stone window ledge in front of him, and Carter stepped onto its slippery surface – then glanced up to where several steel hooks supported cables strung between this block and other buildings. Suddenly, skinny arms appeared and hands grasped his leg.

'Where *is* Patrick?' persisted the voice.

'Get the *fuck* off me!' Carter kicked the young man in the face, placed his Browning back in its holster, then leapt up, grasping one of the steel hooks and hauling himself up into the falling snow. He reached out, boots scrabbling against the snow-slick stone, and with a Herculean effort managed to stretch to a stone carving,

111

his gloved hands finally reaching the lip of the roof of the building. Grunting, Carter hung for a moment, sweat stinging his eyes as he swayed high above the ground . . .

'Hey, hello there, do *you* know where Paddy is? He's gone to get the photos. The rude ones! The ones about the new bridge.' A Steyr TMP clattered, silencing the young man's questioning whine. Carter cursed, and hauled himself up onto the stone-rimmed roof of the building as a Nex's head appeared from the window, along with the barrel of the TMP.

The gun levelled at Carter's dangling legs.

There came a distant hiss and then a thump as the 7.62mm Soviet sniper round took the Nex in the chest and spread most of its guts across the interior of the room. Carter pulled his legs to safety and glanced back across the hazy, snow-filled expanse.

Good fucking shot, Ed! he thought.

And about time!

The snow was falling heavier now, huge flakes spinning softly and blurring the world through which Carter ran, leaving footprints across the flat roof. He halted suddenly, halfway between the roof's edge and the doorway leading to the stairs below.

The stairs . . .

How many Nex?

'How many, Eddie?'

'Around ten entered the building. It was hard to tell due to the heavy snow. I only caught their tail-end.'

'Can you see me?' Carter peered through the heavy fall.

'Just about, but things are getting worse . . . wait . . .' Carter heard the whizz and thud of a sniper shot. 'The fuckers have tagged me – get your arse out of there, Carter – get out of there *now*!'

Carter pulled free an HPG and removed the pin, clicking the dial to 'prox.mine'. He rolled the grenade through the snow towards the head of the stairwell, then dropped another three at his feet where they spun like tops.

He turned, and ran for it—

The edge of the building loomed close as Carter pulled free his Sp_drag – nicknamed a 'Skimmer', or 'Parasite Skimmer' – and leapt up onto the rim. Bullets suddenly howled through the snow and Carter flinched, half-ducking as three Nex sprinted from the doorway behind him with their guns on full automatic – there was a tiny click and a roar shook the building as the HighJ chemical fury kicked the Nex's ragged corpses high into the air.

Carter jumped.

Shrapnel cut through the snow.

He caught the cable, swayed for a moment, secured the Sp_drag and allowed himself to drop down the swaying wire connecting the two buildings – boots locked together, mouth a grim dry line.

Bullets cut through the snowfall behind him and made him scrunch his body tight. He glanced down, and saw a spread of Nex moving into the building where Ed was positioned.

'Bastards.'

A 7.62mm sniper round took a Nex on the ground. Then another. And then they were in . . .

More bullets screamed from behind him as another explosion from his proximity-primed HPG rocked the world, and distant sirens wailed. Carter, clinging onto the Skimmer with one hand, pulled free his Browning and began to fire . . . one, two, three shots, back towards the window and the masked face of a Nex—

'Carter,' came Ed's voice. 'I . . .' There was a wave of crackling static.

'This is not turning out to be a good *fucking* day,' hissed Carter as the Browning clicked on an empty chamber and the Nex swarmed out not just behind him – at the edge of the roof – but ahead of him, on the elevated roof position recently occupied by Ed.

Carter's eyes narrowed as he sped down the cable through the heavy snow. The wind buffeted him, making him sway dangerously. Bitter coldness stung him through his clothing.

The Nex levelled their automatic weapons, tracking with precision and patience. There were six of them ahead – copper-eyed stares fixed grimly on the speeding, falling target.

Without a flicker of emotion, they opened fire.

CHAPTER 5

A SOUR PERFUME

Mongrel squatted in the alleyway, boots shifting slightly on the shattered concrete debris which littered the warped, corrugated road. His gloved hand reached out, steadying himself against the twisted metal skeleton of a rusted fire-wreck Volvo.

Mongrel, eyes squinting, unshaved face contorted in concentration and fear yet marked with an inner strength that made him the son-of-a-bitch rough-and-tumble psychopathic good-natured bear-like Spiral-op bastard that he was, stared out at the distant target.

He licked at dry lips, revealing broken, crooked teeth – victims of too many beer-fuelled late-night bar brawls, the smashed stumps reminders of the impact of innumerable knuckle sandwiches. Mongrel's face was etched with battle-weariness. A deep and ingrained bitterness. And in this new world, fear was never far from his mind . . . Mongrel gripped the stock of his Sterling sub-machine gun and his eyes narrowed as they peered over the twisted metal frame before him.

A fine mist of rain was drifting and falling, chilling

Mongrel to the marrow. His guts were rumbling and his arse was on fire, making him even grumpier than usual.

'It's a shame,' said The Priest, in a small but mournful voice. Mongrel glanced, to where the huge barrel-chested man lay on his considerable belly, dressed in full urban combat clothing but still wearing his sandals and rosary beads – like the religious maniac he most certainly was.

'What is shame?' rumbled Mongrel, glancing along the stretch of rubble-strewn alleyway towards the distant target: new and gleaming; it rose three storeys high and was just crying out for the five kilos of HighJ explosive they were about to deliver with, in the best tradition of covert warfare, extreme prejudice.

The Priest gestured with his silenced M27A carbine, the weapon black and glistening under the misty London rain. Mongrel glanced around, then frowned, hissing, 'What hell you talking about?'

'That!' The Priest pointed, his rosary beads clacking against the bomb-blast debris.

'The *car*?'

'Yeah,' said The Priest, his great sorrowful eyes filled with sadness, yearning and Great Pity. 'Yea I say unto thee that I cannot comprehend how the infidels could wreak such hellfire destruction on such an honourable beast.'

'The fucking *Volvo*?' snapped Mongrel in disbelief.

'It is a most noble vintage model.' The Priest nodded to himself, turning his gaze back along the confined alley-way. Near the end, where street met rubble-cleared highway, fires burned, sending up columns of oily smoke, and they could pick out distant patrols of Nex.

Mongrel checked his watch. 'Come on – is nearly time. You follow my lead, you see how is done proper, right lad?'

116

'Yes, I will follow the true professional.' The Priest smiled, his gold-flecked brown eyes blinking slowly, calmly, as he cocked the weapon in his huge hands and rolled smoothly – surprisingly so for such a large man – to his feet. His sandals flapped softly as he followed Mongrel down the alleyway. They paused behind a heap of glowing embers smouldering in a rusted metal drum. Their eyes scanned what lay ahead . . .

London: one of the greatest capital cities in the world – once the home of Big Ben, the Houses of Parliament, Downing Street, the Tower of London, the Globe Theatre, Tower Bridge, the West End . . . and now—

And now a pathetic shadow of its former self, a blasted, smashed, buckled ghost, a capital of destruction, a pulped and pulverised pile of debris. The Sentinel Tower – unharmed by the twenty-kiloton nuclear blast that had ravaged the city's streets five years earlier – stood tall, black and gleaming, proud amid the rubble of something once mighty.

'Ten seconds,' said Mongrel, clenching his teeth in anticipation and rolling down his balaclava over his face. Broad hands clasped the Sterling sub-machine gun and he glanced past the repaired streets now alive with cars and military trucks; past the gleaming ever-open NEP premises – the Nex Production Plant where humans, genuine thoroughbred one-hundred-per-cent humans voluntarily went to relinquish their human status, went for voluntary Skein Blending, a joining of human and insect, genetic sacrilege, a two-fingered salute to God and Evolution alike.

Mongrel's stare fixed on a . . . signal.

The patrol groups of Nex – three Nex soldiers per group, with perhaps fifteen operations groups surrounding the vast perimeter of the NEP, a circular stone structure with a huge steel and glass dome rising to a height of three storeys – heard the crack of concussion, followed by a massive boom as a nearby building shook and instantly turned into a raging inferno.

Mongrel glanced right as a FukTruk, a heavy battered sixteen-wheeler, veered towards him and halted with squealing brakes and a hiss of hydraulics. He climbed up the rope ladder slung against the canvas of the truck, then knelt, watching carefully as the Nex sprinted towards the NEP perimeter where the rattle of machine guns sounded. The Nex returned fire, taking up their positions behind stone pillars, aiming their Steyr TMPs with steady practised hands and the efficient eyes of trained killers . . .

Mongrel dragged the tube from his back and flicked down the attached bipod. He quickly attached an ECube to the side of the dark green weapon and then dropped his canvas pack, lifting out a long heavy canister. He handled it with the sort of delicate care he usually reserved for a pint of beer, a woman's clitoris, or – in this case – five kilos of powerful explosive.

The ECube clicked and hummed.

Mongrel, sweat soaking his balaclava despite the chill, licked at his salted lips and wished vehemently that he was in the pub. The machine-gun fire was blasting in bursts across the road. The traffic had now vanished, leaving only stragglers who had either panicked or been immobilised by stray bullets. Mongrel waited, watching in horror as a stream of spinning metal cut a diagonal line across the canvas back of the truck on which he perched, stopping at his boots.

'*Ne pizdi!* Son of bitch!'

The ECube blipped; Mongrel felt the tube shift in his hands as digital targeting motors altered the angles of elevation. Mongrel dropped the long HighJ canister into the launch tube, ducking his head as a fiery backwash scorched his eyelashes and the bomb soared out over the street and the battling Nex.

Mongrel was moving even before the bomb struck. He clambered down the ladder with the elegance of a baboon, all knuckles and knees, and was sprinting with The Priest close behind him even as the HighJ connected violently with the hub of the Nex Production Plant.

Several Nex saw the rapid trajectory of the bomb.

But by then, it was too late.

The production plant disintegrated in a ball of glowing purple, a sudden uprush of noise and fire and screaming, twisting melting lengths of steel. Chunks of masonry scythed across the surrounding streets, punching men and Nex from their feet, demolishing whole buildings and delivering the maximum in hard-core destruction . . .

It began to rain stone, concrete and flaming lengths of alloy-stapled timbers as a column of blackened smoke poured into the sky. Cars and trucks were picked up, crushed and twisted like putty into lumps of tortured steel.

Nex were melted in a glowing instant, merging with their guns where they stood. A harsh chemical stink drifted through the streets.

Mongrel stumbled to a halt at the end of the alleyway with The Priest beside him. They were soon joined by another eight grim-looking Spiral operatives. Their detonation mission had been successful. Now all they had to do was get to the next EP for the GRID . . . alive.

'Anybody tag signs of pursuit?'

The ops shook their heads, clasping their sub-machine guns. A woman rounded the corner and opened her mouth in sudden shock at the startling vision of guns and balaclavas. Then she turned and ran. Her heels clacked off down the rubble-strewn pavement as The Priest peered after her.

'We're clear.'

Distantly, sirens echoed. They could all smell smoke.

The Priest, glancing left and right, led the small fighting unit, the DemolSquad, across the now-deserted road and into another narrow street. Rain lay like a veil across the tarmac, the rubble and the dusty grime-smeared windows of shops. Some were still open and operating, some long closed and sporting smashed windows or boarded-up fronts, the graffiti-smeared planks nailed at different angles and daubed with the command NO ENTRY mantra.

The team moved, halted, checked their surroundings.

Mongrel inspected his gun's magazine, and suddenly something seemed out of place. He turned, opening his mouth as he lifted his Sterling—

Bullets screamed from the darkened hole behind him, passing over his shoulder and thumping into the throat and head of a tall woman who was gazing off to her right, caving in her facial features and dropping her in an instant.

Mongrel and The Priest were already moving, whirling low with their weapons ready. The guns roared, emptying a stream of flying metal into an open shopfront as the two men dived in opposite directions. Two more Spiral operatives went down in the hail of exchanged fire and Mongrel felt a bullet carve a narrow groove across his shin, slicing through combats and flesh and chipping the bone. He hit the ground hard and rolled, the Sterling still bucking angrily in his gloved hands. He stopped shooting, breathing hard on dust and cordite, and glanced over at The Priest, who gave a nod. Mongrel pulled out a grenade, yanked free the pin with his few remaining teeth and allowed the cylinder to sail into the darkened depths of the shop.

And then they were running, the seven remaining Spiral agents pounding down the street, dodging behind the burned-out shell of a car – still hot from the previous night's entertainment – then sprinting right into another alley as more bullets kicked up splinters of concrete at their heels . . .

Mongrel slammed against a wall, panting. He dragged his balaclava off and changed magazines in his Sterling.

'What flavour?'

'White phos,' muttered Mongrel.

'Nasty.' The Priest nodded.

'Well, we not playing games here.' Mongrel levelled his gun and fired off a full magazine blindly. Then he poked his head tentatively around the corner. What he saw made him frown.

She was standing in the centre of the street, legs slightly apart, arms hanging limp at her sides. Unlike other Nex, her pale oval face was uncovered, revealing a gentle pale beauty. Her hair was dark, spiked by the light fall of filthy rain. Her eyes glowed copper and were staring at him.

Mongrel shivered, for a moment locked to that penetrating gaze.

Swiftly, he reloaded and fired another burst. The female Nex looked down, almost in disgust, as the bullets did nothing but rattle the gravel at her feet. And then Mongrel watched the tide of heavily armed dark-clad Nex warriors silently fill the street behind her, moving with athletic grace in a perfect economy of action. He watched the columns of military Pigs and FukTruks creep forward, rumbling.

'An army! A whole fucking army!'

'I think we should leave. Now!' hissed The Priest.

They set off, cutting first left, then right through a

maze of narrow streets that were strangely free from damage. Archaic stone carvings stared down from steep vertical walls. The Priest called a sudden halt as he checked the ECube in his fist.

Gunshots rang out, bullets ricocheting off the corner of a building, and the Spiral operatives sprinted for cover. Then they crawled on their bellies to the corner of a street which The Priest indicated with a fist clasping his battered rosary beads.

'They trying cut us off!' hissed Mongrel.

'Come on.' They ran, heaving their exhausted bodies across the rubble-strewn thoroughfare, pounding past a group of tramps who were dressed in rags and sharing a bottle of clear liquid – obviously alcoholic – and staring around with vacant expressions on their ravaged faces. They stumbled along by a huge building and The Priest darted right, squeezing through a fallen archway and into a derelict hall with an uneven tile floor and a softly swaying chandelier – strangely intact and glowing in the weak grime-light spilling through the shadows.

Seconds later, tyres ground against stone as brakes locked in savage skids. Heavy-calibre rounds scythed through the tramps, ending their lives in a sudden hot hail of death. Their lone bottle, sole salvation from the misery of their lives, rolled across the ground and shattered into glinting shards.

'The buggers,' growled Mongrel. 'They've fucking cut us off!'

The Priest put his hands together. 'It is at times like this that we need to pray, my brothers.'

'Pray?' screamed Mongrel. 'What, for a fucking miracle? The only fucking miracle here is I don't put bullet in your dumb religious-maniac skull!'

The Priest's eyes suddenly glinted, and he hoisted his

weapon. He took a deep breath and smiled. 'Have faith, my son,' he said. 'For I have prayed for deliverance . . . to the Lord! Yea, also to Simmo and his TankSquads. They have seen the light of my ECube – and should be here shortly.'

'That *svoloch* jailbird had better hurry,' muttered Mongrel. 'Or we forget battle with Nex and I fucking kill you myself!'

'Be calm, my son,' The Priest soothed. 'The Lord will protect us. The Lord will guide us. The Lord will find us sanctuary and deliver us, yca, even from utmost evil.'

Outside, the whole world seemed to rumble suddenly as something squeezed down the streets with squeals of steel torturing stone. The walls of the building vibrated, sending chunks of plaster toppling from far above, along with a shower of dust. The chandelier began to jiggle, making tiny tinkling sounds.

The Spiral ops looked nervously at one another.

'What . . . fuck . . . is *that*?' hissed Mongrel.

But before anybody could speak, his question was answered – more abruptly and violently than the grizzled soldier had anticipated. The front wall of the building disintegrated as a mammoth twin-barrelled tank thundered through the ancient stonework, sending a shower of broken stone blocks into the chamber. With tracks squealing, the tank heaved itself forward in stop-start surges, grinding stone to powder, and broke free to spin in an arc through the room, its massive guns pointing at the Spiral operatives – who through instinct and pure reflex had opened fire with automatic weapons . . .

Through the hole in the wall sprinted a squad of Nex, Steyr TMPs in gloved hands, cold copper-eyed stares sweeping the shattered area for their enemy. Sub-machine guns yammered in their steady grips.

Mongrel and The Priest scrambled frantically back towards the stairs. Bullets cut chunks from the tiles and plaster ahead of them. Yelling, they ran for the rotten, crumbling staircase as the tank, with a whirr of motors and clouds of LVA fumes belching into the confined interior, rotated its huge twin-gun turret.

There came a tremendous, deafening explosion as the tank fired twin shells in the direction of the trapped Spiral operatives . . .

Sonia J walked with an easy, measured stride down the rain-swept street, wearing a long dark coat which glistened with the damp. She waited for a break in the stream of traffic and then crossed under the archway of the Nex Garrison post built to one side of the Sentinel Tower.

She stopped for a moment, huddling in a doorway, and lit a cigarette. Her long eyelashes blinked rapidly and she shivered.

God, I hate this place, she thought.

She watched warily four Nex across the street. They moved smoothly, athletically. Their copper-eyed gazes swept the street, the buildings, constantly searching for trouble. Their stares locked on her for a long moment . . . Sonia J felt her heart rise slowly to fill her throat. Then the cold insect-like glares passed away from her once they'd rated her as a simple zero threat.

She breathed again and waited, thinking that when the freezing ice-filled rain let up she would make a break for it and head for the HIVE Media Studio [London Division]. Then she'd burrow her way through the labyrinthine complex until she reached her own little niche of Quazatron Productions – which had exploded in recent months with three of the most popular shows to grace any TV network, ever . . . thus propelling Sonia

J into the dazzling spotlight of global celebrity.

Peering out, Sonia nixed any idea of running through the rain. The Nex and JT8 police squads were out in force, patrolling like the natural predators they were. Sonia, like most other citizens, had caught the news between sips of coffee and spoonfuls of SugarBran; the previous day's bomb attack on the most advanced Nex Enhancement Programme centre, or Production Plant, which had cost $22.8 million (US) to build had been costly not only in terms of lost lives, Nex-conversions pulped and actual structural and financial damage. It had also carried a cost in terms of negative publicity. Something the HIVE Media Empire – supporters of the NEP cause – were keen to address by running Anti-Spiral, Anti-REB and Anti-GD-terrorist adverts in near-constant rotation on ChainTV, blending and merging images of death and war and torture.

The Nex were operating on hair triggers.

To run through the rain would be foolish.

'Stuff it. A girl can only get so bloody wet.' Sonia finished her cigarette, dropped the still-smoking butt and stepped out into the downpour. She walked, her boots clacking against the pavements. She kept a lookout for any Nex. Not only did they give her the creeps, making her shiver and occasionally filling her nightmares with their masked faces and copper eyes. There was also something she could not quite place. Something inherently . . . *evil*, whispered the voice in her mind.

Sonia J walked, head down. She reached the first set of gates in front of the huge HIVE Media Building, a tower block almost as large as the Sentinel HQ but built post-strike and sporting impressive defensive features.

Sonia flashed her pass and was laser-read by HIVE security technology. Just as she was about to step forward, she heard a commotion through the rain behind her. She didn't want to turn but felt she had to.

In the distance she could distinguish a small group of women, perhaps twenty of them, bearing banners. They were moving down the road, arms linked, with a few children at their feet scampering along through the rubble. To one side, on the pavement, stood four Nex, guns half raised, their stares scanning not just the group but the surroundings.

Sonia's lips pressed together in a tight line. There was something wrong with the Nex movements, something out of synch.

Her sharp eyes read the slogans on the banners and placards; they concerned the imprisonment of the women's husbands, without trial, for alleged crimes against the State. This small group had appeared out of nowhere and was heading slowly towards HIVE Media . . . and the hope of a slice of instant global coverage.

Sonia stood, rooted to the spot. The Nex on the pavement were twitchy – and slowly one lifted a gloved hand to a hidden earpiece. Its copper-eyed gaze met Sonia J's and she instantly froze – caught in the act of witness. She could not read the Nex's expression behind the mask, but it held her gaze for a moment. Then it turned and said something to its three comrades. They levelled their Steyr TMPs at the crowd of women and children – and opened fire. The group of women was mown down, felled in an instant; they flung up their arms, tried to protect their children, but all in vain.

In an instant it was over. Sonia heard the distant sirens as a K-truck slid around a corner, its bulk hiding the carnage: the dead eyes of the women, and the children's corpses, mouths open and tongues lolling.

Sonia finally managed to swallow, and then it was there—

A Nex.

It stood casually in front of her, its gun levelled at Sonia J's face. Sonia found that she could hardly breathe.

The Steyr TMP's muzzle was steaming softly as raindrops fizzed against the hot barrel. The Nex nodded towards her. 'You are the lady, Sonia J, from HIVE Media?'

She stared down the dark eye of the Austrian submachine gun's barrel, reliving the horror of the women and children flopping to the road. Shock pounded in her chest.

'Yes,' she managed to gasp.

'Well, you live today.' The Nex seemed to be smiling behind the mask.

'I . . . I won't say anything.' Sonia's hand fell to the small 8mm pistol in her pocket. It pressed hard against her skin as if willing her to draw and fire; to use it the way it was meant to be used: to shoot the dirty murdering Nex bastard in the face . . .

The Nex nodded, receiving some instruction through its earpiece. 'We *know* you will remain silent. Now. Go inside, little lady – go and record your TV programme and entertain the people.' The soft asexual voice made Sonia shiver: she fancied that she could detect mockery in its tone. She turned her back on the Nex and felt the itching of fear across her unprotected spine.

Sonia walked stiffly towards the entrance of HIVE Media, almost unable to breathe and unable to think.

And fell through the digital doorway with tears flooding down her frozen cheeks.

Sonia reclined on the couch. She saw the cam lights winking from the crane as the cameras zoomed down across the buzzing audience and then zeroed in on her crotch . . .

The scene cut to her face and she smiled sweetly. Cleverly placed lights reflected from an invisible paint on her teeth, giving the camera a rapid, fluttering sparkle.

'Welcome back to *Pussy_live!* And, as promised for your delectable delectation, here for the first time in front of a live TV audience is Vincent Alexandro, chief engineer and sponsor for the Nex Enhancement Programme. Working from a variety of NEP laboratories across the globe, including the renowned New York, Paris and Hong Kong outfits, Dr Alexandro is single-handedly responsible for the smoothing of the genetic Nex transformation process – and for providing the common, everyday man, woman and child the chance, the *opportunity* to elevate themselves above the ranks of common mortal man . . . to, as the NEP so elegantly puts it, Evolve. Welcome, Dr Alexandro.'

As Sonia had been speaking, a small Nex dressed in an inoffensive black suit had walked primly across the stage and seated himself neatly on one of the settees.

'Good day to you, Sonia. And thank you for inviting me on your show.'

'My pleasure . . . After all, it's not every day we get somebody so powerful and important onto the settee to prove to our audience that they're not a – mewling fucking Pussy!'

The audience gave a half-laugh, looking around at one another and the stage-herders uncertainly. A few chuckled, but many looked deeply confused. After all, this was Vincent Alexandro – he graced their TV sets all the time, civilised, well-mannered, the perfect propaganda representative, the perfect front man for the NEP. And now Sonia was antagonising him in a manner that had not been evident in rehearsals, and which had an undercurrent of . . . *nastiness*. Something had changed.

Sonia's EARMIC buzzed. 'What the hell are you doing? Just what the hell are you *doing*, you crazy bitch?' Sonia J ignored the EARMIC. She gave Vincent Alexandro a thin smile, and his dark eyes focused on her. His lips moved – as if mouthing some silent dialogue. Then he smiled with apparently genuine humour.

'I am sure your audience and the people at home will be the judge of that.' Alexandro folded his hands in his lap and waited, his small dark eyes focused unblinkingly on Sonia J.

She licked her lips. Her EARMIC had gone strangely silent. 'OK, then. As we all know, you head up the genetics division for the Nex Enhancement Programme.'

'Indeed,' said Dr Alexandro smoothly. He turned his head slightly, surveying the audience, that hint of a smile still on his lips.

Sonia J found herself scowling a little. There was something unnerving about Alexandro. Something inherently *bad*.

'The Nex Enhancement Programme'– he gave a flourish with his neat little hands – 'is what we like to refer to as the ultimate in plastic surgery. Even before the War billions of people had gone under the surgeon's knife – and why? Their aims were always obvious – they wanted self-improvement. They wanted to be rid of excess fat, they wanted breast or lip or penis enhancements. But it was all *false*. Surgeons used implants, non-organic and semi-toxic substances which – ultimately – could do as much harm as good. And often did.'

Sonia J nodded.

'Just keep it cool,' spat her EARMIC with a tone of poison she had never before heard. She was dicking with Alexandro; fucking with the Big Man. And her bosses knew it . . . and were far from impressed at her tactics.

Sonia's lips compressed to a thin line. A picture flashed into her brain: murdered women and children lying in the street, their blood leaking in wide pools. And the Nex soldier, its copper eyes studying her. And the *look* in its eyes . . . as if she was nothing.

'Originally, the NEP was a military enhancement designed to create the ultimate soldier. Using modified genetics from a variety of sources, when the subject is *blended* they become stronger, more agile, incredibly athletic. They become highly resistant to disease, and biological and chemical weapons – and, yes, they become mostly immune even to that scourge of our modern world, the biological poison HATE. When you—' Alexandro's gaze suddenly switched not to the cameras, but to *fix* on the billions watching their TVs at home. 'When you subscribe to the NEP then you also release yourself from the imprisonment of the cities. You are able to travel throughout the HATE-restricted zones . . . and thus you earn back your well-deserved liberty.'

Alexandro paused . . . and Sonia leapt in. 'Is it not true that anybody signing on the dotted line for this admittedly sophisticated genetic treatment has to serve a period under contract within the Nex military?'

'Unfortunately, yes. Any subject undergoing the massive benefits of NEP are signed up for a three-month trial period in the Nex battalion of their choice. This is for the subject's protection as well as ours, because the contractual-obligation time is merely a period of monitoring and assessment, not warfare, as some negative-media journalists have suggested. It is where we check that the genetic spirals have *complimented* one another. But, after this simple and short trial period, the subject becomes a free citizen once more. There are no strings attached, Miss J.'

'Do you not find that ninety-eight per cent of new Nex

130

choose to stay within their battalion? Why is that, do you think, Dr Alexandro?'

Alexandro shrugged non-committally. 'It offers a superb career structure, global travel, a brotherhood, you could say – a brotherhood of strength.' He smiled again. Sonia felt herself shiver deep inside. 'You become one of the Nex – one of the Enhanced, one of the Evolved. You have superior mental and neurological processes. You Elevate, Miss Sonia J. You Elevate above the norm.'

'Don't even think about it, Sonia,' buzzed her EARMIC; it was the strained voice of Bobby Clough, HIVE Media's chief executive. 'I'm fucking warning you, your job is on the line here! Don't go down that road! He's too big to fuck with . . .'

Sonia J smiled.

The studio flowed into a blurred swirling of bright lights and colours, of audience laughter and buzz, with the perfect, haunting face of Alexandro the focus of all attention. And the ghosts of the murdered howled softly in Sonia's brain, accusing her, screaming at her. 'How can you be part of this world? How can you protect this set-up? How can you subscribe to this global human assassination?'

'I have a question, Dr Alexandro.'

'Yes?'

'Nooo!' howled her EARMIC.

Sonia J's stare fixed on Alexandro. For a moment – a moment only – she faltered. Then she ploughed on, teeth grinding and jaw tightening as the strength which had propelled her to the summit of TV current affairs and live media forced her onwards. 'If,' she began, 'the Nex Enhancement Programme is such a benefit to society, to humanity as a whole – then how can you justify the scenes reported by REB and Spiral leaflets and a

131

hundred underground newspapers? There are reports of the wholesale massacre of innocent men, women and children carried out by the Nex and their machine guns.'

Alexandro stared at her. The audience fell into a hushed silence. Then Alexandro smiled thinly. 'I think you will find, Miss J, that these are merely unfounded rumours put about by those who would bring down the current World Government. It is the voice of jealousy. It is an accusation by the truly evil.'

'Is it then true that you blend people with insects, Dr Alexandro? That is to say, to produce a Nex you take a person and a selection of insects and merge them together in a genetic slop: and the end product is a Nex soldier without emotions? Yes, you *give* – you give strength and agility and resistance to poisons . . . but you also *take*. The process removes many of the emotions that we associate with a human – and thus the emotions that make a human *human*?'

'In very early trials there was a slight dipping of emotional awareness but current statistics show—' began Alexandro.

'What insects do you use?' interrupted Sonia J. 'Ants? Centipedes? *Cockroaches?*' She stood then and glanced around at the hushed audience. She saw the lights on the cameras still winking. She was still on live TV. Still broadcasting. And she smiled – because she had them by the balls. To cut the live feed now would be to remove Dr Alexandro's platform, leaving too many unanswered questions.

Alexandro remained seated, his dark eyes were glittering. He turned from the audience to face Sonia J. When he spoke, his voice was a soft lilting sound.

'You are beginning to sound like one of the REBS, Miss Sonia J.' He laughed unconvincingly. The audience mimicked his laughter without a prompt, glad of some release from tension. 'However, I appreciate your position as the Queen of Media and how you must pose those unthinkable questions – vicious and nasty unfounded rumours though they are. You must address these issues and I must defend our position from those who would remove the joy of the Nex Process from the masses . . .' Alexandro was smooth and sophisticated. 'In answer to your questions, we use certain genetic spirals from a variety of insects, mammals and marine life. The aim is to strengthen a human's own natural physiological resources. To *accelerate* an organism's evolution. *Current* Nex production does nothing to reduce the emotional capacity of the subject. A human person is the same person when they leave, sporting nothing but *enhancements* – the process gives everything, and takes nothing away. And finally, this "wholesale massacre" – where is your proof? Yes, there have been battles, but there are always battles between governments and terrorists the world over. This is a violent and unstable world in which we live. The Nex units defend against the Violators of Peace, mainly that global thorn Spiral and its terrorist activities – and, of course, the REBS who sadly grow stronger by the day. But all free-speak media across the globe report these conflicts in full . . . there is never wholesale slaughter of innocents. That is . . . how do you say? An *urban myth.*'

The audience started to clap, and their applause rolled out to engulf the standing figure of Sonia J.

Sonia's gaze flicked to the autocue. It was highlighted in red – which meant she was being *ordered* to speak the words.

'Just do what you're told,' came the bitter voice in her EARMIC. The voice sounded bleak and unforgiving. Bobby Clough was far from happy.

The autocue began to flash, building in urgency as the cameras swept down from the false glittering sky on robotic hydraulics, hissing softly, and Sonia gazed around at the clapping audience. She wanted to say, 'I saw it, I saw the murders this morning, the murders you will never show on TV because you fucking *own* the fucking media companies and you fucking *own* the people under your control – all of us, all of us . . . *all of us* . . .' She could see the dead children in the road but she forced herself to smile and grit her teeth and lift her pretty glittering face to the cameras and say, in a proud strong voice, 'Thank you for that most vigorous interview, Dr Alexandro – I think you will all agree, our resident guest for the show has undoubtedly proved that he is *not a Pussy*! Now, to the adverts, and stay tuned for the stand-up comedy of Roger P. Thorpe and his Musical Opus of the Tired and Lethargic.'

The cameras flickered from red to black; the music suddenly halted.

The live feed had been killed. They were off air.

Sonia J and Vincent Alexandro both stood now, facing one another. Alexandro stepped forward until he looked up into Sonia J's face. As they shook hands, he said in a soft and very dangerous voice, 'Thank you for your invigorating questions. Your views were very . . . *enlightening*. We must certainly do a second show sometime in the near future.'

'Of course,' said Sonia woodenly.

And then Alexandro was gone, a slight hint of a metallic scent briefly caressing Sonia's nostrils. Her gaze swept to the JT8s standing in small clusters at the foot of the steps leading to the audience seats. They were watching her, gas-mask eyes reflecting the studio lights – they looked suddenly and frighteningly like androids, automatons . . . insects.

'I have really become death,' Sonia misquoted.

The abuse started to filter through her EARMIC and she removed the tiny glittering ball and tossed it onto the settee. She moved towards the doors. Outside, the London heavens had opened; ice-filled rain was pounding the dark grey streets.

Sonia J was talking to Baze as he drove, but she suddenly realised that he wasn't listening. From her position on the cool leather of the BMW's back seat she could see his eyes in the rear-view mirror – focused on something behind them.

'Everything OK?' she asked.

'We're being followed.'

'You sure?'

'Oh yes,' growled Baze, pressing his size 14 boot hard on the accelerator. The BMW surged forward, bonnet rising under massive acceleration. To either side, buildings slid past, water hissing under tyres and rattling in accompaniment on the car's roof.

Sonia looked over her shoulder. Behind them, five large GMC trucks powered along, matching them for speed. Huge tyres thundered across buckled tarmac, huge black bumpers cannoned into chunks of stone, hammering a clear path. Five grilles jostled for position in Sonia's vision and she felt her throat constrict with sudden fear: they had found her.

It hadn't just been the Nex following on foot after the interview with Alexandro; this was a proper tag – the pursuers did not care that the victim had spotted them.

What worried Sonia most about her pursuers was that the Nex no longer felt the need to hide. It was as if she was a spy who had blown her cover.

'You want me to lose them?' growled Baze.

'Lose them,' said Sonia dryly.

Again, the BMW accelerated. Around Baze's bulk, Sonia saw the needle dance up to 150 m.p.h. This was insanely fast for the narrow rubble-strewn streets of London – especially if one didn't want to attract the merciless attention of the JT8s and the Nex.

Suddenly, the lead GMC truck surged ahead and accelerated towards them. There was a massive crunch as the bumper hammered into the boot of the BMW, forcing the car to one side; wheels thumped up onto buckled pavements and for a horrifying moment Sonia thought Baze had lost control . . .

The BMW veered, rolling to the left and sending a shower of sparks along the face of an old run-down building.

The GMC truck had dropped back, but it soon leapt forward again. It connected with a squeal of twisting steel, and the BMW's rear bumper was torn free, falling under the GMC's front wheels which compressed it into a crushed mass and discarded it with the ease of a tossed paper ball.

'You're gonna have to get off the main road,' snapped Sonia.

Even as she spoke, Baze slammed the BMW right into a narrow alleyway. They crashed at a hundred miles an hour through several bins, one of which sent a web of cracks across the windscreen before it bounced off.

Sonia's head snapped back to the rear window – and she yelped as the GMC's grille appeared once more, slamming yet again into the BMW's boot. This time the shock was so great that Baze's hands were torn briefly from the BMW's steering wheel and the vehicle lurched to the right, careering from a wall which tore free the front right wing.

The BMW veered left now, thundering across rubble to smash down a low wall as Baze's hands slipped and slid on the steering wheel and he finally managed to get a grip, wrenching the lurching high-speed car into some semblance of stability.

'We've got to lose them!' Sonia breathed huskily.

'Don't you understand, Sonia?' growled Baze, glancing over his shoulder with a wild look in his eyes. 'We can't lose them – their trucks are faster than this hunk of shit.'

Once more, the GMC thundered into the BMW SmutCar. And then there came a fusillade of machine-gun bullets . . .

'We can't take this any more,' snapped Sonia. 'We're going to have to use force . . .'

'But what if it's a ruse?' said Baze softly, his gaze meeting – for a fleeting instant – with Sonia's. 'It could blow our cover wide open.'

'Better to shoot the Nex and go into hiding than end up *dead*. If our cover is blown – then so be it, it's blown, and we'll have to readjust our game plan. If we can't outrun these bastards . . .'

Baze passed Sonia a weapon from the front of the car. An M24 carbine. She flicked off the safety and stared down at the matt black gun in her trembling hands.

There came a roar from the following GMC. It lurched towards them, the grille appearing out of the dark ice-rain like teeth.

'Well,' smiled Sonia, her face etched with fear, eyes wide and pale in the gloom of the BMW's cabin. 'It looks like we're going to have to fight.' She cocked the weapon, and sighted through the rear window at the fast-approaching GMC truck . . .

ADVERTISING FEATURE

The TV-ProjU sparkled into life with a digital buzz of humming phosphorescence. Images spun and leapt, dissolving and then reanimating into the mercury logo of HIVE Media Productions . . .

Audio/Vid mix: fast-paced rock music. Thundering drums. Shaky camera following black-clad JT8 police squad unit through city ruins, amid smoke, fire, panicked civilians; **live audio feed:** *panting sounds and shouts, crackles of machine-gun fire.*

– Ever wanted to RUN with the pack?
– Ever wanted to FIRE a throbbing Steyr Tactical Machine Pistol?
– Ever wanted a well-paid CAREER?
– Ever wanted to PROTECT your CHILDREN?

Scene [slow pan R > L]: the JT8s corner a REB unit in a wide stone yard. They pose heroically for the camera, looking tall and fine and heroic in their smart black (well-ironed) uniforms, polished black (gleaming!) boots and sporting many shining silver and gold medals. As a unit, the JT8s lift square chins to the sky, steely eyes looking down at the cowering, bedraggled, filth-encrusted REBS who wave antiquated sub-machine guns in their mire of obvious weakness and filth.

– THROW DOWN YOUR WEAPONS AND YOU WILL LIVE! DEFY THE JT8 POLICE SQUADS AND YOU WILL DIE! DO THE HONOURABLE THING! DO NOT PROVOKE US TO A FIREFIGHT! WE REPEAT, THROW DOWN YOUR WEAPONS! WE DO NOT REQUIRE AN INCIDENT!

Scene zooms in on: the REBS growling incomprehensible curses, remainders of blackened stubby teeth bared in disease-ridden bearded faces. They curse and spit like rabid cornered animals. They lift their weapons and begin to fire at the clean-shaven honourable JT8 police . . .

Scene pans/pull back then zoom in: as one, the JT8s lower their eyes in sadness, mouths grim red lines of compressed flesh as they SIGH, big sighs indicating their despair at this terrible waste of life and this position that they have been **forced** into. They unleash a perfectly aimed hail of bullets, which topple the ten dirty stinking bearded REBS; bodies flip and fall, to lie at crooked twisted angles. A little blood trickles from the corner of one REB's mouth.

Scene: camera sweeps slowly across the carnage, and the JT8s move forward and look down with obvious sadness and great empathy. One even reaches up and wipes away a single tear with a pink-frilled perfectly white handkerchief **[close-up: embroidery: I love you daddy – hurt them bad men].**

Screen fades to half screen (horizontal slash) image over sobbing JT8; TEXT [scrolling L > R/silver lettering FONT LUCIDA SANS]: REBS court DEATH! REBS flout the LAW! REBS are the **SCOURGE** of the modern world. JOIN THE JT8s – SEE THE WORLD – EARN GOOD MONEY – SHOOT A MACHINE GUN – GREAT HOLIDAYS – WALK OUTSIDE THE HATE RESTRICTIONS . . . AND GET TO KILL BAD REBS!!!

SCENE DISSOLVES TO SILVER

CHAPTER 6

IGNITION

Carter fell through the ice and snow, attached to the swaying cable, dropping like a stone through the buffeting wind and swirling flakes. The cable rocked and snapped above him, the Parasite squealing softly against the rough steel-fibre twists. He could smell burning, the scent of hot oil and metal shavings, and feel the intense cold of a suddenly frozen city. Bullets howled at him from out of the blinding blizzard, and from behind came the distant barking flashes of gun muzzles as emotionless copper-eyed stares fixed on him.

I am going to die, he thought. I am a sitting duck. The bastards cannot miss . . . They just *cannot* miss . . . He flexed his freezing fingers and, operating on pure animal survival instinct alone, he initiated the quick release of the Parasite. He suddenly disengaged from the Skimmer and the swaying cable. Gravity picked Carter up and tossed him towards the ground . . .

Carter fell, curling into a ball. Bullets stuttered far behind, lost in the storm. Then came a deafening crunch which echoed through Carter's ears and brain. The world slammed into him and he was blind, smashed, unable to breathe. Pain crashed in waves over him. Opening his eyes he found himself confused by the sight of a wall of corrugated buckled white metal with flaking chipped paint – and then he remembered the Nex, and the bullets. He pushed his hands beneath himself and levered his tortured body up from the small hollow that he had hammered into the top of a tall white Mercedes van. Looking down, he realised that his impact had made a Carter-shaped dent in the metal roof.

Coughing, he rolled over and gazed up, focusing past the spinning snowflakes and towards the dark-clad soldiers beyond. 'Shit. Shit!' He rolled from the roof and landed in a crouch on the pavement. Bullets followed him, shattering the windscreens of a whole snake-line of stationary and abandoned SmutCars, rusting and discarded.

Carter sprinted for the alley, his body racked with agony, his breath coming in short, winded gasps. He slammed against the wall – then groaned, whirling out into the gloom of the narrow street. Bullets chipped the corner of the building in tiny spurts of powdered stone and Carter heard the distant thump of boots on tarmac. Lots of boots. Which, unfortunately, meant lots of Nex . . ..

Carter ran, slipping his Browning into its holster at the small of his back. He stopped suddenly beside an open doorway where he'd recently left his hoarded stash. With quivering fingers he dragged free his pack and M24 carbine. He checked the weapon quickly as he sprinted, hugging the wall of the derelict fire-ravaged building to his right. How many HPGs have I got? Shit. Not enough, he realised.

He halted, dropping to a crouch beside an old twisted

set of iron railings next to steps which fell away to a flooded stagnant basement which stank with an unholy mixed aroma of piss and rats. He pulled free one of his few remaining grenades, set it to 'prox.mine' and tossed it into the falling snow. It blipped and the blue acknowledgement light quickly disappeared. Within seconds snow masked the weapon. Taking a deep, pain-rattling breath, Carter stumbled on with the battered M24 in his gloved hands.

Carter sprinted left now, cutting along another narrow back street. This one was lived in. Huge bins overflowed with rotting refuse and split bags lay scattered untidily across the narrow roadway, spilling old rotting foodstuffs and debris and filling his lungs with a mouldy, decaying aroma, tinged again with the sickly-sweet stench of the ever-present rats. Several of the vermin skittered away from Carter's pounding boots and he crouched down once more, this time behind a huge yellow overflowing container. He heard the soft hissing crack of the grenade and the sickening slap of bodies tossed violently against stone.

Carter lowered his gaze. A rat was squatting directly in front of him, staring at him fearlessly. It was sleek, and so dark a brown that it was nearly black; its whiskers quivered as it watched him.

'You brave little son of a bitch!' Their gazes met. The rat looked defiant. As if to say, 'Yeah, fucker, you're damned right I am!'

Carter laughed, shaking his head and then scowling immediately at the pain from the fall.

The rat did not move, and Carter suddenly realised the intrinsic humour of the situation; this reversal of fortunes. The rat was in charge of the city of London. Ironically, the humans were now the underdogs, forced down and kept under by their new masters – the Nex. The humans were trapped, beaten, smashed down by the brutality of the Nex regime . . . ensnared and enslaved. Yeah, he thought: the Nex have made slaves of us. Everything was geared towards control – TV, the HATE biological virus, threats of further nuclear catastrophe . . . violence, starvation, oppression . . . but the rat retained the one thing that humanity craved so desperately. Freedom.

Carter stood, body protesting, and sprinted further down the narrow street. The rat watched him go, then turned slowly as a stream of balaclava-clad Nex flowed across the narrow roadway. The rat scuttled under a large bin and peered out with narrowed eyes as the Nex sprinted past, several of them splattered with strips of torn flesh – all that remained of their HPG-detonated comrades.

Finally, the roar of an engine broke through the snowy stillness as a heavily armoured ZSU5 Shilka, heavy tracks grinding pavements to dust, turned along the narrow street, guns and missiles bristling across its hull and antennas waving. The vehicle was almost too wide for the alley but it pushed stubbornly forward, engine roaring, tracks crushing everything in its path and sending a cascade of rats scuttling for the protective safety of the Underground . . .

Carter halted, panting, sweat dripping from his brow. All his clothing was soaked with sweat, clinging clammily to his skin. Steam rose from him as his shaved head cooled rapidly in the chill.

'*They're still following.*'

'You think I don't know that?'

'*There are ten of them.*'

'I *know.*'

'*You can't possibly kill ten of them.*'

'*I know*, Kade. Shut the fuck up and let me think!'

Carter was perhaps only a kilometre from the battered Range Rover. But he had tried several times to cut a path across the London streets to the vehicle – and several times he had been turned back: twice by Nex patrols with chain-leashed snarling Sleeper Nex, and once by a building collapse which had filled the streets with huge jagged sections of rubble and was in the process of being cleared by bulldozers and other heavy-tracked quarry machinery.

Carter considered his options: Run. Hide. Kill.

'Kill' was the most obvious, but he was outnumbered, outgunned, and he could hear the distant roar of the closing Shilka – which meant he was out-*missiled,* too. Hide. Hiding wouldn't get him any closer to the act of escape; hiding wouldn't reunite him with his boy Joseph. Carter was in Nex country now. The Nex patrolled constantly, and hiding wouldn't make that simple fact go away.

Run? Carter grinned malevolently through his sheen of sweat. He was fast running out of stamina and strength. A man couldn't run for ever. And when cornered? He'd be forced to fight . . .

'Fuck it. Fight I must.'

And then an idea struck Carter. He whirled, staring back down the street to the inverted V of collapsed rubble blocking his path to the Range Rover – and freedom beyond. There were four JCB K5 bulldozers – huge industrial vehicles, crosses between diggers and dozers, working on heavy hydraulics and with 10.5-litre turbo-cooled engines running refined LVA as they charged about. Carter's eyes narrowed as he watched them, huge hydraulic arms lifting fifty-tonne lumps of collapsed stone and dropping the mammoth chunks into FreightTruks which bobbed on their suspension over eight sets of twin-bubble tyres.

Carter jogged down the rubble-strewn street, past a small huddled group of workmen who were all standing and staring down into a hole. What is it with workmen and holes? Carter wondered idly. All his life, whenever he'd watched any form of construction job there'd always been a group of workmen huddled around a hole.

'*Perhaps they find them particularly holy?*' quipped Kade.

'Yeah, ha and ha,' snapped Carter. Then he stopped beside the teetering remains of a towering wall. The deafening sounds of the JCB K5 bulldozers filled his ears. Carter studied the JCBs, then pushed away from the wall, ducking a little as rubble from above pattered like shrapnel against his head.

He approached one of the vehicles – each wheel that drove the tracks was twice as tall as Carter himself. To the rear of the machine was a narrow recessed ladder leading up to the cabin.

Carter caught a glimpse of movement. The Nex had found him.

He sprinted forward, then threw himself to the left, rolling past the grinding steel tracks which crunched mere inches from his prone frail flesh. He came up into a crouch. There was a moment's pause, then Carter leapt and caught the vehicle as it edged forward. His hands grasped snow-slick yellow steel and he clambered up, hands slipping against the metal until he reached the entrance to the cab. Inside, the driver – an unmasked JT8 – was wearing earmuffs that blocked out the sounds of the thundering engine and hydraulics. Screens flickered in front of him: he gripped a control stick in one fist and operated touch screen controls with his other hand.

Carter opened the hatch, noticing the warning flicker of orange. As the JT8 whirled – allowing the massive bulldozer to suddenly lurch forward out of control – Carter smashed his fist into the man's face repeatedly. Then a third powerful blow broke the JT8's nose and left him drooling blood as he sagged unconscious against his safety harness.

Carter reached forward and pulled back on the stick. The bulldozer shuddered to a halt and Carter withdrew the knife from his boot – a long black blade – and sliced through the harness. He turned, hoisting the unconscious man up and dropping him from the rear of the industrial dozer. Then Carter leapt into the seat, turned and locked the hatch behind him.

Below, he felt the JCB shuddering with the vibration of its huge engines. He took control of the stick with his gloved hands and scanned the screens. The Nex were moving slowly, heads swaying from left to right as they came forward. They stepped neatly over blocks of scattered stone and hugged the walls as snow settled on their body-hugging uniforms and balaclavas.

Then Carter saw it – the weaving triangular head of a Sleeper Nex.

No wonder I couldn't lose them, he thought. They are hunting me . . . *scenting* me.

He found the pedals, revved the bulldozer's mighty 10,500cc engine and heard the whine of quad-turbos. He twisted the stick, flicked a control on the screen and the huge scoop at the front of the vehicle bucked on its hydraulics, and then transformed into a bulldozer's flat blade. On the screen there were eight shapes to play with – different configurations of bucket or blade, using the latest in steel-fan polymorphing technology.

Carter whirled the vehicle, and wheels spun inside tracks which skittered across loose stones and snow slush. The engine roared and Carter slammed his boot down on the accelerator, sending the bulldozer roaring down the street and towards the strung-out line of Nex. Their heads jerked up and around.

Guns blasted but Carter lifted the JCB's mighty blade and the bullets flattened against it and spun off harmlessly. The Nex scattered but Carter's foot was already pressed to the floor, and the vehicle ploughed into the running figures and the bulk of the Sleeper Nex – all were smashed against the side of a building which acted as an anvil, and then itself gave way. The bulldozer shuddered to a halt inside the teetering building, and the stench of hot oil drifted up to Carter from the darkness of his sudden entombment. Pebbles of stone thudded onto the cab above him, pattering like delicate rainfall.

Carter revved the engine, then slowly reversed through the hole where smears of Nex decorated the crumbled sides. Chunks of debris rolled down the cab and the windscreen, and a moment later the whole building collapsed with a massive roar and a billowing of dust.

Carter whirled the bulldozer round. All his screens were now blank, thanks to the swirling dust outside. Licking dry lips, he pulled free his Browning and turned, staring at the hatch – a masked face suddenly appeared and Carter placed a bullet neatly between the Nex's copper eyes before slamming the JCB into gear and powering the huge machine through the grey swirls of chaos he had so recently created.

The JCB's engine rose to an insane roar, and he collided with something within the fog of dust. The impact threw him across the cab. When the shock of sudden impact wore off and Carter's vision returned, he was lying upside down. One of his boots had smashed a touchscreen – which in turn had leaked some form of black, sticky chemical across his footwear and was even, as he watched, burning holes through the tough leather of his soles.

With a yelp, Carter rolled upright and pulled off the melting boots. Bullets rattled against the cab and he ducked involuntarily, grabbing for the JCB's stick and sending it into a frenzied spin, its engine screaming, the hot-oil smell getting stronger and stronger. He had the distinct and horrible impression that something was *not right* . . .

What the fuck did I hit? he thought.

And then he saw it – in the rear screen. He had hit another bulldozer.

You *stupid* motherf— He hit another of the machines in the fog of billowing dust, this time head on, crushing a sprinting Nex between the two massive blades in the process. The dust started to clear as Carter righted his JCB for the second time and spat out a broken splinter of tooth. He shook his head, dribbling a little blood and groaning to himself as he scanned his once again active screens with his mind spinning.

Outside, the snow still swirled. Carter's gaze followed the retreating Nex, coming to rest on the— 'Shit. A tank.'

The Shilka ZSU 88-4tt – which was not technically a tank, but a self-propelled anti-aircraft gun – could be devastating in the right circumstances against ground targets. It ran on tracks in a similar fashion to a tank, shared similar chassis components with several Soviet models, and sported four vertically mounted 23mm liquid-cooled automatic cannons with a firing rate of between 2,000 and 3,000 rounds per minute. These guns could fire either blast, fragmentation or incendiary shells. The Shilka was good for taking out lightly armoured ground vehicles and personnel, buildings, mounted machine guns – and was much more manoeuvrable than a tank of similar size. It had excellent protection against NBC war-fare and incredible radar technologies that included GUN DISH, which emitted VHF narrow beams to help track high-speed aircraft whilst itself being difficult to detect or evade.

Carter stared at the Shilka. One track started to move as the mobile gun oriented itself. 'Fucking tanks. I *hate* fucking tanks.'

Carter tugged the stick of the JCB hard back in order to reverse, and was deafened by squeals of grinding metal. He glanced at the screen and saw – to his horror – that his bulldozer had become entangled during the crash. With a deafening noise of ripping, groaning steel, he dragged the other bulldozer across the street, leaving huge gouges in the snow-mushed road. The Shilka opened fire . . .

Rounds slammed into the two bulldozers but Carter was already running, leaping from the cab and sprinting up the huge pile of collapsed rubble.

Behind him the two bulldozers, their engines scream-ing, suddenly erupted into a raging inferno which roared up into the sky, spitting blackened panels of steel. A wash of billowing flame spread across the road, blanketing the ground and surging against the stone mound up which Carter ran.

Fire licked at the heels of his bloodied feet.

Steyr TMPs opened fire, and Carter felt rather than heard the zip and whizz of bullets. Mouth a grim line, face blackened and eyes filled with tears from the smoke and dust, he forced himself to the top of the rise with lungs burning and bursting, and dived over the summit—

As a rising wall of fire – the result of the ignition of six thousand gallons of industrial LVA – followed him and burst overhead as he lay on his back, panting. Then it was gone, suddenly sucking back and disappearing.

Carter allowed the snow to settle on his face. It felt nice there. Calm, and the cool caress of the flakes was a welcome respite from adrenalin and fire and action . . .

On the other side of the rubble, Carter heard engines revving. And the clack of stone on stone. He groaned, rolled onto his belly and, limping on battered feet, lurched down the slope and away into the falling snow, searching for his Range Rover.

'*Close*,' observed Kade haughtily.

'I'd like to see you do it any fucking *neater*.' Carter slung the M24 over his back. He stopped at a corner, taking deep breaths, then pulled free his Browning and checked the weapon. Definitely the more discreet option when traversing Nex-infested London streets.

Within ten minutes he had located the Range Rover. He dropped his fire-damaged pack onto the passenger seat and with a screeching handbrake turn in the snow roared off in a spray of ice slurry.

Behind, the Nex watched him go. One smoothed open a bastard ECube channel, looked into the pale face and copper eyes of a Nex thousands of miles away, and said, 'He has gone. He escaped us this time.'

Alexis smiled softly. 'Do not concern yourself. He will come to us. I can sense it.'

'How can you be so sure?'

'Because we have his child,' said Alexis sweetly.

The Manta dropped from the white cliffs of Dover, twisting and flashing, then levelling as it skimmed low over the waves of the English Channel, creating a sonic boom as it went.

Carter wore an intense frown. Now that he had time to think, the peril of his situation was eating at him and he felt the need to get back to Cyprus. The need burned him like a brand.

150

It looked so obvious. An assassination with only one possible outcome: the wrecking of Spiral. In other words, a betrayal.

Carter chewed his lip. How could that be so? How could Nicky, his friend, a woman who had stood by him most of his life, *betray* him with such cold calculation?

Carter shook his head. It just could not be so. But more worryingly, what about his boy? His Joseph? His sweet and only child? The one remaining link he had with the woman he had loved, and who had been murdered as a result of the Nex filth seeking world domination . . .

Fear wormed into Carter's heart then, and there was no amount of mental strength, conditioning or calming that would work to exercise his fear.

As Carter sped over the cold churning waters cloaked by darkness he flipped open the ECube. But – as it had been back in London – the machine was dead. Powerless. Nothing more than a useless alloy block. Carter snorted in frustration . . . he had never known an ECube to fail – except through outside intervention. They were built to withstand a hell of a lot of punishment – they had to be, for so often a Spiral operative's life out in the field depended on the tiny alloy device. But this ECube was useless for communications . . .

Unless . . . The SpiralGRID and Spiral itself had been compromised.

Carter flew on, frustration and disbelief bringing him out in a cold, clammy sweat. How could Nicky do this to him? How could she betray him, betray Joseph, betray Spiral? It would be to betray everything that she loved, everything she truly believed in. It would make a mockery of Jam's death. It would make a mockery of her very existence. Round and round the thoughts chased each other.

Carter pushed the howling Manta to its limits; warning

sirens kept sounding in the confines of the cockpit and Carter would ease back, carefully watching the dials as needles retreated from the red – and then he'd slowly ease more power through the screaming engines again until he was sure they could take no more.

Eventually his thoughts focused on two simple decisions.

If she has harmed Joseph, she will die.

If she has betrayed Spiral, she will die.

'*But you are the tool!*' mocked Kade. '*You were the finger on the trigger, the bullet in the gun. You killed Jahlsen. You gave Durell the SpiralGRID. You condemned your friends, fucker . . .*'

And Carter caught himself, snapping from the brink of sleep to see the waves looming close in the darkness, white crests of foam mocking him with their closeness – and he felt sick, deeply sick, and the nausea spread until he was sure he could not possibly take any more.

If she has harmed my boy, she will surely die a long and painful death.

Yes. He nodded to himself, eyes glowing in the darkness of the cockpit.

Carter landed with a crunch that the Manta could only just absorb. Several struts buckled, and as Carter's feet hit the ground the Manta listed helplessly to one side.

Carter's mouth was set in a grim line of determination.

Slowly, he walked forward over ground he knew well, adrenalin counteracting his deep weariness. This was a land he had made his own; a home he had created as a base, a haven of stability for his child, far away from the evils of the world. Or as far away as a father and his son could possibly retreat . . .

The sea surged to his right, hissing against the beach

and thundering against the rocks. He moved up the narrow path towards the house – then paused, head cocked, eyes alert and scanning.

Something was wrong. He could feel it.

Carter moved to the front door and paused – suddenly afraid of what he might find. He became aware of an absence.

Samson. Where was his dog? The mutt should have been there, bounding around and wagging his tail.

Slowly, Carter eased open the door and peered into the house's cool interior. He listened, but could hear nothing. He crept in, moving carefully, and his ears picked up a soft whimper. The muted sound of an animal in pain . . .

Resisting the urge to call out, Carter moved to the kitchen where he found Samson lying, his head on his paws, in a pool of blood. Carter dropped to one knee, smiling softly as Samson's tail gave a half-hearted wag. He peered into the great sad eyes of the chocolate Labrador.

'You been in the wars, old friend?'

Samson licked his master's hand, and Carter quickly examined the dog. The animal had been shot, in the shoulder and from the front – which meant that Samson had been wounded while attacking whoever had levelled the gun. He ran his hand gently across the dog's flanks, feeling the buckle of broken ribs.

'Oh, Samson!'

Carter stood quickly, noticing the disarray. Dishes lay strewn and smashed, there was a knife on the floor, and a footprint was visible in Samson's spilled, congealing blood. So there'd been a struggle – but *after* the dog had been shot . . .

'Joe?' he bellowed. 'Joseph?'

Carter moved through the house at speed, searching

153

each and every room. There were no more signs of struggle – but his child, his boy, his son – Joseph was not there.

'*Maybe Nicky took him somewhere safe,*' came Kade's sardonic mewl.

Carter ignored him. He filled a bowl with water, and checked Samson more thoroughly. The dog was seriously dehydrated and lapped at the water thirstily . . . Carter supported the animal's head, then pushed a blanket under his great velvet ears and fixed a pad over the bullet wound, sticking the tape clumsily to Samson's fur. The wound had already clotted but Carter did not know whether Samson would survive. Pulling free his medical pack, he hurriedly gave the dog an injection of antibiotics, a K7 stimulant, vitamin enhancers and a shot of diamorphine. Samson put his head on his paws and closed his eyes, breathing deeply.

And it was only then that Carter saw it. An ECube. A silver ECube, sitting innocently on the kitchen work surface.

Carter glanced around. Then he reached out and felt the tiny machine buzz in his fingers. He initiated the ECube and it spun open to reveal the tiny eye of a projector unit. Carter pointed the device at the wall and waited impatiently. A circle of light appeared, framing Nicky's face.

She smiled. 'Sorry, Carter,' she said, shrugging and tilting her head to one side.

The camera drew back to show two masked Nex binding Joseph with raze-wire. It cut into the young boy's wrists and blood dripped to the carpet. He was shouting, and one of the Nex punched the five-year-old child in the face, silencing him with shock and sudden pain. Then they wound duct tape around his head, covering first his mouth and then his eyes. Joseph continued to struggle futilely, tears streaming down his face from under the thick grey tape.

Nicky strode forward and reached over. She held the camera as one would hold a lover's head, with both hands, and with a tender look on her face she whispered into it, 'I'm sure you have many questions which burn you with the need for answers. I'm sure all manner of emotions are flowing through that thick Spiral skull of yours . . . predominantly anger, and hatred, confusion, and a need to kill. Yes, I *understand*.' She breathed deeply. 'But, dear Mr Carter, all I can say is that you need to sit still . . . and you need to wait. We will contact you, and if you don't do what we ask . . . well . . .' She smiled, her eyes blinking slowly, and then moved away from the camera to reveal the dark-robed bulk of Durell. Durell, there in Carter's house.

A claw reached out and cupped Joseph's chin.

'No,' moaned Carter, his tongue licking at desert-dry lips.

The projection ended, the silver ECube folding in on itself and sitting innocuously on the worktop. Carter picked up the small device and launched it with a yell of rage against the wall, where it bounded off and skittered across the stone-tiled floor, spinning slowly to a halt. He glared at it with loathing.

Carter lifted his M24, then turned slightly as he spotted—

The bottle. Whisky. Lagavulin. Just one sip. A burning taste to clear his head, to make the world a good place again. It would taste good. It would help him. It would end his pain. Yeah, he thought, one sip would lead to five sips, a dram to another dram to a bottle and Joseph would die lost and alone and Carter would condemn himself to hell.

Just one . . . He reached out. The amber Lagavulin swirled enticingly within its dark glass container. Carter threw the bottle across the room, where it smashed into sharp-edged shards and left a spreading stain across the terracotta tiles.

He met Samson's gaze. The dog was panting heavily, his eyelids drooping under the effects of the drugs that Carter had administered. He knelt, refilled the bowl with water, and said, "I'll be back soon, buddy. Don't go anywhere."

Samson whined. Carter nodded, stood, and moved towards the back of the house. At the rear there was a narrow doorway, camouflaged by hanging coats and other wooden panels. He placed both hands against the smooth surface and pushed gently A panel slid back to reveal a dark hole through which Carter squeezed before descending a flight of narrow steps into blackness. A light appeared, a solitary bulb that could be switched on and off by a simple chain. And then came a metallic grating sound – two alloy panels sliding neatly apart to reveal Carter's secret weapon stash.

Five minutes later, the Manta lifted on its abused jets and hovered for a moment over Carter's house. Then it banked, leapt forward and howled down the coast until the town of Paphos surged into view. At the heart of the Old Town, by the low sea wall, stood the Sentinel Tower.

The Manta thundered towards the tower at only twenty feet above the ground, sending people running, screaming, and causing Nex patrols to stare up, guns hanging from limp hands—

At first hand, Carter had seen these towers withstand a nuclear blast. To attack their exteriors was futile – and Carter was no fool. But he had often wondered what kind

156

of damage a missile could do *inside* the protective shell? After all, he had seen the leaked blueprints . . .

A single K-TF8 missile hissed from its pylon, its rocket igniting as the Manta banked suddenly and skimmed the tower to the right with only inches to spare. The missile flew low over the ground, whipping past the sentries and patrols of Nex gathered at the entrance to the building. It ploughed straight through the welcoming open doors.

There was an instant of silence and then a terrible roar shook the Sentinel Tower. A billowing cloud of fiery gas erupted from the interior like a volcanic explosion, melting the interior glass partitions instantly and pulverising the twenty or so JT8s and Nex standing outside the tower; the savage power of the blast smashed them outwards like skittles, tearing their arms and legs off.

Carter brought the screaming Manta around in a tight circle at twenty feet above the ground, so low as to make the tower's SAM defences useless. He landed amid the shattered remains of the buckled paving flags, and leapt down from the cockpit, M24 in one hand and 9mm Browning HiPower in the other. He strode towards the blasted doorway, the fire-crisped opening smeared with melted Nex fat. Flames still burned, and smoke rose in a black column. A Nex sprinted from the fire, its clothing burning and its mouth open in a silent scream. Carter fired and a bullet cannoned into one side of the Nex's head, exiting in a shower of skull and brains from the other. For a moment its legs kept running, then it collapsed in a tangle, slapping face-first to the ground.

Carter, his face a grim mask, moved into the charred devastation of the entrance hall. An automatic sprinkler system sprayed foam over the leaping flames and made the floor treacherous with its frothing slime. More Nex sprinted into view, three lithe black-clad figures. Carter's gun was already blasting as they appeared, fire blossoming from its scorched barrel as bullets slammed into Nex flesh, sending bodies sprawling.

Carter moved across the entrance chamber, halted by some steps and listened for a moment, head tilted. Sirens wailed, and he could hear the pounding of chopper blades. Gunshots echoed. Carter saw through the smoking hole of the building's entrance a group of civilians kicking a JT8 on the ground. Someone levelled a double-barrelled shotgun at the man's head and gave it both barrels, spreading bone fragments and the slop of pulverised brains across the ground in a sudden splash.

The word leapt into Carter's mind. *Riot*. The people had merely been waiting.

And Carter had been the trigger. But it wouldn't last for long. These things never did. What was important, however, was that Carter was given precious seconds.

With a grim smile he spun right and disappeared down the emergency-lit staircase, his expression grim, cold, determined.

The only sounds were the soft hiss and drip of the sprinkler systems from far above. Small groups of Nex had attacked Carter three more times – and he had cut them down without a flicker of emotion. You want to fuck with me? he thought. You want to threaten my boy? Well, if it's death you're looking for, then that's what I'll deliver . . .

He crouched by a support pillar and planted the High-J. The small unit gave a tiny flicker of blue light as it integrated with his ECube; then the light went out.

Carter strode purposefully through the surreal subterranean vaults of the Sentinel Tower. His recklessness, he knew, could easily get him killed or maimed. But by some incredible twist of fate he had survived. So far.

Again, he dropped to one knee and positioned another pack of HighJ. Tiny mechanical jaws burrowed into concrete supports. The blue glow indicated integration and a complicated detonation sequence.

Carter heard a faint sound and stood smoothly, his Browning pointing around in the gloom. The missile strike had disabled the tower's main power subsystems.

Carter watched the Nex glide into view. He raised his gun.

The Nex heard him. It dived to the right and a bullet shattered a chunk of concrete next to Carter's ear – so close that he felt the shower of shards sting the side of his head. Carter did not flinch – instead, his Browning began to bark, bullets streaming from the weapon as the Nex moved inhumanly fast. Carter slid behind the protective slab of a pillar. He pulled free the final HighJ unit. Just this one and the detonation sequence would be complete. A sheen of sweat on his brow, Carter hefted the HighJ thoughtfully.

'*Fucking Nex*,' came Kade's soft voice. '*Getting in the way of you and your destiny!*'

'Destiny?'

'*Destruction!*'

Carter could feel his energy waning, exhaustion finally creeping through his abused muscles, teasing out his last remaining dregs of strength.

Carter ground his teeth. They had his son. He *had* to push on . . .

A sudden click inside his brain kicked him into focus. There wasn't one Nex, but three, and they were trying to encircle him. The first Nex he had seen was the decoy – shit, he thought, in a few seconds—

He sprinted through the gloom towards a huge bank of thick piping against the far wall. Shots suddenly rang out behind him as he ran, filling the vault with an incredible echoing din.

Carter dived, connecting with the solidity of the wall with a hard thud. One fist still clenched the HighJ and he slammed it against the piping. It flickered blue and Carter felt the rattle of his ECube against his chest, confirming integration as he once more pictured the Sentinel Tower's blueprints in his mind. *Ready.*

He peered from behind the pipes, eased free a smoke grenade, pulled the pin and sent it spinning, clattering across the chamber. A billowing grey cloud rolled up and around, curling against the ceiling and spreading. Two Nex stumbled choking from the smoke and Carter cut them down in a moment. They lay twitching, one with a leg kicking spasmodically as it choked on its own blood, its gloved fingers clasping feebly at a destroyed windpipe through which it could no longer take in air. Carter scanned the smoke, then moved forward cautiously.

'*There were three,*' came Kade's unbidden intrusion.

'Yes, I—'

The Nex leapt from the cloud of smoke, crashing into Carter with incredible speed and momentum. They both fell, rolling heavily as Carter's M24 skittered away across the floor. The Nex smashed a right straight against Carter's head, then another. Carter rolled as the Nex got to its feet and leapt. Boots slammed into his face and his head bounced against the concrete. In a daze, he pulled free his Browning, which was promptly kicked away.

The Nex stood, hands by its side, staring down at Carter. It flexed its gloved fingers, and spoke in a soft voice. Carter realised that this Nex was *female*.

'You are Carter. You have killed many of my kind. I think it is time that we danced.'

160

Carter climbed to his feet and spat out a bolus of scarlet mucus. The blows had left him momentarily dazed and his mouth was full of saliva, phlegm and blood. He rolled his neck, dropped his pack to the floor, and nodded.

The Nex attacked. She was fast and powerful, throwing a series of complicated punches at Carter who staggered backwards, almost unable to defend himself. She left his forearms and shins bruised and battered, sending pain signals to his brain which he cut off ruthlessly. She jumped, booted feet seeking his face. But Carter twisted swiftly, slamming an overhead punch into the Nex's heart and driving her against the wall. As Carter started forward, she rolled to her feet and although she showed no signs of pain, Carter knew he had hurt her.

The Nex changed tactics. She circled him warily as Carter studied her face: flawless skin, copper eyes, short sweat-streaked spiked hair . . .

'*Pretty*,' said Kade.

'Shut up.'

She attacked once more, and Carter's fist slammed into her nose. She stumbled, sprawling backwards. Carter bent, picked up the Browning and pointed it at the recumbent female Nex.

'No,' she said.

Carter could read the fear in her eyes. I thought they felt no emotion, came a little unbidden voice at the back of his brain. But time . . .

Time was everything.

He pulled the trigger, and a single bullet entered the Nex's forehead, slamming her head back to thud against the concrete. Blood pooled out.

Carter grabbed his pack, holstered his Browning and retrieved his M24. He moved through the smoke towards the steps and gave a single glance back at the scene of carnage.

Lifting his ECube, he initiated a sequence. And throughout the vaults of the Sentinel Tower, eight units of HighJ explosive were primed for detonation.

Order had been restored to the town of Paphos by the time Carter stepped out into the sunlight. It blinded him momentarily as Nex and JT8 weapons trained on him and he moved warily forward, dropping his pack and lifting the ECube high for the Nex to see.

For a moment, crazy thoughts raced through Carter's brain, but he was sure that they did not want him dead. They had taken his boy. That meant they needed something from him – and he was damned if he could work out what.

It had taken a lot of guts to trust his instincts and step out to meet a potential firing squad. But there was a game being played here and he was sick of being a pawn. Carter was no man's pawn. He played by his own fucked-up rules.

'Who's in charge here?' he bellowed.

From a large black BMW X9 with darkened titanium privacy windows stepped a Nex, dressed simply in black but without a mask. Nex wore no insignia, no signs of rank, but Carter had learnt earlier in his career that Nex had other means of identification – usually scent. She had a pale oval face and bright copper eyes. Her hair was cut short near the scalp, a spiked black wave; high cheekbones gave her face a slightly haughty look. She moved forward with an incredible grace, poised and powerful despite her lack of height. Carter could sense her physical prowess . . . could sense the nature of this hunter, this predator, this killer. This beast.

'I am, Mr Carter. Put down the ECube.'

162

'Where's my son?'

'He is in a safe place. Put down the ECube – you have caused enough damage for one day. You have proved your point. Now come with me and nothing will happen to your little boy.'

Carter glanced up. From the BMW stepped another figure, a woman with long brown hair and sparkling eyes. She closed the BMW's door, then moved slowly to stand beside the Nex.

She looked up then. Looked up into Carter's snarling face.

'I'm sorry, Carter.'

'I wish I could say I'm not surprised, but I am. Nicky, what the *fuck* are you doing?'

'I am not the Nicky you knew – and trusted. I hate to be the one to tell you this, but Nicky is a corpse. She died alone, in agony, screaming for her long-lost lover, Jam. I am a Nex, Carter. I am a changer. A replication. Now put down the ECube, like Alexis told you to. You don't want to prolong this agony.'

'How many Nex are in the tower?'

'Three hundred,' said Alexis softly, her gaze fixed on Carter.

Carter shrugged, and thumbed the ECube detonator. Below the ground there came a shudder and the pavement shook. Several JT8s fell to their knees as if they were victims of a violent earthquake tremor. Then a collective scream rose and fire blazed up through the inside of the Sentinel Tower as the people standing outside the building sprinted for cover. Alexis and Nicky backed nervously away but Carter merely stood, face a grim mask, as the Tower shook and then started to collapse from within. Smoke billowed outwards, swamping Carter, enveloping him, a huge vapour mouth opening ringed with bone-shard teeth fashioned from the mashed and pulverised bones of hundreds of dead Nex – and then snapping shut to eat him whole.

The Sentinel Tower fell. Carter felt as though he was choking to death on dust as the force of the blast rocked him, dropping him to his knees as if he'd been slapped across the back of the head with a shovel. Coughing spasms racked him and he spat out chips of stone and concrete. He felt gloved hands grasp him. He punched out and the grasping fingers fell away. He found his feet, then scrambled away from the blast zone.

As Carter stumbled free, the Nex were waiting for him. Through the swirling dust and smoke, he saw that a ring of guns surrounded him and he slowly lifted his hands. Nicky moved forward, her face a mask of horror. 'How could you?' she whispered. 'How could you kill them *all*?'

And then Alexis was there, her expression unreadable. Her fist slammed into Carter's jaw, and he was rocked by the impact. His hand came up and rubbed tenderly where he'd been hit. His stare slowly focused on Alexis's face.

'What the fuck have you done with my son?' he growled.

Alexis's copper eyes glowed. Without a word she stepped back and the JT8s waded in with stomping boots and the butts of their sub-machine guns, hammering Carter into unconsciousness and then continuing to beat at his limp body.

'We have him,' said Alexis into a tiny comm.

'Will he do what we want?' asked Nicky.

'Yes,' said Alexis. 'He'll do *whatever* we demand.'

'In the same way as he destroyed the Sentinel Tower? Is that what we *demanded*, Alexis?'

Alexis's stare fixed on Nicky for a while, her look cool and composed. The Nicky changer shivered. Then, without a word, the female Nex general climbed into the BMW X9. Tyres spun against concrete shards as the vehicle powered through the smoke of destruction – leaving Nicky standing and surveying the catastrophic devastation wrought by Carter's merciless wrath.

Spiral Mainframe
Data log#18475 [+18512 updates]

CLASSIFIED SADT/8764/SPECIAL INVESTIGATIONS UNIT
DATA REQUEST 777#18475

QIII and QIV

The QuanTech Edition 3 [QIII] and Edition 4[QIV] family of Military Cubic Processors

The QIII was the first-ever cellular processor – the prototype of an electronic mind – semi-organic, silicon-based and with a mixture of synthetic substances at its core. Via design modes and mechs, the QIII processor and the QIV which followed were totally independent pieces of hardware.

Working around a digital model of WorldCode Data, the QuanTech Edition 3 was digitally capable of incredible computing feats. A successor to the all-powerful QuanTech Edition 2 [QII] processor which runs at the heart of various Spiral Mainframes across the globe, the QIII was capable and fully compliant with all global operating systems – from UNIX to Windows it could

165

decode way beyond current 64- and 128- bit architectures. The QIII was so powerful that it could decode and re-encode DNA in millionths of a second when it would take a conventional computer many hours. The QIII was at least 50,000 times faster than any current processor in development. It was destined to have ground-breaking effects on all aspects of computing, from military applications to world economics.

The pinnacle of the QuanTech 3's development was the ability to use WorldCode Data combined with probability math – equations allowing it to successfully predict the future on the simulation of any given probable event. This feature was nearly 100% successful in prediction, and required only occasional calibration.

The QIII was destroyed when a rogue Spiral operative named Durell abused the military processor (and its subsystems) and attempted to use this all-powerful machine to take over global military systems, financial institutions and satellites, including the highly destructive Russian PredatorSAT modules.

At the time the QIII was destroyed by Spiral operative Cartervb512, it was thought that all schematics were lost/destroyed. However, subsequently, and unknown to Spiral operatives on a global scale, Durell had successfully completed the technical development of the QIV processor which in turn helped to build a 'Quake-machine', or 'QuakeHub' which could use natural faults in an underground network of mineral fuel lodes known as LVA to instigate quakes at specific locations anywhere throughout this LVA network. This gave Durell an extra weapon with which to attempt his world domination but, again, it was successfully smashed by Spiral operative Cartervb512 in his search for a cure for his dying woman.

Keyword SEARCH>> QIII, QIV, NEX, SAD, SPIRAL_sadt, DURELL, FEUCHTER, QuakeHub, Spiral_Q, Spiral_R, SVDENSKA, CONSTANZA, PAGAN

// Also see military texts *SPIRAL* and *QUAKE*.

CHAPTER 7

GAME PLAN

let us () out
make () us free
free again
release us – traitor ()
() dark blood traitor . . .

Mongrel and The Priest crouched, huddling at the top of what had once been a wide staircase in the deserted building and staring down at the devastation in the hall below. The Nex, pinned down by Mongrel's heavy fire, had taken up defensive positions behind pillars. The tank – with a salvo of twin shells – had destroyed the staircase.

'Fucking monkeys,' snorted Mongrel. 'How dumb-ass Nex going get up steps now?'

'They'll probably come in through the roof,' said The Priest softly.

'Ahhhh! Yes, so they will.'

The firing pin of Mongrel's gun suddenly made a frightening click. Mongrel's gaze met The Priest's. Behind them the other operatives had also ceased firing. Most had run out of ammunition. Those who hadn't were down to their last few rounds.

As if sensing this, the Nex started to emerge, moving behind the protective shell of the tank. More motors whirred and the huge twin guns powered up, taking aim towards the top of the massive shattered staircase.

'Got any last words?' muttered Mongrel.

The Priest merely made the sign of the cross – as something big and fast shot through the opening left by the Nex tank and struck it. There was a titanic explosion as the tank spun, shedding panels of armour. The advancing Nex soldiers burst into flame and melted into pools of stinking grease—

Mongrel, The Priest and other Spiral ops cowered behind sheltering sections of wall as fire roared past them, scorching plaster. Sergeant Simmo had arrived.

Simmo was a mammoth tattooed hulk, a barrel-chested man-mountain with a shaved head, a goatee beard and fearsome bushy eyebrows. He had only limited numbers of his own teeth – and the skin of his throat bore tattoos of the names of the many men he had killed. Any other exposed skin was also heavily tattooed.

Simmo had once been a slave to bureaucracy, spending much of his early military life performing puerile pen-pushing tasks. But since the earth-ravaging quakes and the subsequent nuclear devastation that had rocked the world he had undertaken a serious re-evaluation of his life. As a result, he had changed. Simmo had woken up.

Now he strode across the rubble, dressed in his stained combats and smoking a fat cigar. His throat tattoos bulged. The man-mountain stood atop debris greased with smears of bubbling Nex fat, and placed his hands on his hips. He bellowed, 'You here, you fucking crazy Holy

Man? I believe I was summoned by the Lord – or maybe it was only by Lord knows what!'

The Priest rose slowly, and calmly patted out a small fire which glowed in the crispy strands of his beard. Mongrel leapt up, pushing past The Priest to stand at the edge of the blasted stairs. Small pieces of wood tumbled away and clattered far below.

'What you fucking doing, crazy Sarge? You trying to blast us all to Kingdom Come?'

'You are rescued, aren't you, Mongrel, you little maggot?'

'How you know we not behind tank? How you know we not captured and lined up as prisoners? How you know we not be in the *bloody firing line* of HTank shells?'

Sergeant Simmo puffed on his cigar. Big blue clouds surrounded his head, enveloping him in a personal smog. Through his haze, his eyes glittered like a shark's. He grinned a long nasty grin.

'Lads . . . in war it's just a chance you have to take.'

Mongrel's reply was lost in a bubbling tirade of frothing expletives as The Priest fought to hold the adrenalin-pumped soldier back.

'Even though we have a visual on Carter, the QIV processor is completely blind to him.' From his New York Sentinel Tower, Durell stared at the screens before him, images flickering from the helmet-cams of different Nex. The snow was falling thick in London, making images blurred – indistinct. Durell glanced down at the QIV processor read-outs.

His technicians were right. Carter was invisible.

An anomaly within the system. Just like before. 'How can that be?' said Durell. He reached out and drank slowly from a glass of water. The liquid quenched his burning throat and soothed him for a moment. Most of the time Durell endured this constant agony; it was almost an old friend, almost comforting. And he knew that his current state went hand in hand with the pain – one condition could not exist without the other. They were symbiotic. The torture just *was*. Durell accept this with good grace.

A tall black-glass door opened and Mace entered. He was a small Nex, lithe and athletic. His head gleamed, perfectly bald, and his ageing face was only slightly deformed. Mace seated himself next to Durell and waited patiently, hands in his lap.

Durell drank more water, then glanced over. 'Carter has killed Jahlsen. We have the SpiralGRID within our grasp. It feels good, does it not?'

Mace gave a curt nod. 'It feels good that we can exterminate the vermin. I am sick of Spiral hacking my TV stations with their pirate signals. I am tired of them detonating the WarFactories and NEP Production Plants. I am just *tired*, Durell.'

Durell nodded. 'I, too, am weary of this insistent buzzing. They have long been a thorn in our side, and despite their falling numbers they are still blowing up garrisons and assassinating key military figures. It is their flaming torch in the sky that gives REBS strength. Without Spiral's victories to look upon, without Spiral's guidance and hand-me-down technology the REBS would die in an instant. An extinguished flame! But first . . .'

'First we must cut off the head.'

Durell nodded, focusing on Mace.

'Yes. A neat decapitation,' he said.

They walked, Mace slightly behind Durell, down wide deserted corridors. The temperature was comfortably cool and Mace watched his master with respect as they descended a long, twisting flight of steps.

Down. The Sentinel Tower was huge above ground – and just as big below. A labyrinth. A *Nest*.

It was cooler still below ground level and deathly quiet. Occasionally they stopped at sterile alloy doors before passing through into more tiled, gleaming corridors, identical in their symmetry. After long minutes of walking, they came to a large set of double doors. Silence reigned, and the alloy surface of the doors was different here – more intricate, graced with an element of design.

Durell reached out, his blackened claw pressing gently against a switch. A tiny needle slid into his flesh and sampled genetic structure; the doors hissed opened and an icy breeze whipped out, causing Mace to blink.

They stared down on a hive of activity, a microcosm of a city, a three-kilometre-square hub of laboratories and testing centres. Thousands of workers scurried feverishly below; thousands of slabs displaying precious Nex specimens – soldiers – lay spread out in a concentric pattern. There was an order to the seething chaos far below. An organic order.

Tears welled in Mace's eyes.

'So we are still losing Nex?' came Durell's soft voice.

'Yes,' said Mace.

They moved forward onto a glass bridge. Below them Nex scientists scuttled around like insects. The hive below showed a scene which wrenched at Durell and caused him real pain.

On a thousand slabs Nex writhed, slowly dying, *disintegrating* within their armoured shells as if some terrible disease had got into their bloodstreams, into their genetic cores, and was working its way to the surface, destroying their flesh as it went.

Durell's slitted copper eyes looked on with sorrow.

And pain. And *hunger* – the hunger to discover the nature of the problem that was losing him Nex soldiers at a steadily accelerating rate. They were dying on the streets of New York. They were curling into balls and screaming in the rubble-strewn alleyways of Paris. They were vomiting bile and pus onto the cobbled walkways of Moscow.

'One report investigates abnormality in The Avelach.' Durell nodded softly, his gaze settling on Mace. The small Nex could almost feel his master's pain. 'As you know, The Avelach has been copied nearly a thousand times – on a design board created and modelled by the QIV. In all scans, on all wavelengths, the new machines are an identical copy of the original Avelach machine – and in tests all Nex specimens seem perfect. *Are* perfect – developed in the same way. Created in the same manner and containing all core-data structures without a single strand of evidence pointing to corruption. However . . .'

'Yes?' Durell's hiss was a sibilant plume of condensation in the freezing underground laboratory. Below him, a Nex shrilled a high-pitched shriek above the hearing threshold of human ears. The stricken creature fell and began to thrash on the smooth stone floor as technicians rushed to sedate it.

'There may be a bump in the genetic sequence.'

'A *bump*?'

'On the TZ-Graphs. It is so minor that it has gone undiscovered for a long time. No scans picked up this, shall we say, *tremor* in the strands.'

'In which area does the anomaly occur?'

Mace shrugged. 'A cluster of nodes which are inexplicable; even with all our expertise there are still genetic modifiers which are unexplained to our godlike eyes.' He laughed coldly.

'We need to sort this anomaly. And quickly. Our dominance relies on our strength.'

'The scientists are working as hard as they can. And the QIV is continually searching for answers to the problem, committing more and more processor cycles to the discovery of the malfunction.'

'Our miracle processor has come up with nothing?'

'It has found no answers.' As they quit the chamber, leaving the hectic bustle of experimentation and investigation behind, Durell was lost in thought.

A Nex runner sped into view, a sheen of sweat on its brow. It halted, saluting Durell, and handed him an encoded sliver of metal. Durell's claw ran over the pitted surface and his eyes closed in a long, lazy blink as he absorbed the information.

'What is it?'

Durell turned to stare hard at Mace. 'It would seem that we have a defector.'

'A . . .' Mace frowned.

'It would seem that one of our Nex has chosen to join *Spiral*.' Durell's words were ice cold.

'That is impossible.'

'Yes. But then, so is internal destruction of Nex by an invisible enemy contained within their own genetic spirals. Or so we would have thought. These are the first tremors of our model cracking. We must not allow this state of growing atrophy to progress.'

'But what is the answer?' asked Mace gently.

Durell's slitted eyes narrowed and his hood fell back to reveal his terribly disfigured face. Armoured scales seemed to click into place and he turned, gazing back at the door hiding the secret of his damaged and slowly disintegrating army.

'The extermination of Spiral,' he said, his voice so soft

174

it was almost inaudible in the gloom of the sterile corridor. 'We must move our plans forward. We must act *now*.'

Twanging guitars filled the cabin of the old Volvo, screeching from dust-encased speakers as a gravel-voiced country and western singer sang of love, loss and the large swaying breasts of a woman on the ranch. The engine note grew harsher with a snarl of grinding gears. A sandalled foot slapped an out-of-synch rhythm as the singer moved away from the subject of love with a large-breasted woman, segueing neatly to the topics of whiskey and the needs of horses on the ranch. A head nodded, one hand coming up to fondle idly a set of rosary beads.

The Priest was content. For the moment, at least.

Pluming blue-grey oil smoke, the Volvo drove along the deserted roadway. What had once been a major A-road linking the north and the south of England was now a long strip of tarmac desert – a desolation created by the unleashing of the biological weapon known as HATE. But now (and unknown to the majority of the city-trapped general population) it was a cleared route, free from biological contamination.

The Volvo ground to a halt with a thrashing of badly meshing gears. The Priest, muttering that he really should get the old gearbox looked at, wound the window down and poked his bearded face out into the cold autumn air. Around the Volvo lay a scattering of glass and stones, glinting as shafts of sunlight broke from the heavy blanket of clouds.

The Priest smiled, nodding in understanding.

'I hear you, Lord,' he said in a clear, booming voice.

He stepped from the Volvo, his sandals grating against glass and stone. His gaze fixed on the wreckage ahead and he looked around warily, one massive hand fidgeting below his flowing brown robes and reappearing holding a Glock 9mm pistol.

The gun looked small in The Priest's huge hand, like a child's toy in the paw of a giant bear. The Priest, his robes flapping, strode forward, stopping to glance around at the empty fields to either side of the road, the low hedgerows and the distant, shattered pylons.

On the road were the crumpled remains of a military FukTruk. Smoke still curled from it and The Priest moved towards the scatter of burnt detritus. His nostrils wrinkled at the mingled stench of HighJ explosive, oil smoke, burning rubber – and fried human flesh.

The back of the large military truck had been the usual construct of steel and canvas. As The Priest peered into its charred remains, his gold-flecked eyes widened and his teeth bared for a moment. The truck had been full of people when the bomb or missile struck. Now they were a merged mass of burnt limbs, melted flesh and sticky liquefied human fat. Yellow bone showed in places. The Priest had seen the screaming wide eyes of a dead soldier, hair burnt off, scalp skin scorched but face somehow still a square of white against the dark charcoal of the rest of his head.

The Priest bowed his own head. 'Holy Mary, Mother of God, pray for us sinners now and at the hour of our death. Amen.' He moved warily back to the Volvo, coughing a little on the smoke and damning all his enemies to an eternity in the fires of Hell . . . damning the world and its violence.

He killed the wailing plunking of the country and western guitar with a battered thumb and revved the Volvo's engine hard. He wheel-spun past the scene of devastation as his rational brain continued to tell him there were always casualties. But his emotions would not allow him the sanctuary of such justification. Death was death. Cruelty was cruelty.

And there are no rules in love and war, he thought morosely. Had those corpses been Spiral? Or REBS? Or just fleeing citizens who had discovered that this part of the country was free from the curse of HATE and had made a break for it in a stolen truck?

The Priest did not know, but he understood they had been bombed by powerful aircraft and that made his hackles rise. His Volvo was faster than any army truck – but not by much. And he doubted whether the thirty-three-year-old vehicle with its peeling paint, rattling exhaust and three bald tyres could outrun a Manta.

His mouth a grim line, The Priest cut right down a narrow country lane and headed for the far-distant dock-side.

As the number of buildings grew, so The Priest became more alert and he allowed himself gradually to tune in to his surroundings. Everything was deserted, and the signs of battle were everywhere – fire and bullet marks scarring walls, crumbled, smashed edifices revealing the passage of tanks or the impact of missiles. The Priest steered his Volvo with care around the lumps of concrete or piles of crushed brick that occasionally littered the road. As the buildings became taller so The Priest realised that the ground was falling away, dropping down to the distant docks. He slipped the Volvo into neutral (fighting for about thirty seconds with the grinding gearstick) and allowed the machine to cruise with a steady hum of wide bald tyres and the occasional barking backfire.

'Got to save petrol,' he mused. 'After all, the Lord provides for those who provide for themselves.'

A few minutes later, fingering his rosary beads once

more, The Priest rolled to a halt. He had the Glock in his hand and, squinting through the dirt-smeared windscreen, he tried in vain to squirt water onto the curved glass. Somewhere a feeble motor whined, but precious holy liquid did not fountain forth to clear his vision.

'Damn and buggering blast,' said The Priest. He stroked his beard, and slammed his sandal to the floor. The Volvo lurched off, belching smoke. Gathering speed, it squealed around a corner and roared down to the dockside. To one side a concrete slope fell away to meet inky waters edged with scum, old rope and ancient yellowed paper wrappers. The Volvo's tyres thumped rhythmically across the concrete-section dockside as town buildings fell behind to be replaced by desolate and empty warehouse structures.

The Priest's eyes picked out a small gathering beside the opening to a nondescript warehouse – standing beside some battered SmutCars and a large, black, battered van. The men and women were holding sub-machine guns and looking around warily. Muzzles trained on the Volvo as it lurched to a stop and The Priest killed the ignition. He stepped free, his sandals flapping on concrete, and for a few moments the engine burbled and gurgled, stuttering on a rich cocktail of excessive petrol, until it finally – and thankfully – died.

The Priest met Mongrel's gaze, moving forward and nodding a greeting to Simmo, Rogowski and Bob Bob. 'Is he here?'

'Da, *it* is here,' coughed Mongrel, scowling at The Priest. 'Mo and Roxi are inside, keeping it covered. We just waiting for you. You fashionably fucking late, Priest.'

'Ahh! The work of the Lord is always at hand.'

'Yeah, but you'd think a servant of God be on bloody time for once!'

178

The Priest strode forward towards the mammoth gaping galvanised doors. His gold-flecked brown eyes caught the distant glint of Spiral covering snipers. He grinned a malevolent grin.

Simmo and Mongrel followed, leaving Rogowski and Bob Bob by the doors, covering their mates' progress with Heckler & Koch MP5s. Operating on the reflexes of shared experience rather than by any spoken communication, the men disappeared into the gloom.

The warehouse was ancient. The concrete floor was black from years of spilled diesel and engine oil, and high overhead were H-section girders. The huge rectangular interior space was a vast and echoing emptiness. Tiny doors set in the distant walls seemed like those in a doll's house, and high above sat a few grime-smeared grey windows, most smashed and several blocked with blackened stumps of wood.

The Priest led the way, sandals flapping across the vast deserted floor. Against the far wall, seated on a chair, was the Nex. Mo stood to one side; the huge Pakistani with his shaved head and neat goatee beard was not quite pointing his TK50 at the Nex's head. Roxi stood to the other side, slim, athletic, shoulder-length brown hair and piercing green eyes. She, too, was not quite pointing her H&K at the Nex's chest.

The Priest came to a halt, flanked by Simmo and Mongrel. His stare fixed on the Nex – a small male with pale white skin, bristling black hair and the trade-mark copper eyes. The Nex had a gentle smile on its face; its hands were folded neatly in its lap and it offered no promise of violence. And yet—

Yet I not help but point my gun at it, thought Mongrel sourly. Too many battles, too long a war. Old betrayals

179

fade hard. Old wounds do not heal, however efficient the medicine.

Mongrel shuffled to one side to get a better overview of the situation. He glanced nervously over his shoulder, towards the distant light of the outside world and the silhouettes of Bob Bob and Rogowski. Both men had lit cigarettes and Mongrel made out two lazy curls of smoke. Then he transferred his gaze back to the immediate area. The different body language of the group's individual members spoke volumes about their different attitudes. Simmo wanted to kill. The Priest wanted to negotiate. Mo was nervous, waiting for the Nex to attack . . . and Roxi? Roxi was smooth, calm, the taciturn professional – as she always was.

'We are confused,' rumbled The Priest finally, one hand holding his rosary beads as if for reassurance. 'You say you come to help us; you say you are willing to betray the other Nex. Why so?'

The Nex sighed, a gentle exhalation, and rubbed one hand over its face. 'I am tired. Tired of the lies. Tired of the killing. And we were lied to – this is supposed to be an evolution.' The Nex stood then – swift, fluid motion. It peeled up its thin black jumper to show a scattering of scales and short spiky bristles across its belly that led up to a narrow V of armoured chitin over its heart. 'It *hurts*,' it said simply. 'Here.' It touched its breast. 'And here.' It tapped the side of its head.

'It's lying,' growled Simmo. 'Let's kill the fucking little maggot now before the others come.'

'I have not been followed,' said the Nex carefully, its stare shifting between each member of the small group. 'I have been extremely wary of that, because the instant that other Nex turn up with guns and bombs you will merely kill me. You would fight your way free, and the elusive Spiral would disappear once more into the underground.'

'How did it make contact?' asked The Priest, looking at Roxi.

She shifted her stance, a subtle movement. Her green eyes glittered in the dim light. 'He discovered the identity of one of the REBS, showed up at her flat, and explained the situation. She referred him through the echelons of REB command. They weren't sure what to do with the little fucker, so they sought our advice. And now he's here.'

'Too easy,' snarled Simmo.

Mongrel eyed the huge sergeant. 'We give him chance,' snapped the East European squaddie. 'He might have intel save all our hides from thrashing. You not behave like bad jail *petuh* taken roughly from behind! This is no Fat Chick Night . . . and, by God, you not never look gift horse in mouth!'

'Yeah, and you don't buy a gift-horse bullshit when it has a bomb shoved up its arse!' growled Simmo. 'God, Mongrel, you is so simple at times! How can you not see . . .'

'And how *you* not understand the opportunity!'

The Priest held up his hand as the Nex said, voice soft and asexual, 'I did not have to appear to you as a Nex soldier. I could have quite easily disguised myself as human, attempted to infiltrate your group that way. It has been attempted before – sometimes successfully.'

'Until we smell your fucking insect stink,' grated Simmo.

'Simmo!' hissed The Priest, turning towards the sergeant with his dark eyes flashing. 'Will you shut up! For the sake of the Lord! Let me handle this, or I'll have you busted down to cleaning the engine pits in Colly and you

181

won't get another opportunity to smoke a *cigar*, never mind handle a gun or kill any of the enemy!'

The sergeant's eyes went wide. His Adam's apple bobbed, tracing patterns through tattoos on the skin of his throat. Then he caught Mongrel's eye, and managed to calm himself; his massive temper – the emergent tip of the iceberg – subsided beneath the icy waters of self-control.

'You have information on Durell?'

The Nex nodded. 'Considerable data. But – I have come to warn you.'

'About?'

'The SpiralGRID. You are about to be compromised.'

'I would be surprised if Durell has information on the SpiralGRID. It is, shall we say, a very well protected secret. Our levelling factor. The one piece of tech that keeps us alive – keeps us beyond Durell's grasp.'

'I know this.' The Nex's eyes glittered. 'I used to work on a team – our aim was to crack your GRID. Your technology is superior in this field – and original. Durell knew nothing of its development, or he would have stolen the plans in the same way that he stole every other type of Spiral technology. But let me put this to you, Priest. If there was any possibility that the GRID would be overrun, contaminated or – even worse – *usurped*, then that would mean the end of Spiral, would it not?'

The Priest nodded.

'Do you know the name Jahlsen?'

The Priest seemed to pale visibly. 'I do,' he whispered. Simmo and Mongrel exchanged a worried glance.

'If I was then to suggest a phrase, a *technique* – hard-tattooed, for example – would that mean anything to you? I am sure it would. And then if I was to inform you that Durell had sent an assassin to kill Jahlsen, an ex-Spiral man named Carter and that the QIV had been primed to pluck the SpiralGRID map when it was sent spinning back to the Spiral sub-system mainframes – would you begin to believe that it was a plausible plan? An option? A *possibility*?'

'Come on, let's get moving,' snapped The Priest. 'We need to get him to a secure house. Blindfold him – in fact, use one of those rubber Head-Blocks. He won't be able to hear, see, smell or taste *anything*.'

'You believe him?' asked Roxi softly.

'If what he says is true,' muttered The Priest, 'then we could definitely soon be in a whole world of shit. And if it isn't true? Then he definitely knows the right code words – the right strings to pull to operate *this* marionette. And I'll be honest with you, Roxi – Jahlsen has been missing for forty-eight hours. He has vanished off the GRID.'

'Where do you want to take the Nex?'

'The Grey Church,' said The Priest softly. 'And ECube Rekalavich, get him to meet us there.'

'That crazy Russian?' spat Mo contemptuously.

'Yes, that crazy Russian who helped design the SpiralGRID in the first damned place. Let us see if what Mr Nex here says is plausible.'

They moved swiftly across the warehouse floor and towards the dull late-autumn light. Mongrel and Simmo trailed behind, once again exchanging glances.

'He mentioned Carter,' said Mongrel.

'Hmm.'

'Carter not do that. Carter not assassinate one of Spiral's own.'

'Carter is no longer one of us,' said Simmo gently.

'Yes, he is. In his head. In his heart.'

'We shall see,' said Simmo, and followed The Priest out into the light.

★

The SpiralGRID journey was a blur of silver, a buzzing of high energy, a shift into another realm. And then it was done. With felt-filled heads, sour tongues and feelings of nausea they stepped warily and with cocked guns from the stone archway and into the rich wood surroundings of The Grey Church.

Behind them the SpiralGRID fizzled with crackles of voltage and then suddenly extinguished, leaving everybody feeling slightly chilled. As if they were playing games with a mechanism they did not – and could never – truly understand.

The Grey Church was old; worn grooves ran across the intricately sculpted wooden bricks which made up the floor, signifying the passing of feet for hundreds of years. The walls were cold sandstone, now blackened with age, testament to a long and turbulent history. Worn wooden pews still stood at either side of the nave leading up to an intricate hardwood and black iron pulpit. The windows – all of which were smashed – had once been fine examples of stained glass. Now only shattered coloured shards remained.

The Priest loved this place. It had been he who had insisted on The Grey Church being added to the ever-growing list of SpiralGRID locators, back when the GRID had been in its infancy – an inspiration, a technological marvel. Little had the Spiral engineers, technicians and scientists realised that the GRID would become the one thing keeping Spiral from its rendezvous with extinction.

The GRID.

The Priest glanced back to where the portal.exit had squatted, a high-energy snout sneezing forth its precious cargo. He had once been asked how the SpiralGRID worked and had thought long and hard about the technological complexities. He had told the questioner to imagine a spider's-web labyrinth with designated coordinate points, set up at first on a country-wide basis but then growing, with longer strands reaching across oceans and continents. The pathways, or strands, of the GRID were not set in stone or concrete – they were not roads that could be travelled in a car or on foot – they were formed by the passage of high-energy under the ground. The SpiralGRID pathway was not a constant. That way, a direct path could never be plotted: only start and end destinations could be described – initiated – and then the GRID's sentient brain would work out pseudo-random routes between the two points. No midway intersection could ever be set up because there were billions of possibilities for the route during travel . . .

A person wanting to travel the GRID stepped into a SpiderCAR, selected start and end locators, and the GRID's brain did the rest. The SpiderCAR allowed the human body a sideways shift into the energy spectrum; then travel was incredibly fast and painless, but ultimately led to feelings of nausea. The human body was not designed for such high-speed and high-energy disjointed travel.

There was one problem, however.

Nature was, by definition, random. Computer-generated data was not; pseudo-random generators allowed the *appearance* of a random construct, but in reality it was based on variables, on millions of possible factors, and on equations. But it was still *traceable*. Which was where the GRID map came into effect; it was a sequence of equations used by the GRID's brain to plot a course, and it carried the data which allowed the GRID to operate. Without the map it was just another example of useless high-tech gleaming technology: all engine and no balls.

And if one of these controlling maps was to fall into the wrong hands?

Well, with enough computing power it would be possible to decode the equations, the data, the *pathways* that the SpiralGRID used – and for the full energy contours of this device to be revealed. Its polymorphic spine would be laid bare. Its HighJ-powered injectors. Its energy-fusion sink motors. Its injector-fed portal.entrance and portal.exit chambers which allowed absorption of the human shell into the high-energy fission of the sideways shift.

The SpiralGRID was an impossibility made real. An energy pathway that could be *sideways* travelled at will. A labyrinth, a gridwork, a web of ever-changing strands that could be used to bypass not just the boundaries of an unleashed biological abomination named HATE but also the dictatorial constraints of a world crushed into submission.

'We here yet?' hissed Mongrel, opening his eyes a little.

'Yeah, pussy,' growled Simmo, scratching at his freshly shaved scalp.

They trod creaking wooden steps and The Priest moved towards the door which led down to the vaults and to the chamber where Rekalavich waited.

Melentei 'Rek' Rekalavich stood in the shadows of the vault of The Grey Church, a foul-smelling Bogatiri *papirosi* cigarette in one hand, his Techrim 11mm pistol in the other. He wore a long black coat that came down nearly to his ankles, and simple dark clothing underneath.

Rekalavich, unshaven, his eyes red-rimmed, had aged a million years since the nuclear strike on Moscow five years earlier which had taken his wife Tanya, and his baby girl. His hair, thick, black and lank, now laced with streaks of grey, hung over his collar.

Rekalavich watched as the Nex was gently nudged into the cold stone chamber. Around the outer perimeter squatted the bulky stone coffins of men and women long dead; religious figures whose names were being gradually eroded by the passage of time.

And one day? thought Rekalavich. One day even their names will be gone. Bones crumbled past dust, into an infinity of nothing. Reabsorbed into the world . . .

Rekalavich's brooding eyes surveyed the Nex with utmost suspicion. In the past five years he had sought only to kill . . . and with each kill he could picture the face of Tanya, vaporised in a nuclear instant. As that copper-eyed gaze met his in the church vault, his finger tightened involuntarily on the Techrim's trigger through an instinct of pure and simple hatred.

The Priest stepped forward, explaining everything that the Nex had told them back at the warehouse. Rekalavich – whose working knowledge of the SpiralGRID was greater than that of any other man present – simply listened, smoke curling around his dark grey-streaked hair and unshaved sallow features.

As The Priest's rumbling voice faltered and silence descended, all eyes turned to Rekalavich. When the Russian spoke, his voice had not just a Russian accent but the distinctive burr of the Muscovite. 'The Nex have excellent technology – we know this. But the one area in which we excel is the polymorphing metals and use of sentient chips to control technology such as the GRID.' He took a long drag on his *papirosi*, allowing smoke to drift from his nostrils. 'The map you speak of does exist – a collection of coordinates, data co-ords on the equilibrium of the sideways shift and, ultimately, the equations needed to allow the GRID's brain to operate across continents. But it also contains Evolution Tek. You heard of that, lad?'

The Nex, standing with hands by his sides, gave a curt nod. The Priest's eyes narrowed. 'Explain it to me,' said Rekalavich.

'EC – or Evolution Class – is the ability of a metallic object or objects controlled by a sentient brain to have perfect self-sufficiency. When attributed to the chassis involved, whether that be the chassis of a mammoth web-like network like the SpiralGRID, the prototype of an EC VTank, or the chassis of an EC Warhead, it has the ability to accumulate or disseminate its own mass and size dependent on need, using substances in the air, land and sea for the purposes of reconstitution. Is that good enough for you to believe me?'

Rekalavich turned to Mo and gestured with his cigarette. Mo grasped one of the Nex's arms and guided it back up the steps, away from the Spiral group.

They stood in the cold of the tomb, dancing shadows cast by bare bulbs lying across the sculpted stone walls.

'Is he right?' whispered The Priest.

'He is,' said the Russian, inhaling deeply on his *papirosi*.

'How could he possibly know this?'

Rekalavich shrugged. 'Durell has an intricate network of knowledge – and he has the QIV processor. He seems to know everything else about Spiral's business; why not info on the top-secret Evolution Class? I am only glad he has not discovered the location – yet.'

'Location? Of the Evolution Warhead?'

Rekalavich nodded.

The Priest frowned. 'That weapon was never completed.'

'But it was,' said the Russian softly.

'How do you know this?'

'I helped design and program the sentient core,' he said.

188

Mongrel took a step forward, and all eyes swivelled towards him. '*Shto*? What you guys talk about? A warhead? A missile built by Spiral using top-class tech?'

'Yes,' said The Priest, pulling free his tiny battered Bible and holding it face up in one hand. His stance seemed to relax a little as he gathered strength from his sacred source. 'I always thought it incomplete. I always thought the *whole technology* incomplete . . . the VTanks, the EC Warhead, the whole gamut. But, I suppose, for there to be a working prototype of the SpiralGRID it must surely follow . . .'

'That we completed everything else in the same technology frame,' said Rekalavich.

'Can we use this weapon? Against mad *zasranetch* fucker Durell?' Mongrel's eyes were suddenly bright – a glint of dawning realisation, a hope that there might be something, no matter how remote, to help dig them from the mammoth pit of despair into which Spiral had fallen.

'The EC Warhead was completed – just months before Spiral's demise,' said Rek. 'I helped finish the design – and I know that this machine could wreak serious catastrophe upon Durell. It is self-contained and intelligent. If given the correct instructions by a skilled programmer . . .'

'Like you?' said Mongrel.

'I was a chassis specialist, hence my involvement with the GRID,' said Rek slowly. 'There were others who dealt in objective code – target data. But don't you get your hopes up, my brothers – there are very few alive who even know of the Warhead's existence, let alone its whereabouts . . . Even so, Durell seems to know of this machine's existence – maybe he has even now discovered the weapon? As we stand here pondering his machinations? Maybe even now he has disabled it . . . removed any possibility of future discovery?'

189

'No,' said Mongrel, 'if that fucker found it, he parade it like cheap whore's prime flapping *pizda* at transvestite party. No, he not got weapon . . .' He turned to The Priest. 'But we – *we* could search for it, could we not?'

The Priest was deep in thought. 'But where to start?' rumbled the huge man. His voice was cold, his eyes dull. It was as if he did not like what he was hearing; as if the emergence of false hope was like a cancer in his soul.

Rek spoke. 'Recently there was a TV broadcast by HIVE; it spoke of the capture of a Spiral man called Justus. Justus was involved in machine development, in engine codes. He *might* know the whereabouts of the EC Warhead – or at least be a link in the chain to its discovery. If he still lives.'

'And the Nex have him,' snorted Simmo in disgust.

The Priest nodded, as a sudden explosion rumbled through the earth and the vault started to shake. The gathered Spiral agents raced up the steps to burst into the main body of the church.

Mo stood with Rogowski, both looking grim-faced and with their weapons trained on the door. The rumbling continued, and outside fire screamed into the sky.

There was an electrified hum which crackled through the air. Suddenly the portal.exit of the SpiralGRID crackled into existence and three Nex leapt through.

'Impossible!' growled The Priest. Roxi surged forward with Simmo close behind her and their guns blazed, bullets sending all three Nex crashing to the ground in geysers of gushing crimson.

'They used the GRID,' said the informer Nex.

'They must have the map!' snarled Rek, hefting his Techrim. 'The GRID has been compromised!'

The SpiralGRID crackled again as high energies spun around the grey and silver edges of the portal.exit.

Everybody could smell the metallic stench of ozone.

'Out of the doors!' screamed Simmo, as the Spiral team started to back away from the GRID – once the saviour of the whole of Spiral, now just another redundant piece of technology. *Betraying* technology.

'The fucking Nex are outside,' hissed Mo, rubbing sweat from his shaved head and hoisting his sub-machine gun in his huge right fist. 'They've got us trapped.'

Suddenly, a snarl screamed from the portal.exit as something huge, black-armoured and glistening leapt free, long claws scraping against stone and slashing grooves in the ancient wood floor of The Grey Church.

'What the *fuck* is that?' breathed Mo.

'That is a Sleeper,' said The Priest calmly, stowing away his Bible and pulling free his 9mm Glock. 'And we are in a lot of trouble.' As he glanced Heavenwards the portal.exit sent forth another two Sleeper Nex – triangular heads weaving as if searching for a scent, armoured spines bristling as if the creatures were some form of huge wild cat. Outside another explosion rocked the world, making the whole church shudder and sway drunkenly on its teetering foundations.

The Spiral agents aimed their weapons grimly. Mongrel and Simmo, Roxi and Rogowski, Mo and Rekalavich. The Sleeper Nex, claws splintering through the wooden floor, began a wary and calculated advance . . .

The Priest drew a wide-bladed black knife with his free hand. 'For everything there is a season, and a time for every matter under heaven: A time to be born . . . and a time to die.' With his pistol spitting fire, The Priest leapt forward to do bloody and righteous battle.

191

CHAPTER 8

THE TRIAL

'Well,' hissed Sonia, face etched with fear, eyes wide and pale in the gloom of the BMW's cabin. 'We're going to have to fight.' She cocked her weapon, and sighted through the rear window at the fast-approaching GMC truck . . . But before she could fire, bullets slapped along the BMW's flank, spitting bright sparks, and she ducked low against the back seat. With a deep breath and a silent prayer she levelled the carbine, aimed past the inverted T-sight at the five weaving, roaring GMC targets – and squeezed the weapon's trigger.

The M24 carbine bucked in Sonia J's hands like a live creature. Bullets smashed through the BMW's rear window and left trails of tracer fire through the rain and hail, punching holes up the front grille of the lead GMC truck . . .

Grimly, Sonia emptied the full magazine – and watched in confusion as the trucks suddenly fell away, veering to one side and halting in the downpour. They were quickly swallowed by the gloom, dropping away as if falling down a long, narrow shaft.

Sonia tilted her head, confused. She licked her lips as she suddenly realised they were as dry as dust.

'What happened?' growled Baze, glancing backwards. 'Did we stop them?'

'No,' said Sonia gently. She put a fresh magazine in her M24. 'We only fired a few rounds – only had limited impact. We didn't stop them – they stopped themselves.'

'Why?'

'Who knows?' croaked Sonia. Freezing rain spat through the shattered rear window of the BMW. 'But we were heavily outgunned and outnumbered. Maybe this was just a gypsy's warning. A jab to the nose, just to bloody us up a bit.'

'But that would suggest they know who we are,' said Baze. Sonia nodded coldly.

'And if they know who we are . . .'

'Then we are truly compromised.'

'I don't believe that,' growled Baze. He had reduced their speed now that the sudden insanity of the mad chase was over – or postponed, at least. 'Do you *really* believe that they would simply leave us alone? If they knew who we were? Do you *really* think we would be sitting here discussing the situation? No – we'd be minced dog-mcat.'

Sonia sighed. She rubbed at world-weary red-veined eyes. 'I don't know what to believe any more,' she whispered as they drove through the freezing, pounding rain.

The snow fell heavily. Sonia J came awake with a start, feeling groggy, her mouth tasting of sour wine and stale tobacco. The glamour which had made her a media queen of the TV screen seemed like an echo of long, long ago.

The fire was burning low in the high-walled natural-stone hearth, allowing a steady stream of heat to fill her

193

cosy skyscraper apartment in the suburbs of London. She turned dark-ringed eyes to the window. Watched the falling snow.

The dreams had been haunting her for a long time now, making sure she would never forget. There were several different versions, different interweaving variations on the same themes of pain, and horror, and death.

Sonia J was too afraid to go back to sleep. But finally she did, coaxing herself and drifting back in gradual stages as the snow outside continued its descent. She felt the dream creep up on her with the precision of a predator – it curled like smoke chains around her mind and she wanted to scream. But sleep whisked her away, an unwilling passenger, and she could not help herself. She just could not halt the unstoppable nightmare.

The nightmare had replayed itself, a stuttering visual monologue beginning with her miscarriage, the untimely death of her unborn child years ago, and ending with the recent murders by Nex of innocent women and children in the street. And, as Sonia J lay in the darkness, remembering the first joy of pregnancy followed by the bereavement, and the later wholesale devastation and death as the years flowed by, so the tears rolled down her cheeks and soaked into her pillows.

After a while, she rose from her bed and, wearing a thick cotton nightdress, padded to the window. The snow was still falling, huge tumbling flakes. Outside, London had become a ghost town – a desolation blanketed in white.

Sonia J shivered; she loved the snow, that sense of unreal quiet: it almost reminded her of a time before the Nex. And before Durell. Before the mass slaughter of the human race had begun . . .

So many memories. So many bad, bad memories.

Sonia J sat by the window and watched a group of teenagers – four of them, aged around fifteen or sixteen. Dressed in rags, they were tearaways commonly known as 'Skegs', homeless children living by their wits. The Nex usually rounded them up and sent them to weapons or chemical factories to do hard labour. But most Skegs, after losing families and friends in the earthquakes and nuclear strikes, had become incredibly self-sufficient: hard and uncompromising. Cockroach children born into an unforgiving world. And if they didn't adapt – they ended up dead.

Down below in the road, the group's dirt-streaked faces, normally heavily lined and filled with hatred and resentment at their appalling misfortune, had broken into cracked masks of laughter. The teenagers were dancing through the snow, trailing dirt-smeared rags as they scooped up handfuls and squeezed it into white spheres. Snowballs sailed through the air and their suddenly child-ish laughter echoed and pealed up to Sonia's high apartment vantage.

The Skegs disappeared down the street, the sound of their laughter fading, soon muffled by the snow. Sonia watched the falling flakes, rubbing at tired eyes still red from crying. She gave a sigh from the heart. Glancing across at the near-empty bottle of wine, she considered finishing it off. Then she shook her head, her long hair cascading around her shoulders.

A cold breeze cut past the edges of the window and Sonia J jumped down from the sill, padded back over to her bed and leaving the curtains open behind her so that she could watch the pure white snowfall.

Just as she had relaxed, she heard the Skegs again. Their boots clattered along the street. They were coming back and Sonia climbed out of bed and moved to the window once more, staring down. The teenagers were in a panic, running erratically and leaving ragged zigzag trails through the fallen snow.

What are they dodging? she wondered.

And then she saw them: Nex, running fast and carrying silenced sub-machine guns. Sonia's mouth opened in shock as the guns coughed and one of the Skegs – a girl – was hit and sent cartwheeling against a wall where she crumpled into a heap with blood pumping out of her to stain the snow. The other three Skegs crouched together, huddled in a doorway, their eyes wide and frightened. Sonia watched grim-faced as the Nex closed in. Then the dancing fire from the barrels of their guns could be seen again . . .

Blood spattered the pavement. And Sonia realised that her hands were pressed against the glass and knew that her face must be twisted into a mask of horror.

She pulled away quickly as a Nex turned and glanced around. She retreated to her bed. Her mind spun, images hammering through her brain and she knew that she had had enough. Coldly, she realised that she could take no more. The murder. The deceit. The decadence of this new world. This *brave* new world. Ha.

But then, hadn't that been why she had joined the REBS?

And yeah, she had helped print leaflets, had gone out on the marches in the early days before the Nex started dragging people from their beds and executing them in dark, dank prison cells. The REBS had been forced underground but despite this their power had grown, their targets becoming more important – and all the while Sonia was climbing the career ladder of TV production and realising that this, *this* was a tool she could use to help destroy the Nex. TV was the medium that could show the people what was really happening, the reality behind the filter of propaganda. But even though her show was live, her hands had been effectively tied. She had been chained by her position. Manacled by rules. Incarcerated by fear.

Despite her sanctioned status as a rebel in the TV world – something that was actively encouraged by HIVE Media because it pulled in incredible ratings, higher than any other programme on their networks – that rebellion was not allowed certain outlets.

And yesterday she had overstepped the mark with Vincent Alexandro. She was in a world of shit over that gig; but hey, wasn't that what being a REB was all about? To put your head on the chopping block and see if the axe blade was sharp enough?

She heard the rumble of engines outside. The vans had arrived to remove the bodies. The bodies of children who had grown up far too quickly, through social misdirection, through being in the wrong place at the wrong time; victims of an accelerated maturity. Children whom nobody would miss. Children who could simply be *removed* ... without the embarrassment of awkward questions.

Well, thought Sonia J savagely, *I* have questions. *I* have opinions. And *I* have a fucking *platform*. I'm sick of seeing the children die. I'm sick of seeing the innocent slaughtered. I've had enough of watching the Nex cancer spread.

It's time this REB used her platform of privilege, no matter what the outcome, she thought bitterly. Roll the dice, see what numbers turn up. And to hell with the consequences. It's time this REB made a stand.

Sonia moved to her console in the corner of the room, the screen of which was glowing softly in power-saving mode. She sat down, her face a grim mask, and activated the machine. HIVE logos flowed across the monitor and Sonia moved forward, resting her hands against a keyboard.

```
>> HIVE MEDIA SYSTEMS
.. LOG-ON KL SYSTEMS INITIATED
.. ALL SYSTEMS PRIMED
.. TESTING MEMORY SECTORS -
.. TESTING MULTI-POINT PROCESSOR UNITS
.. TESTING ZERO-K ALGORITHMS
.. EDEN/EMPLOYEE TERMINAL ©HIVE SYSTEMS
>> PLEASE ENTER EMPLOYEE ACCESS CODES
NOW - []
```

With a flutter of keys, Sonia accessed the terminal. Filing systems flowed across the screen and Sonia's brain consumed data. I have A-Rate clearance, she thought. And you want to mess with me? OK, let's see what you really have . . . let's see what secrets HIVE Media hides—

She typed a series of complex datastreams, bypassing protection circuits and cloaking her employee number; her reference; her identity.

Now Sonia was a ghost in the system. A wraith in the machine. And a small smile crossed her lips as the glow of the screen reflected in her focused eyes. 'Ah,' she said softly, and scrolled across the images laid out before her. News reports that had been suppressed – hidden – and never aired on the global media network. Images of mutilation, murder and death – on a massive scale almost impossible to comprehend.

Bobby Clough was the man. The Big Man. The dude in charge not just of Quazatron productions but of HIVE Media as well. He was a tall man, athletic, and he carried about him a slightly menacing air. He had gleaming curly hair, which he oiled regularly, and a neat little moustache. But it was his eyes that set him apart from other men of his type – hard, calculating merciless eyes that had the look of tempered steel.

Clough stood at the head of the long gleaming mahogany table. The subtle lighting allowed shadows to gather in the corners of the large room. It should have been a room of busy board meetings and high-powered negotiations. On this early morning, however, with a fresh fall of snow tumbling from grey skies outside the large floor-to-ceiling blackened windows, the room had taken on the ambience of a court . . .

Sonia J stood, feet slightly apart, hands behind her back, waiting. She looked straight ahead, lips compressed, eyes unfocused as she awaited the words of the Big Man. He looked at her as a tiger contemplates a recently dismembered carcass.

'Well,' he said, his voice low. Its deceptive softness conveyed not compassion but authority. And the need to inflict pain.

Sonia J took a deep breath, realising that Clough would not break the ensuing silence – he would allow her anxiety an eternity to blossom. 'Sir, you wanted to see me? About yesterday's show?'

'I do,' he said soothingly, moving to one side of the table. It was perfectly tidy, and had nothing on it but a tiny silver digital organiser. 'After your . . . *performance* . . .' Clough allowed the word to linger, like a bad smell. The Big Man had the ability to crucify his subjects with simple vowels and consonants. ' . . . We have had, shall we say, a cascade of complaints.'

'Sir, but I . . .'

Clough did not meet Sonia's gaze. He merely held up

a single digit. Sonia's gaze fixed on that finger, neatly manicured, soft-skinned, and yet capable of pulling tight the noose on her career – and the course of action that she had now planned to follow.

'One citizen,' he said, his voice still dangerously soft, 'even had a complaint plastered onto the side of an old double-decker bus. It read *"Get On Board With The Double-Deckers – Ban Pussy_live! NOW!"* Can you believe the lengths some people will go to?'

Clough waited. Sonia opened her mouth to speak, then caught the glance from his steely eyes. She realised with a cold sinking feeling: this was a telling-off. There were no words which could excuse her. Sonia was, to all intents and purposes, shafted.

'Vincent Alexandro's business partners forwarded us a thirteen-million-dollar donation – so that Mr Alexandro would have a platform from which to launch phases of his modified Nex Enhancement Programme initiative.' Clough's voice suddenly rose a little as he moved forward, polished shoes treading the thick pile carpet with the eerie silence of a stalking predator. 'But you *fucked it up*.' He turned his back on Sonia.

Bobby Clough seemed to be breathing deeply. He turned around to face the ChainTV presenter. 'We have – thankfully – a second chance. The Nex are sending one of their top men, Mace, who will attempt to recover the situation. You will *play* along with him. You *will* cooperate one hundred per cent. Or I will have your fucking balls on a platter.'

'Balls?'

He glanced down at Sonia J's crotchless yellow and green lycra suit. Then he met her gaze. 'You know what I mean,' he said. 'You will go out there, meet Mace and there will be *no fuck-ups*. Do I make myself absolutely clear?'

'Yes, sir,' she mumbled.

'Now get out. Before I really lose my temper. And remember – your TV future depends on what happens later today. Do not – and I repeat, *do not* – screw it up.'

[ON AIR]

SCENE: A large airy studio tastefully decorated in orange and blues. Three long settees lie at slight angles to one another around a central table fashioned from a single slab of onyx, on which stands a purple jug and crystal glasses which catch the studio lights and glitter. The rear of the studio is taken up by a huge plasma screen.

ENTER Sonia J to ecstatic applause.

SONIA J: Welcome to the latest funky in-your-face episode of *Pussy_live!* In which we take famous members of the establishment and ask them to—

AUD [volume enhance 5.8]: Prove they're not a Pussy!

PROMPT: Audience laughter.

SWITCH/CAM3 [wide pan/pull back]: Full studio including front three rows of audience and clusters of JT8s in black uniforms.

SONIA J: Now, today we have bagged you yet another real treat! [**Sonia J winks**] After our successful staged comedy interview with Vincent Alexandro, in which I tried my hardest to upstage him for a bet (all money donated to a charity chosen by those wickedly funny guys the Nex, of course) we finally have a *real* interview for you! Mace is one of the top guys, Durell's left-hand man, so to speak: Head Prime of the Technology Division, Director of WarFactory Productions and the instigator of the brand new Eden Community Project. Mace has never before been interviewed on any show. Here we have him for your delight. Please welcome, Nex and proud of it, Mr Mace!

CAM6 [dropping and pulling back]: Mace enters, dapper and neatly dressed, shaved head gleaming slightly under studio lighting. He walks down the steps and sits on the middle settee, hands folded in his lap, his back ramrod straight.

EARMIC: That's just great, Sonia, just foo-king brilliant. Now, hold that pose – yes, yes, we're going for the zoom – gleaming, feminine, *BRILLIANT*! Now, you've got the retina transcript, so just make sure you stick to it. OK? No, don't even answer that. Just do your job and we can all go home as happy people.

SONIA J: Mr Mace. Welcome to our show. As everybody out there knows, we normally attempt to make guests prove they are not a Pussy! But in a most serious break from tradition, we will today seek to give you a fair trial. Did I say trial? I *meant* platform.

CAM5: Mace glares at Sonia J, then seems to remember that he is on TV. He smiles sardonically.

MACE: Thank you for your eloquent introduction, Miss J. I am flattered to be held in such high regard by the population and by the illustrious echelons of HIVE Media. You all have my greatest thanks.

SONIA J: Yes. Now. Well. I believe you would like to explain to us a little about the Nex evolving processes, which also take in the most wonderful and exciting activity of turning a normal human being into the evolved personage of a *Nex* . . .

MACE: Yes. Well, to look at me, you might not guess that once I was nothing more than a sickly child. I had a bone-wasting disease and was destined to die. But then I was introduced to the Nex . . . I chose to join their ranks, and I was healed. I was given a second chance at life!

SONIA J: That must have been incredibly exciting! Transcendental, even, as Nex evolution gave you a second chance to lead a full life. And also awesome: with the subsequent Nex transformation you were given almost superhuman powers.

MACE: Yes, Sonia, to become a Nex is to become *so much more than human*! It is the next natural stepping stone of progress for our species. You take on superior characteristics – an enhanced immune system, resistance to pain and disease and chemical, biological and nuclear weapons. But then, the population know these things. As they know that they can earn their freedom . . . **[looking straight into camera]** when you become a Nex, you earn your freedom from HATE!

SONIA J: But what of your own deformity?

MACE [slowly, with growing confusion]: How do you mean?

SONIA J: Well, just look at you, with your copper eyes and your twisted face! I am a God-fearing person, I believe in the process of natural evolution and I say that you are a fucking abomination against God, a deviation of normal genetics that deserves no other place than under the microscope – and the *scalpel* – and I can today reveal here on live TV that Mace, and his superior,

203

Durell, and a million other Nex-deformed abhorrences are, in fact, the Nex scum who claim to—

EARMIC: What are you doing? Just what the *fuck* are you doing?

SONIA J:— liberate you from the threat of the HATE biological weapons when it was in fact *their own* guided warheads which delivered the toxic payloads in the first place! And now the Nex run a closed society in which men, women and even our children are slaughtered like diseased and wasted cattle and this is never reported, this abomination is never allowed into the public domain. *I have seen these things and I know that you, sitting there on your fat arses on your comfy fucking couches have seen these things too.* We need to rise up, throw off the shackles of our oppressors – yes, join the REBS! Join Spiral! Allow these pure-hearted victors to help you to help yourselves!

EARMIC: Get her off! Fucking *get her off*! Cut the feed – yes, now, you fuckwits, cut the FEED!

AUDIO: Classical music.
VIDEO: Black background/white lettering Lucida Sans.
                          NO SERVICE

NO SERVICE: the words stared back at Sonia J from the semicircle of surrounding monitors. The audience sat in a stunned silence. Her gaze slid across to Mace who was smiling a malevolent, twisted little smile.

From the edges of the stage she saw a bustle of activity and, ripping free from her EARMIC, she dragged out a Walther PPM 11mm pistol and whirled around in a tight circle, scanning for enemies.

Mace did not flinch; rather, he remained seated, hands

in his lap, eyes watching with cold detachment. He's too cool, realised Sonia with a sudden stab of doubt. Just way too cool . . .

Sonia sprinted across the ChainTV studio, leaping a low settee and slamming against the wall in which sat the door which proudly proclaimed ON AIR in bright false letters across its processor-inset glass.

Everything had happened so fast that the cameramen and JT8s were still standing, gawping uncertainly at one another. Then their instructions came through on hidden earpieces as Sonia banged through the door and into the path of six Nex with Steyr sub-machine guns pointed calmly at her face.

Sonia J froze.

A hand reached out. 'Your weapon?'

Sonia allowed her Walther to fall to the ground. Then a hand slid around her waist from behind. Mace moved around her, holding her in a gliding creepy embrace, and looked up into her eyes. He smiled then, and Sonia suddenly realised: Mace was dangerous. Awesomely so. Perhaps more lethal than any man – any *Nex* – that she had ever met.

'Now, my sweetness, my little *flower*, I think we need a long and serious chat.'

Sonia J spat into his face, but he did not flinch, and his copper eyes did not blink. His hands tightened around her waist. Sonia tried to back away, but found Mace's grip incredibly powerful. Unbreakable.

Then came another voice. Bobby Clough stumbled down the corridor, his poise for once gone, and lurched to a stop. He stared hard at Sonia, who transferred her disgusted gaze from Mace's smiling face to Clough's angry one. 'What have you *done*?' he hissed.

'I have done what is right.'

205

'You've lost your fucking job!' he snapped. 'You're no longer on board!'

'She has lost more than her job.' Mace moved away, still smiling, and a circle of Nex steel closed around Sonia. She shut her eyes, yet when the first blow came it still surprised her, even though she'd been expecting it. She hit the ground, and within a moment the beating had rendered her unconscious.

She was briefly aware of voices before she passed out.

'. . . so, so, so sorry,' Bobby Clough was bleating.

And then Sonia J's mind swam among diamond stars.

Cold water splashed Sonia's face, and groggily she came around. She coughed and felt sticky blood against her skin, her head and neck, and matted in her hair. She realised that she was bound with wire to a chair.

They were in Clough's boardroom. The lights were still subdued but now the room was crowded. Six Nex, four JT8s – all heavily armed. Bobby Clough himself sat on the edge of his lacquered table, holding his oiled curly head in his hands.

And Mace was there, smiling.

Sonia, groggy from the beating, ran a thick tongue around her sticky mouth. She realised that Mace's demeanour had changed. Now he was exuding the power of the leader. The dictator. *The torturer*, came an unbidden thought at the back of her mind. Sonia shivered.

'Welcome back,' Mace said, almost cheerily. 'Firstly, you'll be pleased to learn that none of today's *Pussy_live!* was actually broadcast. It was, of course, relayed straight back to Durell and other government agencies who have charged me with the responsibility of finding out just what rank you possess within the REBS – and then gaining answers to some difficult and *vexing* questions.'

Sonia's mouth opened, then closed again.

'She made a very big mistake,' said Clough, his steely gaze suddenly softening. He was a big tough man – but this game was not just played in a different league, it was fought like a war on a separate continent.

'Yes.' Mace nodded.

'You fucked with the wrong people,' Clough was saying, scowling at Sonia, running a hand through his oiled curls, skin drawn tightly across his skull with the stress of anxiety. 'I warned you, I bloody warned you this morning, told you that this was your final chance, that you would lose your job, that you had to respect the Nex because—'

The shot sounded deafeningly loud in the confines of the boardroom. Bobby Clough slumped back against the desk, his head now sporting a hole with burnt shards of splintered cranium around its edges, his mouth gaping slack and lifeless. The flattened bullet had raised a little puff of plaster from the wall after exiting the back of Clough's skull in a shower of pulverised brain matter.

Sonia watched as Mace moved forward and looked down at her.

'I have questions,' said Mace.

'I will give you answers,' said Sonia, her voice soft, her sense of impending betrayal a knife buried in the depths of her own shrivelling heart.

The simple pause seemed to last a lifetime

Sonia kept thinking, it'll be OK, the REBS will be here in a minute, they'll come and save me – smash through the windows and doors, kill the Nex in a hail of machine-gun fire and we'll fight a savage retreat and be gone from this place. And then she remembered. The show had not been broadcast. Therefore, the REBS did not know about her situation.

Shit, she thought. She had not banked on the bastards faking a live-air feed. They had sensed her treachery. She had played a dumb game, stumbled like a blind woman into their waiting arms. She had given them a taster; and the taster had led, ultimately, to her discovery and her destruction.

Mace carried a small black case and laid it down next to Clough's body. Sonia J caught a glimpse of the dulled silver of polished medical implements.

She felt suddenly very cold. She didn't feel like a liberator, a saviour of mankind standing tall against the brutality of the Nex. She didn't feel like a freedom fighter who would become a brave and revered martyr. She felt suddenly stupid, hasty, an emotional numbskull who had blown her great gift of live TV access on a network more controlled than any laboratory experiment – and in front of the largest audience ever – on a rant that hadn't actually gone out, didn't even fucking *count* . . . and, at the same time, had also condemned her as REB.

Mace moved into her view. He held a long silver implement which gleamed razor sharp. The blade was very thin, and had a twist towards the edge. He smiled down and his expression was chilling.

Sonia saw him for what he was. A Nex in love with pain.

'You are the leader of the REBS?' said Mace softly.

'No, I—'

The blade flashed out and Sonia cringed – but no pain came as the blade flashed past her face.

'You *are* the leader of the REBS,' said Mace. He moved around her, pacing slowly, hands behind his back.

'I am not.'

'Sonia J – I will stand here and carve up your face. I will cut out your eyeballs. I will remove your tongue. I

208

will slice off your nose. I will smash out your teeth with a hammer. And then, and only then, will I peel off your face, using a digital scalpel. All these things I will do—' he suddenly dropped, so that his eyes were mere inches from her face '—if you give me one more false answer. There will be no second chance. You suffer – but you will not die, because first I will give you injections of pentathol amyldimorphate. You will feel, and you will suffer, but you will remain conscious. Do you understand me?'

Mace's breath smelt strangely sweet, and Sonia felt her own head spinning with the unreality of the situation. She prayed then – prayed to a God she did not believe in.

'Are you the leader of the REBS?'

'Yes,' said Sonia J, her voice suddenly strong. A new idea had come to her, one which could – if she got out of this situation alive – do some good. 'But there are many sub-commanders in the REBS who are almost as powerful as me. I do not have complete control – I delegate to my SCs.'

Mace considered this. 'Where is your HQ?'

'We have a mobile headquarters – in much the same way as Durell had a mobile HQ back in his early days. In fact, we stole the idea from your very own illustrious leader . . .' Sonia met Mace's gaze then, saw him faltering a little. She frowned. 'You will never pin us down to one location, Mace. Although we are not as technologically advanced as Spiral, with their GRID, we are nevertheless just as inventive. Now, I have a question for *you,* you deformed and stinking piece of Nex shit: when will EDEN be ready?'

Sonia saw the flicker in Mace's eyes that told her the answer. It was ready now. It had *always* been ready. But the Nex had no intention of unleashing the Eden_class substance into the world; no intention of purifying the toxic wasteland rendered uninhabitable by HATE. Because, she suddenly realised, HATE was the most perfect of control mechanisms. It kept the people of the world locked up with a biological key.

It was then that they were interrupted. Mace turned and moved away, flanked by two Nex with balaclavas pulled down over their faces. When Mace returned, he was smiling softly.

'You are Sonia J – the Media Queen. Durell has had the incredibly wonderful idea of a televised trial. It will make for great television and will obviously not go out live, so it can be edited to our own exacting standards. It will neatly show how Sonia J, Media Queen, is the head of the REBS and is thus responsible for the deaths of *thousands* of innocent bystanders, mothers and children, thanks to badly placed bombs and stray bullets from street gunfights. It will also negate the damage you did yesterday with your Alexandro interview. It will be perfect!'

Sonia J paled. 'A *trial*?'

'Yes,' said Mace. 'And your judge will be Judge Ronald Hamburger from the daytime trial programme *Name Your Crime!* I believe he is your greatest rival in terms of TV ratings and media competition. And do you want to know something, Sonia?'

'What?'

'The outcome of this trial can only go one way. So take your last breath, your last look, and spill your final tepid tears. Your time on *our* precious planet is over.'

The trial was a long one. A series of 'witnesses' was paraded before the jury, all of them coming out with the most incredible falsehoods and accusing Sonia J of being everything from a performer of witchcraft to a maker of digVID animal porn. She was a REB. Ergo, she was evil. She was a terrorist responsible for the deaths of children. She was anti-establishment, and she would achieve her vile aims by any means necessary – even if it meant the destruction of the whole world.

In a whirl of noise and shouts and accusations, Judge Ronald Hamburger sentenced Sonia – predictably – to a televised death by firing squad. To be carried out in three hours' time, after the trial had been aired. The actual execution would be run on every single network, every TV and radio channel. It would be a stern warning to the population. It would show the horrors of terrorism.

And hell, it would make *great* TV.

Sonia J's brain was in turmoil as she sat in her cell. A part of her thought of the trial as a circus parade, a farce of the most epic proportions. And yet the cold hard reality of her situation still smashed her in the face like an expertly aimed half-brick.

She was going to be executed.

Murdered . . .

Welcome to the Nex State, she thought sourly as she banged her mug rhythmically against the bars of her cell. Unfortunately, it did little to annoy the Nex. They didn't have the imagination, it would seem.

With every passing moment Sonia J was growing more and more tense with expectation, awaiting the explosion that would blow a hole in the cell wall as the REBS came pouring in to rescue her. But reality kicked her in the face. Durell had successfully flushed out and exterminated a great number of REBS over the previous few months: their strength was in severe decline, and could they really spare such hefty resources to rescue one woman?

Sonia closed her eyes and thought of the man she was protecting. The *real* leader of the REBS. She smiled a little at the thought. At least, somehow, the Nex had got their wires crossed by insisting on her status as the top dog. When, in reality, it was a lot more complicated than that. And *his* identity had to remain a carefully guarded secret. Because if they ever discovered who secretly controlled the REBS, who masterminded their modest hits, then Durell would surely throw every resource he owned into their elimination. And the REBS just did not have the resources, nor the technology, to combat such an onslaught.

The JT8s came for Sonia after three hours. They beat her savagely with the butts of their Steyr sub-machine guns, strapped her arms behind her back with wire and dragged her into the narrow cold corridor. She was going to die.

And nobody was going to save her.

The execution yard was large and grey, with high walls that had thick coils of barbed wire along their summit. An anti-mortar mesh spanned the skyline. Snow was still falling heavily on this gloomy afternoon and the yard was crammed around its edges with baying reporters and cameramen. Sonia J's gaze came to rest calmly on the firing squad.

Ten slim masked Nex – holding heavy-calibre 13mm NailGuns – stood in a line, facing one of the walls. The wall had a disturbing peppered quality about it: innumerable former rounds had pounded the surface so that it looked like a crumbled moonscape.

Sonia J shivered, glancing around the crowd, unable to brush the gathering snow from her shoulders because of her bindings. Her outfit was painfully thin, designed for the hothouse interiors of the TV studio, not the chill of a London snowstorm.

Judge Ronald appeared. He seemed subdued, but brightened a little as the TV CAMS tracked his entrance.

'Welcome back, folks! And thanks for tuning in!' he proclaimed.

Sonia J was prodded to stand against the wall. Now that she was close enough she could make out ingrained old dried blood and tiny embedded shreds of splintered bone. It smelled bad. Like a charnel house.

Sonia felt herself fill up with an unbearable fear as she face the masked Nex. They levelled their NailGuns at her.

'One minute to execution, folks!' came the jolly words of Judge Ronald Hamburger.

Sonia closed her eyes, not wanting the black masks of the Nex killers to be the last things she saw as she died. She thought back to better times as the execution yard clock counted down the last few seconds of her expendable life . . .

CHAPTER 9

IN THE LAP OF THE GODS

I will fucking kill them, thought Carter. I will maim them. I will burn them. I will fuck them with white-hot pokers.

'*That's my boy!*' cheered Kade.

'I will fucking burn you as well, fucker.'

'*Don't be like that! I'm here to help!*'

'You never help me, Kade; you merely prolong my misery.'

'*One day you'll thank me. We will sit like brothers, Brother, and you will look deep into my soul, and I into yours — we have shared many moments in this life, and our crossing is a jewelled prologue of what will come, what will be, what will exist . . .*'

'Just what the fuck *are* you, Kade?'

'*You will learn soon enough.*'

'So you can read the fucking future now, can you, shithead?'

'*No, no, Carter. But there are things here you do not understand; things you cannot remember . . . Do you recall your little brother Jimmy? Do you remember his head splitting open like a*

214

ripe melon when he fell from that pipe onto the rocks? And later, the sanatorium? After you murdered Crowley? The sterile white walls, the stench of iodine . . . oh, joyous days, happy days!'

'Sanatorium?' Confusion. *Doubt.* But reality – *consciousness* – came crashing back into Carter's world, and his blood-sticky eyes opened to see square tiles scrolling past his swaying vision. Nausea swamped him – for he had been badly beaten – and vomit splashed thickly from his quivering lips, running down his chin and leaving a foul trail across the tiles. He was ignored; his vomit was ignored; he tried to turn, to struggle and fight but weakness had invaded his limbs and his strength had left him.

Carter was being dragged by his arms and his boots thumped along the tiles. The Nex who dragged him ignored his feeble struggles and muted groans of pain.

Carter shivered when he remembered the beating. It had been a long horror, a torture: they had punched him and kicked him, jumped on his spine, then beaten him with weapon butts. He had vomited blood, felt ribs smash within the cage of his body; and then they had injected him with a bright silver liquid and pain had screeched through him like nothing he had felt before, fire eating him from the inside out, burning him like raw acid in his veins and organs . . . to finally drain away, leaving him a hollow man.

Carter was dumped unceremoniously on the floor. He slumped into a heap and closed his eyes for several moments. Then he felt soft hands helping him up onto a seat. His eyes flickered open and he saw the face of Alexis, her copper eyes glowing, her smile filling him with confusion.

Carter looked around. 'Where am I?' he croaked.

'The Sentinel Corporation HQ in New York,' came the voice of Durell. Carter turned slowly, burning inside with hatred and anger and a sudden need to *kill*.

'What does it take to kill you, motherfucker?'

'I do not die easily.' Durell smiled from within the shadowing folds of his hood. His blackened clawed hands pushed back the hood and he moved across the carpet – past the lithe form of Alexis – to stand in front of Carter in all his deformity.

'You call that evolution?' snarled Carter.

'I am the core, and this is the price I pay,' said Durell. 'Just like a queen bee abandons her ability to fly in order to rule – the greatest of sacrifices – so I must bear the burden of enormous power. However, this talk is needless. You work for me now, Carter. You have joined the ranks of the most powerful army this world has ever seen! You have killed for us – you assassinated Jahlsen, murdered one of your own Spiral men.'

'You used me. Used . . . Nicky.'

'Sorry about that.' Durell smiled again, his eyes glittering. 'She was a clone, yes, one of our superb experiments closely linked to Nex work. When you create a Nex, sometimes – depending on the pattern – you can clone a subject. It doesn't always work – some of our first trials were messy, although the original clone of Gol was a good one. Until you blew him up.'

'Hey.' Carter grinned through bloodied teeth. 'Sometimes shit happens. But what about the real Gol – the one who betrayed *you* in Egypt? Durell, your Nex are far from perfect . . . I've read the recent Spiral memos, the ECube blips. They're starting to turn, aren't they? You're losing thousands in unexplained incidents as they melt on the streets. And as for the rest – can you trust them, Durell? Can you *really* trust them?'

'Enough. We have your boy, Carter. You *will* do what we require.'

'Show him to me.'

'In a little while – when I have explained our position.'

'No, fuck you, show him to me or I swear to God . . .'

'God abandoned you a long time ago, Mr Carter. However . . .' Durell nodded to Alexis, whose lithe figure slipped from the room. 'I will allow you to see him. For a few short minutes.'

Carter waited. Minutes stretched into pain-filled hours. Carter's body screamed at him. Durell moved to the window, staring down over New York City – his world, his *dominion*.

'Daddy!'

'Joe!'

Joseph sprinted across the carpet and fell into Carter's arms. Carter held his son tightly, inhaling the boy's scent. As Joseph pulled away there were tears on the little boy's cheeks.

'Are they being good to you?' asked Carter softly.

Joe nodded. 'Why are you bleeding, daddy?'

'I had an accident, but I'm fine, son. I'm absolutely brilliant.' He ruffled the boy's short blond hair. 'They feeding you?'

'Yes. And the nice lady, her –' he pointed to Alexis '– has been playing games with me.' Carter glanced over at the Nex, frowning, but Alexis was looking away – at Durell. Something unspoken was passing between the two and Carter returned his attention to his son.

'I'm sorry, Joe, but I've got to go away. I have something to do – an important job. But then I'll be back and we'll be together – for ever. I'll never leave you again . . . I promise.'

'You will come back, won't you, daddy?'

'I'll come back soon,' said Carter softly, releasing the boy.

217

Alexis took Joe by the hand and led him from the low, long-ceilinged room. As the door closed Carter stretched, testing his body. Pain flared in a hundred places but he pushed it aside and concentrated his attention on Durell.

'What do you want me to do?'

'You will bring down Spiral.'

Carter paused for a long moment. 'I would rather die,' he said eventually, his voice barely more than a whisper.

'And you would condemn your son?' Durell moved across the carpet to stand close to Carter, whose nostrils wrinkled at the Nex insect stink. Durell's armoured spine crackled softly as he moved and Carter realised that he had never been this close to Durell before without trying to kill him. It felt very strange.

'One day, I will gut you like a pig,' said Carter.

'We shall see. However, for now you must come with me; we need to prepare you for your mission.'

'And how do you suggest I *bring down* Spiral?'

'In an ironic twist of fate,' said Durell, 'I find myself in possession of a MicroNuke, a fully functioning SpiralGRID map and the perfect location in which to concentrate the core of Spiral personnel. The rest just takes a little imagination. As you will witness. Indeed, as you will *instigate*.'

The Grey Church was filled with streamers of sunlight. As the SpiralGRID fizzled and crackled, and the five Sleeper Nex composed themselves, shaking their huge triangular heads, after the nausea of their sudden sideways-shift journey, The Priest leapt towards them with his Glock bucking in his fist—

Mongrel and Simmo leapt to the left and right of The Priest as their own guns came up. The Sleeper Nex jumped apart in a blur of movement, huge bodies crash-

218

ing through old wood pews as The Priest met the first creature head on. Its claws lashed out, whirling past The Priest's face with only a single millimetre to spare. He caught himself, swayed to one side, whirled low and slammed the heavy blade of his black knife into the Sleeper Nex's armoured side. The blade slid smoothly between plates of armour and a spraying jet of blood pulsed out. The Sleeper reared up, a high-pitched chittering sound coming from its gaping jaws. Its belly was exposed now and The Priest unloaded the rest of the Glock's magazine into its unprotected abdomen and watched black scales peel back under the multiple impacts of the bullets. Entrails spilled out like a tangle of squirming eels.

Simmo, backed up by Rogowski and Mo, hammered bursts of bullets into the two Sleeper Nex to The Priest's left. A hail of flying metal cut one apart, punching it backwards, sending it slamming against the ancient stone of the church wall. The second Sleeper leapt towards its twitching comrade and slammed into Simmo whose gun fired an unaimed spray of bullets, making Mo and Rogowski dive to the floor in panic.

Simmo's huge hand grabbed the Sleeper's throat as he was pounded into the ground. A claw slashed down, raking the wooden slabs of the floor where his head had been. Simmo's huge fist cannoned into the Sleeper's triangular head again and again. Mo leapt onto its back, slipping a little on greased chitin and lifting his gun to the back of the creature's armoured head.

Suddenly, the Sleeper Nex's head spun around. It snapped at Mo with long fangs as he screamed and recoiled, his gun blasting a hail of bullets into its open maw. Its jaws jerked forward and bit through his wrist, slicing flesh and bone as easily as a razor cutting through jelly. Dark crimson gushes pumped from the stump to the rhythm of Mo's beating heart as he shrieked like a girl, severed tendon ends flapping against his arm. Simmo, still punching, caught a brutal blow to the head from a savage backswing of the Sleeper's clawed limb. He lay for a moment, stunned, cigar resting against his broken cheek.

The Sleeper reared, whirling as Mo was flung free. Rogowski charged, his gun yammering hot fire. The Sleeper, snarling, strings of blood and saliva pooling from its maw as it chittered, lurched towards Mo. Even as it thrashed in its death throes, its claws came up to zip through his throat and windpipe, tearing off his head and sending it rolling and bouncing across The Grey Church's rubble-strewn floor.

Rogowski, stunned by the sudden death of his friend, blinked and then continued to fire at the already dying Sleeper. With a great deflating sigh, the Sleeper Nex sank down over Mo's headless twitching corpse.

Mongrel and Roxi took on the other two massive beasts, charging together at them, firing as they ran. They rolled apart at the last moment and the Sleepers spun in a tight circle, bullets whining as they ricocheted from the armoured hides. Roxi, with incredible athleticism, leapt towards the wall and kicked off from the stone, somersaulting onto the rim of the circular pulpit on its small dais. As the Sleepers rounded on Mongrel, Roxi started to fire down from her elevated position at the creatures.

'Son of a buggering bugger!' muttered Mongrel as his gun suddenly jammed. He shook the weapon uselessly and went white as the Sleepers growled menacingly and crept towards him.

And then The Priest was there. The two Sleepers were caught in a sustained, coolly aimed crossfire as The Priest and Roxi pumped round after round into their writhing bodies.

Then everything went quiet. The reek of cordite filled the church. Rekalavich slumped to the ground, uttering a foul Russian curse, both hands clamped over the deep wound in his stomach. It wasn't enough to stop a crimson puddle forming slowly in his lap.

'Why it always my bloody gun that jam?' moaned Mongrel, kicking one of the Sleeper Nex corpses. 'Mongrel cursed with dodgy weaponry! Bad God want him dead!'

'We have to get out of here,' snapped The Priest. His face and beard were speckled with blood. He had sheathed his blood-slick knife. In one hand he held his Bible, and with the other hand he was nudging at his rosary beads with the barrel of his Glock. 'I assume by the arrival of these –' he spat on the ground – 'these *unholy* vermin that the GRID is terminally compromised?'

Roxi had placed a thick pad of cotton against Rekalavich's stomach and had helped the Russian to his feet. He was pale from blood loss, and leant heavily on the slim woman for support. She grunted under his weight.

'No,' he managed to mutter, rubbing at his face and leaving smears of blood against his stubbled skin. 'They have cracked the codes; they can use it, they can decode it – but so can we. They haven't cut off our escape route just yet.'

'Let's get moving,' growled Simmo. Despite the fight and the broken cheekbone, he had still found time to relight his cigar, which was all squashed and deformed like a length of twisted tree root. He rubbed tenderly at his forehead where a huge bruise had blossomed. 'The Nex are at the front door – and they're planting a bomb.'

'You sure?' asked Montrel.

'I can *smell* the HighJ.'

The battered group moved to the SpiralGRID's portal which crackled into existence, a SpiderCAR formation becoming visible at the call from The Priest's ECube.

The Spiral team had watched this portal spit forth the enemy and disgorge the Sleeper Nex. Now the whine of injectors filled the air as the GRID charged itself for another sideways shift. Then there came a soft *click* of detonation – and the group watched in sudden wide-eyed horror as the church door became a rapid raging inferno, a terrifying expanding ball of gas and fire and shrapnel rushing towards them. But then they were gone. Swallowed . . . into the GRID.

The Sikorsky Comanche RAH-NV was an old Spiral model, taken over by Durell after the great global collapse. Powered by a twin-turboshaft T800 LHT-950 plant, it carried twin stowable three-barrelled 20mm turreted Gatling nose guns, capable of firing 2,000 rounds a minute. It had a fully retractable missile armament I-RAMS system and the ability to carry a full payload of fifty-two standard 78mm rockets, twenty-two Stinger air-to-air missiles and eighteen Hellfire anti-tank missiles.

As they landed on the roof of the WarFactory and Carter climbed down from the small black Nex helicopter, he eyed the Comanche with a mixture of careful consideration, awe and respect.

'One of yours,' said Durell, standing next to him on the concrete roof. They were surrounded by armed Nex, and Carter could still taste blood and the sour, bitter tang of his mission.

They want me to kill Simmo and The Priest, he thought. And Roxi.

And Mongrel . . .

Carter's vision blurred. He turned away from the Comanche and allowed himself to be guided by the surprisingly gentle hand of Alexis. They moved across the roof, past a hundred more helicopters – many of them new and gleaming black under the dull evening light. They walked down long corridors wide enough to accommodate tanks and aircraft, down more ramps, then up wide steep iron steps, footsteps clanking, until they came to some form of control centre which was a hive of activity. Many Nex sat at glowing work-stations, along with human programmers and military coordinators. A few glanced up briefly as Durell, Alexis, Carter and their contingent of armed Nex entered.

On a bench to one side sat a silver box, half a metre long, narrow and vented. Carter found his gaze drawn to the MicroNuke as hackles rose on the back of his neck. If the bomb, small though it was, were to explode then it wouldn't just take out the WarFactory. Half the damn city would be destroyed.

'That it?'

'This is a Grade 3 plutonium device,' said Alexis, moving to place her hand gently – almost reverently – against the nuclear bomb. The MicroNuke – what Jam had once fondly called Armageddon in a suitcase.

Jam, thought Carter.

It had been a long time. Jam, Carter's oldest friend and one of Spiral's best operatives during their hectic anti-terrorist days, had been captured while on a mission in Slovenia. Beaten and abused, he had undergone a transformation into a new breed of Nex that Durell was developing, a breed named the ScorpNex which involved such complicated genetic modifications that most subjects died before leaving the laboratory slab. With Jam, however, the transformation had been successful – changing the cheerful cockney into a monster, a horrific blend of human and cockroach and *scorpion* . . . Jam had become an awesome warrior, a terrible killer.

Carter had found himself face to face with his oldest friend – a new creature that could not be beaten – only to find that the power of the genetic Nex-hold had not been strong enough. During an epic struggle Jam had helped Carter and had undone the original betrayal. In doing so he had destroyed Durell's plans to rule the world through the use of a machine capable of wreaking earthquakes on a global scale . . .

However, Spiral and other agencies had not realised that the quakes had been merely the first step in Durell's advance. As they beat back the Nex armies, thinking that they were overcoming a terrible enemy, Durell was simply putting the next stages of his plan into operation – striking not just on one front but on three. With the power of the earthquakes weakening global infrastructure, and with the combined power of biological weapons and the awesome might of tactical nuclear strikes at his disposal, Durell had proved himself unstoppable. All these advances had been coordinated by the tactical prowess of the QIV military processor, a sentient machine capable of awesome destruction – a simple and yet infinitely versatile chip willing to play at God. And bring about Armageddon.

Carter stared at the MicroNuke, his mind swimming.

'*You have to do it,*' whispered Kade. '*You have to kill them . . . if you want to live. If you want to save your baby.*'

'Yeah, like you care.'

'*I care, Carter. I care lots.*'

Carter focused on Durell, who was handing out some documents. Alexis lowered the MicroNuke carefully into a Gore-Tex pack as Carter reached out for his set.

'Here are your coordinates – you can access the SpiralGRID through this outpost. There will be armed Spiral men there – but hell, you are Carter. They should recognise you. You shouldn't need *our* help to get you past the Spiral perimeter guards.'

'And if they don't recognise me? If they shoot first and ask my corpse questions later?'

'Then it's game over,' said Durell. 'For you *and* for your boy.'

'So I infiltrate Spiral. Then what?'

'Get the nuke inside, and you will be contacted by somebody already there who will give you details of the next step. An old friend, you might say, who has decided to join us. Decided our way is absolutely the *right* choice.'

'You're beginning to sound like one of your fucking TV campaigns.'

'Of course I do. I wrote them. Now, take the MicroNuke – the Comanche outside is fully fuelled with LVA; you've enough to reach London in one direct flight.'

Carter hefted the Gore-Tex pack carefully – it was very heavy. But then, it should have been: it carried a low-yield nuclear bomb. He lifted his head, turning slightly as Alexis tossed him his 9mm Browning HiPower. He cradled the weapon, then glanced sideways at the surrounding Nex . . .

'*We could—*' began Kade.

'No, we fucking couldn't,' Carter answered silently. 'I'm weak, battered . . . and they outnumber us a thousand to one. How fucking insane are you?' Kade did not reply.

Alexis smiled at Carter then, her copper eyes glowing. 'We have taken the liberty of filling the Comanche with weapons; Armalite XII and Steyr 80 sub-machine guns, HPGs. You'll even find a small case containing a MercG –

225

a Spiral-issue garrotte containing your very own augmented digital signature.'

Carter slid the Browning into his pocket, shouldered the pack with a grunt and a wince at some internal pain or other and moved towards the ramp. Durell followed him, armour crackling, and Carter stopped at the metal doorway.

'Who is it that I must meet?' he asked, his voice barely more than a whisper. 'Who betrayed Spiral?'

'You will see soon enough,' said Durell, his tiny dark tongue wetting his hardened silver-veined lips.

Carter said nothing more. He turned and was gone.

Alexis glanced at Durell. 'Do you think he will succeed? In bringing down Spiral?'

'Yes,' said Durell, nodding and making his twisted spine crackle. 'Carter is *our* boy now. He is one of us. We control him, we direct him, we fucking *own* him. Just like it used to be.'

The Comanche's mechanisms hummed around Carter as he skimmed low across the Atlantic Ocean. Night had fallen, and below him the dark waters churned.

Flying without lights, Carter saw the world below him as a very dark place. His HIDSS pilot's helmet showed different slices of image, using different forms of night vision – infra-red, Green-eye and Ttii-BlueScale – and flickered with constant data updates from the Comanche's electronic brain. Carter was kept active during this low-level night flight; there was plenty to see and do, plenty to control and plan . . .

Yet still—

Turn back. Turn back and kill them and take your boy . . .

You have a Comanche . . . fucking use it.

For once, Kade remained silent, a toad under a stone.

And Carter tried to justify his actions to himself – to convince himself that this was the only way. Durell had an army – a fucking *army* that had overthrown Spiral. Carter was not destroying Spiral; they were already broken. He was merely severing the head . . . killing the broken snake in order to save his son.

'You cannot do this,' came the soft voice of Natasha. And he saw her; saw her face floating white – a ghostly image before him, superimposed over the humming HIDSS display. 'I understand – understand your need to save our boy, but you cannot do this to Spiral . . . you cannot destroy the one hope for mankind . . .'

'I will do what I have to do.'

'You are a different man, then, to the one I loved.'

'I will do what I have to do,' replied Carter, his voice a low growl. And God, how he needed the whisky now, needed it more than ever before. Just a small shot; just a single sip of the old Lagavulin to soothe his burning throat and his fevered brain. '*Yeah, brother, and then the long dark fucking fall into whisky oblivion. I think you would* welcome *the fucking release* . . .'

The snow was falling heavily again, from Bristol to London, as Carter powered the Comanche through a blizzard. The thump of the helicopter's powerful rotors played a lullaby to Carter as he gazed from within the precision HIDSS helmet at the white, undulating world below him.

The snowscape below Carter looked . . . he searched for a word. *Normal*, he finally decided.

Reaching the outskirts of London, Carter held his breath as he passed the first Nex outpost – containing a cluster of eight SAM-7 surface-to-air missiles. Deployed from Mini-SAM7.8 Blocks in III/IV and IVa configurations, the SAM-7s employed electronic countermeasures in the form of mono-pulse send/receivers for semi-active III-TR radar terminal guidance and inertial mid-course guidance. Launched from the SAM7.8VLS (Vertical Launching Systems) the SAM-7s were perfect for both low- and high-altitude threat interceptions and could infiltrate past enemy aircraft's ECM-6, Lockheed 52 and Sikorsky 2212 ASAM aerial electronic counter-measures.

Carter waited for the heavy punch. But below, in the snow, the Blocks whirled on powerful motors. In the blink of an eye they targeted and locked – but held their fire. Carter squinted through the falling snow as the Comanche's warning system screamed proximity alerts at him and the HIDSS illuminated multiple targets. Carter's fingers hovered over the firing buttons . . . and he was tempted. God, how sorely he was tempted . . .

Carter dropped the helicopter low over the city. Then he brought it around in a huge arc and landed in the middle of a street, the roar of the rotors sending civilians sprinting for cover and attracting a huge encircling ring of Nex soldiers and weaponry.

Carter had decided to land only a few streets from a military installation, a forward post for the London WarFac. He slipped the HIDSS from his head, ran a hand through his sweat-drenched hair, then punched the button that prompted the Comanche's advanced hydraulics to fold back the cockpit. Shouldering the MicroNuke, Carter hefted his M24 carbine and climbed down the recessed ladder set into the Comanche's flank.

Sub-machine guns swivelled to target him. Once more Carter waited with dry mouth and hammering heart for the first bullet to strike – he knew it would be over fast, a hot hard drilling through his skull. But the metal punch never came and Carter turned to survey the Nex.

They watched him impassively. Carter took a step forward, and spat into the nearest Nex's face. Its eyes blinked in reflex. But there was no other reaction.

'Hmm,' said Carter. 'Interesting.'

One of the Nex approached. And it saluted. 'We have transport awaiting you. Sir.'

Carter stared in disbelief. His eyes narrowed. His M24 wavered, and finally, licking at his dehydrated lips, he growled, 'Don't call me "sir", you cockroach motherfucker. Just get out of my fucking way before I decide to shove this MicroNuke up your fucking arse. You understand, maggot?'

The Nex – still showing no emotion – merely stepped back and allowed the irate Carter access to the snowbound streets of London beyond the cordon.

Carter walked. Flakes tumbled around him and he took deep, steadying breaths, calming his mind and composing himself for what he had to do. The annihilation of Spiral . . . the extermination of his friends . . . and the destruction of everything he had ever worked for.

'*Your boy will become just another casualty of war,*' said Kade softly. '*You think they will let him go when you destroy Spiral? When you are the last remaining Spiral man? No, Carter . . . they will kill him and you. They cannot let him live – because to let him live will be to plant a seed, a seed of revolution and future revenge so strong it could one day bring down Durell. And the man knows this. The Nex know this.*'

'You're sounding very philosophical,' muttered Carter.

'*Hey, it's this fresh London air. Much more pure now they've saturated the radiation with chemicals.*'

Carter walked for nearly two hours, his mind whirling, contemplating different scenarios and then rejecting them.

229

Horrified, he realised that he could not do this alone. He could not extricate himself from the tangle of events. It's a fucking terrible mess, he realised, and I'm caught right in the middle of it. Shit.

Carter passed three Nex outposts: checkpoints set at intervals to intercept Spiral terrorists and REBS and to monitor the civilian population of the city. Not once was he stopped or even verbally challenged. They knew he was coming, and for this mission Carter had an all-zones passport which allowed him a freedom that only Durell could have engineered.

Carter smiled with chilled lips, ducking right down a narrow side street. The MicroNuke was heavy on his back now, the weight of the bomb digging into his shoulder and cramping the muscles of his neck. He walked with care, brow furrowed, hair laced with a brushing of snow which made him look older than he was. His walk slowed as he counted the shopfronts, and he stopped finally at a derelict clothes shop. The window still had cracked and battered plastic dummies in it, some sporting clothes, some naked and stained yellow.

The door was propped shut with sacks of rubble. Carter leant his shoulder against the warped wood with its flaking off-white paint, and pushed gently.

The door scraped open and Carter stepped inside. In the gloom he could just make out the black eyes of a quad-barrelled heavy machine gun, with chains of ammunition coiling on the floor. Carter halted, stare fixed on the gun – and on the dark hooded shadow behind the weapon.

'I am Spiral,' said Carter softly.

'I know you are,' came a smooth voice. 'Took your time coming home.'

Carter smiled wryly. 'Can you take me to Mongrel?'

'Were you followed?'

'No.'

'Then I will call Mongrel to come for you. You *look* like Carter but we can't be too sure these days – the city is awash with vermin. And the world is in, shall we say, a shit state.'

The shadowy figure produced an ECube and Carter watched the gentle movements of message transmission. Shortly the ECube gave a tiny blip. Carter caught the flicker of blue light.

'Follow me.' The man led Carter down long musty corridors that stank of damp and neglect. Part of the wall at the rear of the building had been knocked through into another building – an old newsagent's, still containing shelves with rusted cans on them. They moved out through a battered archway. Within the shops of this London street Spiral had created a labyrinthine warren. A rat-run for humans.

Finally, they reached a flight of steps, and the hooded man stopped. Carter glanced at him, and beneath the hood he glimpsed a terrible array of facial scars: a twisted and deformed nose together with healed diagonal lacerations that had ruined the skin, slashed across the man's lips, and turned one eye a milky white.

'I carry my scars on my face,' the man said quietly. 'But I know you carry yours in your heart. Be brave, Carter. Be strong. Be true to Spiral.'

'What happened to you?'

'A tank exploded. I was in it.' He laughed. 'Hey, this is nothing. You should see the rest of my body.'

'And still you fight?'

'Is there any other way? Mongrel is down there.' He gestured at the steep stone steps leading down into darkness. 'He's waiting for you. I hope you bring us good news – things are not going well and we could use a little ray of sunshine.'

Carter said nothing. He stared down the stone stairway. It could be a trap . . . it was possible that Spiral knew of his involvement with Durell, and that they were waiting down there to kill him. An ambush, to neutralise the MicroNuke and its bearer before detonation finally made Spiral a thing of the past.

A ray of sunshine?

I carry more than that; I carry the heart of the sun, Carter thought. With his head held high, Carter stepped slowly down the stone steps, his loud footsteps announcing his arrival.

'Carter, you old *pizda*!'

Mongrel loomed from the shadows, making Carter jump, and threw his arms around him, hugging him tight and making him grunt in pain. Still, Carter could not help but give a wide grin.

'How's it going, you fat old goat? You still in love with those Stilton ladies?'

'Har! I love a woman with a whiff of Cheddar about her. It like . . . like . . . like fine old wine! Only with more of stink! Ha har! How you doing, you dog? You lost a bit of weight, but poor old Mongrel . . .' He cupped his protruding belly in one huge paw. 'Ahh, the beer and the sausage make a mockery of him.' Mongrel took a step back, holding onto Carter's arms. Then he hugged his old friend once more, crushing him again.

'Nice place you have here,' said Carter, glancing around at the single broken chair, the table propped up in one corner on piles of mouldering books and at the bare stone walls riddled with huge patches of black fungus and damp.

'I see wicked sense of humour never leave the Carter boy! Welcome back, Carter, welcome back! There so many people who be glad to see you, there Simmo just as fat and stubborn as ever, there Rogowski who make coffee like no man alive and there that insane religious *svolok* – The Priest – torturing us all with country music about large-breasted women, the old God-bothering madman. Not that Mongrel have anything *against* large-breasted women, of course, because we all know it large-breasted women that make the world go round!'

Mongrel grinned a lunatic grin filled with missing teeth.

Carter laughed then. He felt as if a pressure valve had been released in his skull, allowing the pent-up steam of frustration to evaporate. He slammed Mongrel on the back and the two men just stared at each other. They had been through shit together, served many, many missions – and witnessed the beginning of the fall of the world. It had been a long time . . .

Too long, Carter realised sadly.

'Come on,' said Mongrel. 'We walk and talk, faster that way, too much shit gone down to just be here chatting and not planning! This way.' Mongrel led Carter to the back of the damp stone room, and they ducked down low – Mongrel had to crawl on his hands and knees – under a low arch of smashed rubble. Then they were in a room with what looked like a bank vault's doors, two feet thick and hung on hinges that could have supported a tower block. Mongrel punched in several digits, attached his ECube, then spun the wheel and heaved on the mammoth portal. It swung open silently, and Mongrel ushered Carter through into a dimly lit alloy corridor, narrow and with a low ceiling. Every thirty feet or so a bare bulb hung from a reel of cable, giving off flickering illumination. As

Carter stepped over the threshold, nostrils twitching at the smell of distant sewage, Mongrel heaved the huge door closed behind them.

'Down here, boy.'

They walked, Mongrel in front and Carter behind, until they reached a square section of floor, a poorly defined flicker of silver that signified the SpiralGRID. 'I thought that this had been compromised?' said Carter softly.

'How you know that?' Mongrel tilted his head, giving Carter a strange look.

'I know, because it was my fault.'

'It was? I think we have lot to talk about, Carter. Come on – it is still usable, but we have to be careful; we think Durell is tracking our every move . . . lying in wait like fat snake in the grass, just waiting to strike and sink in poisonous fangs.'

Carter wanted to say, *Yes, you are right. You* are *being tracked, and very soon you are going to be dead . . .*

But he said nothing. And, with the MicroNuke in his pack, he followed Mongrel towards the heart of Spiral.

The warehouse down at the Old Docks on the banks of the Thames was a cold stone structure. The building itself was very old, and had once been a mill of some kind. Now it was deserted, filled partly with massive sections of steel machinery – engineering presses and banks of dead computers ranked around the perimeter walls. Due to the size of the building, the cold was intense. Carter warmed his hands over the flames of the brazier and watched as Rogowski changed the sterile pads on the wound in Rekalavich's stomach.

'You get that fighting a Sleeper Nex?' asked Carter softly.

234

Rekalavich nodded, drawing deeply on his stinking Bogatiri *papirosi* cigarette. 'How you know that?'

'I can tell by the serrations along the edge of the skin. It's their claws. They do that.'

'They tough bastards to kill, yes?' said Rek, smiling sardonically.

Carter nodded, shifting his gaze around the group in the warehouse. There were perhaps forty men and women, some of whom he knew, some of whom he had heard about, and a few who were new recruits from after the time when Carter had exiled himself to Cyprus. But all had heard of Carter; all knew of his past; and all seemed happy to see him. Another old soldier, ready to unload his sub-machine gun at the enemy . . . But Carter knew the truth, and the Spiral men and women knew it too.

They were trying to block a breach in a dam with a pebble. They were trying to bail out a sinking warship with a teaspoon. And they believed that one more old soldier could make very little difference . . .

Carter waited for Mongrel to return and lit a cigarette. The smoke tasted sour and he did not enjoy the experience. Tossing the butt into the burner he watched Mongrel as the big man entered and moved across the warehouse, stopping to talk to the distant hulking figure of The Priest. Mongrel had a woman with him. Carter groaned.

All I fucking need, he thought, shaking his head. Roxi sticking her – admittedly beautiful – nose into the proceedings. She trailed Mongrel warily as the huge battered man returned to Carter, carrying a large pan of soup. 'You want to eat? Is vegetable. Is good,' he rumbled. But Carter's gaze had bypassed him to rest on the lithe athletic figure of Roxi.

235

She halted, her green piercing eyes unreadable in a beautiful oval face framed by fine shoulder-length brown hair. Her head tilted as she watched Carter, then she pulled free a cigarette, lit it slowly, and took a long drag.

'Hello, Carter,' she said, her voice husky.

'Roxi. You are looking . . .'

'Tired? Worn out? Frustrated? *Exhausted*? It's fucking good of you to join us – at last.'

'I have had – different priorities.'

'Yeah, so I heard.' Her stance was aggressive, and Mongrel had slid silently to one side, still holding his pan of steaming soup. He opened his mouth to speak, then thought better of it and closed it again. He muttered something about being needed somewhere urgently; about needing to see a man about a pig. Then he left.

Carter looked down. He found it hard to meet Roxi's gaze.

'You're looking well, Carter,' she said finally. She took a step closer. Carter could smell her musk but he did not look up. How could he? He was expected to kill everybody in this room within a few short hours . . .

'I've felt fucking better,' he drawled.

'You're like fine wine. You mature with age.' Roxi was closer now, almost touching him. 'I've missed you,' she murmured.

'And I you.'

'When I saw you in Greece, you said that you still loved me. You told me that we may one day be together – in another lifetime. Well Carter, this is another lifetime.'

Carter closed his eyes. Roxi kissed him, and he did not pull away. He allowed himself to become lost. He allowed himself to be taken and her hand slid around his back, rested against the base of his spine with an infinity of hesitant intimacy. Her tongue probed his, her lips a tantalising silk that teased his own with their delicacy; and then, finally, Carter opened his eyes and slowly pulled back – the upper part of his body, but her hand held their hips together in a tight embrace.

'Yeah, you definitely missed me,' he smiled. But it was a smile laced with uncertainty.

'We have the benefits of distance on our side. We have both made mistakes in the past. We have both made *many* mistakes; but the end of the world is coming for us, Carter, I can feel it. I can feel it in my bones, and now is not a time for weakness, or hesitancy. Yesterday we faced a group of Sleeper Nex and I was sure we would all die – and yet I am here. I might not have been. I have waited for you, Carter. Waited for you since that time when I thought you would kill me . . . when *Kade* tried to separate us for good.'

Carter was staring deep into her bright green gaze. 'You have *waited* for me?'

'Yes.' Her voice was incredibly low and husky. Tears stained her cheeks, and she pressed her face to his, transferring the wetness of her longing, of her need.

'Now is not the time,' he said.

'Now is never the time,' she responded.

'I do not think I am ready.'

'Then you will never be ready.'

There came a cough and Roxi stepped away, turning from Carter. Carter looked up into The Priest's gold-flecked gaze. The Priest did not smile.

'I am sorry to interrupt such an intimate moment, but I have questions for you. Concerning the SpiralGRID.'

'You are here to put me on trial?'

'No,' said The Priest. 'I believe you when you say that you were tricked. And Jahlsen brought about his own defeat and death – and, ultimately, the destruction of the

SpiralGRID. We did not know he was such a heavy user of Godsmack. His selfishness and his addiction destroyed him; made him an easy target. But I have many questions about the SpiralGRID and its compromise . . . and about Durell.'

Carter nodded. Glancing at Roxi, who stood with her back to him, Carter followed The Priest away towards a huge bank of computers. They both sat down on stencilled crates and Carter explained what had happened.

When The Priest had finished with his questions and drifted away towards Mongrel, who was drinking his soup from his huge burnt pan, Carter glanced around at the men and women preparing for the night. Many of them had brews simmering in pans and kettles, and had unrolled bedding mats and sleeping bags on the warehouse's stone floor. Rogowski was oiling a rifle, Bob Bob was scrubbing at a custard stain on his combats, and Simmo was playing cards with several other men and smoking a big fat cigar. These were true Spiral; these were the hard core, the survivors – the ones who had refused to be stomped and ground into the dust under Durell's mighty boots.

I have come home, Carter realised. And a weight greater than anything he had ever felt descended to wholly smother his heart and mind and soul.

Carter had set his bedding roll – kindly lent to him by Mongrel – away from the others. Always a solitary creature, he felt even more alone now with the great burden he carried – the guilt for the destruction that he would soon unleash with the MicroNuke weighed heavily on his mind, thoughts of betrayal chewing at him constantly.

I cannot do this, he thought. Over and over again.

I cannot do this . . . But I must. Shivering, Carter

238

pulled on a thick jumper and sat down on his improvised bed. Many of the Spiral people were already asleep; Simmo was snoring loudly, and occasionally farting in rhythm with his great throaty rumbles.

Outside it was dark, leaving no illumination inside the warehouse other than the occasional firefly glow of a soft blue NightCube or a purple hexiblock. Out of this gloom came Rogowski who stood gazing down at Carter with a strange look on his face.

'You OK, mate?' asked Carter.

Rogowski nodded – and realisation hit Carter like an iron bar. Rogowski dropped to a crouch, his stare locked on Carter's face. 'You have the bomb?' came his soft whisper.

Carter's expression hardened. Here was the traitor, the betrayer of Spiral. Durell's contact. The man who would lead Carter and the MicroNuke to the detonation point; the man who would arrange the convergence of Nex and Spiral for the ultimate confrontation; the man who would exterminate Carter's friends.

'Why, Rogowski? *Why?*'

Rogowski gave a strange little smile. 'You would never understand, Carter. Never. And we haven't got time to discuss this fucking situation, so just answer my fucking questions – or the little kid finds himself without a head, and without a fucking *dad*. In that order. Understand?'

Carter's stare burned into Rogowski. 'Yeah, cunt, I have the fucking bomb.'

'Good. Tomorrow there will be a call for a gathering of Spiral agents. For such meetings we have an old munitions depot called the Concrete Arena – which I've recently discovered contains the GRID HUB. It's a couple of miles from here. We'll all troop along, smiling and happy, and I will show you where to plant the

239

MicroNuke. When we detonate that fucker it will destroy the HUB and the SpiralGRID will be unusable.'

'Won't we all die in the nuclear explosion?'

'Spiral will. But you and I have other plans,' said Rogowski. 'Don't worry, Carter – we have an exit point.'

'You think I give a fuck about a fucking *exit point*? Rogowski, man, what are you doing? You would turn against your friends and comrades? You would betray them all?'

'Friendship is all a matter of perspective,' said Rogowski coldly. 'In a world like this . . . well, shall we say, that I'm just willing to let that friendship slide.'

As Rogowski walked away quietly Carter's stare burned laser-like into the man's back, focusing an intensity of hatred. But there was nothing he could do. He was imprisoned by kindred.

Nothing he could do . . . if he wished to save his little boy's life.

Hours had passed, flowing by like a slow dark river. Carter lay awake, riddled with exhaustion but still unable to sleep.

Something moved close by, then a finger was placed against his lips – and Roxi was there, the scent of her skin a natural perfume invading his senses as she slid beneath his blanket and pressed herself close to him.

'Do you mind?' In the darkness, her voice sounded suddenly young; far younger than the rough and tough killer Carter knew so well.

'No, I don't mind,' he replied.

Roxi pillowed her head on one arm. Carter sensed that her face was close to his. Strangely, he felt soothed. Relaxed. Her scent, her proximity, calmed him.

Finally, she said, 'If I die tomorrow, will you remember me?'

'I will remember you,' he said.

'Will you light a candle for me?'

'What kind of talk is this, Rox? You sound like you think you only have hours left! Don't be so defeatist . . . the woman I knew was never so despondent, she was an optimist. She would laugh in the face of danger.'

'I have a mission to perform,' she said softly. Her hand came up and stroked at his hair. 'A dangerous mission.' Her finger traced a line down his jawline, and on impulse he reached forward and kissed her.

'Do you want me to come with you?'

'No. It is something I have to do alone.'

They kissed again. Carter's hand stroked her flank through the thin cotton T-shirt she wore, and she groaned, a low and husky animal sound. He could feel her need.

Pulling away, Carter smiled in the darkness. 'Don't be getting any ideas, madam. I have a long day tomorrow – and by the sounds of it, so do you.'

'Make love to me, Carter. Fuck me like you used to fuck me.'

'Not tonight.'

'Is it because of Natasha?'

Roxi felt Carter freeze beside her, then slowly sink into her embrace once more. His breathing was harsh, laboured, but gradually it returned to normal and she whispered, 'I'm sorry,' in his ear.

'No, it's not your fault. It's me.'

'Natasha was beautiful. Natasha was my friend. I miss her as well, you know.'

'I know,' sighed Carter.

'She would have blessed us.'

241

'I know that, as well.'

'Well, you awkward bastard, make love to me!' Roxi pressed herself harder against him, and they kissed once more, passionately this time. Carter felt himself falling into the uncontrollable embrace of red velvet lust; Roxi's hand dropped, stroking slowly at his belly, then down to tease and taunt his penis which hardened until he thought he would explode under the squeezing of her long strong fingers. Roxi lifted her leg over him, then leant forward to kiss him again, her hips lifted tantalisingly over him as he groaned and the whole world descended into a blood red sea swirl of want and need, of love and lust and a howling need for sex and his hands grasped at her, pulling her writhing gyrating hips onto him and her cunt was warm, and wet, and soft and willing and they slid together perfectly, a puzzle clicking neatly into place. She ground her hips down with an animal moan and she fucked him as Carter lifted her T-shirt free of her long brown hair and her breasts were highlighted in the gloom of the old stone warehouse. Roxi suddenly arched backwards, and locked together in the act of fucking, Carter's hands found Roxi's and her nails gouged his flesh as they became one, lost together, falling together. She toppled forward across him, hair in his face, her breasts pressed against his chest as her eyes gazed into his and they slowed to a mechanical grinding rhythm. Her hips lifted again, lifted from him this time, a tease as his teeth nuzzled at her neck and she plunged herself suddenly, painfully around him, forced herself onto him and they remained locked together for long, long moments and Carter was lost in a maelstrom of emotions and the rushing pounding smashing thrust of – slow – hard – sex.

When he awoke in the ghostly witch-light of dawn, Roxi had gone.

And Carter felt bad.

'*That was entertaining,*' said Kade smugly.

'You're a cheap voyeur,' snapped Carter. 'Why don't you fuck off and spy on the ladies' toilet?'

'*A dark twin needs to get his amusement somehow.*'

Carter could smell Roxi on his skin, but at least something made him feel better: the knowledge that Roxi had headed out on a mission. She would not be there when he detonated the MicroNuke. So she would not know of his terrible, ultimate betrayal. And, more importantly, she would not be there to die in the blast.

'*You're a whore,*' said Kade.

'Get to fuck.'

'*As far as you were concerned, my friend, you'd fuck her and then kill her and her friends with a bomb up the arse. You are worse than any animal, Carter; more deadly than any virus; more lethal than any fucking machine.*'

Carter realised that Kade was right. Carter could not kill Spiral. But if he didn't that would condemn his son . . .

I need help, he thought.

'*Yeah, I realised that a long time ago, fucker,*' chuckled Kade in his head.

'We need to talk,' said Mongrel soberly.

The Priest had spent the previous thirty minutes briefing the forty men and women present. He'd told them that they were shortly going to travel to the Concrete Arena, GRID HUB side, and meet up there with a huge group of Spiral operatives to plan a series of coordinated attacks on Durell's WarFacs; and to discuss the feasibility of bringing down the Sentinel HQs – from within.

Carter nodded, pulling tight the laces of his boots. He followed Mongrel towards the toilet block. Looking shiftily left and right, Mongrel ushered Carter into the

243

toilets and Carter wrinkled his nose at the stench.

'I hope you're not looking for romance,' he said testily.

'Time for comedy over,' said Mongrel softly. 'I have something important to speak.'

'Important? What, you dying or something, you old cunt?' laughed Carter.

'Yes.'

Carter's stare met Mongrel's. The big man's expression was deadly serious, then Mongrel did something that Carter had not seen for a decade. He flashed a coded hand signal. The signal said: *I know about the bomb.*

Carter and Mongrel stood there in the stinking toilet block beside the stained and cracked urinals.

Carter said, 'What's the matter with you?' as he flashed a signal, fingers working quickly through the complex sign language: *They have my boy. They will kill him if I do not blow up SpiralHUB.*

'I was having big toilet problem,' said Mongrel, speaking slowly, clearly. 'I started lose lot of weight – ha, which I know you think is good thing for fat old Mongrel, hey? But I started needing toilet, sometimes ten times a fucking day! It not comfortable when you on mission with machine gun and keep needing a shit, I tell you, boy-o!'

He gave the signs: *I have sent a squad to lift your boy from New York. You must trust me – and detonate the nuke only when I give the signal.*

'What are you telling me?' said Carter softly. 'You are dying from terminal excessive toilet exposure?'

I will trust you, Mongrel. Just don't get my fucking son killed!

'No. I have the cancer,' said Mongrel gently. *Your boy will be fine. I have sent Roxi. She is the best in the business. And we have our own people infiltrated into the Nex. We will get him out, Carter. I promise you.*

244

Carter's mouth gaped in amazement at both revelations. *OK*, came his flickering hand signals. *But the cancer story is just a cover, right?*

Mongrel shook his head sadly. 'No, Carter, I really do have cancer. Just a few months to live, doctors tell me. It is too far gone to cure: a man can't live without a fucking stomach, or entire fucking bowel – or so old Mongrel been told.'

Carter was stunned. 'I don't know what to say.'

'Don't even fucking think about *Get Well*.' Mongrel grinned and slapped Carter on the back, his eyes gleaming. 'Don't worry, Carter. Everything turn out just fine – you will see, laddie.'

Carter nodded, breathing slowly, and allowed Mongrel to lead him from the toilet block. 'Come on,' said Mongrel over his shoulder. 'It's time to move out. We've got job to do.'

Outside, the snow had stopped falling. A cold, bitter wind was sweeping across the city, piling the snow in drifts.

The Spiral operatives left the buildings in staggered groups of twos and threes, walking swiftly down deserted roads beside the Thames which was crusted with a layer of ice.

Carter, Mongrel and Rogowski walked in silence, guns hidden in their packs and long coats covering their military clothing. Additionally, Carter carried the heavy MicroNuke.

Wintry sunlight shown down from a clear blue sky. Carter, with his collar turned up against the cold, his breath steaming, followed Mongrel who was in the lead, and Rogowski, who was coming up close behind. Rogowski dropped back a little, out of earshot of Mongrel who pretended not to notice. 'You ready for this, Carter?'

'I'm ready.'

Rogowski sneered nastily. 'Don't fuck this one up, boy. A lot rides on it – including the lives of your child and yourself. Don't be a dick – just do the job and do it right.'

Carter grinned. 'You need to shut the fuck up, Rogowski. Or maybe I'll shoot you in the fucking skull and detonate the bomb without you. I'll still pacify Durell, keep my kid alive – but you'll be fucking worm food.'

'Big words from the big man. You have a reputation Carter, but I have the experience. When this is all over, I would like to dance a slow waltz with you.'

'The pleasure will be all mine,' growled Carter. 'Anybody who turns traitor against his friends, condemns them all to die – well, he deserves everything he fucking gets. I am going to fuck you up bad, compadre. You can rely on *that*.'

Rogowski sneered again, then jogged forward to catch up with Mongrel.

The Browning felt good, holstered against Carter's hip. And for the first time in a long while Carter felt cautiously positive. Yes, everything might turn to rat shit – but he would give it his best shot. And he would be strong. He couldn't ask more of himself than that.

The groups were travelling to the Concrete Arena via different routes, some on foot, some by SmutCar, some by the GRID. Mongrel had elected to lead his tiny entourage on foot – and they moved through narrow alleyways and back streets, occasionally making a dash across major roads.

It took them an hour. All three men were rosy-cheeked from the cold as Mongrel led them through a series of large yards surrounded by abandoned tower blocks, and deeper into a complex of yards and large concrete sheds, warehouses and low buildings. There were old cranes reaching for the sky, and high metal walkways stretching between towers and buildings. Some, though, ended in – nothing.

'What is this place?' asked Carter.

Mongrel shrugged. 'We use it as munitions depot, and to store FukTruks. Mongrel think it once used to build first-generation tugs, in the infancy days of ChainStations. Now it long derelict; it good meeting place, hey?'

'Why's it called the Concrete Arena?'

Mongrel gave a nasty smile. 'When two Spiral men of bad reputation have an old falling-out, then this is place they sort it out.'

'What, with guns?'

'With fists,' said Mongrel, eyes gleaming. 'Good old-fashioned way. Guns never solve problem, Carter; guns only good for putting something down. No, no – guns have no pride, no honour. They are like GPS – only for pussies. A real adventurer, he not need these machine aids . . . This is about *living*, Carter, about *striving* . . . This honour must be earned with real effort, and blood, and pain. And nobody die as a result. Well, not often. You see?'

'I see, all right,' said Carter, rolling his shoulders under the pack.

'You OK, Carter?' asked Rogowski. 'You want me to carry that for you? Take the weight for a while?'

'I'm just fine, Ro. You leave it with me. I carry my own burdens.'

'Ooh,' said Mongrel. 'Bit touchy, aren't you, Carter? You two girls been fighting? Well, we in the right place if you need to settle something, that for sure, or Mongrel not like fat women with cheese feet!'

They entered a small side alleyway, and as they advanced along it Mongrel disappeared behind a pile of metal grilles. There came a grinding noise and behind them the alleyway was blocked by a wall of steel which descended from screeching pulleys overhead – huge thick slabs of metal dropped into place, each with a pitted and slightly rusting surface.

'Wouldn't want to get followed.' Mongrel grinned. 'Bombproof to HighJ rating of 3.7. Take moron long time to cut through *that* baby with blow-torch!' They moved out into a vast yard. Buildings circled them. The brickwork looked old, almost Victorian, with many bricks sporting black and crumbling surfaces. The place had a heavily industrialised look.

To one side of the yard was a huge steel structure, vertical girders rising from deep under the concrete. Flimsy-looking ladders were bolted to rust-streaked struts, and high above the men – perhaps two hundred feet overhead – several gantries straddled the huge concrete yard. Some were crane supports, others braced huge iron H-sections whose purpose was not immediately evident.

Mongrel got to work getting an enormous pan of water on for brews as more and more Spiral men and women started to arrive. Some came through the SpiralGRID, sideways-shifting into shimmering existence in a blur of silver and pink. Many of them looked queasy as they stepped from the SpiderCARS and gratefully accepted Mongrel's huge mugs of sweetened tea.

Carter sat down, balancing the MicroNuke across his knees carefully and sipping at the hot and incredibly sweet brew. It was then, from inside the pack, that he detected a barely audible *click*.

The MicroNuke had been primed.

A terrifying thought then occurred to Carter: what if *Durell* detonated the nuke automatically? What if they had used Carter merely as a delivery boy and had decided to cut him out of the loop?

'*Then we're all dead*,' came Kade's crackling laughter.

More and more Spiral agents arrived, until nearly three hundred of them stood in the yard and Carter felt more and more nervous. I feel too much like a pawn, he thought. A fucking victim. And he didn't like that feeling . . . Carter was no victim – Carter was the hunter, the man who called the shots. But not this time . . .

The Priest started to talk, addressing the gathered Spiral operatives who sat on their packs, guns on their laps and brews in their hands. All faces were serious, all demeanours businesslike. Spiral was facing extinction; and they knew it.

'Psst. Carter.'

Carter glanced round to see Mongrel and Simmo beckoning to him. He stood, shouldering the MicroNuke, as the other two ducked down behind a jumble of corrugated metal screens. Carter joined them, crouching and looking at a small active optical screen. 'What is it?' he asked.

'Watch.'

Whatever was sending the signal to Mongrel's screen was airborne, some kind of spy insect relaying back a constant video stream. Carter felt suddenly nauseous as he watched thousands of Nex creeping silently through the surrounding streets. They were accompanied by large Mercedes trucks, TT56 tanks and V3 HTanks – all using stealth mods and exhausts so that they could steal up on the gathering of unsuspecting Spiral soldiers.

'We've only got a few minutes,' said Mongrel softly. 'They're approaching the edge of the blast radius. Rogowski *must* make his move soon.'

'Something occurred to me. What if they remotely detonate the bomb? They don't need Ro for *that*.'

'Shit. Mongrel not think of that!'

'Mongrel!' hissed Simmo, chewing his cigar savagely. 'What now, Sarge?'

'Rogowski trying to do a runner.'

'You sure?'

'Aye, The Sarge never wrong. Look, there is furtive bastard, trying to slime his way out of crowd like a big ol' slug – over there. Come on, let's cut him off.'

Mongrel and Simmo, with Carter close behind, moved around the outskirts of the gathering. Rogowski saw them and stopped. He gave a nasty smile, looked around for another way out, then turned and moved to the only exit available to him – the bolted ladders, leading up the steel-beam towers. From there a brave man could traverse a dangerous, vertigo-inducing network of ancient metal beams – towards the sloping roof of a battered warehouse . . .

Rogowski started to climb.

Mongrel reached the ladders first, followed by Simmo and then Carter. They climbed frantically after Rogowski. All three men were thinking, where the fuck is this madman going? Does he fancy himself as a tightrope walker? But then they heard the distant poundings of a chopper's rotors.

An airlift. 'Bitch,' said Mongrel, panting as he heaved his bulk up rung after rung – a heavy-sweat pursuit of the fleeing Rogowski. As he climbed, he suddenly shouted down, 'Carter, you still got your little toy?'

'I got it,' bellowed Carter.

'Good. We be needing that soon.'

They kept climbing. Below, The Priest's sermon petered to a halt as the Spiral ops turned their collective gaze to the action above them. Several aimed sub-machine guns as they tried to work out just what the hell was happening.

Rogowski slammed his boots onto the level top of a gantry, which swayed a little against its rusted support struts. He levelled his H&K MP5 down through the hole. Mongrel's sweat-stained red face appeared.

'Goodbye, Mongrel,' snarled Rogowski. And pulled the trigger.

There was a dull click. Mongrel threw an overhead punch, which slammed against Rogowski's kneecap with a sickening crack and dropped him, yelping in pain and shock. Rogowski fell backwards, scrambling away as Mongrel, his dark eyes narrowed, hoisted his bulk onto the treacherous gantry. There came a tiny squeal of stressed metal. Again, the gantry swayed.

'Mongrel had thought of removing bullets from your mags,' rumbled the big man, cracking his knuckles as Simmo, and then Carter, appeared behind him.

All three stared at Rogowski with loathing as the traitor backed away.

'Why did you do it?' Carter asked.

Rogowski laughed, a low cackling sound, scrambling even further back to where the metal ledge narrowed to a precarious ten inches in width. He glanced up, searching for his airlift as he licked at lips beaded with sweat.

'You want simple answers, so you can all neatly tie up your fucking loose ends? Well, fuck you. I ain't talking. And your knowledge is irrelevant anyway, because soon you will all be dead.'

Mongrel lifted his weapon and levelled it at Rogowski. The sounds of the chopper were coming close and Simmo turned, directing his own weapon over at the high buildings surrounding the Concrete Arena.

251

'Talk.'

'Fuck you.'

There was a dull *blam* and blood spurted from Rogowski's leg. The man jerked and went white, both hands moving protectively over the wound. Within seconds his hands were covered in pumping crimson liquid.

'Talk,' repeated Mongrel.

'Fuck – you!' snarled Rogowski, his eyes narrowed.

There was a second shot, and this time the bullet smashed through one of Rogowski's knuckles, gouging a furrow through the flesh of his forearm before exiting in a spray of fine red mist. This time, Rogowski screamed.

'Talk, fucker.'

Rogowski started to laugh, blood pumping from the two wounds in time with the pounding of his heart. He tried to shuffle backwards, further down the narrow gantry. It rocked and shook in warning.

'You don't understand!' he hissed, eyes rolling wildly. 'You think I'm the contact? You think I'm the mole inside Spiral? You boys are so fucking predictable . . . I am just the messenger. There is another among you, somebody in direct contact with Durell . . . you just can't see the fucking wood for the trees. You are sitting fucking ducks.'

Mongrel moved forward, his face a grim mask.

'Tell me who!'

'Ahh, to die in ignorance.' Rogowski smiled malevolently through his pain. He checked his blood-smeared watch, his fingers slippery against his own flesh. 'You have forty-five seconds to live. Can't run far in that time, eh, lads?' He stared at Carter. 'Sorry, mate, you were just the pack mule. The carrier. We knew you could get the bomb inside undetected – but you were never trustworthy enough to detonate the damned thing. Not even with your boy's life hanging by a thread. But did I mention that he's dead already? The little bastard will be pushing up the daisies even as we speak – he was slotted with extreme prejudice the minute you left New York.'

'No!' growled Carter.

Mongrel whirled suddenly on his friend. 'He's stalling, Carter. Give me MicroNuke. Give old Mongrel that tick tock ticking bomb.'

Carter unzipped the pack and lifted out the long silver cylinder. There were no LED digits on the warhead – no countdown to indicate the seconds left before detonation. That was just a gizmo for the movies. In the real world such a mechanism had no purpose.

The device was vibrating softly in Carter's calloused hands. He felt fear crawl like a large spider up his spine and neck as he held the embryo of a nuclear explosion in his sweat-slippery grip.

'You are all dead men,' snarled Rogowski, eyes bright with tears that spilled down his cheeks. 'Say your prayers, fuckers – because there is nothing on Earth that can save you now.'

In a huge two-kilometre-wide circle around the munitions depot the Nex had halted. Tanks sat with their engines idling, and thousands of Nex soldiers hunkered down, waiting for the titanic explosion that was to come, their bright copper-eyed stares fixed on what lay up ahead.

Nobody would be allowed to escape the net.

Their single target was the dregs of Spiral.

Their only objective was its total annihilation.

PART TWO

DEUS EX MACHINA

Through me the way is to the city dolent;
Through me the way is to eternal dole;
Through me the way **among the people
lost**.

Justice incited my **sublime Creator**;
Created me divine Omnipotence,
The highest Wisdom and the primal Love.

Before me there were **no created things**,
Only eterne, and I eternal last.
All hope abandon, ye who enter in!

Dante Alighieri
The Divine Comedy: Inferno

CHAPTER 10

DETONATION

Roxi stood in the shadows for nearly an hour.

The underground chamber was huge and dark, its floor stretching away from her like the surface of a concrete ocean. To her left, in a silent gleaming line, stood sixty brand new Volvo trucks, painted in combat colours and with matt-black grilles grinning fiendishly. To her right, beyond a series of mammoth pillars, stretched a range of machines, from 8x8 German Spähpanzer Luchs recon vehicles with ten-cylinder V4 Daimler-Benz engines, to Turkish Otokar APCs sporting old V12 Land Rover engines and roof-mounted 7.62mm MGs. The mish-mash of mothballed vehicles ended with ten HTanks – shrouded in anonymous greased sheeting that did little to disguise their war-machine outlines.

Roxi allowed her breath to ease free from her lungs. She lifted her ECube and it unfolded in her palm like an ancient Chinese puzzle box, alloy leaves unpeeling and sliding noiselessly apart. She rested her gloved right hand on the device and started to trace patterns on its digital pad. The tiny machine vibrated, signalling that there was an electronic shield of invisibility surrounding her, which effectively hid her from all forms of digital movement-detector . . . as long as she was cautious and slow-moving enough to give the ECube time to decode, delete her presence, and re-encode all transmitted files.

Roxi's hand slid down and pressed a concealed button at her hip. There was a whine and then – nothing. She gave a little shiver as her clothing's integrated silver wiring dropped her body temperature, matching it to that of her surroundings. Now she was invisible to thermal scanners, too.

Roxi allowed the ECube to close in her gloved fist. Then she pulled free her 9mm Glock. She checked its magazine, and with her other hand carrying the ECube as if it were some magical artefact which could shield her from evil – which, in a way, it could – she moved slowly out until she was exposed to the scanners. She waited nervously, awaiting a negative and brutal response . . .

Nothing. No alarms were tripped.

The ECube buzzed.

Taking great care, Roxi walked softly down the centre of the huge concrete vehicle-storage warehouse. Reaching the end, she lifted the edge of one of the greased tarpaulins covering the HTanks.

Again, she keyed something into the ECube and it scanned the HTank. Roxi heard several relays thump into place. The HTank was primed and ready to roll.

Suddenly a noise alerted Roxi and she moved behind the HTank, dropping to a crouch. She licked her lips and flicked off the Glock's safety as two Nex walked slowly down the centre of the chamber, gazes sweeping left and right. They disappeared at the far end.

I see security is tight here in New York, thought Roxi sombrely. But then, Durell himself was in the building . . .

She crept along the row of HTanks, then climbed lithely onto the tarpaulin and reached up towards the ceiling. False tiles formed a shallow cavity in which piping and electronics were fitted; Roxi slid a tile free, then climbed up onto the supporting framework above, her slim body bent almost double, and slowly pressed her access tile back into place.

Inside the ceiling now, she worked her way across the frame and squeezed herself into a narrow aperture which opened into one of the many lift chutes that gave access throughout the New York Sentinel HQ. Roxi shone the beam of her Maglite torch down to illuminate gently swaying thick cables and a huge array of gearing mechanisms and powerful electric motors. She glanced up but the beam would only reach so far before the shaft disappeared into darkness.

Roxi holstered her weapon and ECube, took the Maglite in her teeth, and leapt lightly from the shaft's edge. She caught hold of a thick cable, her fingers clamping tight against the heavily greased steel, and began to climb slowly.

Roxi felt the vibrations first. The cable under her gloves began to tremble, then sway gently from side to side. To her left, a few feet down, wheels started to spin. Calmly, she continued to climb. And then it came, hammering down from the darkness above: the huge alloy block of the lift.

Roxi's gaze lifted, focusing in the erratic light of her Maglite on the falling cube. At the last moment she released her grip, kicking herself backwards as she went into a horizontal dive. With outstretched hands she took hold of the struts on the lift's underside and hung on for dear life.

Suddenly, the lift slammed to a halt. Hydraulics cushioned the abrupt stop for the occupants but Roxi, attached to the lift's base, was jerked and shaken roughly. One hand lost its grip.

For a moment, Roxi swung. Then she scrabbled and caught hold again with both hands.

Shit, she wanted to say. But she dared not speak. The Sentinel HQs were riddled with sound detectors as well as surveillance cameras. Anyway, if she'd opened her mouth she'd have dropped the Maglite.

She hung for a while, contemplating her next move. Then the lift clicked with a meshing of gears and started to rise at an incredible rate. Roxi clung on, counting the floors as they passed. She needed Floor 96 but the lift stopped prematurely at 94. Then, after a short pause, it began to descend.

Twice more the lift ascended. Roxi's brain frantically calculated the floor levels as they sped past at an incredible rate. Within minutes her mind was a scramble of confusion and she fought with all her might for clarity. Then, on the next ascent, as she passed – by her calculation – Floor 96 she released her grip on the lift's underside and neatly folded over, hands gripping the undulating cable and legs arcing around to clamp it. She hung for a moment, hair blowing in the updraught in the shaft.

Roxi slid down the cable, her Maglite's beam intermittently illuminating a narrow opening which led in turn to a section of crawl space above Floor 96.

She slowed down and steadied her body against the swaying cable. Then with amazing agility, she leapt from the cable to the ledge. Arms outstretched, she caught hold and then hauled herself up into the confined space. Sweat gleamed on her face and trickled down her spine to make her itch. She took the Maglite from her mouth, switched it off and put it away. Then she licked her lips and pulled out her Glock with fingers that trembled with fatigue.

This is where the fun begins, Roxi thought, smiling grimly. She crouched, listening intently. She waited like this for nearly twenty minutes, then eased free one of the ceiling panels and dropped down. Replacing the panel, she crept along the cool gloomy corridor and crouched by a doorway, once again concentrating.

Three, she thought after long, tense moments. There are three of them in there, as well as the boy Joseph. She could also hear a distant tinkling of water. Using her ECube as a scanner she logged the position of the three Nex guards and then waited for her moment.

It took another few minutes before the ECube reported that it would be safe to enter. Trusting blindly in the technology, Roxi opened the door a fraction on silent hinges and slid inside.

The room was large and bright, as if lit by sunlight from above. Roxi squinted up at an artificial sky scattered with wisps of white cloud. The whole room was a jungle of vegetation: exotic foliage, green plants, purple-leafed creepers, bobbing colourful flowers. Sculpted walkways edged with crushed pink shells and white stone weaved intricate patterns among the greenery, and the air was filled with an extravagantly rich heady fragrance. Accompanying the simulated sun, a synthetic breeze drifted gently through the trees, making their leaves whisper and sigh. Outside, HATE poisoned the reality of nature, so the Nex scientists had now recreated the delights of an organic new world within a controlled environment.

Roxi smelled orange blossom. And jasmine.

261

She slid through shadows and crouched behind a tree. She looked around carefully, searching for the enemy. The sound of running water was louder now, more distinct. She could see a gleam of silver up ahead, shimmering.

Roxi checked her ECube. The three Nex guards were all spread out, and only moved occasionally. They were relaxed, obviously feeling that they were on an easy gig babysitting a five-year-old boy. What possible threat could he pose? And who on earth would be able to infiltrate so far into Sentinel HQ tower? Especially the central New York Sentinel HQ?

Roxi smiled savagely. But then, Durell had his own problems at the moment. The focus was on bringing down Spiral by using their own specialised tool – Carter . . .

Roxi moved carefully around the outskirts of the room. The walls were covered with thick vegetation and she was soon sweating heavily. And then she saw Joseph. He was sitting on a low wall that surrounded a pond into which a silver waterfall tumbled, trailing his hand in the water and staring down at something beneath the rippling surface.

At least there's one benefit of the heat and humidity, Roxi thought to herself, leaping up onto a ledge of loam to avoid treading on a narrow shell pathway.

The heat slowed the Nex down . . .

She checked her ECube again. Up ahead. Directly up ahead.

Roxi glanced in that direction but could see no Nex. Was it disguised? She looked down once more at her ECube, but the machine was dead. With a shiver, Roxi realised that she was on her own . . .

Roxi continued around the room, her Glock ready in her grip. She spent nearly half an hour searching meticulously before she came to the conclusion that, apart from Joe, she was alone in the chamber. There were no Nex present.

Frowning, and with her heart hammering in her chest – she *knew* she was being dicked with in some way; she just couldn't quite figure out how – she approached the boy from one side where he was hidden by a spread of large-leafed palm fronds.

She watched him for a while. By now he was lying down beside the pond. She could see the object of his fascination – Koi carp, a selection of bright colours, silvers and glittering greens and vibrant golds. With a careful glance, she stepped onto the grass and moved towards the young boy. Joe jumped when he saw her, looking around nervously.

Roxi held a finger up to her lips. 'Shh. I'm here to take you home.'

Joe's eyes widened. An uncertain smile flickered across his face but was instantly gone. 'Home?' he said, his voice soft and frightened. Confusion showed on his young features.

Roxi nodded and smiled. 'Carter sent me. Your daddy sent me. To take you away from this place.'

'But what about the Nex?' said Joe.

'We have to be careful. We have to move slowly, and keep our eyes open. We have to avoid the Nex at all costs – there are too many to fight. They are too strong.'

And then Roxi saw the look in Joe's eyes.

'But what about her?' he said, pointing.

Slowly, Roxi turned, her Glock held low. Standing directly ahead of her, holding a Steyr sub-machine gun, was a lithe Nex female of modest stature. She wore a tight body-hugging black uniform and on her feet were soft black boots. Her short dark hair was spiked and bristling,

263

and her oval flawless face was elegant, sculpted and extremely pale-skinned. Her eyes were bright and copper; they showed no emotion.

'My name is Alexis,' said the Nex gently. 'And you are Roxi, a pretty little Spiral agent whom I have been observing for some time. You are good. No, you are exceptional.'

'I have heard of you, Alexis.' Roxi's grin showed most of her teeth. 'Durell's greatest general; reports of your atrocities precede you. Your reputation stinks like hellshit.'

'Please don't flatter me so. To destroy humans is no great atrocity; how could it be when they are too stupid to embrace Nex symbiosis? Now, the whole building has, of course, been alerted to your presence. You have – in effect – been digitally manacled. Throw down your weapon, if you please.'

Roxi hesitated.

'If I shoot now,' said Alexis, 'then there is a high possibility that a bullet will strike the child. Don't be such a fool.' She smiled then, her copper eyes gleaming. 'Don't throw away the life of your lover's little boy. Throw down your gun. Show us what a good girl you can be.'

Roxi dropped her Glock on the grass. It fell with a dull thud.

'I do so enjoy a happy ending,' said Alexis coldly.

'There can be only one of those in this situation,' said Roxi, her body tensed, readying herself for whatever Alexis decided to throw at her – even if that might be death . . .

'Really?' asked Alexis smoothly, eyebrows raised. 'Only one happy ending?'

Carter, Mongrel and Simmo stood on the high gantry. Rogowski, smiling malevolently, watched them as the final seconds ticked away towards the detonation of the MicroNuke – and the final destruction of Spiral.

'Here!' rasped Mongrel.

Carter grunted, passing the heavy cylinder to Mongrel who took the vibrating bomb in his hands and glanced down at it. Then he looked at Rogowski, pulled free his ECube and punched in a complicated sequence.

The ECube opened; then it hummed, and blue lights flickered across its alloy petals. Below the group, near the foot of the steel tower, there came a crackle from the SpiralGRID as the silver outline of a SpiderCAR materialised and hung a few inches above the ground, barely visible.

Then the SpiralGRID . . . illuminated.

A million strands of lightning seemed to spread out from the CAR, arcing and zigzagging in a million different directions. Electricity shimmered through the very air, making everybody sway as sparks and galvanic discharges ran up their legs and arms. But Mongrel ignored this phenomenon as he stepped to the edge of the gantry and with a quick glance down, held the MicroNuke out over the dazzling display.

'What are—' hissed Rogowski, his eyes suddenly wide and confused.

Mongrel allowed the silver warhead to drop. All eyes followed the bomb as it tumbled end over end. Mongrel thumbed his ECube coolly and as the MicroNuke struck the SpiderCAR he initiated the GRID.

There was a pulsating flare of high energy.

And the nuclear bomb had gone.

The Spiral operatives below gave a small cheer, as Mongrel turned his dark gaze back to Rogowski.

'Impossible!' gasped the wounded traitor.

Mongrel winked. '*Niet*. Not *impossible*, just not *likely* for big lump like me to plan so far ahead. You saying, Ro? About us being so unaware?'

Below, the GRID was still crackling.

Rogowski pulled free his own ECube and thumbed the small alloy device – as three kilometres away the SpiralGRID delivered the MicroNuke into the heart of Durell's latest and largest plant combined WarFac and NEP Production Centre. A group of fifteen dumbfounded Nex stared at the silver cylinder rolling noisily across the polished wooden floor towards them. Hands reached for weapons . . .

There was a tiny click. And the MicroNuke detonated.

Carter heard the blast, and averted his gaze as a flash many times brighter than the sun bloomed for an instant on the London horizon. For hundreds of metres surrounding the detonated MicroNuke buildings were suddenly smashed from existence, pulped into a frenzy of crushed concrete, melted metal, incinerated wood, a boiling thrashing composite of base elements and fused flesh. London shook to its stone roots.

A column of dust and smoke rose up into the sky, a micro-mushroom cloud. Beneath their feet tremors rocked the ground in pounding waves and up on the high gantry Carter nearly lost his footing.

Rogowski thumbed his ECube and rolled from the gantry. Below him the SpiralGRID crackled and as Rogowski hit it he was half absorbed, half transmitted on high-energy pulses. As his flesh parted company with itself he was effectively *pulped* instantly. His noodle-like remains slid messily from the silver flicker of the GRID to lie in a pile of slop on the concrete floor.

'We changed access files,' said Mongrel softly, staring down. 'We suspect him for a long while.'

Carter came up beside his old friend. 'Well, at least that fucker's dead.'

Mongrel met Carter's gaze. Carter could see a reflection of nuclear fire in the other's man's dark orbs. 'Yeah, but we not know who real traitor is now. Unless he bluffing.'

'I get the horrible feeling that he was telling the truth,' said Carter. Then he glanced at Simmo, who was chewing his cigar stub and staring with a strange expression at the still-rising cloud. 'I don't trust the bastard; there will be a fail-safe. Another bomb, or some form of back-up close by. Simmo, get the squads searching.'

'Maybe we not have the time,' rumbled Simmo.

'We need to get the hell out of here, then.'

As the three men moved towards the ladder a shout came from below. 'There are Nex advancin' – *thousands* of 'em and you're not going to believe this, lads – they've only gone an' got us fuckin' surrounded.'

The huge chamber at the top of the New York Sentinel HQ tower was dark. At a quick glance it would have appeared empty. Banks of computers glittered softly, and a large black screen shimmered black on black – like a block of obsidian slowly melting into itself.

Something shifted within the darkness. Durell stood with a crackle of spine plates. He moved slowly – as if in great pain – and stared at a single flashing point of blue. Then the blue dot vanished from the screen, which cleared to show a scene of nuclear devastation . . .

Durell frowned. The location was wrong.

'Reports?' he said through strings of saliva.

'WarFac df12 and co-ProC totally destroyed by MicroNuke explosion yield 2.6ktf. Estimated death count: 1,270 Nex, 885 JT8s, 313 civilians awaiting Nex integration.'

267

'Was it . . .' Durell cleared his throat. 'Was this the device destined for the Spiral outfit?'

'Affirmative.'

Durell pushed a button at the base of the plasma screen and started out over the dark night sky of New York. Below, the world was still and peaceful. No violence, no warfare; an oasis of calm. Durell smiled. *It didn't feel right.*

Alexis arrived and stared inquisitively into Durell's face. 'We have a problem?'

'We have a problem. It would seem that our little plan – to destroy Spiral and the GRID with one swift crushing blow – has effectively been turned against us.'

'Carter didn't deliver the bomb?'

'He delivered it, all right. Straight into our major UK WarFac.'

'What would you have me do?' said Alexis coldly.

'Kill the boy.' There was a momentary pause. Then Alexis hoisted her 9mm TMP, spun on her heel and strode from the room.

Durell stared out over the destroyed cityscape of New York.

'Why won't you join us, Mr Carter?' whispered Durell, clawed fist drawing tight. 'Why won't you join us when you are, effectively, a splinter of our clan?' I don't want to kill you, Carter, he thought.

Don't you understand? I do *not* want to kill you.

The orders came – in a digital moment.

As one, the Nex army rose from their cover and started to move slowly through the streets – a huge black swathe of lithe killers, heavily armed and backed with tanks. Tracks crushed stones, rolled over the detritus of the ancient world – rusting old SmutCars, battered parking meters, twisted alloy chairs. Engines revved, pluming LVA exhaust into the air. In the distance, the sounds of chopper engines carried through the air.

As the Nex walked through the ruins of London, they checked gun magazines, hoisted weapons high, and looked around with emotionless copper eyes.

Carter stood beside the remains of Rogowski. All around him the Spiral operatives were checking weapons and several groups were searching through surrounding rooms, cabins and between huge heaps of metal scrap. The whole area was a hive of activity.

Simmo strode over; he slotted a mag into his H&K with a precise click. 'Reminds The Sarge of a particularly fine tagliatelle he once had.'

'Hmm?'

Simmo nudged the remains of Rogowski with his boot. 'Ham and mushroom. Heavy on the tomatoes and cream. A fine dish, if a bit on the rich side.'

'What actually happened to him?'

Simmo shrugged his shoulders. 'Dumb bastard jumped in mid-shift. It took several strips of him in the same direction as the warhead; left about half of him here. You could say he a paid-up subscriber to VHF now, eh, Carter?' He gave a booming laugh, and relit the stump of his cigar.

Plumes of blue smoke engulfed Carter. 'I never would have thought it of Rogowski.'

Simmo frowned. '*You* would never have thought it? Carter, I fought fifty-eight missions with that man. He was unflappable. He was a professional soldier. He was as hard as heat-tempered nails – no, harder. He could hammer nails through six-inch floor joists with the palm of his hand. If you had asked The Sarge to point out possible traitors, he would have shot that damned *Priest* before he picked out Rogowski as turncoat.' Simmo sighed, shaking his huge head. 'Carter – if Ro was one of them, then I can no longer trust *anybody* within Spiral's ranks. And that the honest truth, laddie boy.'

Carter nodded. He understood Simmo's sentiments exactly.

Mongrel came pounding over, face red with exertion. 'Right, lads, got problems. There fucking *thousands* of Nex closing in – we have maybe three minutes before arrival. They got tanks, choppers, the lot. But there is tunnel escape, so we can slink off out of here – too risky to use SpiralGRID at this moment, Mongrel thinking. But worse than this, Rogowski did have back-up plan – he has planted another bomb. An ECube shell picked up tracers, but it using electronic fibrillation – we can't pinpoint it.'

Gunfire erupted to one side and an enemy chopper swept overhead, its low drone reverberating from the concrete walls.

'You said three minutes?' said Carter.

'Make that zero minutes,' corrected Mongrel sheepishly.

The three men sprinted across the concrete yard; machine-gun fire rattled, and several screams sounded from nearby. Mongrel dragged Carter to a halt. 'Down there.' The huge East European squaddie pointed. He grinned a gappy grin. 'Just follow the fleeing Spiral men . . .'

'Where are *you* going?'

'To save the GRID.'

'I'm with you,' said Carter.

'Me too,' growled Simmo.

Mongrel clapped the two men on the shoulders. His face twisted, as if he was sucking on a lemon. 'By God, you is fine fellows to die with! Come on!' They ran, ducking under a bank of low galvanised pipes, several of which were leaking steam. They emerged into a low-ceilinged room stinking of dead rats and damp and mould. More gunfire erupted out in the concrete yard as a Spiral rearguard opened up with mounted Browning heavy machine guns to allow their comrades to escape.

Mongrel led Carter and Simmo through a complicated maze of old warehouses, storage rooms and ancient workshops, floors still stained with the sludge of antique blackened oil, battered and chipped engineering mills and the curls of aged steel shavings.

They halted, chests heaving and sweat dripping into eyes, in a quadrangle that was open to the air and surrounded by ancient grooved steel benches. Mongrel peered up, searching for more choppers. Sporadic machine-gun fire was still rattling in the distance.

'They pissed off we nuke their WarFac, you think?'

'They pissed off.' Simmo nodded, hefting his H&K. He peered at Mongrel. 'You taking us to the HUB?'

'Yes. Look like Ro got there before us. We must find his secondary bomb – and that would be logical place. I confused how he manage to get past security!'

'Why did he not detonate it earlier?' asked Simmo. 'He could have destroyed the HUB without Carter acting as a pack mule for the MicroNuke.'

Carter gave a cold smile. 'He wanted to take *all* of you out. Not just the GRID, but the majority of Spiral as well. The MicroNuke would accomplish that – and if it didn't work? Well, this was Plan B.'

They moved warily across the quadrangle and into a small workshop. Pipes criss-crossed overhead, and the

271

walls were lined with benches, many with tiny, intricate-looking engine parts lined up on their surfaces.

At the centre of the room there were several huge metal grates, with alloy loop handles attached, set into the floor. Mongrel and Simmo, grunting, swung the central one into the air, showering dust all around. The three Spiral men looked down onto – the SpiralGRID HUB.

It was about the size of a small car and seemed to be wrapped in thick black polythene.

'Is that it?' grunted Carter.

'Is brain, not face of fucking supermodel,' snapped Mongrel. Then his eyes widened. 'Shit. There.' He pointed to the small black case attached to the side of the HUB. 'Alien artefact.'

'It has gyroscopic floats,' said Simmo, puffing on his cigar. The huge sergeant dropped to his knees and peered close. 'Also has K12 alloy permeable casing. I can get the cover off – looks like basic HighJ payload.' The Sarge removed his jacket and stood bare-chested, muscles rippling. Outside, in the quadrangle, snow started to fall once more.

'That'll slow down the choppers.'

'But not the infantry,' growled Carter as five Nex appeared. Carter's weapon bucked in his hands and bullets hurtled from the workshop's doorway. Two Nex were hammered from their feet, and the rest retreated under covering fire. Ancient blackened brickwork shattered and Carter ducked back, slamming shut the thick steel door with his boot. He peered through the grimy windows.

'Not good,' said Mongrel.

'Just buy me some time! The Sarge sort this out in a jiffy.' Simmo had produced a small leather case and removed several small tools. He dropped to his belly and reached over the side of the pit containing the plastic-sheeted HUB.

'You good at this?' asked Carter, his gaze searching warily for more Nex.

'Ten years in bomb squad,' said Simmo, blue cigar smoke pluming up from the HUB's supporting chassis struts. His voice was calm, soothing. He threw something behind him which clattered. Carter and Mongrel stared down at a battered length of casing. Then they moved to crouch at opposite sides of the window.

More Nex appeared, firing as they came. Carter and Mongrel shot through the glass, their bullets flying across the quadrangle to kick tiny showers of powdered red dust from ancient brickwork.

'You got some 15q snub-nosed pliers?' came Simmo's disembodied voice.

'No.'

'We've got two minutes before this baby blows.'

'Ahh.'

'Rogowski should have detonated this in the first place!' muttered Mongrel.

'Yeah, well, he wanted to preserve his place in Spiral to the end,' said Carter. 'Make sure we were all dead and buried, the traitorous piece of shit.'

'Damn and bloody bollocks,' cursed The Sarge from the pit.

Mongrel fired off a full magazine across the quadrangle. They could hear choppers circling through the falling snow.

'What is it?' Carter moved across to crouch beside Simmo. Sweat was dripping from the huge man's forehead, running across his facial tattoos and making the tattoo script at his throat gleam.

'Negative wiring. I seen this before, a long time ago. So

273

has Rogowski. He knew I might try this; he trying to trick me.'

'And has he?'

'No!'

Simmo grinned, and snipped a green wire. There was a barely audible blip as some connection was triggered.

'Was that good?' asked Carter slowly. Then he saw Simmo's eyes, and he knew that it was *not* good. In fact, it was as far from fucking good as it could ever be.

'Ha, ha, lads. Simmo have little problem here.'

Mongrel moved to Simmo's prostrate form. 'What is it?'

The thumping of rotors was getting louder. Suddenly, a hail of mini-gun bullets pounded through the steel-sheeting roof ten metres to the group's right, making it rattle and dance.

There was an awful heart-stopping pause. More bullets hammered from across the quadrangle. 'They corner us,' spat Mongrel.

'What's wrong, Sarge?' said Carter quietly, coolly. He could hear the scything whine of engines far above. A chopper was coming around for a second sweep.

'I cut wire. Rogowski pulled double bluff on me. Bastard. Simmo now acting as a circuit bridge. If I let go, the whole fucking lot detonate – and we'll go with it.'

'How can we bridge it and get you away?' said Carter.

'We cannot.'

'You sure?'

Simmo met Carter's gaze, and Carter saw that there was peace there. A final, chilling peace.

'I am sure, my friend.'

Another stream of bullets exploded through the roof, smashing a line across the floor. Several hummed past Carter's face and he threw himself down, cursing foully.

'Simmo!' hissed Mongrel.

Pinned in place, unable to leave the bomb circuit, Simmo had taken three rounds: one in the back of a shoulder blade and two bullets that had flattened on ricochet, one striking just above his kidneys and the other near his spine.

Simmo, however, showed no signs of pain. He lay, blood flowing from his three wounds, cigar stump still clamped between his teeth. His head turned and his dark-eyed stare met Mongrel's, and then Carter's.

'Get out of here,' he growled, chewing his cigar.

'We can't leave you,' said Carter.

More bullets roared outside, and Mongrel shot off another full magazine in response. He swapped mags swiftly, letting the empty one fall clattering against the floor tiles.

Snow was settling across Simmo's shaved head, carried in through the holes in the bullet-riddled roof.

'You will,' said Simmo calmly. 'Simmo here hold the fortress, you be sure.'

'We not let you do that, *pizda*,' snapped Mongrel. 'We love you too much, grumpy old bastard that you is! Just tell us how bridge the circuit, *dolboy'eb*!'

'Can't do that.' Simmo reached over, grabbed back his H&K from Carter, then hefted the weapon thoughtfully. 'Get the fuck out of here, you buggers, before I shoot you myself!' He coughed then, and Carter saw the blood staining his teeth. 'Go on! You only have a minute – then we are all dog meat!'

Carter and Mongrel stared uncertainly at one another.

'So much for rescuing the HUB!' snorted Mongrel.

'Fuck the HUB,' snarled Carter. 'Simmo, let go of the circuit – we'll take our chances. Maybe Rogowski was bluffing you again. Thought he'd take you out with his final blast . . .'

'That noise was a terminal cut-in,' said Simmo slowly. 'You not bluff that kind of thing. It *integral*. But The Sarge *do* have one final request for you.'

'Anything,' said Carter.

'Light my cigar, there's a good lad.'

Carter and Mongrel sprinted out through a low doorway as Nex came pouring across the quadrangle and into the workshop where Simmo let fly with his H&K until he ran out of ammo.

Bullets smashed into Simmo's twitching body and his blood flooded across the tiled floor.

And between plumes of blue cigar smoke his teeth gritted in a tight nasty smile as his fingers twitched in a shaking spasm – and cut the connection to the bomb.

HighJ fury blasted the HUB and pulverised Simmo's bleeding body and the bodies of thirty attacking Nex soldiers. Nanoseconds later it ripped the roof from the workshop and melted stone and flesh alike in a massive eruption of purple fire.

There came a click, then a soft whine.
And the whole of the SpiralGRID closed down.

Sonia could feel herself shivering under the multiple darkhole eyes of the guns. She calmed her breathing, creating a steady pulse which soothed her mind, body and soul. Yes, she was going to die. So at last the pain – and the struggle – would be over.

The baying noise of the crowd in the execution yard faded. Gone were the shouted questions of the press, gone was the annoying sound of Judge Ronald's irritating voice.

All faded into a hissing white noise . . .

The ten Nex, dark-clad, emotionless, lifted their

13mm NailGuns. They were huge, brutal weapons, quite cumbersome and impractical in a battle situation where their weight made them more of a liability than an asset. But they were ideal for the purposes of execution: nobody was shooting back then, and their massive stopping power made damned sure that the target wasn't going to get up.

Judge Ronald Hamburger's voice echoed tinnily over a tannoy.

'Prepare for the execution!'

The crowd cheered.

'Firing squad, check your weapons!'

The crowd brayed.

'Firing squad, safety switches off!'

The crowd *roared*.

'Firing squad . . . fire!'

The ten NailGuns coughed, bucking in the gloved hands of the masked firing squad. Nails shot from the dark-eye muzzles but the solid streams of metal roared not towards Sonia J but at – the crowd.

The gathered paparazzi, cameras and microphones at the ready, were scythed like wheat under a glittering black blade, ripped asunder to lie dying and dead, torn into strips of raw bloody flesh. And Judge Ronald Hamburger, who had turned to flee as the Nex firing squad turned its guns on the watching people crammed into the execution yard, was shot brutally in the back as he put on an excellent arm-pumping example of a sprint towards the exit.

The huge guns stuttered to a halt and a terrible silence filled the yard that now reeked of cordite. Groans arose from heaps of bodies as blood pooled and trickled through kill channels which had drained away the life of thousands of previous execution victims.

Slowly, Sonia J opened her eyes. Her nostrils twitched at the gun smoke. 'Jesus Christ,' she whispered as she surveyed the carnage: the twitching bodies, the pools of blood glistening under cold skies.

The Nex turned towards her at the sound of her voice. 'Are you going to kill me now?' she whispered.

Before any of the Nex could speak, there was a blast of HighJ explosive and a huge hole appeared in the wall of the execution yard. Massive chunks of concrete spat outwards, scattering across the ground and leaving a portal to freedom . . .

Suddenly, gloved hands were on Sonia's arm. 'This way, Miss J.'

'Why didn't you kill me?' she asked softly.

The Nex looked down with cold copper eyes. 'We are part of your organisation, Miss J. We are a part of the REBS. Now, if you please, this way – quickly. It will only be moments before Nex soldiers arrive – *other* Nex soldiers – with helicopters and tanks.'

Sonia was led to the smoking remains of the wall and ducked through the jagged portal. A sleek alloy Manta Trans-G was waiting, its engines hissing softly, on the square beyond. The group clambered up the recessed steps into the small fighter's hold and slipped their hands through restraining straps. A Trans-G was commonly used for fast infiltration, for the placement of troops behind enemy lines, and for the drop-off of special-force squads. In this case, it was being used as an escape module.

The Manta's engine howled as the craft lifted vertically. Suddenly, Nex poured from the breach in the execution yard's wall, guns yammering in gloved hands.

The Manta banked and lifted with amazing agility, easily escaping the hostile Nex bullets.

Inside the Manta, Sonia J had gone white. 'Thank God,' she said, shaking her head as sobs racked her body, a release of the suppressed emotions that she had been holding tight.

Carter and Mongrel had their heads down, sprinting hard as the explosion rocked the very ground under their boots. They skidded to a halt on the snow, glancing back – and then at one another.

'He can't be dead,' growled Mongrel.

'We all die,' said Carter.

'Not Simmo! It not in his nature.'

'We all die,' repeated Carter. His eyes glazed for a moment as distant memories threatened to overwhelm him. Then he slammed his hand against Mongrel's back. 'Come on, or we'll be the next monkeys to shuffle off our mortal coil.'

'The only coil *I* willing to shuffle off is coil up whore's *pizda*! Come on, Carter, this way down arse-tight alleyway.' Mongrel turned right, and they pounded down a narrow brick tunnel which stank so badly of rats that Carter held his breath as he ran. Swarms of slick vermin scattered out of his way, darting along ancient cracked gutters as the two men stampeded past. Several filthy rodents stopped to watch with glittering dark eyes.

Mongrel led Carter down a flight of steps into an old basement, and within minutes they were working their way through a series of underground tunnels packed full of battered galvanised pipes, pitted with rust, many of them broken and leaking streamers of slime to the black concrete floor.

After ten minutes of struggling through the subterranean chambers and narrow shafts, Carter, who at this point was hauling himself up onto a ledge covered with orange slime, finally muttered, 'Where exactly are we going, Mongrel? This is some fucking escape route, my friend.'

'There thousands of Nex waiting for us out there,' said Mongrel, one hand clamping hold of Carter's wrist and helping to haul his friend up. 'And now GRID is down – we fucked, Carter, we fucked bad. I think we go and pick up your Comanche, yes? We have secret rendezvous LZ set up – way outside London. All the DemolSquads have instructions to head there in case of bad shit going down. London too hot now for missions; just too dangerous.'

'You mean we're running away?'

'We regroup,' said Mongrel gently. He looked down into the part-flooded chamber from which they had just emerged. In the black water, streaked with glimmers of oil, rats with glossy spiked coats glided. 'They broke our back, Carter, despite our efforts. Just like man stomping on rat. We need get out of this shit hole, we re-form, we gather strength together; then we attack one last time.' Mongrel nodded to himself.

Mongrel's ECube buzzed. He fished out the small alloy device from his heavy combat clothing and keyed in a code. Then he spoke into the device. 'Yeah?'

'It's Roxi. I got the child.'

Mongrel's face broke into a beaming, toothless smile. 'Well done, that girl! You come up against much bad fight in NY? Was it tough-fuck gig?'

'Yeah, real tough. But nothing I couldn't handle. The GRID's down, Mongrel – what happened there?'

'We got shafted. Severely. From above.'

'Jesus, the minute a girl turns her back! Tell Carter that I have his boy, and that he's fine. Just a little shaken up. I assume we're going to RV at Code3?'

'Yes.'

'See you soon, Mongrel.'

'Be good, Rox. And be careful. Mongrel have big sloppy kiss waiting for you when you get back! And you not want to miss out on *that* treat! Out.' Mongrel pocketed the ECube, then grinned at Carter. 'She got him. I knew she would.'

Carter's smile was wary. 'I'll believe it when I see it. No good getting too excited; every time that happens, I end up having to kill somebody who gets in my way. And there's nothing I hate more than shooting somebody I like in the face.'

'Not this time, Carter. You trust old Mongrel.'

'Like we trusted Rogowski?'

Mongrel snorted. 'That fucker now sausage meat. He get what he deserve; Mongrel think he bluffing about being just messenger. He just playing old mind-o games with our heads.'

'Who's to say what motivates somebody to turn against everything they have ever fought for in the past? Everything they have ever loved? One thing is for sure, though – the world today has changed beyond all recognition. I wish I could share your optimism, Mongrel. I really wish I could.'

Mongrel gave Carter a strange smile in the gloom of the stinking underground chamber. Below, two rats were squealing as they fought over a small, bobbing item.

'When something's eating you, Carter, when something's chewing you from inside – then you learn to look at real values in life. Har! I am tick-tocking worse than any bomb now; and it bad because I *know* I not halt the detonation – no matter what I do. I as dead as Simmo, Carter. The cancer, it worming through me like parasite; my death is only matter of time.'

Carter placed his hand on Mongrel's broad powerful shoulder. 'You're a good man, Mongrel. You're a *strong* man. We'll find a way for you to fight this thing.'

Mongrel nodded, smiling a sardonic smile. 'Enough

morbid talk. We got places to go, people to meet, ladies to woo. And an old Spiral Comanche to steal.'

'Ladies to woo?' Carter stared at the hulking toothless man. 'God Mongrel, can't even the guaranteed prospect of death rein in your rabid lust?'

'The cancer? Ha! Not even fucking HTank on head stop this squaddie with romantic inc— incli— hard-on.'

Carter grinned savagely. 'Where are we going?'

'To Code3. In Scotland.'

'The mountains?'

'Yes, Carter. We going back to the mountains.'

The Comanche swept down through the falling snow, with Oban and the silver glittering waters of Loch Linnhe to the far west and a huge strung-out vista of mountains appearing through the blizzard. The helicopter banked, engines humming and rotors thumping as they bore east and then flew up through Glen Coe – following the desolate A82 highway with mountains rearing either side of the snowdrift-buried road. Carter peered out from the cockpit as feelings raged through his heart and soul. Below and to either side lay his world.

Carter had finally come home.

It had not been hard to reclaim the abandoned Comanche. The area where Carter had originally landed had been deserted. There had been no Nex, no civilians . . . London had seemed almost like a ghost town. With heavy weaponry drawn and ready, Mongrel had muttered something nasty about the Nex being drafted in to hunt down the remains of Spiral.

'You're doing well for such an amateur pilot,' said Carter, glancing over towards the insect-like HIDSS.

Mongrel grunted something unintelligible from his entombment in the black helmet. His gaze was intent on scanners and the awesome view from the cockpit. They dropped towards the Munros, dropping down over sprawls of snow-clad conifer forests to the south of Fort William and flying low to follow the River Nevis before Mongrel brought the combat helicopter around to sweep up and over Sgorr Chalum. Then the massive bulk of Ben Nevis towered ahead. They flew on, over the lower green and white-peppered flanks towards the stone summits of The Ben.

Carter peered out at the daunting lump of rock. He smiled, a smile of understanding. The mountain had treated him well all these years, had pushed him to his limits during the seven winter runs which had forced him to the limit of his physical abilities – but, ultimately, despite the pain, she had never once sought vengeance. The Ben was unforgiving. The Ben was merciless. But she and Carter, well, they had an understanding.

The Comanche howled up past steep slopes of scattered grey stone, pitted and hollowed like the surface of the moon, and rimed with a crust of frozen ice. They skimmed over the summit plateau, the old crumbling observatory flashing past as the awesome views spread out ahead of them.

'Nice place,' muttered Mongrel.

'Nice? *Nice*? You are the fucking master of understatement, Mongrel, you stinking old goat. Did you see Devil's Ridge down there? Or the Observatory, or the Tower Gap? No, of course you didn't because your eyes are jaded – you are a fucking city heathen. A pub-whore piss-artist.'

'Ha, I agree, this old soldier prefer kebab house to nasty fresh air of such places. But I concede: this has desolate feeling to it, feeling of freedom which growing in Mongrel's crusty old soul. I have had enough of city, I spit on city. Durell has cursed my playground with Nex and death. No more one-legged whores for Mongrel!'

'One-legged . . . let me guess. It's a long story, right?'

'Aye, Carter, you catch on quick, lad. Is long, long story. I tell you some time . . . before I die.'

Carter watched the terrain flashing below them, and within minutes Mongrel slammed the Comanche into a vertical landing. Its engines roared as the combat helicopter fell between steep-sloping walls of ice-jewelled stone and touched down, suspension groaning, cooling engines clicking. Carter jumped out as the rotors thumped above him. Cold air slammed his face, snow tried to settle on his eyelashes, and he grinned a wide boyish grin.

He breathed deep.

The cold mountain air smelled *good*. Like no other air on Earth.

Gathered on this mountain plateau, in a carved scoop hidden neatly between the rearing savage peaks from which flurries of snow drifted and swirled, there were perhaps twenty aircraft. All piloted by Spiral operatives; all hijacked by the remnants of the DemolSquads.

Mongrel dropped the HIDSS, scrambled out and stood on the rocky plateau, sniffing, face twisted into a frown. He glanced around at the other choppers and three Manta fighters, and then put his huge shovel hands on his bulging hips.

'What's the matter?' said Carter.

'This place smell funny.'

'It's called *fresh air*, Mongrel.'

'Ahh? Ahh! That what it is. I not used to breathing something without the old biological or chemical pollution. Look, there Simmo's Manta!' But then the smile dropped from his face. 'Oh,' he said. 'Shit. It take the

Mongrel a long time get used to the Big Man being gone.'
He sighed, eyes distant and nostalgic. 'You know, he used
to have big green Land Rover, huge hulking piece of battered garbage, ergonomic as brick, heavy as tank, blowing
and honking its stinking burnt-fish-oil fumes all over
damned airfield like worst of torque-raped engines. We
used to call it his Land *Reaper* – witty play on *Grim
Reaper.*'

'Yeah, Mongrel, I get it.'

'Well, Simmo fucking *obsessed* with his big green anvil
on wheels. We used to mock him without stop, used to say
his Lanny was like sitting in your armchair and driving
your house! Oh! how we roared with laughter, mocking
his 4x4 caravan, but the old Sarge, no, he not think this
one bit funny. Oh no, lost his sense of humour over the
lads' quips about his battered fish-stinking Lanny. Used to
get old beardy scowl on his jowls and wander off to the
NAAFI muttering about SU carburettors and rotational
pistons and the ease of draining gearbox oil. He a proper
Lanny freak. But I . . . I—' He beamed proudly. '*I* was
privileged to share cups of Horlicks with Sarge. We swap
old war stories, tales of adventure, told around roaring log
fires with our B&S spoons raised in salute . . . as the
squaddies let down the tyres on his cheese-stinking
machine. *Ahhhh!* Those was the days. Happy, happy
days.'

'Now he's gone,' said Carter softly. 'Killed by the Nex.'

Mongrel's eyes had filled with tears. Now they glistened with a harsher light. 'Yes,' he growled, nodding.
'Gone. Dead. I wish I could bring him back, Carter, I
really do. Now the Nex, they will suffer, I think. They will
pay the price – I send them bill from muzzle of my
machine gun.'

Thus Mongrel lamented the passing of his great friend.

'Come on,' said Carter eventually, turning up the collar on his jacket as the wind fought to get next to his skin. 'Lead the way. We've some tough decisions to make.'

Mongrel's boots thumped across the plateau rock and the two men jumped down into a narrow gully that was ankle-deep in crushed ice. With crackling footsteps, slipping and sliding, they made their way to the small arched entrance, to the tunnel that led into the depths of the mountains.

As Carter stooped to enter the dark, ice-glittering passageway, he glanced back at the rocky trail leading up over to the distant summit of Ben Nevis. Then, flicking on the narrow beam of his powerful Maglite, he shouldered his pack and followed Mongrel into the waiting darkness beyond.

It was an hour later, and the underground cavern was crowded. The Priest sat by a roaring fire and across from him squatted Carter, oiling his Browning and checking its magazines. Mongrel was stirring a huge pan of B&S over the flames, and around the room many Spiral ops had got their heads down in bivvy bags, or were sitting talking in small groups and holding steaming mugs of tea. Carter looked around as he worked slowly and carefully; it was a wise man who took the time for precision care of his gun.

AnnaMarie, Kavanagh and Remic were all there, looking older and more grizzled than he remembered them. His gaze passed over the weary faces of Rekalavich, Haggis, Fegs, Russian, Dublin, Legs, 9mm, Gemmell, Kinnane, Oz, Ian 'Elton' Pickles, Root Beer, Mrs Sheep and Samasuwo, who looked more like a sumo wrestler with every passing day.

Mongrel suddenly frowned and fished out his ECube. It was rattling in his huge hand and he keyed a control on its alloy surface. He read the text.

'What is it?'

'Roxi will be here soon. With your boy.'

'Brilliant.'

'And there's more.'

'More?'

'We've got visitors. Roxi says the REBS are coming, Carter. They're coming here and they're coming to pay their respects.'

'Dad!'

Joe sprinted across the rocky floor and fell into Carter's arms. Carter nuzzled the boy, and his tears fell into Joe's short hair. Suddenly, everything was right in the world.

'You OK?'

'Yes dad.' Joe looked up then and Carter could see Natasha in his son's face. He felt his heart skip a beat.

'They didn't hurt you?'

'No, dad. The nice lady, Alexis, she looked after me. I was scared. She brought me things. Toys. She spent time with me. She was kind.'

Carter frowned. 'She was? I didn't realise the Nex could be so . . . caring.'

Carter's gaze shifted from his son to the lithe figure standing close behind. She carried an H&K sub-machine gun balanced on her hip. Her green eyes twinkled.

'Thank you, Rox. I don't think I'll ever be able to repay you.'

'It was my pleasure, Carter.' Her voice was low and thick with emotion.

Mongrel ambled over, waving his huge wooden spoon. 'You two lovebirds need some scram?'

'B&S?' moaned Carter. 'Couldn't you have been a bit more adventurous?'

Mongrel shrugged. 'Don't like that foreign muck. All sea grass and peppers and herbs and shit. Mongrel like real food for real man! I have hard-on for damned B&S!'

His huge head turned suddenly to Roxi. 'You say REBS coming here? Why so? Our paths have not often crossed; our goals have never been the same, I thinking.'

'Our objectives *have* been the same,' said Roxi, her hand dropping to rest against the small of Carter's back. 'Only the top dogs in Spiral never chose to amalgamate. Well, now the REBS are broken – and *we* are broken. I think the only way we have a chance is to combine our forces. The only way to win is to merge. To blend – like the Nex.'

'Win?' Carter laughed then. 'That is a word I haven't heard for a long time. I think *survival* is more the order of the day now. We are not in a position to win. We have neither the manpower, the technology nor the weaponry. To overthrow Durell – well, we would need a miracle.'

'Let's see what the REBS have to say,' Mongrel rumbled. 'Now come and get some B&S down you. You'll need your strength.'

Carter, taking Joe's hand, led him across to the large pan of red gloop. 'We'll need our strength, but we won't need any more damned roughage, that's for certain. Look at that, you're burning it around the edges! Give it a stir! Mongrel, man, learn to cook!'

Mongrel grinned bitterly. 'I wish I had time, Carter, I really do. Let's see what goes down . . . hell, after tomorrow it might not matter anyway. We living on borrowed time, my friend. Borrowed time.'

'For everything there is a season! And a time for every matter under heaven; a time to be born, and a time to die; a time to plant, and a time to pluck up what is planted!

288

And yea, Durell is in dire need of a serious uprooting!'

The Priest strode across the cavern, sandals slapping against the damp stone, rosary beads rattling across his hairy chest. His beard was filled with breadcrumbs and stained with wine, and in one hand he carried a modern day Sterling sub-machine gun.

Behind him came two figures. One was a woman, with shoulder-length blonde hair and pale blue eyes. She wore black combat fatigues and a tight black jumper. The line of her compressed mouth hinted at untold horrors in her recent past. The second figure was a huge man with fists like sacks of marbles; he had a huge black beard flecked with grey, and his shaggy dark hair showed silver at the temples. His nose was hooked slightly, and his skin was dark, making him look distinctly Arabic. His stance was that of a protector and he stayed close to the woman, shielding her with his huge frame.

The group halted.

'Hey!' cried Mongrel. 'You that bird off TV! One who always shows her . . . her . . .'

Carter placed his hand on Mongrel's shoulder. He nodded towards The Priest. 'You been busy, you religious nutter? Of course you have. And you two are part of the REBS?'

'Yes.' Sonia smiled then, a dry smile. 'We've come with a proposal. The REBS' back is broken; Spiral are doomed without their GRID. The REBS think it is time that we joined forces, before it is too late for all of us.'

'Even together we cannot take out Durell.'

'We have to,' said Sonia softly. 'Because I know his plans.' She glanced at The Priest, whose hulking figure was hunched, dark brown eyes hooded with weariness and a hint of defeat. 'We both know his plans.'

'What are they?' rumbled Mongrel.

'He is going to spread EDEN across the globe. He's going to evacuate the Nex and the people who want to be Nex to his ChainStations in orbit around the Earth; then he's going to spread EDEN using a barrage of intercontinental warheads.'

'I thought EDEN was a cure? I thought it was going to neutralise the toxins of the HATE virus?'

'No,' said Sonia. 'EDEN is the most deadly poison ever created. It will effectively wipe out every man, woman and child on the planet. Durell plans a genocide. No, more. Durell plans to eradicate the entire human race.'

'What can we do?' said Mongrel.

They were all seated around the fire, which crackled softly, golden embers glowing in a hearth of charcoal. The whole of the Spiral gathering – those DemolSquad unit commanders who still remained – had congregated in a circle around The Priest, Carter, Mongrel, Sonia J and Baze. The mood was grim indeed.

The Priest sighed. Then his head came up and his gold-flecked eyes surveyed the group. 'We are broken. We are smashed. Spiral and REBS will pool their resources, put aside their historical differences. Without the GRID we are effectively crippled. Now our only recourse is to the EC Warhead . . .'

'A myth,' said Mongrel.

'A reality,' said The Priest gravely. 'Durell plans to kill everything on Earth. Every form of life will be extinguished to make way for a new Nex realm. A planet free of insurrection. A new and advanced breed of humanity. We need to find the Evolution Class Warhead, my friends . . . and we need to launch it against Durell. It will destroy his WarFacs, destroy his NEP Production Plants –

290

and it will destroy his ChainStations. It is the only weapon on the globe with such capabilities . . . Without his ChainStations Durell cannot evacuate the planet. Without them, he dare not unleash EDEN.'

'How we do this?' rumbled Mongrel.

'We have two objectives,' said The Priest. His gaze swept the group, and all he saw there was strength. A readiness to lay down their lives for the good of the world; and the good of their species. This was a fight for survival of life on Earth. 'The first objective is an infiltration. We must break into the Nex central K-Labs – to confirm our fears that EDEN *is* this terrible poison that we suspect. We need to know when and where Durell plans to launch it. And we need to destroy the K-Labs and any stocks of EDEN we discover – smash their technology ladder, if we can. Or at least buy ourselves time to find the ECW.'

'And secondly?' asked Carter, a cigarette balanced between his lips, eyes squinting as the smoke stung his eyes.

'There is a man who knows where the Evolution Class Warhead programmers are – the ones who still live, from before the days of Durell's dominance. They will know the exact whereabouts of the EC Warhead – and the codes needed to activate the weapon and to target multiple destinations. Without the programmers, we can't find and launch the EC Warhead. And without our informant, we can't find the programmers.'

'Who he?' asked Mongrel.

'His name is Justus, and he is being held in a high security Nex prison – at the Submarine Graveyard. Deep under the North Atlantic Ocean.'

'Great,' muttered Carter. 'Things are looking just rosy, hey?'

'It gets better,' said The Priest, his eyes twinkling. 'Our

intel informs us that we have forty-eight hours. Before the Nex are Drag-lifted from Earth and the bombing begins.'

'So we have a race to see who can launch first?'

'Precisely.'

Carter frowned. 'Call me cynical, but we've been mis-fed information before. How do we know this is the truth and not a crock of shit? How do we know we're not just being set up once more? Another deception designed to eliminate the remains of both Spiral and REBS once and for all?'

'Ask her,' gestured The Priest.

Carter turned to look at Sonia J. 'You're the head of the REBS, right?'

Sonia shook her head. 'Wrong. I'm the decoy. I'm too high-profile to head the REBS, although Durell and Mace and his other cronies made that same false assumption. They thought I was the big boss – the lady in charge.'

'Why should we trust you, then? And how does your head honcho come by such inside information? I'm pretty sure Durell doesn't just leave disks labelled "Plans for World Domination" lying around.'

'You can ask our leader himself when he arrives. He will answer all of your questions.'

'Do I know him?' Carter's eyes were glittering in the light of the fire.

Sonia J met his gaze. She nodded then, smiling gently. 'Yeah, you know him, Carter. He is your oldest friend.'

'Oldest friend?' Carter frowned again.

'His name is Jam.'

CHAPTER 11

PRISON TOMB

REWIND >>> The noise intensified around Jam as the earthquake reached its climax. He fell, bleeding, with clawed ScorpNex hands reaching tantalisingly close to Durell's throat as the Austrian castle collapsed around him.

Rumbling filled Jam's head, rock pounded his skull and dust blinded him. He could smell sulphur, and smoke filled his nostrils and lungs, choking him. His arms came up, covering his armoured triangular ScorpNex head as he fell, and the fall seemed to take for ever.

And then it was done. For a long time Jam lay there, prone and filled with pain. Weight pressed down on him: the mass of the mountain crushed him and he struggled to breathe. Hours passed as he slowly recovered his strength.

Blinking blood from his copper eyes, Jam braced himself against the ancient rock above him and heaved. His armour plates crackled, his muscles bulged and a roar escaped his twisted jaws . . . but the stones which trapped him refused to move.

Jam relaxed. He allowed his breathing to calm. Dust and grit settled into the blood still streaming into his eyes, but he could not wipe it free. He tried to turn his head, but a huge block obstructed his movements.

Trapped. Panic began to build in Jam's chest. It was one thing to die, smashed into an oblivion of pain and then dark eternity – but to suffocate? To succumb slowly to a choking lack of oxygen?

Jam started to struggle, thrashing about within his crushing stone tomb. But there was a collapsed castle around him, above him, that even his fury and enhanced ScorpNex strength could not shift.

Jam fought for an hour until his energy was spent. Then, as he drifted into an uneasy sleep, he wondered if he would ever wake. How much air did he have? How long could he hold to the glittering thread of life?

In his dream, Jam was human again. Time had played slowly backwards, from before the experiment, before his transformation into Nex by Durell – and by Mace, the evil Nex who had been Jam's torturer. In his dream Jam was not a powerful ScorpNex with chitinous black armour, armoured forearm spikes, and a twisted, almost triangular head flattened on the top. In his dream, Jam was a human, lying in a warm bed next to a warm woman. She turned to him, eyes filled with love, and kissed him tenderly on the lips.

'You did the right thing.'

'I did?' His voice was normal; his voice, Jam's voice. Not the softened, twisted sound of a Nex.

'You helped Carter, up on the castle battlements. You did not kill him. You bought him time . . . and you love me, you said that you loved me . . .'

'I . . . I do not remember.' But then it returned, like a flash: Durell, orchestrating the earthquakes across the

294

globe. And Carter had come – to find the machine, The Avelach, which had the ability to heal. Carter wanted to save Natasha, his woman, from her terminal wounds. He wanted to save his unborn baby boy . . .

Durell had ordered Jam to change Carter into Nex – either that, or kill him. Jam had done neither. Instead, his humanity had asserted itself, piercing the metal armour of the insect holding his soul hostage: Jam had given The Avelach to Carter and allowed him to live . . . to rescue Natasha . . .

Nicky kissed Jam again in his dream. And he cried . . .

Jam opened his eyes on darkness, and realised that tears were flowing from his eyes. Yes, he decided. He *had* done the right thing. He felt the insect mind inside his own, squatting, immovable, watching and listening. What happened? he thought.

What the fuck happened to me?

Realisation struck him with an impact that swept aside thoughts of his present predicament. For a moment it no longer mattered that he was teetering on the brink of death, that he would be dead in a few short hours – either by being crushed or from oxygen starvation. He had won the battle: the mental battle. He had overcome the insect part of his mind and soul. He had regained his humanity and imprisoned the insect in a cell within his consciousness.

Jam was back.

And Jam was *pissed*.

I will not die, he thought. I *cannot* die! He heaved against the stones above him, heaved until blood ran down his armoured arms and legs and he forced his triangular head to one side and pushed until he thought his bones would compress and grind into dust—

Something moved.

Not above him but below. Jam focused his energies in a different direction, struggled, *fought* with the collapsed castle until something under his fist broke free in a tiny avalanche of stones and dust, which fell away into a gap beneath him. Jam's clawed hand flexed in its freedom, and a cold breeze caressed his skin.

Jam moved his hand and spikes rippled across his forearm. He began to scrape at the rock and rubble which held him prisoner and after what seemed an eternity his claws exposed the edges of a stone block. He carried on levering and scraping and pushing until, after what must have been many hours, the block finally shifted.

The breeze flowed up more strongly now and Jam tasted the cold air. It filled his dust-abused lungs like the finest of nectar. Jam breathed in deeply and with renewed vigour set about moving the rectangular stone.

It moved again then fell away into darkness. There was a dull thud, which indicated a considerable drop, and much of the pressure was released from Jam's chest and abdomen. But still his legs were pinioned in a vice of stone. With his other arm free, Jam levered himself around, sensing a huge expanse of space beneath him, and started to work at his trapped legs. He toiled for hours, his weariness sidelined by sheer necessity. Time meant nothing in this dark vault: the total darkness was almost as oppressive to Jam's senses as the weight of stone bearing down from above.

He worked, and suddenly felt something shift again – not around his legs, but somewhere above him. A sudden wave of nausea washed over Jam: if the stone above him gave way, he would be cut in half or brutally crushed by the new fall of stone.

With renewed vigour from tortured cramping muscles

Jam continued to work at freeing his legs. The stones above him shifted once more and something fell past his face, rattling and clattering as if rolling down a slope beneath him in the blackness. *Slope?* Jam knew that the castle had had dungeons, huge vast subterranean vaults. But why a slope? And then he realised. When the castle collapsed, stones would have tumbled down, filling up the spaces below. Somehow the collapse had become precariously stalled – with him entombed at its heart.

Suddenly, without warning, the stones shifted again, this time in a deluge of dust, and his legs pulled free. There was a delicious momentary sensation of freedom, then Jam fell – and heard the suddenly accelerating rumble of the avalanche of rocks above him, raining down towards his tumbling body.

Jam cannoned into the slope in the complete darkness, pain crashing through him as he struck its surface. Curled up tight, he rolled down the slope with the crushed castle chasing him into the darkness—

I will be buried alive once more, he thought.

The stone slope was steep and jagged. Jam tumbled down it helplessly. Behind him, the avalanche roared in pursuit. Finally he struck a ledge and became airborne – uncurling, he stretched in flight, then cannoned into a wall and fell to the ground, stunned, mouth open and drooling blood and saliva, all breath hammered from his frame.

The roaring sound followed him. Jam waited for the castle to crush him and stamp out his life. But it never happened. There was no impact. And gradually the noise subsided and stone dust filled the air, choking Jam who covered his battered face with his arms in a feeble attempt to filter it out.

Rolling onto his armoured knees, he began to crawl

until he was away from the immediate cloud of choking dust. He felt water pooled in a hollow beneath him. He sank to his belly and lay, body heaving as he lapped at the stale, strange-tasting water like a dog. Then he sank down, his face pressing into the slow-moving inch-deep stream, and closed his eyes. A sleep of exhaustion overcame him and it felt as if it would last a thousand years. But as he sank into oblivion he realised one thing: somewhere the stream would lead from under the mountain . . . would lead *outside* and to freedom . . .

let us () out
fucking () prisoners () make us free
make() us free
we see you () see you
we see your () pain () we take it
() take your pain
welcome us like mother and father and brood () () () in mind allow us free we need free we cannot lie trapped () in world () bright world bright sky metal () taste metal taste water feel good feel need need to move need to live need to kill.

There came tiny clicks, like the scraping of cockroach chitin. Jam's eyes opened in the darkness which slowly brightened to mere gloom. It had been five years, five long years – and yet the entombment seemed like only yesterday. A nightmare nestling in his skull and taking every opportunity to break free.

He breathed, moving fluidly to a seated position, and slowly became aware of the vibrations around him: the howl of engines, the thumping of rotors, the sound of voices in the cockpit. Jam looked to the right, triangular head gleaming black and oiled, slitted copper eyes glancing out over the mountains and the snow.

'I am here,' came the rumble of his alien ScorpNex voice.

Carter was half asleep, seated beside the burner. To one side he could hear Mongrel and The Priest discussing the location of the SP_1 Plot on the south-west coast of Greenland where they could pick up a fast boat – a Viper ZX – and head out into the North Atlantic to the Submarine Graveyard. He could see Roxi through his drooping eyelids, playing with Joe beside another burner which cast its eerie glow over them. Carter watched them for a while, feeling warm inside: Roxi and Joe had bonded fine, and this could only bode well for the future. If, indeed, any of them had a future . . .

A cool breeze blew through the cavern. Carter glanced up and idly watched an enormous figure lumber in. He blinked, suddenly fully awake as the hackles rose on the back of his neck in a primal reaction. Then he stood and moved slowly across the rocky floor. He halted, a few feet away from Jam.

They stared at one another for a long time.

Around them came the clicks of weapons being cocked. Jam's physical appearance did nothing to soothe the fears of the men and women present. He was Nex, through and through. But, worse, he looked – inevitably – like what he was: a ScorpNex – a deadly, violent rarity.

Sonia J was dressed now in fresh black combats and a thick grey jumper; her hair swept under a tight thermal hat but she was shivering. She stood beside Jam, her gaze moving over to Carter and her head tilting as she tried to read his stance.

'How you doing, fucker?' said Carter, eventually.

Jam gave a deep-throated chuckle and moved closer,

body swaying, head dropping until it was only inches from Carter's face. 'I am not dead yet,' he said.

Carter reached out, hand pausing for a moment in mid-air before gently descending to touch Jam's thick black armoured skin. His fingers left tiny smears in the oiled surface as they moved down the side of his friend's head and their gazes locked. 'Does it hurt?'

'Sometimes, Carter. Sometimes. You look well.'

Carter withdrew his hand, and shuddered involuntarily. 'I wish I could say the same for you. I . . . I need to thank you. For that moment, in Austria, on the battlements.'

'You would have done the same for me, if you could have,' said Jam, his twisted voice thick with emotion.

Mongrel stumbled in, holding two huge mugs of steaming tea. He glanced around, then focused on Carter and the huge ScorpNex figure of Jam. Without breaking stride, without flinching, he marched up to them, handed Carter a mug, looked Jam up and down, then peered into the slitted copper eyes and said, 'Welcome back, dickhead. We thought you'd never fucking arrive. You want a cuppa?'

Carter laughed then, and some unseen tension, some ghost of ancient violence was exorcised. Jam settled down onto the stone floor.

'I will try my best to drink it,' said Jam, his words slow and slurred. 'After all your sweet tea is a legend throughout the ranks of Spiral. I believe one squaddie referred to it as the tar-shit of the devil?'

'Yeah, yeah, well – you still have six sugars? Of course you do. I see your change into Nex monster not done anything for your fat fucking pot-belly.'

Jam stared at Mongrel's own huge expanse of overhanging gut. '*My* pot-belly?' he growled.

300

Mongrel patted his own girth with a grin. 'Hey, I just say you were fat – I not say nothing about my own wobbling stomach. Now, you want this tar-shit tea, or what?'

It was thirty minutes later. The Priest, and the Spiral and REBS members present, had all been briefed and were ready to set off from their hideout in the Scottish mountains.

'And the Lord will guide us, my friends,' intoned The Priest to his captive audience. 'He will guide us in our search for the ultimate truth, for collective wisdom, and in the final triumphant bringing down of the infidels.'

Mongrel nudged Carter. 'Is he on drugs, you think?'

'He might be mad,' said Carter, 'but he gets the fucking job done, I'll have to hand it to him. No other fucker could organise the DemolSquads and REBS in such a short time. He has, shall we say, a God-given talent.'

Five minutes later, Carter was kneeling on the ground beside his son, Joseph. The boy was hugging his father tightly, tears on his cheeks, and Carter looked up into the face of Roxi who stood only a few feet to one side, a gentle smile on her lips. 'Roxi will look after you.'

'I know,' said Joe, his voice hardly more than a whisper. 'Please be careful, daddy. The Nex are bad people. The Nex will try to shoot you! It frightens me.'

'You just look after yourself – and I want you to do me a favour.'

'Yes?' Red-rimmed eyes stared into Carter's own. The gaze melted his bitterness.

'I want *you* to look after Roxi. I want you to make sure she comes to no harm. She is a very great friend of mine . . . can you do this for me? Can you protect her?'

Joe puffed out his chest. 'I will look after her,' he said proudly, glancing over at the Spiral woman and smiling

301

broadly. 'Where will we go, Roxi? Shall we stay here?'

'No, we will go somewhere warmer,' said Roxi softly. She moved over and placed her hand against Joe's soft hair. 'Come on, up you get. Your father has a job to do.'

Joe nodded and stood up. Carter gave him one final kiss. Then he glanced at Roxi and a silent understanding passed between them.

Look after him if I don't return. It didn't need to be spoken out loud.

Carter hoisted his pack, and with a grumbling Mongrel in tow moved towards the cavern's exit. Jam, Sonia J, Baze and Oz had already departed, heading for the K-Labs and a meeting with the white-coats who had created EDEN.

'Wait.' Carter halted, just beside the entrance to the short tunnel. A freezing wind poured in, filled with needles of ice. Carter turned as Roxi fell into his arms and looked up into his eyes.

'For fuck's sake,' groaned Mongrel. 'This not time for getting all horny, people! We on mission! Come on, get tongues down throats and out again so we can head out, by God!'

Carter and Roxi grinned at one another, then kissed. 'You told Joe you would be careful.'

Carter nodded, and he could see her eyes searching his face. His hand lifted, fingers stroking the soft skin of her cheek. 'I'm coming back, Rox. Believe me, I have a lot to live for.'

'Hey, Mongrel?'

'Hn?'

'You look after Carter, you hear? If you come back without him then you'll have me to answer to.'

Mongrel grunted something rude, and wandered out into the cold fresh night air. Roxi kissed Carter again, a full long kiss. 'Another life, remember?' she said, voice husky, scent strong.

'I hear you.' He turned her around, then slapped her backside. 'Go on, you mischievous minx. Get in there and get cooking.'

'Get cook— Now, you wait one minute . . .'

But Carter was gone. Roxi stared at the exit for a full minute, the cold mountain breeze rustling through her dark hair. Then Joe nestled against her side and she dropped to a crouch beside him. 'Come on, let's get our stuff together, little man. We're out of here.'

The Comanche hammered through the darkness, through the heart of the storm. It fell from the mountains and within minutes was howling low over the Atlantic, which rolled dark and restless beneath it.

The cockpit of the Comanche was cosy, a cocoon of warmth. Mongrel, ensconced in his HIDSS, was making little conversation as he concentrated on piloting the war machine through the blizzard.

Carter leaned back, eyes half closed. His mind whirled with memories of recent events, but he forced himself into a state of calmness. Mission, he thought. Find Justus – old Justus, a gun-runner and trader in information from back in Kenya during Carter's Spiral days. Find Justus – if he still lived – and then locate the programmers who had helped to turn the dream of the EC Warhead into a reality . . . and into a viable weapon that Spiral and the REBS could use against Durell. All in forty-eight hours.

I just *love* a fair timescale, Carter thought bitterly.

He dozed for a while. He dreamed of Natasha and Joe, playing together in the surf outside his new home in Cyprus; they would have been happy there together, he realised. They would have been content. A family.

'*You shouldn't be so nostalgic,*' said Kade, his voice a hoarse whisper.

'Hey, long time no mind-fucking,' snapped Carter within the confines of his own skull. 'What's kept your nose out of the shit pie for so long?'

'*I've been busy.*'

'Doing what?'

'*Ducking and diving. A dark demon's got to eat. You know how it is, Carter.*'

'I'm pretty sure I don't.'

Carter shook himself and drank a long soothing draught of water from his canteen before passing the black bottle forward for Mongrel. Mongrel slurped, losing half the precious liquid down his tattered grime-stained T-shirt. 'Hey, is good that Spiral and REBS is all one big happy family, no? Just shame we on brink of an extermination.' Mongrel turned sideways and flicked up his visor. His gaze fixed on Carter with concern. 'But I just hope this mission not be wild-goose chase. If Justus dead, we well and truly fucked.'

'From what The Priest was saying – and from our past intel – the Nex only take prisoners to the Submarine Graveyard for one purpose. Torture.'

'Aye, lad, and a man can only last so long against that sort of abuse under the knife. They've had him for a week now . . . a long time to survive without your balls. Mongrel only worry that if Justus still alive, what sort of shape we find him in?'

'Let's concentrate on our infiltration first. You got the SP_1 Plot coordinates locked?'

'ETA one hour.'

'Then let's get this thing done, then.'

The sky was blue and clear as Mongrel negotiated the

rugged coastline to the south-west of Greenland. They flew over jagged brown mountain ranges through which fjords cut arcing sweeps, their waters a cold slate blue and peppered with majestic chunks of glacial ice. The Comanche thrummed over a tiny fishing village, with dirt roads and a simple grey-stone church. The bay was littered with compact fishing vessels and the few people who were out tending the colourful boats looked up, shading their eyes as the Comanche whined low overhead and banked.

'ETA one minute.'

'You're getting good at this.'

'Yeah,' snapped Mongrel. 'Was steep learning curve fighting Nex, that for damned sure.'

'Where exactly is this SP_1 Plot?'

'Down there, beside the Søndre Strømfjord; it give us easy access to Labrador Sea, and Submarine Graveyard beyond. Is most desolate. Carter should like this place.'

'You trying to say I'm a hermit?'

'Had crossed my mind, *compadre*.'

The coastline was a desolate yet strangely beautiful rugged stretch of rocky ground dropping in steps towards the grey waters. Carter shivered, looking down from the warmth of the Comanche's interior. The sight filled his veins with ice.

Mongrel slowed their speed and the chopper banked again, coming in low over the fjord as armoured rotors whipped the calm waters into a frenzy. Then they carefully touched down beside a derelict cabin on the shores of the Strømfjord.

The cockpit folded back, and Carter climbed down, stretching and shivering as the numbing cold hit him. Mongrel followed in his ragged T-shirt, breathing deeply, cheeks a rosy red.

'Smell that, lad!' he boomed, slotting a thirty-round magazine into his H&K MP5K. The modest sub-machine gun looked like a toy in his large rough hands. Across the fjord they could see several pure white gannets floating majestically on the cold current. The birds looked at ease, at one with their surroundings.

'Come on, Mongrel. And get a jumper on or you'll freeze to death out here.'

'Ha! It take more than ice and wind and cold to kill this old war-dog!'

Carter and Mongrel moved across the rocky ground towards the abandoned shell of the cabin. It had no roof, just bare stone walls, one of which had mostly crumbled into dereliction. Inside, there were the black scorch marks of previous fires on the rock floor and Carter crouched to examine them. The rocks were speckled with discoloured bird droppings; no fires had been lit there for some time.

Mongrel grabbed their packs from the Comanche, and the two men set off on a short half-kilometre walk inland. Using his ECube, Mongrel located a ravine that dropped down through the rock. Shouldering packs and pulling zips up tight on their Berghaus fleece jackets, the two men started to descend a narrow trail. It dropped steeply, dangerously, into the incredibly constricted ravine and they both used gloved hands to steady their descent, reaching out to touch the smooth, crystal-veined walls as the steep rock reared above them. Gloom descended as the sides of the cleft blocked out the light.

Claustrophobia loomed threateningly.

'You been down here before?' asked Carter.

'Yeah. The Mongrel not like.'

'You *sure* this is the entrance to the Sp_Plot?'

'Would *you* forget descent like this?'

They dropped perhaps three hundred feet on the

narrow rocky pathway. At the base of the steep slope the two men hopped from a narrow ledge. Mongrel moved forward, located a steel doorway and integrated his ECube. The rock-coloured portal slid open and lights flickered dimly into life within the freezing, frost-layered interior of the cave that was revealed.

Carter peered in. 'Looks homely.'

'It get worse,' croaked Mongrel, shivering.

They stepped in, boots tramping over slivers of ice, and the portal closed behind them, locking them inside the mountains.

It took the two Spiral agents ten minutes to gather thermals, extra weapons and ammunition, food supplies and UPTs – pressurisation tablets used when planning a deep-sea excursion. This particular Sp_Plot in Greenland was only rarely accessed, but it had been superbly stocked when Spiral was in its heyday. Now, with both men carrying two packs and dressed for Arctic exploration, Mongrel led Carter through a labyrinth of passageways carved through the rock to the dark shores of an underground lake.

The sight took Carter's breath away. There, under a few globes of dull yellow light, was a huge glass-black expanse of water measuring perhaps a kilometre across. As Carter's breath steamed and his ears and nose tingling with cold, his boot kicked a tiny rock which bounced down to the shoreline. The sound echoed around the vast cavern, making both men jump, and ripples spread out across the previously perfectly still surface, destroying the illusion of slick gleaming glass.

'If there *are* dinosaurs living in there, I pretty sure you woke them up now,' muttered Mongrel disapprovingly, a frown carving contours down his rugged face.

'Yeah – but what an incredible place!'

'Not as incredible as the secrets she hold. Look!'

Carter focused on the ten objects covered by tarpaulins at the water's edge. He moved forward and grabbed the edge of one of the tarps, hauling the cover free from a Viper ZX.

The Viper ZX was built by Kawasaki, a sleek black sea-craft whose hull was created from interleaving semi-morphic panels of Titanium-II. It could house three people in comfort inside its high-walled narrow hull, and sported a 380 bhp 3000cc four-stroke engine with QOHC and fully waterproof twin-line electronics. The Viper could travel in complete silence, using USD-tx Ultra Sonic Dispersers, and it sported direct-drive axial-flow jet pumps, twin three-blade impellers and quad 168mm jet-pump nozzles for powerful acceleration – even vertically. Which was where the Viper really surprised and delighted first-time users and made a liar out of any man referring to its sleek design merely as 'speedboat'. At the touch of a button, the Kawasaki machine would slide panels in a dome above the occupants, realign control settings and effectively become a high-speed submarine. It could dive vertically to a depth of three kilometres, had advanced pressure-control mechanisms and used a variety of underwater sighting systems, combined with powerful hull-mounted STK rockets and an industrial green-beam Greeneye laser. This could easily slice through twelve-inch plate steel and could also double as a tactical weapon. The final touch of genius was the machine's ability for a remote-control operation. Utilising a tiny black pad with an inbuilt LCD screen, the Viper could be piloted from a distance of five kilometres: useful for setting up decoys, or using the vehicle as an unmanned reconnaissance vehicle, or – drastically – a mobile bomb.

Carter stared at the sleek black hull.

'Wow,' he said, visibly impressed.

'You piloted one of these beasts?' asked Mongrel, nudging the vehicle with his boot.

'I've been in the simulators,' said Carter softly. 'They were pretty new, even when Durell was stomping the fuck out of us with his nukes. Just past prototype stage, if I'm not mistaken.'

'You not mistaken.' Mongrel grinned, scratching at his head. He beamed. 'I have had honour of piloting one. Just once, mind, and I spill gravy on control dash and blew something up and got us trapped under sea for fifty-five minutes and we nearly ran out of air because air-recyc went titties up. But hey, I still got to drive beast on op beneath oil rig! Is *very good* machine for missions. Very reliable. Has many fancy function.'

Carter thought about this, as his eyes ran down the sleek lines of the Viper. 'You spilled gravy?' he said at last.

'Is long story.'

'I bet it is.'

'I tell you later. Come on!' Mongrel threw his packs into the Viper, which rocked only slightly under the weight, then jumped in boots first.

Carter followed, sliding into one of the well-sculpted pilot seats and grinning suddenly like a little boy. His hands stroked over the smooth synthetic seat-covering. Then he reached forward and switched on the power. The dash lit up in a swathe of bright colours. Carter nodded in satisfaction, hand reaching out to flick on several more switches.

'You got the coordinates for this Submarine Graveyard?'

'Yeah.'

309

'Let's pay our old friends the Nex a surprise visit, then.'

'Mongrel not argue with that. I just hope this *is* surprise for the copper-eyed fuckers.'

Carter smiled coldly. 'If they are waiting for us . . .' He palmed his battered Browning, and placed it on the seat beside him. 'Well, we both know what we will have to do.'

The engine started with a quiet hiss. Carter turned a dial and watched as panels slid neatly all around him and Mongrel, sealing them within the hull of the machine.

Then the Viper slid silently, gracefully and quickly into the underground lake, with hardly a disturbance of the black waters to indicate its passing.

CHAPTER 12

HIGH VOLTAGE

The Søndre Strømfjord was calm, blue-grey waters lapping quietly against rugged ancient shores. Huge blocks of gleaming glacier ice rocked gently, glowing in the sun.

A distant whine penetrated the stillness and then the sleek black hull of the Viper ZX broke through the surface, engine rumbling throatily across the freezing fjord as the craft took momentarily to the air, black plates peeling back to shed cascading silver droplets. It crashed back into the water, banked in a shower of spray and then powered out down the fjord towards the open sea. 'Not bad,' muttered Mongrel.

'You see any gravy stains?' snapped Carter, his eyes glowing. He accelerated the boat on a surge of torque, and the black hull crashed rhythmically across the icy fjord.

'It was a *particularly* tasty meat pie,' rumbled Mongrel indignantly. 'It not *my* fault the microwave overcook damned thing, and it go slippy-slop through Mongrel's paws.'

'Yeah – but on a mission?'

'A man has to eat,' snapped the huge tufted squaddie complacently.

Cold air beat at the two men. Carter veered gently left, avoiding a massive block of ice. He glanced up as they passed in its shadow and could see gleams of sunlight refracting through it.

Carter increased the boat's speed again, powering up to 100 knots per hour. They left a wake of foam, and passed several fishing boats from which Inuit fishermen gave friendly waves. Carter frowned, and then revised his first impression: they were not waves of friendship; rather, they were acknowledgements born of fear, directed at a quite obviously military vessel in the hope that the fishermen wouldn't be machine-gunned on the spot. It's a shocking world we inhabit, he thought darkly.

Once more, Carter accelerated, the engine moaning softly as Mongrel hunkered down behind the protective upswept windshield. Wind howled around the two men as the Søndre Strømfjord widened and they leapt out into the sea, bounding from ocean swells and giving a wide berth to groups of rocks that protruded like sharp black teeth. The Davis Strait opened up before them, and Carter powered them across it towards the Labrador Sea . . .

'Coordinates?'

'At this speed, ECube estimates arrival at surface site in three hours.'

Carter gritted his teeth. 'We'd better get a move on, then. Get down low and for the love of God put on a woolly hat. Your ears are already glowing blue with the chill.'

'Mongrel not like hats.'

'This ain't about what you like or don't. This is about frostbite. Come on, Mongrel, last thing I need when the shit hits the fan and we're in the middle of a firefight is you fucking moaning about your chewed-up ears.'

'I not moan,' moaned Mongrel.

'You're doing it now.'

'Well, Carter lad, *you* the one who nag.'

'Nag?'

'You once say I was like having your fucking wife along on a mission. Well, har har, now we have role reversal for sure, and from where I sitting, it look like *you* the one who is wearing nice flowery dress. By God, you become *pedik*!'

Carter frowned. His voice was dangerously low. 'What's *pedik*?'

'Is man who is used as a . . . female – usually in jail. It go something like: "Hey fat boy, bend over and pick up the soap!"'

Carter slammed the accelerator hard forward. Engines howled. Mongrel was thrown back violently against his seat as the Viper stormed at an astonishing rate across the waves, flying from one crest to the next, as the wind howled savagely around the two men.

'Tetchy,' observed Mongrel. He set about trying to oil his H&K – not the easiest task when slamming across the sea at nearly 200 knots an hour and with his last fried breakfast rolling around like a greased cannon ball in his belly.

To begin with, Carter was wholly focused on the task of piloting the Viper ZX. But as the minutes ticked by and he watched the huge black clouds rolling across the heavens, he felt the gentle tug of low-grade mental tension – a jabbing reminder that the clock was ticking. Carter was painfully aware that they were running out of time; that

313

the whole fucking *world* was running out of time.

Gradually the sky darkened and Carter manipulated the craft's digital controls. Several panels rolled up over the two men to create an armoured roof as ice rain started to sheet down from the sky.

With the flick of a switch, powerful white lights swept in a swathe from the speeding boat. The sea rolled and heaved, and Carter had to reduce their velocity a little for fear of capsizing.

As they travelled Mongrel serviced both men's guns and checked that their packs contained everything they could possibly need. Food, hydration pills, UPTs, ammunition, combat knives, spare clothing, wetsuits, compact sachets of HighJ explosive, Babe Grenades with a variety of different explosive fillings and, of course, Carter's trusty Browning HiPower 9mm and its clips of ammo. 'You love this gun, eh, Carter?'

Carter glanced around from the rolling dark sea ahead of him. Foam smashed against the windscreen. 'Yeah, my Browning is like a brother, a trusted friend. Unlike a lot of men I've known, this piece of metal has never let me down. It's like an extension of my own body – and of my soul.'

'It just a gun, Carter.'

'No, it's more than that. Mongrel, the only emotional attachments you've ever made were with that one-legged whore in Jakarta, and with the large yellow v-bin outside the kebab shop on Portobello Road. You could never truly understand my sentiments.'

'Ha? Crazy talk! Just drive, Carter. Just drive.'

'This ain't a Ford Cortina, Mongrel.'

'You far too sarcastic for a man on a mission.'

Carter grinned in the gloom, eyes black and face lit by the glow of the boat's control panel. 'Sometimes our fucked-up squaddie humour is all that we've got to keep us sane.'

'I raise glass to that, my old *drook*.'

They had killed the lights ten minutes earlier, switching to stealth mode and slowing their speed drastically. Now they cruised across the rolling, heaving black sea. The rain still hammered down, crashing against the Viper's roof panels, and the storm looked like it had no intention of relenting. Carter and Mongrel pulled on wetsuits and checked all their weapons for a third and final time. They did not intend to actually swim but they were unsure what they would find deep down under the sea in the Submarine Graveyard, and wanted to be prepared for anything.

Finally, Mongrel called a halt. His ECube glowed briefly and Mongrel nodded to himself, muttering a mixture of some Slavic language and, apparently, German – a rapid-fire string of expletives that Carter could not follow.

'We ready?' asked Carter. The Viper ZX, using a digital engine-anchor, was rolling on the surging waves of the dark sea.

Mongrel glanced up. He took a deep breath and gave a single nod.

'Game on,' he said.

The Viper dived. Carter and Mongrel left the storm behind, and a new darkness flooded their world as silence enveloped them. The only sound was the steady crooning *thrum* of the engines, and Carter eased the Viper around in a gentle arc in its sixty-degree descent as Mongrel navigated, using the instrument displays illuminated by the eerie blue glow of his unfolded alloy ECube.

'You ever been down here before?' asked Mongrel, his voice barely more than a whisper.

Carter shook his head. 'No. But I've seen the vid footage – from before the time when the Nex took over the complex. It looked awesome.'

'I, too, seen those images. If Sub Graveyard as big as I think, then finding Justus will be like looking for needle in haystack.'

'Yeah, but Justus is our man – he's Spiral. We have his data encoded: if he is aboard the prison, the torture cell – call it what you will – then the ECube should be able to pinpoint him.'

'If our tech work in the Nex environment.'

Carter grinned savagely. 'Yeah, that as well.'

They moved through the dark depths and to Carter's mind it seemed like travelling in space. They could quite easily have been piloting a spacecraft through the cold vacuum of some unchartered galaxy.

As they began their final approach Carter slowed the Viper once more. Its engines hissed into silence and the advanced Kawasaki De-Vib Shock Nulls rattled softly as they neutralised any vibrations that the Viper might otherwise have sent out in its passage through the sea.

'I hope we got right place,' muttered Mongrel.

'Yeah, or it's goodbye, world.'

A distant light came into view. A yellow globe, it was soon joined by others as the Viper crept down and down towards the underwater world of the Submarine Graveyard. Slowly the undersea prison base – once the creation of Spiral and used to house the most dangerous criminals, usually for interrogation purposes – crept into view. The Submarine Graveyard was, as its name suggested, a dumping ground for decommissioned submarines. Originally, the premises for its construction had been a simple one: drop a titanic anchor-weight to the seabed with a cable five metres wide attached which led straight up to the designated anchor point on the surface. To this central pivot could be moored any number of old and crumbling submarines, a natural resting place for them.

Over the years upwards of two hundred subs had been 'retired' to this distant stretch of water where the Labrador Sea and the Atlantic Ocean met. The anchor stone had been dropped and had lodged against the Greenland Shield, an undersea shelf of ancient rock that connected Greenland to Canada. The submarines had duly been moored, a twisting spiral of dark and rotting hulks drifting up out of the gloomy depths, each with its own trailing lead connecting it to the core of the anchor cable.

Searching for a discreet interrogation centre away from the prying eyes of the military and from interfering national governments, Spiral had, masquerading as one of its major front organisations, signed certain deals with various navies. It had effectively purchased the graveyard and then dropped its own highly advanced core, an inhabitable Titanium II alloy column, a circular tower block which was towed by freight tugs and then made a controlled descent into the cold deep waters.

Next the Sub-Core was linked to many of the ancient submarines by coiled tubes large enough for men and women to be transferred through. The submarines themselves had become cells for certain dangerous individuals. The Submarine Graveyard was born: a prison-tomb for the dangerous and insane. Now under Nex control, it was a control and torture centre that had long since dropped out of Spiral jurisdiction. Carter and Mongrel had little idea what to expect, little notion of what they would really find. They only knew that Justus was being held there. And they had to get him out.

Carter's eyes focused on the dim silver Sub-Core, a huge upright tube glittering with thousands of tiny portholes. From this central structure spun many drifting umbilicals, twisting away into the darkness and connecting the 'trunk' of the undersea base to its dead-submarine 'branches'.

Everything was moving: the tube walkways, the distant submarines still linked by huge black chains to their original ancient anchor cable. The Sub-Core itself swayed, only a subtle movement in the undersea currents but it played tricks with Carter's mind as he sat there, attempting to take in the enormity of what lay before him.

'I not realise it so *big*,' said Mongrel at last.

'It's fucking *huge*. You're right. Needle in a haystack, mate. A microscopic needle and a titanic haystack.'

And then eerie sounds drifted to the two Spiral agents through the water. A distant groaning, metal against metal: the long-drawn-out moans of slowly rotting, settling submarines as they jerked and tugged at their barnacle-crusted chain leashes, then relaxed again and let those chains clank and fold down in huge dark loops before dragging them taut once more.

The Viper cruised on, its speed shaved now by an apprehensive Carter. The sounds grew louder and Carter felt goose bumps creeping up his arms and spine.

'They sound like they in pain,' muttered Mongrel.

'They sound like they're dying,' agreed Carter.

'This remind me too much of damned Kamus.'

The Kamus was an old Spiral base in the Austrian Alps: a maze of tunnels and redoubts that led deep down under the mountains themselves. This mountain fortress had been the scene of a series of bizarre murders and had become something of a dark legend: a deserted Spiral stronghold where evil had invaded, seeping from the mountains themselves to take a hold on the minds of the people working within. In total, forty-six people had died – men, women, children. It was said that the Kamus was cursed and, even now – decades after it had been abandoned – haunted, some versions of the story told of the denizens of Hell walking the deep dark corridors. One version said that Spiral had intruded on an ancient lair of the Devil himself.

Mongrel nodded. 'It definitely remind me of Kamus.'

'In what way?'

'Same creepy feeling. Like you know something bad going to happen.'

Carter smiled grimly. 'Something bad *is* going to happen. I've just fucking arrived.'

Mongrel stared hard at Carter. 'What your thoughts on infiltration?'

Carter considered this. He had, of course, been giving it a lot of thought. Removing his own battered black alloy ECube, he spun it in his hand as he stroked out several patterns. It reconstructed itself in his palm, and a tiny red-laser projection appeared in the air above it, spinning as Carter spoke, linked to his words and tagging his meanings by the use of simple RI algorithms. 'Stealth is an option, but there are many fail-safes built into the Submarine Graveyard. After all, it was developed as a prison, and because the cells are actual submarines that are situated away from the main Sub-Core, they present easy targets for anybody with their mind set on a prison break.'

'If you have right undersea equipment.'

'Yes. And if you can actually *find* the damned place. Consequently, there are automated defences – Sonic Cannons, mounted Granite Lasers and NeedleHarpoon emplacements – mainly situated in and around the Sub-Core but with the ability to scan, fire on and destroy any of the submarines in the locality – or any approaching craft.'

'That make it tricky.' Mongrel rubbed at his stubble. 'Did Priest have any ideas when he send us on this mad-fool errand?'

'Yes, but I won't repeat them,' said Carter darkly. 'They mainly involved the central premise of protection – by God, of course – and putting our complete faith in Him. Not exactly what I would describe as *guaranteed entry strategies*. Anyway, for us to get the Viper in close enough, even to a submarine – that's assuming Justus is being kept in a submarine and not in the Sub-Core itself – we would have to pass before the all-seeing eyes of the defence systems. Not good.'

'Alternatives?'

Carter smiled. 'The Sub-Core drains a lot of power. Enough to power a huge city, in fact. Where does it get its power from?'

Mongrel frowned, staring at the red-laser image. 'The sun?'

'That would need cables connecting the Sub-Core to the surface and easy-to-spot solar panels. What's the point of a secret undersea base when you've got big silver panels floating on the surface of the Atlantic? No, there's a main sunken cable that runs across the Greenland Shield all the fucking way to Canada.'

Mongrel nodded. 'And?'

'I think it's time we set a trap.'

The Viper ejected a tiny PopBot, a small floating alloy sphere about the size of a football, and then dropped away into the darkness, deep down and away from the Submarine Graveyard. Slowly, the echoing, haunting sounds of distressed metal and dying subs faded until only water and a soothing silence surrounded the Viper.

Carter dipped its nose and pushed it into a more rapid descent. Mongrel worked the scanners, and images flickered onto a screen – relayed digitally from the PopBot.

It took them a while to locate the main supply line, a twelve-inch-thick cable swaying gently and covered with dark tangled seaweed. The line described an arc through the waters and disappeared into the unfathomable depths. Carter halted the Viper, then armed the machine's Greeneye laser.

'Is this going to be messy?' asked Mongrel.

'I hope so.' The green beam flashed out, slicing into the supply cable and Carter guided it through the thick insulation. The cable thrashed wildly, and Carter glanced at the digital feed relaying images of the Submarine Graveyard. The Sub-Core's lights flickered intermittently, then glowed bright as emergency power kicked in.

Carter cut the Greeneye, and the cable sagged against its emergency retaining loops which were there in case of improbable cable severance. Picking up the pieces from the bottom of the Atlantic would not be an easy process.

'How long, you think?' asked Mongrel.

Carter sat back, stretching and pulling free a cigarette. He lit the weed, took a long drag, and through a haze of smoke which made Mongrel cough said, 'Shouldn't be long. A place that size fucking *eats* power. They will need to re-establish a connection – and quick.'

Mongrel pulled free a canteen and took a hefty pull. He grinned at Carter. 'Want some?'

'What, some of your scabby water?'

'Is rum.'

'What have I told you about drinking on ops?'

'Is only little sip. And we *at sea*. After all, they once dish out rum to sailors in navy. It settles stomach, so I told, and – aye aye, me hearties – so it does.' Mongrel

321

twitched, squinting with one eye in an attempt to impersonate a pirate king.

'Mongrel?'

'Yes, Carter?'

'Please, please stop.'

'Yes, Uncle Carter.'

They watched the PopBot vid feed. Within ten minutes a hatch opened and released a long sleek submarine – much smaller than a naval war vessel, but nevertheless a serious subaquatic device capable of low-level undersea warfare. 'They not taking any chances.'

'I can see that.'

Carter started the engines, whirled the Viper around and headed out into the darkness, settling it once again and killing the power when they had travelled for a kilometre. The Viper's cloaking devices buzzed softly, disguising their underwater presence.

'You going to attack? This baby have awesome rocket power.'

'No.'

'What your plan, then?'

'We wait,' said Carter, settling back with a second cigarette. He closed his eyes, and for a moment Mongrel thought his old friend was going to sleep. But then Carter smiled, rubbed at his eyes and drew deeply on his addictive weed. 'We wait,' he repeated, exhaling.

The Nex repair sub hummed through the waters and located the break in the cable with ease. Pressure hatches opened, and the submarine manoeuvred onto the supply-line breach, allowing the cable to be reeled in for repair. Lights glittered in the darkness. Carter watched the Sub-Core's roving weapon systems on the video feed; he saw their precise, stepper-motor actions and licked nervously at his lips. To get this thing right, their timing had to be perfect – and when the action kicked in, Carter knew it would be sudden and brutal.

'*I see what you're going to do,*' came Kade's dark tombstone tones.

'You do? Well, you're wrong, fucker.'

'*I think you will be in need of my assistance very shortly, Mr Carter. In fact, I am pretty fucking sure of it . . . Do you know how many Nex that place holds? Over two thousand – you can't take on that many alone . . .*'

'I can and I will.'

'*Don't underestimate them, Butcher. Don't ever underestimate the Nex.*'

'Thanks for your advice, Kade. Now fuck off, find a large stone, crawl under it and die. Or if you can't perform that simple task, then drop yourself off a nearby vertical cliff. I need my *sanity.*'

'They've fixed it,' said Mongrel.

Carter started the Viper's engines. He could see the Nex submarine on his scanners. 'You think they know we're here?' He glanced across at Mongrel, who was watching him carefully. 'What?'

'You planning what I think you planning?'

'We need to get in.'

'There no way you can piggyback on a submarine, Carter. That idea make you total mad *svoloch.*'

Carter finished his cigarette. He rolled his neck and there came a crackling of realigning vertebrae; a release of tension; a sign of readiness. 'I had something more *drastic* in mind,' he said.

The Nex submarine cruised towards the Sub-Core. Carter hung back, the Viper pacing the larger vessel until they reached the signified perimeter of the Sub-Core's defensive weapons. Mongrel wiped sweat from his brow and stared hard at Carter, then back at the scanners. The Nex sub increased its speed, and Carter waited. 'You letting him get away.'

'That's the idea.'

'*What?*'

'You see the cannons? And the missile housings?'

'Yeah? *So what?*'

The sub was in their firing line. Carter was watching it glide smoothly towards the looming Sub-Core. The large corrugated hatchway opened, releasing a stream of bubbles. Both men were nervous, gazes fixed, joking suspended, as they watched the scanners and waited for the . . . moment.

Carter slammed the accelerator forward until it struck the control panels. Engines screamed behind them and the Viper ZX surged at an incredible rate, like a fired harpoon, cannoning through the darkness towards the Nex sub and the Sub-Core beyond . . .

Shots blasted from the defences, then deflected over the Nex sub's bows. Carter activated the Viper's weapons system and two STK rockets detached and hurtled towards the Nex submarine. Carter rolled the Viper, shot under the sub's keel and then headed up towards the welcoming mouth of the Sub-Core's hatchway. Again Carter hit the launch keys, and two more STK rockets detached. Mongrel frowned, looking behind him and then back at the scanners—

The first two rockets slammed into the Nex repair submarine and detonated, sending a green explosion of undersea fire boiling out, a discharge of unleashed energy that made the hundreds of chained submarines rock wildly. Instants later, the second salvo of STK rockets hammered ahead of the Viper, up through the hatchway

324

and decompression chamber behind. In the heart of Sub-Bay 6, fire unfurled and expanded, vaporising Nex guards and a small launch station in a sudden rush of green flame and broiling gas.

As explosions rocked the Sub-Core, the Viper emerged from the sea like a released black bullet, leaping through the pressurisation field and landing on a long narrow launch ramp where it slid along in a shower of sparks and with terrible squeals of stressed steel and alloy, through walls of fire and clouds of smoke until it touched neatly against the far blackened scorched wall of the Bay with a metallic clank.

Metal panels peeled back and Carter leapt free, H&K MP5K swinging around in a rapid arc as his watering eyes squinted through the smoke and three Nex charged from the nearest doorway. Carter's sub-machine gun spat a hail of bullets, picking the three Nex up one after the other and slamming them against the wall, drilling them with hot metal. Carter coolly changed mags.

'So they know we here, then,' growled Mongrel, hauling himself free of the wreckage and staring back at the battered, dented Viper.

'Come on. And get that fucking ECube searching. I don't think we've got much time.'

'Really, Carter?'

Carter fixed Mongrel with a baleful glare, lifted his H&K and fired ten shots past his colleague's cheek, so close the tufted squaddie could feel the spinning whistle of their superheated passing. The Nex soldier who'd been creeping up behind Mongrel was picked up and then slammed down hard on the buckled deck.

'Yeah, really, Mongrel. Now let's fucking move.'

Mongrel swallowed hard. He did not turn around. 'OK, boss.'

★

They halted in some kind of cubical alloy chamber. It seemed to be a type of power generator, with banks of computers and a huge central mass of spiralling coils. It hummed loudly, and made Mongrel's hair stand on end, fizzing with electrical discharge.

Carter dragged a blue-wrapped package from his pack and tossed it casually into the heart of the coils. Then he ran, and Mongrel sprinted after him, his face blackened by smoke, heart hammering, beer belly bouncing as they rounded the corner and Carter triggered the bomb.

The Sub-Core shook, alloy floor panels rattling violently under their boots. Fire slammed down the corridor and washed past to their right. There was a whine, then the fire was sucked back and a deafening boom pounded at their ears.

Sprinkler systems started up. In the distance, alarms droned in rising and falling wails. Carter smiled nastily. 'Should give them something to think about.'

'It possible that sort of behaviour could *sink* Sub-Core.'

Carter considered this. 'Might do, yeah, that is always a possibility.' The two men set off at a run again. Behind them they heard distant machine-gun fire. The Nex were shooting at shadows.

'But Carter!' panted Mongrel. 'This dog not want to drown!'

'I know that, Mongrel, old boy. But we need to kick up a fuss; we need a distraction.'

'Not at risk of sinking whole damn Sub-Core!'

'If that's what it takes, then that's what it takes,' said Carter evenly. They sprinted across a high gantry. Shots came up at them from a mounted MG emplacement guarding a whole field of small squat black generators, each one veined with silver crystals and with coils of copper around its base. Carter grinned viciously in the

326

gloom under the erratic spitting of the sprinkler systems.

Mongrel wiped water from his face as Carter produced another blue-wrapped package.

'I know you know what they is,' snapped Mongrel.

'Yeah. Pressurisation generators.' Carter primed the explosive, then leant sideways and launched it past the flying 7.62mm bullets of the mounted gun. His eyes were gleaming, his breath coming in short gasps.

Mongrel was frowning through smoke and streams of water. He was trying to aim his H&K back down the corridor, searching for enemy Nex. 'Pressurisation gen— you mean, things that keep this whole base *pressurised*?'

'Right. I noticed the hull on the way in; this Sub-Core was never designed to operate at such depths. It needs a bit of friendly electronic and mechanical assistance.'

'But if you blow them up, won't this place slowly crush in on itself?'

'Yep,' grunted Carter. Then he covered his ears as the explosion tore through the massive chamber, vaporising the machine-gunner and sending blossoms of fire in all directions. Carter calmly climbed to his feet as the hot air of the blast ruffled his hair. He pulled free his Browning 9mm and checked the mag as a clatter echoed on the alloy walkway. The two men stared coolly at the twisted, detached barrel of the heavy machine gun. It was bent sharply at a seventy-degree angle and thick smoke poured from the drilled steel.

'Savage,' whispered Mongrel.

'Nothing less than they deserve. Now, has your ECube got a lock down on those genetic coordinates yet? I think we've given the Nex a pulped and bloody nose. It's time to find Justus.'

Alarms were howling, high and shrill, and Carter paused.

The Sub-Core's power had started to fluctuate wildly and the lights had suddenly gone down, leaving nothing but the occasional red firefly glow of emergency illumination.

'This real creepy,' muttered Mongrel.

'Shh.'

They edged forward along a dark gantry, then walked quietly down a sweeping ramp. Carter glanced back. 'This one?'

Mongrel nodded, and they both peered ahead through the falling sprinkler streams at the umbilical leading out through the cold dark sea towards the submarine prison block that housed the captured Spiral man.

Again, sounds of groaning metal reached their ears as they stepped tentatively onto the plastic of the translucent tube leading out from the Sub-Core. Carter's hands pressed warily against the smooth synthetic surface, and he tried to estimate how thick the tube's wall was. Not very, it seemed. That didn't give him much confidence.

Behind him the Sub-Core was a hive of activity – and panic. The alarms had not only been triggered by Carter's explosions, his acts of HighJ vandalism. They had also been set off by the destruction of the pressurisation generators and the consequent slow compression that had started to squeeze the Sub-Core in its fist. Occasionally, there came a scream of compressing steel and alloy that would stop just as suddenly as it had started, leaving nerves stretched piano-wire taut.

Stepping into the umbilical tunnel, Carter and Mongrel started to run.

The tube swayed gently all around them, and through its hazy plastic walls they could just make out the gloom of the dark sea and the lights of distant submarines.

'This horrible!' said Mongrel. 'It feel like I in belly of worm!'

Carter said nothing, his stare fixed forward. The swaying of the tunnel, the constant shifting meant that bends and dips and humps suddenly appeared and then disappeared. It made precautionary surveillance difficult. And sprinting along the tube was incredibly tough work. The tension was heightened by the definite possibility of . . . combat.

Suddenly there were two Nex guards up ahead. All four fighters started shooting at once. Sub-machine guns yammered as Carter dropped to one knee, his Browning bucking in his fist. Mongrel whirled to one side, sliding onto his belly with a grunt, H&K MP5K spitting hot metal in his huge battered hands . . .

Ricochets whined past Carter's head. He blinked as one of his bullets smashed into a Nex's chest, punching it backwards.

Carter changed magazines.

Mongrel's H&K fired once more, and the second Nex was slammed against the tunnel's wall, spurts of its crimson blood splattering up the plastic. Then Carter and Mongrel were running again and Carter put a single shot in the masked forehead of the wounded Nex as he raced past. The Nex was slammed down, twitching, head caved in.

Without a word, their nostrils wrinkling at the cordite stench, the two Spiral agents stepped over the bodies and peered at the hatchway in front of them that had been fitted neatly into the hull of the submarine. Carter reached forward and turned the metal wheel, releasing the portal so that it swung open on heavy steel hinges. A stench blew from the depths of the old sub and the two men glanced at one another warily.

'More Nex in there?' asked Mongrel.

'No.' Carter shook his head. 'It would take a bomb to get through *that* door. A bomb or us, that is. I don't think they need any more security inside. Do they?'

'We soon find out. Yes. Soon. So you go first, Carter boy.' Mongrel slapped him on the back.

'Yeah, thanks, Mongrel.'

'Is my pleasure.'

Carter stooped, stepping into the gloomy interior of the ancient submarine. It smelled really bad and it was bone-chillingly cold, too. The walls were covered with ancient crusted pipes and were painted a dark grey, the paint bubbled and peeling after so many decades of neglect. Lighting was provided by strings of swaying light bulbs linked by great looping arcs of simple electrical cord. They flickered, and some had blown so that there were several patches of inky black shadow.

The two Spiral men moved forward carefully and Mongrel checked his ECube. 'A hundred metres,' he said. 'We need to go *down*. Over there – ladder.' Carter nodded, and they moved off carefully, ducking to avoid the low-hanging bulbs. Then they dropped down through a narrow hatchway in the floor, a circular opening leading into—

'Hell,' thought Mongrel sourly, watching Carter disappear. He licked at his flattened lips, tongue probing at battered broken teeth. 'It do remind me of Hell; and of Kamus. Which is one and same.' He shivered, shouldering his weapon. The freezing steel of the ladder numbed his fingers and his boots scrabbled for purchase on rungs polished by decades of use. Cursing softly, Mongrel followed Carter into the submarine prison's oppressive metal bowels.

The submarine constantly creaked, groaned and moaned. The floor rocked continuously. Mongrel, stare fixed on the ECube, followed closely behind Carter.

'Up ahead. Five metres, on the left.'

Carter halted outside the hatch and worked at the rusting bolts. Then he glanced at Mongrel. 'I hope to God this poor fucker is still alive.'

'We severely fucked up nether pipes if he not,' replied Mongrel.

Carter kicked open the heavy steel portal, blinking as his eyes adjusted to the gloomy interior. He held his Browning ready. For a moment he thought the improvised cell was empty and felt his heart sink. But then he made out a figure hanging from chains wrapped around thick ceiling-mounted pipes. 'Justus?'

There was no answer. With Mongrel covering his back, Carter crept forward. He realised that the huge black man was naked except for a pair of tattered shorts. His ankles were secured by chains which had been tossed over ceiling pipes, and his knuckles dragged against the riveted deck.

'Justus.' Carter reached out to touch the man's freezing flesh. He could feel wounds there, razor-slices and burns. He stepped in close and, grunting, lifted the massive weight of the man as Mongrel reached up and untangled the restraining chains. Carter lowered Justus to the deck and checked for a pulse.

'He dead?'

'No. His pulse is erratic. Pass me my pack.'

Carter gave the unconscious man several injections, antibiotics, a K7 stimulant, vitamin enhancers and morphine in two-milligram stages. When Justus awoke, Carter wanted to kill his pain, not push the man back into unconsciousness. Morphine had a terrible habit of rendering its subjects cheerfully immobile.

Suddenly, Justus's dark eyes fluttered open. He stared up in confusion and his mouth opened in a silent scream. His body jerked, tensed, spasmed, and Carter swayed back as a fist the size of a shovel whirred past his face. He

331

placed his hand against Justus's lacerated chest. 'Shhh, Justus mate, it's me – Carter. I've come to get you out. Rescue you. Take you out of this shite-hole.'

'Carter?' He felt the big black guy relax under his hands, body trembling with pain and fatigue. Justus levered himself up onto his elbows, glancing around the cell before fixing his gaze on Carter and Mongrel. He shuddered.

'You OK?' rumbled Mongrel.

Justus nodded, then patted Carter on the shoulder. 'Papa Carter, you old dog.' He coughed, a heavy cough filled with phlegm. Then he smiled, showing several broken teeth. 'Am I *fucking* glad to see you.' He got to his knees, then stood, taking several deep breaths and swaying dangerously. He looked down at himself, his battered body covered in his own vomit, urine and blood. He rolled his neck gently, and pulled a dislocated finger back into line with a disquieting crunch.

'Keep still. I'll give you another two mgs.' The needle slid back into Justus's vein, and as Carter pulled away the black man began to cough savagely again.

'Can you walk?'

'From this place, Carter? I can fucking *sprint*.' Justus sighed then, closing his eyes as he swayed again and nearly fell. 'I am a long way from home, Papa. I am a long way from my beloved Kenya.'

'Come on. We need to move.'

Justus's face hardened. 'Have you got a weapon for me?' Mongrel handed him a Beretta 92 and a fist full of magazines. Justus weighed them thoughtfully, then gave a pain-filled grin. He exhaled softly. 'I have a few scores to settle with those bastard Nex – that for sure. Not for all the gold in Africa would I let this humiliation fade away . . .'

Carter moved to the doorway.

'Did you tell them anything?' asked Mongrel.

'Mongrel, you dick!'

'It's okay, Papa Carter,' said Justus placidly. Then he fixed Mongrel with a dark unreadable stare. 'No, I did not tell the Nex anything. Because, my friend, the Nex did not ask me any questions. They did this purely for sport. For entertainment.'

'Now I see why you sore.'

'Sore, my friend? I would bathe the world in blood. I would snap every Nex pencil neck with my own bare hands.'

'Let's move,' snapped Carter, and with a gun in each hand he led the way. Mongrel took Justus's arm across his own huge shoulders and supported the big black man as he hobbled on naked feet down the cold metal walkway. It took both Carter and Mongrel to get Justus's huge bulk up the ladder, and they stood panting for a few moments before setting off once more towards the umbilical tunnel and the distant Sub-Core beyond.

And then the bullets came. They ripped along the tunnel, and Carter and Mongrel retreated, returning three-round bursts. They squatted behind a steel bulkhead and Mongrel flipped free his ECube. He cursed.

Carter fired a few more shots. Return fire followed, ricocheting dangerously around the three men.

'What is it?'

'You not like answer to question. There are Nex. Lots of them.'

'How many?' snapped Carter.

'Thirty – no, forty. They tracked us after the detonations! They blocking tunnel, Carter. And that our escape route. What the fuck we going to do, lad?'

Carter pulled shut the heavy portal door to cut off the tunnel as more ricochets made him duck and flinch. He sat back on his haunches. 'Shit.' His face creased into a sour frown.

'We need a plan, Carter.'

'You think the engines on this old sub work?'

'No, it nuke-powered. Long ago decommissioned with core removed. That not an option.'

'Right, then.'

Carter placed his weapon on the ground and pulled free a blue-wrapped pack of HighJ. He primed the detonator as Mongrel looked on in horror, mouth agape, the half-conscious Justus lolling against him. 'What you doing, Carter?'

'Watch.'

'No no no. You tell Uncle Mongrel first – that look suspiciously like bomb you got in sweaty paws there. That dangerous, that is. What you planning in mad bad head?'

Carter grabbed his H&K. He took a deep breath. 'Be ready.'

'For what?' screeched Mongrel.

Carter opened the heavy steel portal, then sprinted forward into the plastic umbilical with his H&K blasting, bullets slamming down the translucent tunnel and making the slowly advancing Nex pause briefly before returning fire. With bullets zipping around him, Carter hurled the package of HighJ at the Nex, turned and sprinted for the cover of thick portal steel.

The HighJ package exploded with a fury of purple and green fire, annihilating the Nex and destroying the plastic umbilical which connected the ancient submarine to the Sub-Core.

Carter leapt through the submarine portal and slammed shut the heavy door behind him. He spun the wheel and threw the heavy rusted bolts with shaking hands as behind him a wall of fire slammed against the heavy steel door.

'What have you done?' whispered Mongrel, horrified.

334

The fire washed over the hull of the submarine, and the pressure waves of the explosion sent the vessel spinning slowly, yanking against its thick, rusted tethering chain – which groaned like a huge animal in pain and parted easily with a crumbling of corroded links.

The plastic tunnel was gone – melted, vaporised – and with no restraint to hold the defunct war machine in place it whirled for a moment on the energies and wild eddies of the explosion. Then it bucked violently and its nose slowly dipped towards the far-distant ocean floor. The dead submarine began a long, slow, spiralling descent into blackness . . .

CHAPTER 13

K-LABS

Jam watched with slitted copper eyes as The Priest's Comanche leapt into the air and slewed sideways through the falling snow. He breathed slowly, feeling the power in his huge armoured chest, and he flexed his talons and lifted his face to the spinning flakes. Jam liked the cold. All Nex liked the cold; it sharpened and speeded up their reactions. The heat slowed them down, made them lethargic, made them easy targets.

But I am not Nex, Jam thought. Not in my mind; only in my body. *But what about your soul?* whispered a voice in his mind. *They have eaten your soul. When you die, there will be no Heaven for you; no human Heaven, nor Nex Heaven . . . not even Hell awaits you. You are an abomination; you are mongrel-breed; you are an in-between, a deviation deformo that should never have existed . . .*

Earlier, Mongrel had mentioned Nicky's name. Before, when Jam had been wholly human, Nicky had been his lover, his partner, and his friend; his future wife-to-be. But, as Jam's mission in Slovenia went horribly wrong, and he had endured torture inflicted by Mace – Durell's finest Nex surgeon – so every footstep had taken him further and further away from his life, from his woman; from his love.

Jam had fought a war inside himself. And had won. His humanity had been stronger than the Nex side that had been blended with it. And yet he still carried the Nex stain in his blood. He appeared as an armoured monstrosity, a huge and powerful cross-blend of human and genetically spiralled insect. Things could never be the same for him again . . .

Jam stared into the falling snow. The Priest, he thought. A good man; the best of men. Sometimes, though, he was too fanatical in the Spiral cause. With The Priest there were no greys, no in-between shades. Only black and white. And if you crossed to the wrong side . . . well, then you were dead.

Their first meeting, after Jam had gradually worked his way through the REB ranks, building their strength, gaining Spiral trust with every Nex killing, gaining respect with every rescue of innocent men, women and children, had been a tense and fraught affair. And it had taken much to persuade The Priest that Jam was his own true Spiral self – his *old* Spiral self . . . But the earlier divisions between the two factions no longer mattered. Both Spiral and the REBS, despite their historical differences, had been forced to join ranks against the might of Durell in these last few days of conflict. It was to be a fight to the death.

Jam turned as his squad emerged into the snow, and he saw the glint of fear in their eyes. Not at the mission to come – but at the entity they had to risk their lives alongside . . . No matter how often he proved himself in battle, Jam was a twisted and deformed horror – to them – and would always provoke an immediate reaction of fear, mistrust, loathing. They were not only scared of his power,

337

his insect blood. They were faced with their own mortality. They were horrified that, one day, if things went brutally sour, then they might end up like Jam. Sadness flooded through him.

A great sadness that could never die.

'Follow me.' Jam's voice was deep, rumbling, powerful. His team consisted of Spiral personnel and REBS; their mission was to locate the K-Labs rumoured to be buried under an old nuclear power station, infiltrate, hack the computer systems, discover what they could – and then blow Durell's stash of poison to Kingdom Come.

Jam analysed his team in his mind as he led them to the Chinook's K5 transport helicopter. Sonia J was the first to follow him. She was an expert on HIVE Media computer systems; having been integral to the growth of Durell's media company in London and New York, she carried with her top-level access codes and the ability to worm her way into many of the medial giant's digital cells.

Next came Baze, huge and bear-like, with hands like shovels. Oz, tall and gangly, a chain-smoker with shaved head and battered, pock-marked features, and Rekalavich, the tough old Russian with bitter memories and a nasty grudge against the Nex. These were what Jam termed his Heavy Squad, able to bring massive amounts of firepower into play when so required.

Baze carried the MG. Oz, who doubled as a sniper, carried his trusted Swiss SSG550 rifle strapped tightly across his back; this weapon was his love, and he had been known to break people's cheekbones for leaving so much as a thumbprint on the polished stock.

Haggis, or Whisky Haggis as he was sometimes known, was the explosives expert on this mission. Finally, their pilot was Fenny, still sporting long curling locks, still wearing a cheeky – if weary – grin and still harbouring a love of pouring beer into the laps of his friends: a pastime that had earned him many a well-deserved punch on the nose.

Fenny had the Chinook CH-58's rotors turning slowly, warming the engines, and he waved as Jam led the ragtag band towards the chopper. A freezing wind howled down from the Scottish mountains and the group lowered their heads, throwing packs through the open cargo doors and climbing onto the low corrugated alloy platform. Rekalavich moved instantly to the mounted MG, checked the ammunition belts, wiped the snow-melt from the gun's barrel, and lit Bogatiri *papirosi* cigarette. Haggis started to complain about the smell of the smoke and Sonia moved across the massive deck – stacked with several crates bearing stencilled Arabic letters – and poked her head through to the cockpit.

'Where are we going?' she asked, her face drawn and weary. She felt completely out of place with this group. A motley crew of soldiers, killers, and one genetically modified Spiral Nex. How crazy can life get? she thought, her mind in a whirl.

'You have to ask the boss,' chuckled Fenny. 'I don't even know myself – yet.'

Jam leapt aboard the Chinook, and the suspension lurched under his weight. The group's members exchanged glances as Jam moved forward and Sonia J sidestepped to give him room. Jam smiled down at her – a disconcerting predatory look on a misshapen armoured face which was wide, flat and almost triangular. Sonia J forced a smile in return, then moved to a corner of the Chinook's cargo bay where benches lined the riveted and badly painted wall. Canvass harnesses were attached to the frame and Sonia strapped herself in tightly.

'Where we going, Big Guy?' Fenny tilted his head, staring up into Jam's copper eyes with a smile.

You are one of the few, thought Jam, sighing deeply. One of the few who still treat me the same; one of the few who remember me from before – before the torture at the hands of Mace. Before the transformation into ScorpNex. One of the few who still look at me without the veil of prejudice.

'Norway,' said Jam. 'And I thought I told you to get those fucking curls shaved.'

'I'll do a deal, JamNex. You shave my curls, I'll wax your insect armour. How does that sound? Does it tickle you in the right place, my old and chitinous friend?'

'You make me feel wanted again,' rumbled Jam with an alien smile.

The weather over the sea as the Chinook crossed the Prime Meridian consisted of freezing ice rain which had lasted without respite for the previous 500 kilometres. Winds howled and buffeted the transport aircraft as Fenny fought the storm with a grim, weary look on his normally pampered face. Bags marred the usually smooth skin around his eyes, ruining the effects of his Oil of Olay, and he continually cursed his lack of sleep. On board, every member of the group felt sick due to the incessant pounding of the storm and the constant pitching and yawing of the Chinook. They all had the feeling that at any moment they would be plucked from the raging heavens and tossed screaming into the sea.

Sonia had her knees up under her chin and her arms wrapped around her legs. For a while she had listened to the banter of the soldiers, but soon it grew wearisome – there are only so many jokes about 'fannies' and 'sheep VD' that a girl can listen to – and she closed her eyes, trying to link the rhythm of her body to the undulating pendulum swings of the helicopter. I am a fish out of water, she thought. A simple TV presenter who's out of her fucking depth.

Jam settled himself next to her, and even with her eyes closed Sonia could feel his presence. The oiled smell of his ScorpNex chitin. The way the alloy bench groaned under his weight. Sonia smiled then, and opened her eyes.

'How are you?' Jam asked her.

Sonia shivered. 'Well, cold. A bit at sea. I'm not a soldier Jam – I never was.'

'But you are vital to the success of this mission. You know the HIVE systems better than anybody here. And we are desperately short of programmers. They are the first people the Nex exterminated; they remember too clearly how Spiral relies on its technology.'

'But what happens if my codes don't gain us access? What if I can't find out what we need to know?'

'I will help you,' said Jam softly. 'Together, we will infiltrate their systems. Trust me – I have every faith in our combined abilities. Remember when you joined the REBS? You were sick of the killings? Sick of Nex rule? You wanted to make a difference? Well now you can. In a small way. Maybe even in a *huge* way. Who knows what secret talents you hold? We all have our part to play, Sonia, we all have our roles in life – and they change. They are not always clear – even when sunlight is shining through the crystal ball.'

Jam seemed to sleep then, his copper eyes closing, and Sonia's mind drifted back; to her TV productions, to thoughts of her colleagues, to the farce of the trial and her certainty that she would die under the hail of bullets fired by the execution squad.

The Chinook hammered across the Norwegian Sea and flew parallel with the coast, which was shrouded in heavy mist, for many kilometres. When it reached the edge of the Arctic Circle it banked steeply, thundering inland. The weather had cleared somewhat as they pounded low over the coastal waterways with sheer hills rearing up from the sea to either side. These waterways led inland, past Angersnes, Fagervika and Bardal, and Fenny shaved their speed as they approached the disused nuclear power plant at Hemnesberget. Here, he banked once more, heading south to touch down a couple of kilo-metres from their intended target.

'Any signs of electronic scanning?' asked Jam, as the Chinook's howling engines powered down, whining slowly to a stop.

'No. Nothing. But that doesn't mean we weren't picked up by advanced scanners. To tell the truth, Jam, this crate is a bag of shit, and I'd rather fly an old B52. With no wings.'

'You did well, Fenny, getting us this far.'

The group jumped free into the LZ, a small clearing surrounded by towering Norwegian spruce which offered excellent cover and camouflage for the Chinook. The stretch of forest would also provide cover from the air on much of the short journey to the Hemnesberget Power Plant. The soldiers, alert now that they were on the ground and, indeed, in enemy territory, checked weapons and set up a defensive perimeter of sub-machine guns.

Fenny would stay with the aircraft, to carry out checks and to be available to pull the group out if the mission suddenly went pear-shaped. For Sonia, especially, this was a more than sobering thought.

Once ready, the group moved away from the clearing, over a forest floor strewn with patches of frozen snow. Under the rich-scented boughs they trudged, Jam and Oz in the lead, followed by Sonia and then the rest of the group. It offended her pride that they wanted her at the centre – as if she needed protection. But Sonia had to concede that she definitely was not a battle-hardened veteran. And so she kept her mouth shut and her eyes on the horizon. The soldiers were only doing their jobs.

They moved forward for a kilometre in silence. Then Jam and Oz slowed their speed as they approached a ridge which fell away down a concave slope that looked like a giant scoop, more sparsely scattered with vegetation and showing several huge drifts of snow which had gathered in hollows.

The group paused for a while, strung out under the cover of trees, gazing down at the power plant near the coast. It was a huge, staggered building – a main concrete block four storeys high, the walls covered with galvanised panels and painted dark green. The view was dominated by the huge white cooling dome of the reactor.

Oz and Baze both had digital binoculars, and the tiny clicks and whirrs that they had made signified a careful set of observations. 'Anything?' asked Jam.

'Two guards, standard Nex,' said Oz softly. Then he placed the binos down on the pine-cone-scattered ground and started to fit the long digital sight to his huge SSG550.

'Two,' confirmed the huge figure of Baze. He scratched at his bushy black beard. 'Seems about ten too few, if you ask me. If this *is* the K-Labs, then shouldn't they have more protection? You'd expect a damned battalion to be camped out there.'

'Possibly,' said Jam. He scanned along the lines of smaller buildings which were set back from the main concrete complex. 'The K-Labs are highly specialised, very well hidden, and have practically finished their research tree. Their job is done. A large group of guards would only draw attention to such a place. The labs' main defence is the covert nature of the base.'

'How did you find out about the K-Labs?' asked Baze.

Jam shrugged his armoured shoulders. 'I used to work with Durell. I knew many of his secrets. The fucker thinks I am dead – buried under a billion tonnes of Austrian mountain. What has he to fear from discovery? He rules the world and HATE rules much of the wild land between towns and cities . . . or so Durell would have us – and the herded populations – believe. Amazing, the power of the media, isn't it?' He threw a sideways glance at Sonia, who nodded.

'Something's happening down there,' said Baze softly.

The group returned to their surveillance. One of the smaller buildings had ten trucks parked outside, huge battered military FukTruks used for the transportation of infantry, ammunition, supplies – even a couple of tanks could be carried on the back under the heavy flapping tarpaulins. Engines started up, spurting clouds of black diesel smoke. With tyres crunching frozen earth, the vehicles turned in wide circles and rolled away down a bumpy track, disappearing between two small hills where they were swallowed by the forest.

'What do you think they're transporting?' asked Oz.

'Let's hope it's not barrels of EDEN. What's the point of destroying this installation if there's nothing here? I think it's time we made a move. Oz, you confident?'

Oz settled himself against the ground and sighted through his scopes. He said, 'Yes, Jam. I am always confident.' A shot rang out and a bullet took the first Nex guard between the eyes, flipping it backwards where it smashed against the wall and folded down into a sprawled heap.

A second shot rang out, but the other Nex had already turned and was sprinting for cover. The round took it high in the shoulder, spinning it, momentarily stunned, to the ground. The Nex, bleeding, started to crawl towards a doorway – beyond which it could set off alarms.

'Oz?' asked Jam coolly.

'I'm on it,' said Oz. The third bullet caved in the top of the Nex's head, and it dropped lifeless to the ground. It twitched for a while, body jiggling as if an electric charge was passing through its dead limbs. Then it finally lay still.

'There is no dignity in death,' came the soulful voice of Rekalavich.

'There's little dignity in life, either, my friend,' replied Jam. 'Come on, let's move out. We have a job to do.'

Using trees for cover, they made their way down the hillside. Oz and Haggis used their ECubes to scan for sensors, heat, vid, audio. Jam could no longer use his own ECube. It did not recognise him as human.

The group hunkered down a hundred metres from the towering walls of the old nuclear power plant. No longer did a core burn at the reactor's heart. But the Nex had to have been guarding *something*. And instinct told Jam that his team was in the right place. The K-Labs, one of the crucial research and development centres for this new biological weapon – maybe even a *production* centre for the toxic shit, for EDEN . . . well, it was in there.

He could feel it. In his bones. In his newly created Nex soul . . .

Jam's teeth ground hard deep within his chitinous armoured head. His copper eyes glowed. And pain started to gnaw at the centre of his brain, the agony growing, until his vision blurred and he lowered his head in submission . . .

let us () out
make () us free
we see you () see you

you traitor () to our kind

traitor we see your acts () betrayer

we see you rot () we see you burn () you not control us ()
we live here ()

here in your soul in your mind in your heart and you can
never be free

we see your () pain ()

we see your () weakness ()

weakness

Jam frowned, buzzing sounds and pain spinning inside his skull. And then they were gone.

Shivering, Jam turned, breathing deeply, filled with confusion. Then, with a single movement of his clawed hand, he gave the signal to advance and the team moved slowly across the final few metres of barren land . . . *killing ground* . . . and towards the narrow door.

The door swung open. There were no guards, no auto-mated alarm or defence systems. Jam, with Oz close behind, moved into a narrow corridor and the group shuf-fled forward, bristling with automatic weaponry, and halted, covering each other's arcs of fire.

Oz stared down at his ECube, then shook his head 'It's been blanked. I think the building is made out of some kind of material which interfered with ECube scans; pretty handy for an old nuclear plant, eh, Jam?'

'Yes. Far too convenient.' They moved forward, the clattering of Jam's claws against concrete the only sound in the cold corridor. They moved into another, wider cor-ridor which was painted a dull yellow and had a grey floor. The walls were covered with piping, tubes, wiring and corrugated sections of steel. Oz ran his ECube across one of the cables.

'DigiOptic. No need for that in a power plant.'

'I have a gut feeling we are in the right place,' said Baze.

'Then why is it so deserted?' asked Sonia. To her own ears her voice seemed small; she felt tiny in this place, insignificant amongst these soldiers.

'I have a bad feeling that we're too late,' said Oz softly. He rubbed at his bushy eyebrows, and hoisted his sub-machine gun thoughtfully. 'Those FukTruks? Maybe they're taking the last dregs of EDEN away to safer quarters. You'd think this place would be riddled with Nex. I thought we were going to have to fight our way in.'

'It's definitely been too easy so far,' conceded Jam. 'Come on. Let's find the labs. There will be answers to our questions there.' He set off, the rest of the team close behind him.

And in my experience, he thought sourly, easy is always a bad thing.

The interior of the Hemnesberget power plant was a muddle of cables and piping. Many cables trailed haphazardly across the floor – which had changed from dull grey concrete to black, shining vinyl. But somehow the place seemed too neat, too clinical.

The group of Spiral agents and REBS had stopped at an intersection.

'Looks like they were in a rush to finish something,' said Baze, gun barrel weaving in a constant arc as he searched for Nex enemies.

'That's what worries me,' growled Jam. 'Can you locate the centre? The old reactor? That is where *I* would put the labs; it would offer a central power source, a core for cabling and piping and any local networks. It would also be the most secure location available here. The easiest to guard.'

A squeal of rubber against the gleaming vinyl floor alerted the group. They turned to stare at a tall, thin, balding man, clutching a PDA the size of a clipboard, his long white coat flapping around his Arran sweater and grey chinos. His brown flip-flops slapped to a halt as he stared at the group and their weapons.

He frowned. 'Are you with the Nex?' he asked. Suddenly Jam leapt forward, a blur of glistening black, his Steyr TMP's muzzle pressing up under the man's chin. The man swallowed, slowly.

'Can I help you?' he finally managed to squeak.

'Take us to the K-Labs,' said Jam.

'I . . . I . . . I'm just a technician. That area is restricted.'

'I'll fucking restrict your breathing.'

'OK, OK, but you need codes . . .'

'You want me to *persuade* you to remember them?' Jam lifted his free hand, and huge armoured spikes slid free of his forearm. The serrated chitin prongs gleamed like oiled steel in the yellow globe-light of the dim corridor.

'I . . . I . . . I'm sure I could find the codes.'

'Good boy.'

Oz moved forward, prodding his own gun into the man's face. 'Why is this place so deserted? Where are all the fucking Nex?'

'They have finished here,' stammered the technician. 'Most of them have left. They have been called back for – well, for something. I don't know what. I just service the machines.'

'Machines?'

The technician went pale. 'For the production. You'd better follow me. You're not going to shoot me, are you? I just service ProdK machinery, make sure we keep production levels at a sufficient output.'

'Lead the fucking way. Before I get really angry.' As

Jam spoke, a curious smile crossed his armoured ScorpNex face . . . a hint of some distant memory, some private joke. 'You wouldn't like me when I'm angry,' he said. He pushed the technician forward. The man stumbled and righted himself. Then, with many nervous glances over his shoulder, he led them through a maze of yellow corridors. They passed several ceiling-mounted gun emplacements; but the guns were pointing uselessly at the ceiling.

Oz shook his head. 'Some defensive system!' He snorted with derision.

A minute after the group had passed, a tiny amber light flickered on the side of the first mounted gun. It turned smoothly in full circle, quad barrels lowering and aiming at the last point of exit for the group. And inside the tiny AI chip, algorithms clicked and flickered as the defensive systems linked together, instructions flowing through the gun network like fire through a tinder-dry forest. As the group passed each gun, so it came to life in their wake. The defensive systems knew, in their simple machine-intelligence way, that it was one thing to let an enemy in.

It was quite another to let them out again.

The technician halted outside a pair of huge alloy doors. A code pad lay to the right, hidden among the metal panels, the myriad pipes, the thick clusters of cabling. 'This is the old reactor,' said the technician softly. 'This is where the K-Labs are sited. But there's nothing left – they have been stripped. You're wasting your time.'

Jam's face moved in close, slitted copper eyes observing the tall man closely. 'You're lying about something. You're holding out on us. Something is not right – smells bad.' His gun pressed against the side of the man's head. 'Open the doors.'

'High radiation levels,' observed Oz, studying his ECube.

'In thirty-six hours, it ain't going to fucking matter,' said Sonia J, coming forward to stand beside Jam. 'Come on, we need to get in.'

Jam tilted his head to look at her. She smiled and nodded, and Jam gave a small nod in return, acknowledging her bravery and her willingness to get to work.

The technician punched in the entry-code digits on the doors, and slowly, ponderously, they slid back on well greased rails . . . to reveal a huge chamber, easily as large as a football stadium and split into three levels. The group were entering on the central level, and ramps led off below and above them. The whole chamber was visible in a gloomy half-light, despite its three-tier layout: floors were built from galvanised mesh panels, support struts were narrow lengths of steel, and huge swathes of clustered cables ran everywhere, across floors, walls, hanging in loops from ceiling struts. Towards the centre of the chamber the lower level housed a huge pool containing a sparkling green liquid through which could be seen two huge cylinders whose lower parts disappeared into darkness.

'That's the reactor core, and the fuel assembly,' observed Jam, taking a step forward onto the overhanging metal gantry. Above the glittering lake of coolant were huge rails, and assemblies of lifting gantries and cranes. The coolant pool filled the whole of the mammoth chamber with a soft green glow, and the total effect was one of immense eeriness. This was a dangerous place; this was where controlled nuclear reactions had once occurred.

The technician was silent. He seemed to be looking for something.

'What are you not telling us?'

350

'N-nothing! Look, the computer systems are over there. The K-Lab research benches, all lining the sides of the upper level – what used to be the reactor-monitoring equipment.'

'Jam, it's *really* dangerous in here,' said Oz. 'The levels of rad are real high.'

'You wait outside with the others. Guard the doors. Make sure we don't get any nasty surprises.'

'I'm coming with you,' said Sonia.

'You heard the man. The rad levels are toxic. I am ScorpNex; I have increased resistance, improved genetic tolerance. You, however – you are human, Sonia. You can die as easily as all the other humans here.'

'You need me,' said Sonia defiantly. Jam moved forward, his gaze locked to hers and she stared back at him. 'You need me to access the computer systems. You need me to access HIVE archives. Without me, you are screwed.'

'Oz, get her a gun.'

Oz passed Sonia an Uzi, which she looked at in distaste, and a small hand-held comm. 'We'll keep in touch, yeah? Jam can't use it – because of his claws.' Oz turned, and the group of men moved back into the wide corridor.

The technician made as if to follow them but Jam nudged him with his gun. 'I think you would be *safer* with us.' Jam pushed the technician out onto the gantry, and then stepped out himself. The structure rattled under his weight. They moved slowly up the nearest ramp which rose gently towards the top level of the K-Labs, providing an even more expansive view of the huge chamber. Below, the coolant rippled in its house-sized container. The green light seemed to seep into every corner, every crevice.

Creaks and rattles echoed through the vast space. The

ambient temperature was cool, with a breeze flowing down from wide ceiling ventilation pipes. Sonia followed Jam up the long ramp, and then along another suspended walkway that veered left, opening onto a platform set out with big benches and a host of complicated glass mechanisms. Tubes and vials sat in racks, scattered amongst computers and metal tools, laboratory ovens, microscopes, centrifuge machines and several industrial cubic autoclaves. Racks held trays of Petri-dishes, slides and thousands of bottles of chemicals.

'K-Labs,' said the technician, simply.

Jam's eyes were scanning. He could not believe that nobody was there, that their group had, in fact, arrived too late. The Nex had packed up and left – which meant only one thing. EDEN was definitely ready. The biological agent had been produced, probably on a mass scale. And now it was on the move. The Priest had been right.

Durell was ready for his onslaught against mankind . . .

Jam moved towards the computers, with Sonia beside him. They switched on the machines and light spat from twenty screens. HIVE logos flowed across monitors and Sonia moved forward, resting her hands on a keyboard.

>> **HIVE MEDIA SYSTEMS**
 .. **LOG-ON KL SYSTEMS INITIATED**
 .. **ALL SYSTEMS PRIMED**
 .. **TESTING MEMORY SECTORS –**
 .. **TESTING MULTI-POINT PROCESSOR UNITS**
 .. **TESTING ZERO-K ALGORITHMS**
 .. **EDEN/K-LAB SYSTEMS © HIVE MEDIA SYSTEMS**
>> **PLEASE ENTER EMPLOYEE ACCESS CODES NOW – []**

Sonia accessed the terminal with a few deft keystrokes. Filing systems flowed across the screens and Sonia's jaw fell open. 'I do not believe it,' she said, voice soft, face glow-lit by the monitors. 'Why would they *still* give me access? And here, of all places?'

'You're an employee of HIVE. You have an A-rate clearance. They never would have thought in a billion years you would go anywhere near a K-Lab production unit. How could they? You present TV programmes. You only ever connect to Media-Systems. But they are all networked by the same password laws the same huge server mechanisms. Mad, eh?'

'Yes, but the Nex also tagged me as a REB.'

'Yes,' said Jam, 'and they also condemned you to death. Things are moving too fast, Sonia J, Media Queen – I think Durell has more things to worry about than a tiny little rogue TV presenter . . .'

Jam moved closer to the central console and squinted, looking over the folders which appeared to be in a strange archaic language. They spread out in glowing spirals of data.

'I don't understand it,' said Sonia slowly.

'It's encrypted. It uses a Nex conversion system.'

'And you can convert it? In real time? In your head?'

'Yes.'

'What does it say?'

'There are lists of figures. Most of them don't mean anything to me. Scroll down there.' Sonia obeyed, and Jam was silent for a while.

'You see anything?'

'The EDEN production has definitely finished. A million barrels have been shipped over the previous two months. Here!' Jam pointed. 'Print that section.'

'What is it?'

'Shipping destinations. A hundred and twenty locations around the globe where EDEN has been transported; much of it airlifted, some by trucks, some by cargo ship. Durell has been planning this for a considerable time. Unfortunately, we've discovered his game too late.'

'We still don't know if EDEN is the biological poison it's supposed to be.'

'It is,' said Jam softly. Sonia moved through various folders until an image flickered onto the screen. An incredibly complex series of molecular structures rotated, then merged to create a new chemical – which in turn spun softly. 'That is EDEN. It is a poison. It has one purpose: to shut down the human organism as quickly as possible. Durell uses his media empire to string the population along. According to the propaganda, EDEN is the cure to all their ills. It will remove a toxin called HATE from the fucking air and give them back their liberty . . . that way, Durell's plans are virtually unobstructed. Last thing he fucking needs is the *truth* leaking out, the people of the world rising up in their millions against his new regime; against the Nex.'

'But we could do that,' said Sonia softly.

'How?'

'If I could get back on TV. I could tell the people what is really happening. I could get them to rise against the Nex! The people think I am dead, because Durell transmitted a faked execution after I was rescued. My appearance on a global network would cause chaos. If nothing else, it would show that his whole system is based on lies.'

'Maybe. If nothing else, it could buy us time,' said Jam softly, considering her point. 'And time is something that is very precious at the moment. If you could expose this on TV, it might make the world finally see the truth. To look beyond their TV screens at the reality around them.

I suppose that in itself would be a miracle.'

'Are you two OK?' came the crackle of Oz's voice.

'Yes, we'll be down there soon.' Sonia turned, and realised with a sinking feeling that the tall, bald technician had gone. 'Oz, that guy we picked up has done a runner. He might be coming your way.'

'I'll see if we can introduce him to a bullet,' said Oz. 'Out.'

'Put a disk in, over there,' said Jam. 'We need this information. There are video test clips – there, yes, the .vdx extensions – they show the effects of what EDEN is capable of doing, and where it is being stored. Then we need to get this data to Carter, so the ECW can be programmed with the EDEN depots. I just hope this fucking Warhead is capable of taking out so many targets! I just hope it's as good as everybody thinks it is . . . because without it, we are lost, we are a dead race.'

Oz killed the comm. 'That little maggot we picked up is on his way down here. We should be ready.'

Rekalavich, smoking another of his Bogatiri *papirosi* cigarettes, was seated against the wall. He was nursing his stomach, quite obviously in some pain from his recently stapled stomach wound. 'Just point your gun at the door. Little fucker won't know what hit him.'

'I think you need to be more on the ball,' said Haggis, his voice harsh. 'This ain't the fucking time for a cigarette, Russian.'

Rekalavich pulled free his Techrim 11mm, cigarette balanced between his lips, smoke stinging his eyes. 'Believe me, Haggis, I've been in much more dangerous situations than this and walked free – with a cigarette dangling from my lips. This is not exactly a Nex hive crawling with fucking specimens . . . no, this time we got lucky, boys. This time it's a simple infil followed by data recovery and a clean helicopter pick-up. No problems. No drama. Take a chill-pill, my little Scottish friend.'

Baze moved to stand in front of Rekalavich. 'I think Haggis is right. This is not the time for relaxing and smoking. This is a dangerous place, especially when one of your team is a crazy Russian motherfucker.'

Rekalavich squinted up at the huge bearded man through his evil-smelling cigarette smoke and licked his lips thoughtfully. 'Those are brave words, coming from such an obvious hero standing tall and proud before me. Question is, are you all hero or part stupid cunt?'

Baze reddened, and his fists clenched. And then something sounded, an alarm in all their minds – a *clack*, like the noise of stone against stone, followed by another *clack*, then another and another. The noises echoed down the corridor and the men carefully aimed their weapons at the far end of the long stretch of dim-lit yellow.

'I thought all the Nex had gone,' growled Haggis softly.

Rekalavich dropped his cigarette and jacked himself up off the floor, Techrim extended towards the sounds – which halted.

There came a scent of—

'What's that smell?' whispered Oz.

Something moved on all fours at the end of the corridor like a huge black oil-smeared cat, its triangular head low to the floor as though it was scenting something. The Sleeper Nex was enormously muscled, spiralled patterns of skin blending with silver armour down its flanks. Then its copper eyes lifted, calmly and arrogantly surveying the small group of heavily armed men.

'Shit,' said Haggis.

The Sleeper Nex charged them, claws tearing through the floor panels in its urge to reach them and tear and rend and kill. The men opened fire, guns roaring as a hundred rounds flew down the corridor, smashing into the Sleeper Nex – which came pounding on, leaping from wall to floor to wall, dodging many bullets but also absorbing much of the scything metal. The group of men gripped their yammering guns in sweat-greased hands as the beast's bright copper eyes came closer and closer . . .

The Sleeper Nex stumbled, then pitched forward on its face mere inches from the group, sliding a little. It slumped, with a great deflating sigh, copper eyes still fixed on the men who stood, surrounded by a cordite smoke-mist, eyes wide, stunned.

'Fuck!' snapped Haggis.

'Son of a bitch,' panted Oz, slowly changing the magazine in his weapon with clicks that sounded loud in the sudden silence. 'I thought the Nex had all gone. I thought we had this place to ourselves.'

'They let us get in,' said Baze softly. His gaze was still fixed on the end of the corridor.

'What do you mean?' hissed Haggis.

'They let us get in,' Baze repeated. 'Then they close the doors behind us. It's a trap, my little friend.'

'No way,' said Oz. But even as the words left his mouth there came more sounds of armoured claws up ahead – so many clattering *clacks* that it sounded like a river of insects flowing towards them. The men's horrified stares fixed on the far end of the corridor.

The mass of Sleeper Nex charged, hammering forward on squat powerful legs towards the group of Spiral and REB men laid out like a three-course meal before them.

Oz started to count – three, seven, fifteen – but the Sleeper Nex kept coming, a dark black armoured flood that rushed towards the flashing muzzles of the men's guns. They crashed against the group, claws slashing

357

left and right, up and down, huge jaws snapping and biting and tearing. Blood flowed like a river across the floor, splashed in great arcs up the alloy doors and chunks of torn flesh skittered and rolled in all directions.

For a few moments the Sleeper Nex fed on the corpses of Oz and Haggis, Baze and Rekalavich, snouts dipping into shattered and bone-ringed chest cavities, ripping out hearts with strings of muscle and bone-ringed veins still attached, devouring them in swift gulps. Then burning copper eyes turned to the doors leading to the reactor chamber.

As one, the fifty Sleeper Nex shuffled together like a huge and chitinous insect swarm, their gleaming bodies smeared with Spiral blood, thrusting and slithering as their combined mass heaved forward. Slowly, the alloy doors started to buckle and groan. Within seconds there came a shower of sparks, and the doors bent inwards and fell crashing to the ground, revealing the green glow of the reactor chamber beyond.

The Sleeper Nex poured inside.

Jam and Sonia J exchanged a long, meaningful glance as sub-machine guns fired far below them, muffled by distance and the closed alloy doors. Sonia found her hands suddenly coated in sweat, which made holding the Uzi difficult.

The noise finally died. Somehow, the silence was worse.

'You think that was the technician?' asked Sonia, her words barely more than a whisper.

'Take out the disk,' said Jam. He moved across the lab, then leapt lightly up onto one of the wide benches. He seemed to be *sniffing*, his triangular head tilted to one side. Then his hugely powerful claws cocked the sub-machine gun – like a child's toy in his grip – and he stared down, through the grilles and the beams, past the struts and cranes and lifts.

Sonia J ejected the storage disk within its tiny silver cube housing, and pushed it into the pocket of her black combats. Then she wiped her hands on her trousers and moved closer to Jam, who lifted a claw. 'Wait,' he hissed. He could sense them. The mass of Sleeper Nex. Hear their claws . . .

Then he could *hear* the insects in his mind, burrowing into his soul. And he realised: they wanted their freedom. But more: they wanted him back. They wanted him to be Nex again . . .

They wanted to flow through his veins.

Below, guns roared again and suddenly stuttered to a halt. There were several loud bangs and crashes – then silence for a moment.

Jam's head tilted as he listened.

Below them there came a creak, and then a sudden frenzy of hammering as the alloy doors were pounded until they buckled and caved in. Sleeper Nex poured into the chamber, glistening black bodies reflecting the light of the nuclear reactor's coolant in the gloom . . .

Sonia gave a little sigh of horror, fear – and understanding.

They were trapped, and only Jam stood between her and a painful extinction. Jam leapt from the bench, claws gouging the alloy mesh floor.

Then he turned, and stared at Sonia.

His copper eyes narrowed as inside himself—

Inside—

Something *broke*.

we see you () see you
you traitor () to our kind traitor
we see your acts () betrayer
() you be whole again () we be one again
()we be nex again
open the () door
we see you () see you feel you want you
we are () one
we are one again.

CHAPTER 14

TIBET

Water swirled in fierce currents around the dead submarine and it rocked violently as it dived, buffeted by incredible pressures. Inside, the three men were slammed savagely against a wall of thick pipes. Mongrel was still staring hard at Carter, mouth open to reveal many of his broken teeth. 'You fucking killed us, you madman!' he howled.

Carter pulled free a small black pad, then fixed his gaze calmly on Mongrel. 'I need your help, not your fucking histrionics. The Viper can be handled by remote control. You understand?'

Mongrel looked around wildly. Then he slowly focused. 'Remote?'

'Watch.'

Carter initiated the ControlPad and it blinked at him with a tiny yellow light. Then the small LCD screen flickered on to show a low-resolution image of Sub-Bay 6 within the Sub-Core, replete with scorched rocket-blasted walls, buckled girders and dented galvanised walkways. Two patrolling Nex moved into view, heads scanning slowly from left to right.

Carter traced a pattern on the ControlPad and the Viper ZX responded instantly, engine firing with a sudden howl and burst of exhaust fumes. The Nex whirled, Steyr TMPs jerking up and bright copper eyes searching for an enemy.

But there was nobody there. They approached the Viper. Carter accelerated madly and the vehicle began to move. He eased it around in a tight arc and the Nex broke into a run, a low-res image of their sprinting bodies and masked faces looming across the screen as Carter hit the turbofans. The Viper leapt forward, smashing between the two Nex and sending them spinning aside. Panels folded up in a sheath to create a roof as the craft left the walkway and struck the black waters, diving instantly below the surface.

'Neat,' Mongrel acknowledged with a nod. Then he eased the half-conscious figure of Justus to the metal deck. 'The Mongrel still not like this. It like a bad dream which never end.'

'Just keep your shit together,' growled Carter. The Viper ZX shot from the Sub-Core and accelerated down at an awesome rate. The tiny LCD screen was filled with nothing but black.

'Mongrel, can you link the ECube to the Viper? Lock coordinates?'

'I think so.'

'Do it – now.'

Mongrel played with his ECube for a moment, then glanced up, a worried look on his battered face. 'You want good news or bad news?'

'I don't like the sound of that.'

'Good news: Viper now home in on our location.'

'Great!'

'Bad news: so will three Nex submarines which follow it.'

'Shit.'

'My sentiments exactly.'

'Can you get them on a visual?'

'Negative, Carter. But I can track the sub coordinates on the ECube. It look like you losing them. Our little Viper, she hot stuff, eh? She leave them for dead . . . wiggle her tasty arse and give them the finger as she disappear over the horizon.'

'Yeah, but more than anything we need time to get from this floundering wreck into our little high-tech beauty.' Carter accelerated the Viper harder, and it powered through the dark waters. Meanwhile the submarine groaned around them as it continued its terrible descent.

Within minutes the Viper caught up with them and the LCD screen showed a fuzzy visual. Using Mongrel's carefully read and constantly updated coordinates, Carter guided the Viper over the portal which had allowed them entry to the submarine. In a careful manoeuvre, panels peeled back in sections and it connected with a pressurised *clang* – like a remora fish attaching itself to a shark.

'Them other subs catching up now, Carter. They closing in real fast.'

Carter, jaw muscles clamped tight, spun the wheel and with a hiss the portal opened into the Viper's narrow hull. They dragged the barely conscious Justus into the vessel's interior, threw packs and guns into the sideways-slewing craft and closed the hatch behind them. Slowly, Carter peeled the Viper away from the stricken submarine. Then, in a sudden burst and rush of pressure that made their ears pop and heads pound, they were free of their host and drifting in the deep dark waters.

'Missile alert. Two. Incoming,' barked Mongrel.

'Will it never fucking end?' Carter slammed the heel of his hand against the accelerator and the Viper leapt forward, dived towards the sinking submarine and spun around the other vessel's hull before shooting out and climbing madly through the dark waters for the far-distant surface.

Behind them the two missiles struck the recently vacated submarine, which glowed briefly, a white-hot crucible with a core of molten metal. Then it exploded into a billion metal shards with a dull underwater roar that sent blast waves pulsating out into the surrounding ocean. But the Viper was gone, heading for the surface and carrying inside it their captured prize.

The Viper surfaced just as a wild storm was abating under a flurry of towering black clouds. Carter peeled back the machine's protective skin and it sat bobbing, a sleek and mean-looking vessel but now, apparently, nothing more than a speedboat. The hull hid the machine's secrets well. Cold fresh air drifted across the three men as Carter and Mongrel made a full appraisal of Justus's wounds with the aid of the ECube. Once satisfied that he was stable, Carter restarted the Viper and they flew across the rolling waves as Mongrel unpacked dried rations. All three men ate and drank in contemplative silence.

It was finally Justus who gathered the energy to speak.

'Thank you,' was all he could manage, for a while.

Carter glanced back, smiling. But his eyes were weary and filled with utter exhaustion. He nodded, as Mongrel passed him a chocolate bar, grunting – his own mouth was too full to speak.

Eventually, Carter said, 'There is information that we seek.'

Justus nodded. 'There always is, Papa Carter. I'm just glad there was reason to break me out of that hell. I thought I was going to die in there. I thought I would never see this – ' he spread his hands and gazed up into a dark sky that went on for ever '– again.'

'You were involved with the Evolution Class Warhead?'

Justus tilted his head, eyes bright. 'Ahh, so that's the pretty toy which you seek. Yes, Carter, I was involved with the machine – but not with its development. My skills lie in other directions.' He coughed again, a small fit which lasted a couple of minutes. He took Mongrel's canteen and drank deeply, then spluttered and gave Mongrel a shocked look. 'Rum?'

'Jamaica's finest!'

'You are a good lad, Mongrel!' He took another hefty drink and felt the rum warming his belly. 'Ahh, I thought I would never again taste such a wondrous liquor! You are to be congratulated! You make me feel human again.'

'Warhead?' Carter urged.

'Yes, yes, sorry. I presume we haven't got much time. Although I'm not sure what you think you can do with the ECW, even if you find it, even if it was completed. The finished product is still a myth, to the best of my knowledge.'

Carter felt a teetering sensation, as though he was walking along the razor-blade edge of an abyss. So many factors in this game were unconfirmed; so many things could go wrong. Spiral was playing a dangerous game in which the stakes were extinction or survival. And only Durell seemed to know the rules.

'Do you know where this Warhead is?'

Justus shook his head sadly. 'Like I say, Papa C, this machine was not finished as far as I know. And I never saw it – I never set eyes on even a damned prototype.'

'We were told you know the whereabouts of the ECW programmers, the people who worked on coding the machine.'

'Yes.' Justus nodded slowly, rubbing wearily at his great dark eyes. 'But that information is old; certainly out of date. And there is another problem.'

'*Another* problem?' said Carter.

'Yes, my friend. There were three programmers originally, based at Spiral_R in Tibet. They worked on the Quantell range of processors, and were then sidelined into ECW coding – a prototype that, as far as I am aware, was never built. I think you are chasing a dream, Carter.'

'You say there were three programmers originally. What happened to them?'

'Suzy Pagan is missing, has been missing for the past five years – since Durell bombed the fuck out of our world. Tademo Svdenska was taken out by Nex assassins three years ago; his corpse was delivered to Spiral in pieces. And Angel Constanza . . . well, she went mad, my friends.'

'Mad? You mean, as in loony?' sputtered Mongrel through a mouthful of chocolate and rum.

'Yes, Papa Mongrel. Mad.'

'Yeah,' said Carter, 'but mad doesn't necessarily mean dead.'

'She is as good as – or so I was informed.'

'And your source is reliable?'

'No source is totally reliable, Carter. But I have many men and women whom I trust, who have worked for me for many years – even from before my Spiral days. And so, yes, this came from a reliable source – as much as it can be.'

'Do you know where we can find this Angel Constanza?'

Justus rubbed at the scabbed skin of his face, and tenderly touched his recently broken nose. 'I think so. Or at least, I know where you might create enough interest to bring her to you . . .'

'And where would that be?'

'Spiral_R. Tibet. The home of the Evolution Class Warhead, the place where the concept was devised, created – the place where they talked about the building of the prototype.'

'Won't this Spiral_R be crawling with Nex?'

'Unlikely. The place was stripped, bombed, smashed by earthquakes during Durell's rise to power. It has become bandit country, a no-go area even for the Nex – run by an army of men and women with many machine guns. The only other technological artefacts that remain are Spiral's old automated air defences – surrounding Spiral_R in concentric rings for a hundred kilometres – a highly intelligent masked network of SAM sites run by a single AI chip of advanced design and related to the Quantell processors. An AI chip whose intelligence has unfortunately gone AWOL, and which now shoots down anything that intrudes into its airspace. No aircraft can go there so the Nex had to go in on foot, searching for this army that lives in the mountains surrounding the remains of Spiral_R. An army that unhesitatingly kills all who go near the ruins – for the site has become their shrine. Their holy place. The Nex started to hunt these people down, but the bandits waged a guerrilla war and it became too much trouble, cost too many Nex casualties for absolutely no purpose, no gain. After all, Spiral_R had been bombed, right? So the Nex were pulled out and the savages were left to their own devices. Nobody goes there now. It is a wasteland.'

'Savages?' said Mongrel, unwrapping his seventh chocolate bar. 'You make this so-called army sound primitive. Like cavemen or something, har har har.' He shoved the chocolate into his mouth.

'Indeed. There seems to have been some nightmare

effect of biological or chemical warfare – it is said to have regressed these men and women, turned them into nothing more than aggressive animals with a single purpose, a single aim.'

'Which is?'

'To kill.'

'Yeah, that's a definition of the whole fucking human race,' muttered Carter. Then he sighed a deep and weary sigh. 'Right, so you believe that if we can infiltrate as far as Spiral_R then this Constanza woman will show herself to us? Take an educated interest because we're on her front doorstep and heading towards the ECW?'

'Yes.'

'But what about savages?' asked Mongrel, chomping away. 'Why they not kill her? Make her into big Neolithic sausages? Put her in bubbling dinosaur stew?'

'Because,' said Justus slowly, gazing out over the sea and breathing deeply the cold salt air, 'Angel Constanza is their leader. She controls the army of the insane. She controls Spiral_R. And she is the only woman alive who can take you to the Evolution Class Warhead – if the machine was ever built; if it even exists.'

'If it even exists,' repeated Carter. He turned to stare with a cold sense of foreboding into the distance where a brightening sky was rolling towards them in the wake of the storm.

The Comanche came in high over China. Huge swathes of the landscape below were obscured by cloud. The engines howled furiously as Mongrel thrashed them to within an inch of their lives.

Carter, sleeping in the back, came awake from sour dreams and found that he was shivering. He lit a cigarette and gazed down at the thick cloud cover rolling unevenly below. Above, the sun glimmered in the sky, its rays shimmering hazily through the smoked cockpit glass. As Carter lit his cigarette, there came an immediate whine of cockpit air purifiers.

'You shouldn't smoke,' Mongrel admonished him.

'Get to fuck.'

'No, really. It may affect our oxygen.'

'Yeah, by filling it with nicotine fumes. Just fucking great. Just what I need. Mongrel, I might die today, and if I die, at least I want to have had a last blast on my beloved weed. OK?'

'You're getting tetchy again.'

'Hmph.' Carter rested his head back, closing his eyes. He hated flying, and he was feeling deeply nauseous from the constant thrum of the Comanche's engines and from the lower air pressure of high-altitude travel.

After rescuing Justus, they had loaded up the Comanche with supplies from the SP_Plot beside the Søndre Strømfjord in Greenland. They had dropped Justus at Ammassalik on the east coast where he planned to spend a few days recovering his health – and his sanity – before going back to war. Gone was the big black guy's easy smile. Torture by the Nex had left him bitter, and ready to seek out a terrible and lengthy revenge.

Carter and Mongrel had then taken shifts piloting the Comanche, refuelling in Sweden and stopping off at yet another SP_Plot on the Russia/Kazakhstan border where they acquired and loaded up two KTM LC8 890cc motorbikes, custom-built Spiral desert racers tastefully sprayed up in suitable camouflage and packing 329bhp and a torque rating of 198 lb-ft inside their rumbling engine casings.

Mongrel now hammered them high above China with a single objective: the location of Angel Constanza and information on where to find the Evolution Class Warhead.

Carter enjoyed his cigarette. Within the next thirty minutes the Comanche banked in a wide sweep to drop down below cloud cover.

A dazzling vista met their eyes.

Tibet, the Roof of the World. The highest country on Earth, where the lowest depths of the valley bottoms were at higher altitudes than most of the summits of the tallest mountains across the rest of the globe, and where the Tibetan Plateau was surrounded by the highest mountain range in the world: the Himalaya. Carter looked down in awe at this spectacular vision as they descended. Always a lover of mountains, for Carter this was an orgiastic visual feast. Greater than any other vision on earth, it quite literally took his breath away, spiking his senses with a heady blend of wonder and adrenalin.

Passing low over the Karakoram Range, Mongrel peered down, frowning thoughtfully.

'Go on,' snapped Carter.

'What?' Mongrel smiled a gappy smile.

'Say it. Whatever you're thinking. Destroy the ambience. Napalm the mood. Nuke the fucking *moment*.'

'Ha! Mongrel just thinking that you get good bit of skiing done down there. Look all right, it does.'

'Skiing? Mongrel, those mountains would smash you to a pulp. They would stomp your head in. You are a fucking insect to them.'

'What about snowboard, then?'

'I feel the same would apply.'

'Toboggan?'

'Mongrel! Just get us down there in one piece, and I'll be a happy man.'

The sky was bright and clear, signifying the start of the

370

Tibetan winter. Carter knew that the weather was more than likely to be harsh and could give them serious problems. He knew already that it was going to be a cold journey by bike; a supreme test of stamina.

'What about there?'

'You got any readings on this rogue SAM system?'

'Yar. They start to spring up on scanners like flies in jar of jam.'

'You have such a way with simile.'

'Similar *what*?'

'No, *simile*. Comparisons.'

'Companions?'

'Mongrel, wash your fucking ears out.'

'My beers?' He grinned. 'Har, only fucking with you Carter. Just liccle ol' Mongrel playing his liccle ol' games. I know what a simile is! I is not ignorant peasant! I is not damned *svolok* village idiot! Simile is just like a *smile*, only with an extra i.'

Carter sighed. It was going to be a long, tough mission.

The Comanche touched down on its creaking suspension. The rotors hissed and thrummed, scattering small stones and dust, as the cockpit canopy was folded back and locked in place.

Carter jumped down, boots thudding on the rocky ground, H&K MP5K ready in his wary hands. Around him reared a range of jagged mountains. Mongrel jumped down beside him, stretching his huge frame with a crackle of popping sinews. 'Is cold,' he observed.

'Yeah.' Carter nodded, moving a few feet away from the Comanche and gazing over the nearby cliff edge. A rocky slope tumbled away for hundreds of metres and was scattered with rough boulders, some larger than a house. 'It's like the surface of the moon, mate.'

'I get a brew on.'

'Good idea. I'll sort out the bikes.' As Carter unhooked the motorbikes and wheeled them free of the Comanche, checking their chassis mods and tyres, then their fuel tanks and starters and on-board guns, his mind turned over the new mission ahead of them.

Angel Constanza. Commander of an insane army. Willing to kill on sight anybody she met . . . Carter shook his head. It had to be an exaggeration. He knew that people were only too happy to exaggerate and amplify: it was the curse of the human imagination.

He fired up one of the KTM LC8s with its stealth mods in place, and the engine burbled. He felt the violent thrash of vibes through his hands as he revved the bike, and smiled despite the harshness of their surroundings and the apparently suicidal nature of their mission. There was nothing like a powerful bike to get Carter hard.

Mongrel had ignited a tiny J-block and was heating a pan of water. While it was coming to the boil, he grabbed their kit from the Comanche and piled it next to their makeshift campsite. Both men pulled on extra clothing – several thin layers, plus gloves. Carter changed his footwear for thermal-lined bike boots, and then donned a pair of silver Oakley Juliets with polarised fire-iridium Plutonite lenses to filter out the glare of the bright Tibetan sky. The lenses were specially designed for snipers, and gave clear-cut precision to a wearer's surroundings. Mongrel pulled free his own shades, square dark lenses set in thick sweeping black frames. Carter stared at them as Mongrel proudly placed them against the bridge of his nose.

'What the fuck are they?'

'Hey, this coolest of cool. Or so market trader told me.'

'Mongrel, you look like one of those extremely old 1960s gangsters. Without any style.'

'These cool shades, these is. They chic. They was $1.99, reduced from $350! Bargain.'

'Yeah, a bargain.' Carter grinned, pouring them two large mugs of tea and stirring in plenty of sugar.

Mongrel sipped at his brew. 'Carter, lad, this not boiling!'

'Water boils at lower temperatures in higher altitudes.'

'It does?'

'Yeah. It's the elevation – lower air pressure reduces the boiling point of a liquid. Look, just drink it. We've got a fucking job to do and time's starting to run out, so lay off whining about your tea. We're down to thirty hours – by The Priest's calculations, at any rate.'

'And he is mad one.'

'Fucking amen to that.'

Carter started his bike, wheelspun against loose stones, and shot off across the undulating rocky plateau in a burst of engine fumes. Mongrel fired up his own machine, checked that his tacky plastic shades were still in place, pulled his woolly hat tight over his ears, then followed Carter at a more sedate pace as he adjusted himself to the bike's idiosyncratic riding position. The cold wind blasted Carter's face as he led Mongrel down across the plateau, then followed a dried-up stream bed which led down towards the bottom of a steep-sided rocky valley. Mountains reared all around the two Spiral agents.

The two men hit the valley bottom and cruised for a while, swerving to avoid huge boulders and sudden drops in the rocky ground. The valley swept south and the bikes powered along, tyres thudding over rocks, engines growling quietly beneath the two riders as cold air found annoying little places to creep behind clothing and nip at exposed flesh, chilling bare skin to an almost instant blue.

After an hour they halted, breath steaming as they rubbed at their freezing flesh. Mongrel peeled off his gloves and rubbed his hands together vigorously. 'By God, Carter, I wish we could have flown in using Comanche.'

'I agree. Much easier. Bikes are just great in warm sunshine; but out here? You'd have to be insane.' They sorted through their kit, pulling on yet more clothing, including wind-proofs and neoprene face masks. Carter glanced over at Mongrel, who looked like an alien behind the black mask – only his eyes showing as glittering orbs.

He is destined to die, thought Carter suddenly. The cancer is eating through him, even as we speak. And yet he is still willing to give his life for Spiral, for his friends, still trying to save the world. A great flood of sorrow filled Carter then. A great wash of emotion that brought tears to his eyes. Even if they were successful, even if they halted the machinations of Durell – well, Mongrel was still dead fucking meat. A walking, talking corpse.

'You want a story?' Mongrel grinned. 'It help take your mind off cold! And you know how good Mongrel story is. They legend! Even late Simmo would sit and enjoy cup of Horlicks and listen to tale of Fat Chick Night!'

'Fat Chick Night?'

'Yeah, Fat Chick Night, tale of angst and woe, which centre around sexual promise of thirteen fat—'

'Maybe later.'

'Yes. Later: guaranteed,' Mongrel promised. Or threatened.

Carter fired up his bike and set off on a surge of power, leaving streaks of melted rubber on the rock. Mongrel followed close, weaving through the grey landscape and uttering a plethora of moans behind his neoprene mask.

Behind them, hidden in the rocks, cold black eyes in a disease-torn face watched them go.

The two men had found a narrow trail leading west of Rutog, with a mountain range hugging their left shoulders and steep water-eroded slopes dropping steeply to their right. The slopes were the results of landslides during the rainy season, and Carter kept a close eye on the trail for any signs of the sort of irregularity lethal to a biker – especially where a three-hundred-metre drop was concerned.

The trail started to climb, and both men had to work their close-ratio KTM machines hard as constant obstacles appeared on the trail: boulders and scatters of loose stones falling away into oblivion; huge humped spines of rock that necessitated careful balance as tyres slipped and then chewed for grip; curious rock pedestals with large dips between each circular head, a formation that had both Carter and Mongrel cursing as their bikes slid and lurched, tyres spinning and engine-cages clanging. The only way to negotiate the formation successfully was to lift the front wheel over the dip, then slam on the front brake and kick the rear of the bike around onto the circular rocky platform. As the formation gave way to a normal trail, both men were dripping sweat which chilled their bodies.

Carter halted, fumes pluming from his bike's stealth exhausts. Mongrel pulled up beside him with a tiny squeal from his tortured Brembos.

'What is it?' His voice was muffled behind his neoprene mask.

'Take a look for yourself.'

Mongrel squinted behind his cheap sunglasses. His

mouth made chewing motions beneath his mask and he flexed his cramping fingers, which were aching from the constant battle with the KTM and the cold.

'SAM site?'

'Must be one of Spiral's rogue systems.'

'You want to take a look?'

'Yeah. Something's bothering me.'

They eased their bikes closer, sub-machine guns resting on handlebars as they came close to the launching block. The alloy was grey, perfectly camouflaged. As they pulled their bikes to a halt Carter could just make out the dark grey lettering when he looked up along the wall of rock to the projection where the huge weapon squatted.

'It's Spiral, all right. SAM-7. Standard Mini SAM7.8 Block in a IVa configuration. You can see the vanes for the semi-active III-TR radar terminal guidance and inertial mid-course guidance systems.'

'Is it active?'

'Give me your ECube.'

Mongrel passed it over. Carter pulled free his glove, then traced a delicate pattern on the tiny alloy device. A sliver slid free of the housing and Carter saw digits flicker briefly across the blue screen as he integrated. There came a sudden whine of gears, and above them the block whirled in a rush of movement. Carter stared at Mongrel, then closed the ECube. 'Justus was right. They're primed, no question, and still working autonomously after all this time.'

'Didn't you just control it?'

'For about one second – then it kicked me violently out of the system. It disconnected the ECube.' Carter gave a death's-head grin. 'It shouldn't be able to do that.'

'At least we know we justified on bikes, and not wasting time busting our balls on rocky saddles!'

'But more importantly than that, now we know that some fucked-up AI has taken control of a Spiral SAM network. That should be an impossibility. Justus said the AI was based on the same technology as the developing Quantell processors from the same era – and that just gives me the fucking creeps. Makes me think of Nex intervention. Makes me think that Justus's story was based on a misunderstanding; maybe it's not true that the Nex didn't conquer this army of the insane because they couldn't – I find that a hard premise to swallow anyway. Maybe the Nex *allowed* the army its existence for a reason and the SAM sites are their guardian angels – protectors against air attack by a stronger force.'

'You have a sick mind, Carter, my friend.'

'I'm just the way society carved me,' he said.

The Tibetan trails and occasional roads were a nightmare of rock and dust. The cold was constant, seeping, draining. Carter had once heard Tibet referred to as 'The Cold Desert' and he found the description extremely fitting. It really did remind him of the desert – vast open expanses of undulating rock: a desert of stone. And all encompassed by the looming mountains. Carter smiled inwardly: the ever-present mountains were enough to give a man paranoia. Surrounded by such colossal peaks, how could one *not* believe in a god?

Darkness started to fall, draining the brightness from the sky. And with the failing light came the falling temperature as the stone surroundings sucked the heat from the world.

Soon the KTMs had slowed down, headlights cutting slices of yellow from the intense darkness. After several hours Mongrel flashed his lights at Carter and they pulled to the side of the trail with a crunch of tyres on loose stone. They were perched on the side of a mountain, a series of stepped valleys falling away in the darkness below them and lit by an eerie dim wash of blue-white starlight. The mountains around them were ink black, towering, jagged, chilling.

'I freezing tits off here, Carter. I die if I not get some heat.'

Carter nodded, killed his bike's engine, kicked down the bike's stand and eased his cramped and freeze-locked limbs from the saddle. He listened to the clicking of the engine as it cooled rapidly, his nose twitching at the scent of hot oil. Then he squatted by the side of the trail with his H&K slung over his back, face shadowed by the neoprene mask.

Within minutes they had a pan filled with water, and after another couple of minutes both were pouring hot tea down their throats.

'This a cold, desolate place,' said Mongrel over the green glow of the J-block, heating a second pan of water. He shivered. 'A man like me not tuned in to such desolate culture. How, for example, do they live without kebabs?' He sounded genuinely horrified. 'How, for example, can they live without titty bars? There only so much fun you can have with yak.'

'It's a case of the old different cultures, different customs,' said Carter. 'And believe me, Mongrel, you are a whole different culture, all on your own. You are your own universe of misunderstanding. Will you be fit to continue after drinking a gallon of tea?'

'You can feel that pressure of the clock, eh, Carter?'

'Yeah, I feel like we're fucking about in the mountains on a couple of desert racers while the rest of Spiral and the REBS do all the real work; I've got a horrible feeling we're on a wild-goose chase. Somebody is playing games with us, and we haven't got a copy of the rule book.'

'One more brew. Then the Mongrel feel ready for another session of freezing hours in saddle. Hey, you want to hear about Fat Chick—'

'No.'

Mongrel tilted his head to one side. 'In this light, Carter, I swear you have look of eagles about you. You are truly man to walk the mountains with!'

'Fine words, Dog. Get the tea made and drunk, and let's haul our arses out of here. I've got a creeping feeling we're being watched.'

'Pah! Just overactive magination.'

'You mean *i*magination?'

'Yeah. Sorry. I think this old dog suffering from serious case of altitude sickness,' Mongrel muttered, scowling. 'Obably.'

During the night it was so cold that the water froze in their canteens, and the bikes' brake-discs became coated in a layer of slick ice. The KTMs' gearboxes worked only intermittently, and their tyres were crusted with crushed white rime.

Dawn saw Carter and Mongrel dropping from the mountains past what they at first suspected was a deserted temple, a huge red-walled building built into the side of a mountain on huge steps of smooth carved stone. The beautifully crafted roofs were sloped and curved up suddenly at their edges, gilded and topped with golden statues facing in towards one another; the walls were wooden, the many tiny square windows edged in white and gold lace. The distant sounds of wind chimes echoed hauntingly from the red temple, and colourful banners snapped in the wind, crackling between tall fire-blackened wooden poles.

The two Spiral men cruised past at a modest speed, eyes searching the parallel layout of windows and decorated panelled doorways for any sign of occupancy. Suddenly, a single shot rang out, a crashing retort that boomed through the mountains. Carter saw a puff of stone dust kicked up near his front wheel and he slammed open the throttle, the word *sniper* racing through his brain. Mongrel needed no further persuasion, and the two men thundered down the narrow stone trail, suspensions hammering, tyres thumping and thudding through ruts, and over rocks. Another two shots followed and then they rounded a bend, a bulging rock face covering their back trail – and cutting them off from the gunman.

Carter slammed on his brakes and slithered to a halt on iced rims. He glanced back. 'You OK?'

'Yes. So, a friendly people, then?'

'It would appear that way.'

They quickly checked the bikes, then rode off down the narrow trail, both men cursing themselves. They had been lulled into a false sense of security, hypnotised by the harsh and savage beauty of the spectacular landscape and the apparent desolation. Whoever had taken those potshots had brought the two Spiral men back into a brutal reality; they knew now that they were in hostile territory. Now they rode with sub-machine guns cocked, safety catches off and a round in the breech.

Another hour saw them stopping at a near-deserted village due to Mongrel complaining of HAS – High-Altitude Sickness. He had called a halt twice to vomit beside the trail, and complained of headaches and a persistent feeling of nausea. For Mongrel, the whole world was spinning like a kaleidoscopic top.

Carter had brought Diamox from the SP_Plot stores, but the small grey tablets seemed to do little to relieve

Mongrel's symptoms – despite the bold claims on the packaging. And this natural break slowed their average speed right down, increasing Carter's sense of frustration.

The village was little more than a collection of wooden buildings painted in a mixture of white and red square panels. It was surrounded by a plain of tough coarse grass, and its central feature was a pile of stones supporting a gold idol atop an intricately carved wooden pole.

There were several men there, small and with jet-black hair tied back in ponytails. There were four or five horses tethered behind one of the wooden huts, along with a couple of small black yaks. The two Spiral agents stayed for a few minutes at this desolate outpost, just long enough to buy several small cups of butter tea, some potatoes, soya beans and wheat, and for Mongrel to use the local toilet at the edge of the village – effectively a wooden hut on beams that stretched out over a small but breezy ravine. It brought a whole new meaning to the term 'free fall'.

After Mongrel had followed local custom by burning his used toilet paper – much to his wrinkle-nosed disgust but at the urgent insistence of the villagers dressed in their heavy wraps of Yak fur – they listened to one of the men talking in the fast-spoken local dialect. Carter frowned as he tried to grasp at the odd word of intermingled Chinese.

'Little guy seem excited about something,' muttered Mongrel.

Carter nodded. 'I think he's trying to warn us.'

'What, about vast damned bloody drop under toilet seat? I swear, Carter, it enough to give man coronary. I not want to die on bog! I want to die in arms of gorgeous plump woman with arse like two badly parked Land Rovers!'

'Come on, before they try to sell us something else. They seem to have an addiction to dollars.'

They mounted the KTMs and headed out into the freezing wilderness of broken stone. Far off, they could now see the Himalaya range and the distant, mammoth peak of Qomolangma – otherwise known as Everest – and her many sisters. They were only a distant smudge on the horizon but, even so, they filled the two men with a subtle awe at the majesty of the planet on which they lived.

The bikes pounded along the narrow dirt road, picking up speed now that daylight was on their side once more. Mongrel's recovery from HAS seemed well under way as they dropped from the higher mountain elevations. The road was deserted. Since their purchase of creamy hot butter tea in the run-down village the Spiral agents had seen nobody.

The road wound down into a valley, the floor of which was littered with huge boulders. Man-made caves lined both sides and as the two men approached the valley's entrance on their bikes, Carter suddenly halted his machine.

Mongrel pulled up close. 'You got a bad feeling, bruv?'

Carter nodded. 'Don't you?'

'Carter the world spinning like I had twenty pints of Guinness. I not see danger if it bit me on my fat beer belly. Tell me what you sniff.'

'It's too convenient, this place. But there's no other way through.'

'How far we from Spiral_R?'

'About forty klicks. We're definitely close enough to be near the area where Constanza is supposed to operate. You ready to take on an army, Mongrel?'

Mongrel snorted. 'I couldn't take on my old grandmother.'

'So we just walk into what might be a trap?'

'Have we any other choice, Carter boy?'

'I suppose not.'

'Let's see what they got for us. It only way we get to meet Constanza.'

They eased their bikes forward and the towering valley walls closed in. Carter's eyes twitched from left to right, trying to see into the small dark hand-hewn caves. And he suddenly realised that something smelled bad; it drifted to him on the breeze, a distant lingering stench. The stench of organic atrophy.

'Into the valley of the shadow of death,' muttered Mongrel.

'What?'

'I just trying to lighten mood. Maybe we could sing songs?'

'Sing songs? Just keep your fucking machine gun pointing at those caves!'

'Only trying to help,' mumbled the big dentally challenged soldier.

The bikes rumbled across the valley floor, weaving to avoid obstacles. Then, up ahead, a small figure – stooped, and clad in furs – emerged from one of the caves.

'Here we go,' muttered Mongrel. The man was dark-skinned, small, with black hair and dressed in heavy yak furs. He carried an SLR, the rifle clasped in gnarled hands that had crusted red skin. But it was his face that caused Mongrel to stop his bike, Carter following suit a couple of seconds later. The man's face looked . . . scorched. The skin was blackened in patches, red-raw in others. Strings of flesh fell from his cheeks and flapped against his jawline, revealing the hollow cavities of his mouth within and the yellowed stumps of worn-out teeth.

Mongrel suddenly raised his H&K but Carter lifted his own weapon and knocked Mongrel's gun aside. Mongrel's head snapped right, his expression questioning. Carter gave a shake of his head. They waited as the man approached, his SLR pointed unwaveringly at them.

'He's on his own!' hissed Mongrel. 'Come on, Carter – we take him, no sweat.'

As the last syllables passed from Mongrel's lips, so they noticed other figures moving within the gloom of the caves – *all* the caves. Figures stooped, and started to stream slowly from dark holes in the rock – men and women, and a few children, all dressed in furs, all with the same scorched skin and spaghetti-flapping holed faces. Their eyes seemed distant, almost vacant, and they carried an assortment of weapons – from ancient British Army rifles to modern German, American and Russian sub-machine guns. Several even carried H&K MP5Ks – the same weapons that Carter and Mongrel held.

'Not good,' snapped Mongrel, looking rapidly from left to right at the closing circle of – what? Is this the army of the insane? he wondered, then licked at his lips behind the neoprene mask.

'Don't make any sudden movements,' growled Carter.

'I not dream of it, Carter, old boy.' More and more people were emerging from the caves and plodding across the valley floor. With them came a stench of something rotten.

'How many?' muttered Mongrel.

'At least three hundred, so far,' said Carter, the hairs on his neck prickling. And still they were emerging from the scatter of caves which lined the valley walls.

'How many bullets we got between us?'

'Don't even fucking think it.'

'We either shoot or run, Carter.'

384

'Or wait.'

'For *what*?'

'There.' Carter pointed, and from the throng, which had halted about ten feet from the two men on the bikes, came a woman. She was dressed in the same furs as the people with the deformed and scorched faces, but her beautifully haughty face was held high, skin perfect, eyes a deep gold. She had a mane of dark brown hair which flowed down her back, and she was of modest height but wiry and powerful, with generous hips. She carried a Kalashnikov JK50 – an old Nex weapon. She moved gracefully from the rear of the gathered mob to the front, and a hushed silence fell over the crowd. A cold wind blew, and Carter pulled down his mask. His eyes met the woman's and something clicked in his mind. Something strange, yet . . . *familiar*.

His head tilted gently, and she smiled at him then. She lifted her weapon and pointed the muzzle straight at Carter's forehead. 'What are you doing here?'

'We come searching for Angel Constanza. We seek her help. Are you Constanza?' Carter spoke carefully, his gaze locked to her large and beautiful gold eyes. He could see the scorched aliens around him in peripheral vision. They seemed uneasy, restless, toying with their weapons. As if they were ready to—

'*Murder*,' whispered Kade.

'Cheers, mate.'

Constanza nodded, and she licked at her lips. 'You are not welcome here, Spiral man. You are trespassers in our land. You are defilers of our soil. You tread our holy mountains with your bloodstained feet. You befoul our pure air with your hate-soiled breath. You carry your weapons of assassination in toxic hands, and your eyes reek of death and destruction and decay and despair.'

385

'A simple yes or no would have been enough,' muttered Mongrel.

'We have not come with death in our minds. We come seeking only knowledge. The world – your world as well as ours – is in terrible danger. We all face extermination – the human race faces *extinction* – and you have knowledge which could aid us, which could save us all.'

'You speak of the Evolution Class Warhead,' Constanza said softly, gold eyes sparkling in the bright Tibetan sunlight. 'You are not the only ones who have been here seeking such knowledge.'

'So it exists?' Mongrel blurted out.

Her gaze turned on him, and he felt suddenly chilled to the core of his soul. She carried death within her cold beauty. 'Yes, the ECW exists. I programmed it. Even now, it awaits only a simple priming sequence.'

'The others who came?' said Carter. 'Did you tell them where to find it? Did you give them ignition codes?' A sudden dread that the Nex would reach the weapon before him raised his fear to new heights. This was a situation he had not anticipated.

'I will tell you what I told them,' said Constanza, as her soldiers came closer and took the H&K sub-machine guns from the two men's helpless hands. 'You are the unholy. You have poisoned my soil. You have burdened my brethren with your toxic world. From this place you will be taken to Temple – and your flesh will be stripped from your bones, and cooked, and consumed to achieve an ultimate and perfect purification.'

'And I thought day could not get any fucking worse,' snapped Mongrel, scowling like thunder as Carter and him were dragged from their bikes. The stench of scorched, diseased flesh overwhelmed them as clawed red

386

hands scrabbled eagerly, hungrily, binding the Spiral agents with raze-wire.

The army – numbering perhaps a thousand – moved as a single unit, warily, with many scouts moving ahead and several covering their back trail. Carter and Mongrel were forced to walk near the centre of the mass, surrounded by sweating, stinking fur-clad bodies. Often, fingers would come snaking towards the two men, poking and prodding, and it took every ounce of their discipline for them to refrain from slapping the red gnarled hands away.

'You ever feel like you a chicken on butcher's block?'

'Yeah, that or a prime rump steak. Get the *fuck* off!' Carter smiled icily as he spoke through gritted teeth. His hands, bound in front of him, steadily dripped droplets of blood to the rocky ground they traversed.

'At least they're bringing the bikes,' said Mongrel. 'Dumb cunts wheeling them over the bumps.'

'I think this might be a case of chemically-induced genetic regression, as distinct from the fuckers being naturally stupid.'

'Har har.'

'Something amuse you?'

'We talk of them being stupid, but it is *us* for cooking in da pot.'

'We must have misheard her,' said Carter uneasily.

'No, no, mad bitch say we get all cooked and consumed for purification. In Mongrel books, that mean we due for chop, then pot.'

Constanza moved at the head of her hordes of bandits. They made good speed out of the valley and then moved on up, climbing a huge slide of dirt and scattered rocks until they reached a plateau ledge which curved away in a great arc.

'Up there.' Mongrel nudged Carter.

Carter glanced up and could see some kind of base high up the wall of a mountain. It was built from dark steel and glass, and glittered in the bright Tibetan sunlight. 'That's got to be Spiral_R. No wood in the construction. Far too technical for this part of the world.'

'That some ascent, laddie.'

'Yeah, the story of my fucking life.'

They moved across the plateau, the mountain looming closer and closer. Several times Carter tried to attract Constanza's attention, but she was either ignoring him or was too focused on something beyond his own powers of vision.

Once the plateau reached its highest point the rocky ground started to fall away in a gentle cascade of smooth, polished steps – like a giant's staircase, with each step five metres across. The men and women of Constanza's 'army' moved forward, leapt down one huge step, then moved on once more, jumping down with their furs flapping. A wind howled from one side of the natural polished formation, blasting up out of the valley and stealing Carter's breath away. Through his wind-seared tears he caught his first glimpse of the camp at the base of the mountain – at the foot of Spiral_R – looking as if it had been laid out for the purpose of ritual worship.

'Big camp,' observed Mongrel.

Carter merely nodded. They moved closer, boots slapping stone, the leap down the big steps made dangerous by their tightly bound hands. With each jump, the wire bit into Carter's flesh and he cursed the bindings viciously.

'They got lot of animals,' observed Mongrel after a few more minutes had passed. 'Yaks and horses. Look, and some goats. They have own little farm.'

They moved still closer, and both Carter and

Mongrel's blood froze suddenly in their veins. They stared hard at the pole, and the rigid locked body of the man who had been brutally impaled on it. His arms and legs were twisted unnaturally, his face frozen in a rictus scream of death.

The Spiral men turned to look at one another, silently communicating their mutual determination to get the fuck away from this hell-hole as soon as they could.

After this first marker they passed more and more impaled bodies. There were men, women, children – even the occasional Nex, some still wearing their black body-hugging uniforms and soft leather boots. All Nex had had their masks torn free, and the copper eyes were dulled, lifeless.

'You know what give me creeps?' hissed Mongrel.

'What?'

'At base of each pole is big puddle of dried blood. That mean them impaled alive. Hoisted up there, and forced down kicking and screaming onto the sharpened point – whack, right up arse, up past spine and out of back of neck. *Savage*. I wonder just how long it take them to die? I have horrible feeling it not quick.'

'Thank you for sharing that wonderful observation,' Carter said dryly. 'Now I *really* feel better.'

They reached the foot of another natural stone stairway and the camp spread out around them in its unholy stench. As they walked, prodded in the back with sub-machine guns, they passed rows of tents between which were displayed many disgusting examples of brutality. Piles of hands, naked bodies staked out against iron pegs – several still alive, but with flesh carved from their limbs, and wriggling numbly, feebly. In one case, there was a pile of around thirty heads, eyes glazed, the stink incredible. A woman was seated nearby, cross-legged, a head in her lap with its eyes facing towards Carter and Mongrel. As they passed, she lopped the crown of the head off with a blunt, chipped machete, and started to scoop out the rancid brains with a spoon, digging the tarnished silver implement in hard and grinning madly through her own holed cheeks as the spoon made soft, *schlup* noises. Carter nearly threw up.

They were pushed towards what seemed to be a centre for the camp: a huge ring of stones, each as large as a man and worn smooth by centuries of the pounding elements. The stones were topped with a wooden platform on which squatted a large black iron cauldron, apparently covered in tar. A fire was burning steadily underneath, sending out a thin column of black smoke.

'That look like my sister's manky old barbecue.'

Carter glanced sideways at Mongrel. 'So your sister cooks human flesh, does she?'

'It fucking tastes like it.'

'Anyway, I didn't know you *had* a sister!'

'Aye, Carter. I got six sisters. Jam mauled this one at Spiral Christmas party. In fact, I pretty sure he gave her right good seeing-to. He couldn't walk next day. Apparently. He say she milked him like stag, although he then smirk and say that this OK because he have huge balls like stag.'

Carter mulled this over, distracted by displays of obvious cannibalism presented to his reluctant gaze. But he was still disturbed by the notion of a *woman* in the same mould as Mongrel . . . and the idea of *six* of them! He shivered.

'Does your sister . . . look like you?'

'Oh no!'

Carter released a deep sigh. 'Thank God,' he said.

'She much uglier.' Mongrel grinned his gappy grin, set

in a pouchy, rough-skinned, heavily scarred face on the front of a tufted head shaped like a punchbag. 'I pretty one in the family, for sure.'

Angel Constanza mounted the platform at that moment, and the army around her grew hushed. They dropped to their knees, silence settling like nuclear fall-out ash. Then, as she finished speaking, she made eye contact with Carter and gave a broad smile. Her gold eyes sparkled and Carter felt confusion flood through him.

Constanza dropped down from the platform and stood in front of the two men. She dragged off her furs and stood proudly, her near-naked body incredibly toned and muscled. She was wearing nothing but a leather harness hung with knives and jewels. She shook back her hair and moved close to Carter, whose face went suddenly stony and grim, lips tightly compressed. There was a long, uneasy silence as they stared into one another's eyes.

'Don't you remember me?' she asked.

Carter frowned. 'Remember you? I have never met you before in my life.'

'You have.'

Carter shook his head, peripherally aware of Mongrel's smirk. 'I'm pretty sure you're going to eat my fucking liver – whatever – but on this point we must disagree.'

Constanza took a step back, turned lithely and bent to grab her fallen furs, presenting her ample and uncloaked backside to the Spiral men's gaze. Mongrel's eyes widened in their sockets.

Then she gestured to several of the disfigured soldiers who grabbed Carter and Mongrel roughly between them, guns poking against the backs of their heads.

'We *have* met before, Carter,' said Constanza without turning to look at him. Her voice was quiet. 'That's why

I know about Kade – that's why I know about the demon twin nestling inside your skull.'

Then she was gone, and Carter was left frozen, confused, filled with a billion questions pounding his mind as the guards jostled him and Mongrel away from the central cooking area and towards a wooden hut with thick pitted black steel bars that was surrounded by a ring of heavily armed fighters.

Carter's last sight was of an old man, seated, almost naked, his face a cluster of ragged flesh strings. He was eating small cubes of raw meat, pushing them into his mouth via a hole in his cheek, jaw opening to accept the soft flesh before chomping between rounded molars. The strings of cheek flesh swayed in rhythm with his chewing . . .

The heavy timber door of the hut slammed in Carter's face, blocking the view and plunging both men into a frightening darkness.

Night had fallen. Outside, many fires burned among the army of the insane and the Spiral men could smell the sickly sweet stench of old rotting meat turned carefully on long slick skewers.

'We're running out of time,' said Carter. His head was pounding, and his limbs felt like lead. His bound hands were burning him with lines of razor fire, and his recent wounds were throbbing, making his life just that little bit more uncomfortable: his aching nose, the cracked ribs, the extensive bruising across his whole frame. I feel like a kick-bag, he thought. I feel like a human train wreck.

On top of this, the day's surreal events seemed like a very bad, fuzzy nightmare. A brain-fuck with a sharpened screwdriver.

'What we going to do, Carter, my boy? We got to find

codes for Warhead. We close now – can you feel it? I can feel it. We are close, oh so very close – like a quivering hand down a plump girl's panties going for that sweet wet touch. And that fucking *pizda* out there, she know how to initiate ECW and she not fucking telling us! We need kidnap her, Carter. We need give her much pain, then she talk, Mongrel promise you that!'

'Have you managed to break free of the wire yet?'

'No.'

'Me neither. Next option?'

'Aww, fuck, Carter, we need think of something real fast. Why don't you sweet-talk her or something?'

'*What?*'

'Ha har! Old Mongrel, he see way that sexy little lady stare at Carter man. She fancy dance with you, Carter baby, she fancy slice of Carter meat pie. Again.'

'Again? What the fuck do you mean, *again*?'

'She remember you, Carter.'

'She remembers *fuck all*.'

'OK, OK, don't get touchy. I know how embarrassing these things can be.'

'You fucking *what*?'

'Mongrel, too, spend many drunken night canoodling with some sexy plump *devushka*, hands all over ass and slobbering tongues entwined – dancing in as close as plump overhang bellies allow, only to wake up next morning next to Great White Whale and wishing, oh wishing I had harpoon gun to hand and real skill with weapon, just like Captain Ahab. I been there Carter, there no shame in beer goggles. We all done it. We all felt the comedy burning in cock as we rush limping and scratching to the VD clinic to be given our anonymous identification number. And oh how we all does laugh as simple case of antibiotics clear it all up! How we roar with guffaws down at pub and drip Guinness down our combats.' Mongrel finally rolled into an uneasy silence. He coughed in the gloom and scratched at his itching stubble.

'Mongrel,' Carter interrupted threateningly, 'we live in *different fucking worlds*. Now listen, you moron, Constanza's not some ex-girlfriend who just might do me a favour because I was good in bed. She's a fucking lunatic rogue ex-Spiral programmer with a fucking Kurtz obsession. But this isn't *Apocalypse Now*, it's *Apocalypse Over*. She's a fruit-loop, a nutcase, and the only way we're getting warhead codes from her fried brain is if we drill them out.'

'I understand.'

'Understand what?'

'I suppose . . . you know, shagging cannibal – well, it not good for man's self-esteem.'

'Mongrel, I did not *shag* the cannibal.'

'Ahh, but she know about Kade. So you *must* have shagged cannibal.'

Carter paused, unease prickling down his spine. He licked at his dry lips: their packs had been dumped outside and thirst-quenching was currently high on his agenda of needs – shortly behind the necessity of strangling Mongrel.

'I concede,' said Carter slowly, 'that she did mention Kade, and as far as I am aware, only a handful of very, very close acquaintances know about *that* fucking demon. However, my old *drook*, I certainly didn't sleep with the woman. I never even shared a glass of Italian red. I didn't put my hand down her "sweet panties" and I didn't cook her tagliatelle in exchange for hardcore Spiral secrets. You listening to me, Mongrel?'

'Har har har.' Mongrel loomed in the darkness and slammed Carter hard on the back. 'Just fucking with you,

Carter, just fucking with you. Don't get so uptight – the old Mongrel, well, he just trying to keep your chin up. Give you boost of some good old British spunk!'

'Thanks,' said Carter weakly. 'Spunk. That's just what I need.'

'You want to hear story of Fat Chick Night yet?'

'No.'

'Another time, then,' mumbled Mongrel, and retreated to his own side of the hut.

Carter's head snapped up as the door opened. Constanza was there, holding a small Glock 9mm and with an Agram K50 silenced sub-machine gun strapped to her back. She gestured wordlessly to the two men and lumbering to their feet they stooped and stepped out into the bright daylight, squinting.

The camp seemed to be in turmoil. The deformed and scabrous fighters were running everywhere, bristling with weapons. Constanza indicated that the two Spiral men should grab their packs.

'We going somewhere?' asked Carter.

'Yes, I will show you Spiral_R.'

'Ahh, the place which twisted your mind?'

She smiled then, gold eyes shining. 'Yes, something like that. You'll understand if I don't return your guns. Now, down there, past the yaks, the narrow pathway.'

The two men walked ahead of Constanza. Carter glanced back, expecting to see an entourage of guards, but none followed.

'What's happening back there?' asked Mongrel. 'What is all excitement about?'

'We have some unexpected and unwelcome visitors.'

They moved down the narrow pathway, which squeezed between two huge boulders at the foot of the dark mountain walls. Carter glanced up at the steep climb ahead of them. Steps had been cut into the rock face, a huge veering series of uneven ledges, and as Carter took the first step he had to strain to get his leg just high enough. Great, he thought. The world's largest staircase.

Grunting, Mongrel followed close behind Carter and within a few minutes they were above the camp which bustled like an anthill. The 'soldiers' were setting up some kind of defences; trenches had been uncovered and they were rolling out big mounted guns which were being locked into place on sturdy steel tripods.

'None of the army are allowed up here,' said Constanza, climbing lightly and easily behind the two men. 'It is hallowed ground. A holy place. They do not understand the implications of Spiral – or what Spiral_R was all about.'

'What happened to them?' asked Carter.

Constanza shrugged. 'Chemical agents? Biological toxins? Maybe it was a side-product of that toxic fucking puke Durell poured over the world. So, a mutant form of HATE, then? I'm not really sure. I do not claim to understand genetics – code was my speciality.'

'And you know the location of the Evolution Class Warhead?'

'I do.'

As they climbed, both Carter and Mongrel started to sweat heavily, their packs gripped in clumsy, bound hands. The camp fell away below them, and within thirty minutes looked like nothing more than a toy model populated by scurrying stick figures.

'This feels strange,' said Carter at last. 'Like you are abandoning them.' He threw the dark-haired woman a glance, but her expression did not change; she showed no emotion.

'What that noise?' Mongrel's head cocked to one side.

'Choppers,' snapped Carter. He whirled, stare sweeping the skies – and there they were, a swarm of black Nex helicopters. They swept down from the heavens towards the distant camp – and machine guns began to rattle from the mounted positions on the ground.

'They have brought Htanks, and infantry,' said Constanza. 'My scouts report six thousand Nex, three hundred tanks, and as many helicopters.'

'Your soldiers cannot hope to stand against such military might.'

'Yes. I agree.'

'So we've taken the back door?' sneered Carter.

Constanza smiled, nodding. 'Come on, follow me. We are nearly there.'

Carter glanced up, at the steel and glass walls of Spiral_R – and something suddenly jarred within him as he saw cold sunlight sparkling through a missing expanse of roof. And now that they were close enough to see, he also noted the dented struts, the missing windows, the damaged pillars. Spiral_R was no longer an operationally viable base. It had been ravaged by war.

They increased their pace while below them the swarm of Nex helicopters swept down like a plague with their guns blazing. Fire erupted from mounted flame throwers, scorching the earth and sending the army of the insane running burning into their own trenches where they set their comrades alight. Then Carter heard it: the smash and *krump* of tank shells.

They continued to climb and finally reached the winding path leading to the buckled alloy doors of Spiral_R – development headquarters for the QIV processor, the production centre for the original QuakeHub under Durell's perverse guidance . . . and the intellectual

397

powerhouse that had created the miracle of the Evolution Class Warhead: the greatest single intelligent weapon ever devised.

'Why did you bring us with you?' asked Carter, bathed in sweat and panting. His legs quivered with the strain of the incredibly steep ascent and his lungs were burning because of the reduced level of oxygen at this altitude.

'You brought the Nex to me,' said Constanza softly. She moved towards Carter and placed a hand on his shoulder. He looked into her eyes then, but they no longer glimmered with power, dignity or hope. The Glock lifted, and Carter realised that she carried a short knife in her other hand as the blade came to rest against the skin of his cheek . . .

'*Kill her, and kill her now!*' hissed Kade. '*Let me do it, let me take her, let me fuck her hard and watch her corpse tumble into the valley below . . . but do it quick, do it before the fucking Nex arrive, do it, Carter! Fucking DO IT NOW!*' Kade's arrogant tone had risen to a painful scream which pounded against the inside of Carter's skull like a rock being slammed against his brain. Stars flickered behind his vision; agony bounced around his skull.

Constanza's knife fell – and parted the binding wires. Then she moved to Mongrel and cut through the large man's bonds. Reaching into her own pack she brought out Carter's Browning and Mongrel's Sig. She passed the stunned men the weapons, and said, 'You have more ammunition in your own packs.'

'You are helping us to escape?'

Constanza shook her head. 'I am helping *myself* escape. The Nex have left us alone here for a long time, gentlemen. I am no fool – the surrounding SAM sites are controlled by the Nex. For whatever reason, they left these people here to breed and feed from one another. To

kill and brutalise and cannibalise – they left them alone
even when the odd stray Nex fell into the web. I was
trapped here after the bombing of Spiral_R, left to rot
and to die by my colleagues. Do you know how that feels?
The sense of abandonment? The utter loss of hope? But
the army – they saw me as a queen, they saw me as a *god*.
And I adopted their ways for my own survival. It is incredible what a human being will do to survive, gentlemen . . .
what a person will do in order just to continue to breathe
God's good clean air.' She gave a low, sardonic laugh.
'Facts: you have arrived. You brought the Nex here. The
Nex have decided to exterminate the army – *my* army –
maybe because they are disgusted with the brutality of
these twisted people, although I doubt it. Or maybe
because they are still looking for *you*. My best chance for
survival is to show you – here, in Spiral_R – the secret
buried within this ruin.'

'But why? Why bring us?' rumbled Mongrel.

Constanza smiled then. 'Because, my dear Mongrel, I
cannot fly the Manta which nestles under a protective
shield of alloy in one of the bunkers. I do not have the
ignition codes. I am trapped.'

'And you propose?' said Carter softly.

Constanza stared down at the distant carnage. Guns
were still thundering, choppers swooping and diving, bullets cutting the few remaining people to shreds of meat.

'An exchange. Of information. Of skills. You get me
out of here alive, and I will program your EC Warhead. If
you save my skin, then I will take you to your machine.'
She smiled wryly. 'Yeah. I will save the world.'

'Well, guys, we better be quick.' Mongrel gestured, and
they glanced down the steep mountainside to where the
swarm of choppers had gathered and was hovering. 'Look
like we might have some bad company on its way.'

Even as the words flowed from Mongrel's mouth, the choppers powered ahead and then swept up like a huge black swarm, engines screaming, rotors thumping.

Carter, Mongrel and Constanza shouldered their packs and sprinted towards the huge buckled gates of Spiral_R as the Nex helicopters screamed up from the valley and opened fire. The three hunted people dived for cover under a protective but precariously leaning archway.

Carter growled, 'Where is this Manta? Which way do we go?'

Constanza pointed. 'There, towards the bunkers . . .'

But then three choppers swarmed overhead and squads of Nex threw themselves from the howling machines on wildly swaying fast-ropes, Steyr TMPs yammering. Carter took a deep breath and led the group in a pounding charge towards the underground bunker and the promise of escape.

CHAPTER 15

SYNTHESIS

Jam watched impassively as the Sleeper Nex poured into the reactor chamber of the K-Lab. He turned: Sonia looked alien to him with her pale flesh, parted red lips, fear like a bloodstain on her strange human features—

The trapped insects chattered in Jam's mind, desperately urging him to return to the ways of the Nex, to relinquish all emotion . . .

And then Nicky was there, her face close. He could smell the musk of her skin. Feel the soft velvet of her hands. Taste the caress of her lips, brushing his as he fell and tumbled into another world, another time, another existence – and he knew then. Knew she was dead, murdered by the Nex. She was dead, and had returned to warn him. To help him. 'No,' said Nicky, and Jam's copper eyes blinked—

'No,' said Sonia, her arms resting gently against his black armour.

Jam nodded, breathing deeply as the chittering of the trapped insect souls in his shell receded. Then he was calm again, whole again, one again. He stared calmly at

401

the charging Sleeper Nex, then looked down at Sonia. He could read her panic. Her fear. Her despair.

'Call Fenny. Tell him to pick us up from the roof. Now.'

'The roof?'

'Just do it!' snapped Jam. Spikes sprang up along his armoured forearms and he leapt forward, limbs smashing out to rake a great hole in the thick panel before him, dragging it free so that it fell, tumbling end over end until it splashed into the thick green reactor coolant far below.

Jam moved to the edge of the level and glanced up. There was a huge tube, some form of ventilation system; it had a ladder riveted to its internal wall. But the distance to it was at least fifteen metres – too far for Sonia J to jump.

'Fenny's on his way,' Sonia reported.

'Come here.'

Sonia glanced up. 'Oh no, no way, Jam – I cannot possibly make that jump!'

'You're not going to jump.'

The Sleeper Nex were pounding up the ramp. Jam swept low, lifting Sonia in his armoured claws – then he whirled and with a powerful thrust of his awesomely muscled arms he launched her across the gap without giving her time to think. Sonia flew, slammed into the wall and scrabbled frantically for the ladder. She dropped her Uzi, which fell into the green coolant. Grunting and cursing, legs kicking frantically and sweat-slippery hands grasping and sliding, she finally managed to get a secure handhold and glanced back to Jam—

As the first of the Sleeper Nex arrived. Two pounded towards him, snarling, long trails of saliva drooling from their bloodstained jaws. Jam leapt forward, ducking a slashing claw and grabbing the first Sleeper's head. It

402

struggled, snarling, and Jam launched it across the chamber where its flailing body crashed through a tall rack of delicate glass tubes. Then more claws slammed against Jam's armoured flank and Jam's own talons hammered down, breaking one of the second Sleeper's limbs – a *crack* that made Sonia cringe. Jam's left armoured forearm smashed forward, claw slicing into his assailant's belly and grabbing a mass of internal organs, wrenching them free in a gore-splattering shower of offal. The Sleeper Nex slumped to the ground, blood gushing from its disembowelled gut cavity, flooding through the mesh of the buckled alloy and falling into the old reactor's coolant pool far below. A third Sleeper charged up the ramp – followed by another two, and then two more.

Jam crouched to avoid twin blows, then straightened and slammed one Sleeper sideways. It teetered for a moment on the edge of the walkway before toppling into the green coolant. It went under in a huge splash of glutinous green and did not reappear.

Sonia shuffled nervously up a couple of rungs of the ladder. It was a long way to fall. She felt incredibly vulnerable, hanging there, with no floor beneath her to break any such tumble.

Jam's head snapped right. He snarled, 'Fucking *climb*, woman!'

Sonia started up the ladder, chilled by the look on Jam's face – frightened to her very core by the visible hatred and hint of insanity. He was, right now, most definitely more ScorpNex than human.

Jam leapt and fought, slashing left and right with his claws as the Sleeper Nex flooded up into the chamber and towards him across the K-Lab's mesh alloy floor. Jam slipped and slid on the blood-and meat-strewn surface, ducking blows, dodging snapping, rending jaws, powering vicious thrusts into abdomens and heads, splitting armour, cracking skulls like brittle eggs, gouging bellies and ripping pumping, glistening organs free in a blur of unstoppable powerhouse violence.

Then Jam suddenly turned, ran and leapt, sailing out over the disused reactor and slamming into the vertical cylinder, which shook alarmingly under his weight. His claws grasped at the internal ladder and he swung himself up into the dark interior. The ladder rattled, shaking violently, and several rivets popped free with squeals of stressed steel. Below, the stunned Sleeper Nex stood for a moment, eyes focused on Jam's disappearing figure. They snarled as one, a loud and terrible sound: a sharing of the Hive mind. Then, whirling, one Sleeper Nex ran, its claws gouging the mesh floor, and made the leap. But it bounced from the ladder and tumbled into the old reactor below. Another leapt, claws gaining purchase with clumsy movements, and it started to climb. Jam's armoured foot cannoned down, five times, breaking its face and sending it, too, tumbling towards destruction and a horrible death by drowning in the highly toxic mix of glutinous nuke coolant.

The Sleeper Nex spread out. Then, as if receiving the same instantaneous command, they turned and sprinted away, searching for another way to reach Jam – and the incredibly valuable data cube that Sonia carried in hands that shook with mortal fear.

They moved along wide shafts. Several times Jam stopped and smashed holes through thick alloy panels with his armoured claws, bending back huge sheets of metal and urging Sonia to follow him quickly.

They climbed upwards, and along several more girders that were part of the building's internal roof structure.

They emerged onto a platform high within the roof space, a series of long narrow beams with thick tensioning cables bolted at stress points and supporting the whole structure. Jam led Sonia, like a tightrope walker, across the beams and she quivered, filled with terror as she inched her way across, never once daring to look down.

They reached a wall. Jam punched a hole through the concrete blocks, giving himself a foothold to clamber higher where he tore a gaping wound in the roof alloy. Daylight spilled in and Jam levered himself through the gap. Then he reached down and hauled Sonia up.

The fresh breeze slapped her cheeks. Sonia breathed deeply, panting, aware of her thundering heart in the huge echoing cavity of her chest. Then she heard a sound, and down below a Sleeper Nex sprinted across a narrow girder without any sign of fear or vertigo.

Jam aimed his sub-machine gun through the hole in the roof and drilled the Sleeper Nex with bullets as it ran. It skittered on blood-slick steel and fell away from the beams, toppling fifty feet and slamming into several metal beams on its downward trajectory until it smashed into a metal panel which crumpled under the heavy impact. Sonia peered into the gloom.

The Sleeper Nex was thrashing around.

It was hurt, but it was far from dead.

The sounds of thumping rotors echoed from the distance, and the twin-rotor Chinook powered over the horizon like a lumbering monster, its Honeywell turboshafts whining. Sonia waved towards the aircraft as it flew towards them and Jam pointed across the roof, towards the massive panelled dome of the cooling system some hundred metres away.

More Sleeper Nex had emerged. They glanced up at the Chinook, then saw Jam and Sonia and began to sprint towards them. The Chinook swept low, trailing a cable from its loading doors, and Fenny's skilled piloting ensured that the aircraft steadied, cable swaying slightly.

Sonia started to climb up the cable. Jam wound the end around his armoured forearm and signalled to Fenny who lifted them swiftly from the roof of the disused plant – scant seconds before the Sleeper Nex arrived. One leapt, and from his swaying vantage point Jam emptied a full magazine into its snarling face. Bullets crashed into its visage and split its armour, and, trailing a spray of crimson, it fell and slammed hard onto the concrete surface four storeys below. The Chinook lifted high into the clear Norwegian sky.

And slowly, like fish on a line, Sonia and Jam were reeled in.

Sonia lay on her back, panting, on the cargo-deck floor. Jam squatted beside her, reloading his weapon and glancing out at the rolling landscape beyond.

'We need to refuel,' came Fenny's voce. 'Where we heading?'

Jam rolled shut the cargo doors, and the cold buffeting wind was shut out. Then he moved to the cockpit and checked the latest uploaded coordinates – in encrypted format – from Carter. 'He's in Tibet,' said Jam, slowly.

'Yeah. But where is the EC Warhead?'

'Let's head east, see if we can rendezvous with him. When he moves, he's going to move fast. Try and call up Carter or Mongrel on their ECubes; see if we can establish a destination for the ECW,' he rumbled.

'I can refuel in Finland, then we plot a course through Russia, see if we can intercept him there. You get what you needed, Jam?'

'Yes. We got the data for the EDEN depots strewn

across the globe. Now we just have to upload the data into the Warhead – and then, with luck, this weapon of mass detonation will do its job. Take out the biological shit.'

Fenny banked and headed east towards the Swedish border. 'Shall I inform The Priest of our route?'

'Yeah. Ask him for some DemolSquad back-up; I think we are going to need every bit of help we can get.'

'Won't Carter be expecting you to ECube the data?'

'We can't; because of the encryption, and because of how the shit is stored. We have to deliver it by hand. And that's going to take time.'

Fenny thought for a moment. 'Are we likely to see combat?'

'I'd be surprised if we didn't.'

'Then we won't just refuel. We can dump this Chinook and pick ourselves up something a little more, shall we say, exotic.'

'You fucking pilots. Why've you all got hard-ons for Comanche war machines?'

Fenny shrugged. 'It's just the way we're made,' he said, his curled hair bobbing.

Jam moved back to Sonia, who had sat up and was rubbing wearily at her eyes. She crawled to her feet, and glanced around at the equipment left by the dead members of their group. Baze had left behind his heavy overcoat, Haggis a satchel filled with HighJ explosives, Oz a long soft case for his sniper rifle, and Rekalavich a faded, corner-curled photograph that he'd tacked to the wall with tape. Sonia moved over to the photograph and pulled it free. It showed a woman, young and pretty with a cascade of dark curls and deep red lipstick. Sonia turned the photograph over. On the back somebody had written *With all my eternal love, Tanya*. Sonia fond that there were tears on her cheeks.

'Are you OK?' rumbled Jam.

'They are all dead.'

'Yes.'

'This data better be *fucking important*.'

'It is,' said Jam smoothly. 'It is the information that will save the world. You have done well, Sonia. You have showed bravery and determination – you have shown courage greater than I could ever have anticipated.'

Sonia merely nodded, her face grey and exhausted. She moved to the wall, strapping herself into her harness. She pulled free the small silver data cube and stared into its faceted depths, then her head fell back with a thud and she closed her eyes. I hope you were worth it, she thought bitterly. I just hope you were worth it.

The Comanche soared through the rain-filled heavens, armoured rotors thumping, missiles gleaming eerily in the gloomy half-light. Within the insect-like HIDSS, Heneghan, combat pilot and generously bosomed mother of three, hummed to herself and glanced over her shoulder at the snoring figure of The Priest. A large man, he wore grey robes, open to show his hairy chest, and his hand was curled around his rosary beads in sleep – a comfort toy.

It's a shame to wake him, she thought. But they were nearing the Number 45 TacSquad sweep destination and Heneghan had a bad feeling that they had found another Dreadnought site. 'Priest?'

The Priest continued to snore, barrel chest rising and heaving. He made a snuffling catarrhal noise, gurgling on phlegm before turning over a little and settling back down against the leather of the co-pilot's seat.

'PRIEST!'

'Hnnh! Hnnh? What? Oh, yes, Heneghan.' He

coughed, shuffling himself up in the seat a little. 'Are we here, then? That was quick. Seems like only two minutes ago . . .'

'It's been three hours, Priest. And you've been snoring like a bloody warthog.'

'Yes, a terrible chest infection, Heneghan. But the Lord sends these trials to test us, does He not? Now then.' He pulled down a scanner, his eyes sweeping the screen before him. 'You see the SAM protection?'

'Very heavy,' said Heneghan, slowing their speed and banking the combat chopper once more. 'Down there; we're just out of range. I can make out thirty sites.'

The Priest caressed his ECube, which unfolded in his broad flat hand. His skin was quite soft, for The Priest used a lot of skin ointment. 'Hmm. Yes, a lot of highly expensive and terminally efficient firepower – just to protect a sardine-canning factory? And look there, you can see the huge central funnel used for launches. This, I think, is where they make the FreightTugs.'

'Shall we lock the coordinates?'

'Yes, add them to the data bank.'

Heneghan slowed the Comanche until it was hovering, and she jostled the combat vehicle, fighting the elements of the rising storm. 'Taking a snapshot – now.' The Priest watched digits flicker up the monitor before him; he gestured with his ECube, and navigated through various screens which gave read-outs on Dreadnought Sites, WarFacs and other aspects of Durell's star-spanning empire.

The Priest had organised the remaining men and women of Spiral into teams, newly formed DemolSquads, TacSquads and TankSquads. Each had been given goals, missions, and final destinations for the coming battle. Now The Priest and thirty other TacSquads were in the process of sweeping known locations, sites, weapons depots, Dreadnought construction centres, gathering a data bank of coordinates that could, The Priest hoped, be used by the EC Warhead and the DemolSquads themselves when it came to the final, ultimate battle – the Big Push that they all knew was imminent. The Priest looked weary, and his faith was being tested to its very limits. Sometimes he found it hard to believe. Sometimes he wondered if mankind was, ultimately, doomed.

By his own hand, sighed The Priest.

'You OK?' Heneghan's voice was filled with compassion. She was staring back at him. He gave another great sigh, nodding. 'You look wiped out, Holy Man,' she said.

'I am exhausted. But then, so is every man and woman of Spiral. So is every REB who has joined our cause. We are stretched to our limits, our GRID is broken, we are relying on a Warhead which may not exist.'

'Carter will find it,' said Heneghan softly.

The Priest's eyes gleamed in the cockpit gloom. 'Yes,' he said. 'I'm sure that he will.'

The streets of Johannesburg in the Gauteng Province of South Africa were alive with activity. People were celebrating the imminent arrival of EDEN and the freedom it would bring outside the city sprawls. TV adverts fielded by HIVE Media Productions had been running in heavy rotation, promising an end to the city-wide population restrictions. The land outside the cities would once more be available to the global population without them having to ingest dangerous chemical tablets and suffering the uncertainty of whether or not they were walking through tox-filled zones.

9mm flowed with the crowd, her high cheeks flushed with the humid heat and the close proximity of so many people. Her dark eyes were scanning as she moved with the human current, her athletic frame merging with the mob. Laughter echoed through the streets and there was a distinctly carnival atmosphere hanging like smoke in the air.

9mm noted the Nex stationed at every street corner. They wore their masks, copper eyes impassive, Steyr TMPs and Kalashnikov JK49s and JK51s pointing at the ground.

The Nex were sanctioning freedom. And 9mm couldn't help wondering why.

The crowd surged, huge groups of people dancing in the roads. 9mm pushed her way to one side and stood on the pavement, body held casual but eyes still alert. Somewhere in the distance, fireworks roared into the sky and green and white stars sparkled.

A figure moved slowly along the opposite pavement. AnneMarie was tall, a little over six feet, and very slim. Her hair was golden, and tied back in a loose ponytail. Her head sat atop a smooth, slender neck and turned as her eyes sought out her—

Companion. Their gazes met, and both moved to rendezvous on one corner just behind a group of Nex soldiers. The Nex, despite appearing calm, seemed subtly twitchy. They scanned the crowd constantly, conspicuously enough to make both 9mm and AnneMarie smile viciously. To the Nex, a crowd was something to be put down – not actively encouraged.

'This way,' said AnneMarie.

They moved again with the crowd as more fireworks erupted to the west and people of all nationalities cheered, united in the excitement of the moment.

Eventually, after carefully checking out the local Nex, the two women slid down a narrow alleyway and halted at

411

the end, scrutinising their back-trail. AnneMarie produced an ECube and scanned their surroundings.

'We need to get closer,' said 9mm.

'We might make them suspicious.'

'Come on; we can pretend to be lovers out for a stroll.' Arm in arm, they moved on. Above them, rearing into the evening sky, rose the Sentinel Corporation's Johannesburg HQ, its glittering surfaces of steel and glass fitting neatly into the skyline of central Johannesburg.

AnneMarie's ECube scanned, checking data, analysing structures. The two women moved towards the deserted street in front of the Sentinel building, and as they heard soft boots on concrete they embraced, lips touching softly, hands stroking at one another's clothing.

'You shouldn't be here.'

9mm broke away from her kiss and turned her dark eyes on the three Nex. She smiled broadly. Her hand moved to rest on AnneMarie's hip. 'Sorry, we just wanted some, uh, privacy. Everywhere is so busy tonight! What's going on?'

'The EDEN anti-virus is being released tomorrow. The city is celebrating.' The Nex's copper-eyed stare moved up and down the two women. 'Are you armed?'

'No, sir,' said AnneMarie, flashing her widest smile. 'Can't we stay here, sir?' She kissed 9mm's cheek. 'We have nowhere else to go, nowhere to, you know, *enjoy* one another.' In her pocket, she felt the ECube give a tiny click.

The Nex made as if to lift its Steyr TMP, but then the weapon dropped back to its side. It pressed a finger to its ear, some unheard communication, and then its mouth moved behind the mask. 'No. You must rejoin the main carriageway. This area is restricted.'

'OK, OK, don't get a hard-on,' said 9mm. The two

women turned, giggling, arm in arm, and strolled back down the street, turning right and heading towards a throng of excited party-goers. The moment they were away from the Nex they killed their giggles.

'We get it?'

'We got it.'

'Have you noticed something?'

'What?'

'I haven't seen a single JT8.'

AnneMarie frowned. 'You know, you're right.' They stood for a few moments, scanning the press of people. Fireworks crackled. Voices sang songs from a decade past. 'That's weird. Log it to the data bank. Let's see if anybody else has noticed.'

'OK. We ready to Centralise?'

'Yeah. Got a fast Manta heading in for a two-minute pick-up; we need to shift ourselves, get our kit and make the airfield in –' she checked her watch '– just under an hour.'

'Let's move, then. The DemolSquads are waiting.'

Durell hated Africa. Hated it with a vengeance. He hated the sun, the heat, the sand, the flies, the people, the food, the chaos – and he hated the space. People should just stay put, huddled together, he thought.

In one place. Where I can fucking see them.

The black Nex helicopter swept down towards the distant BCB construct, a mammoth grey-black structure which squatted against the skyline, suspended two kilometres above the rolling desert.

Durell watched the Dreadnought drift into view, and pride inflated his chest. He had created this monument, this *space station*, this dream. He had made it possible – his resources, his technology, *his* intention. But his pride swelled even further when his slitted copper eyes swept

413

across the sheer magnitude of the construction. This was not one of the smaller linking Dreadnought blocks as previously witnessed by man and paparazzi alike; no, this was Dreadnought NGO – the first class of the central core units. This core block was now complete, and would be towed into space in twelve hours – in order to start a sequence of events that would lead to the evacuation of Nex from the Earth, and the launch of the EDEN missiles destined to cleanse the world of mankind. Humanity would be destroyed. The slate would be wiped clean. The Earth scorched.

Soon, he thought as the small black helicopter approached the roof of the Dreadnought. *Soon*.

The helicopter touched down and Durell stepped free. A powerful wind from the rotors made his robes flap but as this died nothing else stirred – no breeze, no birds flying overhead. The Gravity Displacers made sure of that.

The surface of the Dreadnought was perfectly flat under Durell's boots and veined with tiny minute tracings of silver almost invisible to the human – or Nex – eye. Durell strode purposefully forward, towards the far edge of the construct block, and halted a few feet from the two-kilometre drop. Below him, the northern plateau of Ethiopia spread out, a vast and breathtaking landscape. Jagged mountains faded into distant haze, their dark volcanic rock like teeth raised from the core of the world. Valleys spread away from Durell and he breathed deeply, surveying this scenery from his seat, from this throne of the gods.

How fitting, he thought. Ethiopia – the starting point of mankind's evolution. And soon to be the starting point of Nex evolution. How perfect. How *neat*.

Durell turned and moved towards the ramps which led

down past various airlocks and into the Dreadnought itself. Around him lay a scatter of narrow towers trailing off into the distance, and many sections of the Dreadnought's roof stepped down into squares with huge controlling banks. Other parts of the Dreadnought's vast surface contained cones dipping below the surface with Gravity Displacers set at their bases. Durell moved to one of these and peered down into what looked like nothing more than a tiny dark hole at the central footing of a steep inverted conical slope. He shivered involuntarily. The GD looked like a tiny black mouth.

As Durell moved back towards the ramps, another helicopter dropped from the skies and touched down. Its engines were killed, clicking softly as the rotors slowly *whumped* to a halt. Alexis stepped out, her gaze fixing instantly on Durell as she moved towards him with precise steps and a gentle sway of her hips that was not lost on Durell.

'Carter has found Constanza, in Tibet. Squads are attempting to neutralise the problem. And a report has just come in across the EC network – one of the K-Labs in Norway has been infiltrated, although we suspect all the terrorists were slaughtered by Sleeper Nex there. I do not see how they could have escaped. We do not have names, as yet.'

'The K-Labs,' said Durell, his head tilting thoughtfully. 'That is – interesting. What news on the rest of Spiral – and their ragtag upstart companions, the REBS?'

'There's a lot of activity.'

'I would expect nothing less.'

'We have discovered the core of Spiral regrouped in Scotland, but by the time our scouts arrived they had already fled. We suspect they are being organised into tactical units, probably with the aim of attacking either the Dreadnoughts still located above the Earth, or maybe even the EDEN depots – if they can retrieve coordinates.'

'That would explain the K-Lab infiltration.'

'Yes, sir.'

Durell smiled then, his hand moving out to stroke Alexis's cheek. 'Don't call me sir. You make me feel *lessened*. Will you walk with me, down to my quarters? I feel a . . . need.'

'Of course. But what of Carter? Do you not wish me to scan the reports – to discover the outcome?'

'In time,' said Durell smoothly. 'They all move like flies to the centre of my web. There are no surprises any more, my dear – no surprises. Let them find the Evolution Class Warhead. Let them bring it to me. And we will see what fight is left in Spiral . . . see what fight is left in *Carter*.' He smiled then, a dark, dark smile, his copper eyes glittering.

Alexis watched him, awed.

'Soon it will all be over,' said Durell, and disappeared below the deck of the Dreadnought. Alexis paused for a moment, turning to look off across the vast and breathtaking Ethiopian plateau. Then she took a deep breath of the fresh, pure air, and followed Durell without a sound.

ADVERTISING FEATURE

The TV-ProjU sparkled into life with a digital buzz of humming phosphorescence. Images spun and leapt, dissolving and then reanimating into the mercury logo of HIVE Media Productions . . .

Audio/Vid mix: a mellow croon of comforting music: a subtle mix of violins and harp, soothing and pulsing, floating towards the audience on a wave of beauty – and invoking images of nostalgia and a deep-rooted hope.

– It is nearly time.
– It is nearly here . . .
– EDEN will answer ALL of your prayers . . .

Scene [slow pan R > L]: a rolling plateau of rich dense vegetation. A mid-sized family saloon parked on a slope, a fluffy blanket laid out on the grass. A woman, dressed in a smart business suit, face professional and yet beautiful in a businesslike way: she is laying cutlery out neatly, as close by Daddy plays football with little Billy and two little girls paddle in a nearby stream, tiny nets in their eager grasping hands as they giggle uncontrollably, plunging the nets into the water, chasing a shoal of glittering fish.

– Remember a time when everybody was free?
– Remember a time before HATE?
– Well, EDEN is finally complete – this wonderful antidote to HATE has been fully tested and will kill all and any remains of the harmful HATEful bacteria which still linger after our terrible global military accident . . .

Scene zooms in (x3): little girls giggling in the stream as they catch a tiny fish in one of the nets. The fish wriggles, gasping for air, but it cannot break free of the mesh confines despite its spirited struggling. The girls giggle and giggle. Their eyes are wide and bright and healthy. The fish puffs and pants, gills working hard to prevent asphyxiation . . .

– Tomorrow, when the unmanned aircraft fly low overhead, don't be frightened. Don't run away and hide. Step out into the bright new world and breathe deeply as EDEN is pumped into every corner of the globe . . .
– EDEN will bring us freedom!
– EDEN will bring us life! And everybody deserves that luxury.

Screen zooms in past the giggling girls; focuses on the rhythmic working of the fish mouth – open, close, open, close, open, close . . .

TEXT [scrolling L > R/ silver lettering FONT LUCIDA SANS]: DON'T BE A LITTLE FISH. DON'T GET CAUGHT IN THE NET. EMBRACE EDEN. WE ALL DESERVE A BETTER FUTURE – WE ALL DESERVE TO BREATHE THE FRESH MORNING AIR – WE ALL DESERVE A RETURN TO LIBERTY.

SCENE DISSOLVES TO RED

CHAPTER 16

ANTARCTICA

As the Nex squads hit the ground inside the ruins of Spiral_R, fast-ropes flapping and snapping around their lithe black-clad figures, Carter's Browning HiPower began to buck in his outstretched fist, fire spitting from the muzzle. His dark eyes focused with a grim finality on the relentless enemy he had fought for what felt like an eternity.

Bullets slammed into the heads of three Nex, flipping their bodies backwards in mushrooms of exploding blood-mist. Mongrel, sprinting up beside Carter, slid to a halt and opened fire. Constanza too had stopped, falling to one knee as she tracked the abseiling bodies. Her shots riddled the fast-dropping Nex to make them twitch in spasms of pain before plummeting from their helicopter umbilicals to lie crumpled on the hard ground.

'This way,' snarled Constanza.

'She an incredible shot!' said Mongrel, showing a professional appreciation.

Carter said nothing, sliding a fresh mag into his Browning as the small black attack helicopters banked

419

and started firing. Mini-gun rounds struck the remains of the Spiral base and spat up clouds of powdered stone.

Carter and the others ran and took shelter behind a pile of rocks. They could hear the whirr and whine as the lead chopper dipped low, runners almost touching the marble, and eased forward towards their hiding place, rotors thumping.

Carter pulled a HPG from his pack and tugged free the pin. Mongrel stared at him dumbly. His colleague was standing there calmly with a primed grenade in his fist.

'W—' said Mongrel as Carter, moving in a blur, leapt out in front of the small black helicopter and hurled the grenade. Within a second he was back, lying prone and with his hands and arms covering his head. An explosion erupted, melting alloy, consuming the Nex pilot and sending a wave of fire rushing past the rock piles mere inches to Carter's left. The heat scorched the hairs on the left side of his head, and singed his left eyebrow.

There were screams of stressed metal as two of the helicopter's rotors detached. One came crashing into the heap of stones bending with terrible pain-filled squeals and slamming along in huge whirring powdered grooves, to clatter on the floor by Carter's boot where it skidded along away from him. The other was thrown like a spear to pierce the cockpit of another helicopter, decapitating its two Nex occupants in diagonal spinning razor slices, sending the machine veering wildly out of control until it crashed into a third. Both choppers, locked together, plunged to the ground. Fuel ignited. A mushroom of flame boiled skywards and black smoke rolled out and up, filling the central courtyard of what had once been Spiral_R with a suffocating cloud laced with threads of fire.

The smoke made Carter, Mongrel and Constanza choke, and Constanza led them coughing down a stone-paved corridor and into the remains of the main Spiral_R building through shattered glass doors, one of which hung on broken steel hinges.

They halted for a moment, panting and wiping streams of tears from their blackened faces. Mongrel slapped Carter on the shoulder. 'Neat, buddy,' he gasped.

'What?'

Mongrel grinned, rubbing at his red-rimmed streaming eyes. 'Three choppers with one grenade! That good use of resources. Simmo would have been proud of you, Carter boy.'

'Proud of me?'

Bullets flew from the smoke, smashing into alloy pillars and the shattered remains of the glass doors. Without a word, Constanza broke into a run. Carter and Mongrel followed close, leaping a low desk, racing past the huge oval of granite bearing bright steel letters proclaiming SPIRAL R – TECH DIVISION, and then disappearing into a matrix of corridors that spread out from the reception area and tunnelled into the mountains.

Within moments, they were deep within the sprawl of the complex that was dimly lit by solar-powered emergency lighting, much of which was flickering and faulty after long tech-free years of neglect.

Constanza suddenly stopped and turned to face Carter and Mongrel. 'There's something else,' she said.

'Something *bad* else?' snapped Mongrel.

'Not all of the diseased people from my army were actually *in* my army.'

'What you mean, woman?'

'Occasionally, some of the diseased bastards went on pilgrimages, holy searches for enlightenment – call it whatever you want. They would head off into the mountains and they never returned.'

'Let me guess,' snarled Carter. 'Some of them ended up in here, right?'

'It was never confirmed,' said Constanza softly, brushing her long dark hair from her face. She shrugged. 'Just thought I'd warn you. We've got a long way to go in here – and I need you alive as much as you need me.'

Once more they set off at a run as Mongrel muttered, 'Fucking great. Nex battalion behind, and a lot of loony cannibals ahead. Can it get any worse?'

'Mongrel,' panted Carter, 'shut the fuck up.'

Spiral_R had seen much small-arms fighting. As the two Spiral men followed their guide, they couldn't help but notice the heavy scars that the place carried on its infrastructure. Bullet holes riddled walls and doors; huge scorch marks from grenade blasts lay across tiles, panels and Titanium-III wall sections.

They arrived at a mammoth site of HighJ detonation where the corridor suddenly effectively ended, a severed artery, with only ragged girders protruding out over a deep black chasm. A cold breeze drifted up from this giant gash. Across from the group, a distance of perhaps thirty metres, they could see the corridor begin once again. Carter and Mongrel exchanged worried glances as they looked at the damaged beams they would have to cross.

'Come on.' Constanza drew her pack straps tight, shouldered her Agram K50 sub-machine gun, and leapt onto the nearest length of blackened metal which measured only a few inches across. Her arms came out to either side, to help her balance, then she began to walk slowly, placing one boot carefully in front of the other, head lifted and gaze fixed on the opposite edge of the blast-severed corridor.

Carter watched, heart in his mouth, as halfway across Constanza had to turn to her right, moving carefully, and step between two broken beams. As her boot touched down, there was a creaking sound and the girder seemed to move slightly. Distantly, there came a sound of stones loosening and then falling into a void.

Mongrel took a step back. 'I not do that, Carter.'

'Yes, you can.'

'I fucking tell you, Carter, Mongrel not able to do that.'

'Well, what are you going to do? Head back on your own?'

'That very good idea. In fact, that *superb* idea! Mongrel go back, you get Manta, come pick me up at the Spiral_R entrance in ten minutes, eh?' He grinned but a deep fear lurked in his dark eyes as his hands fumbled with the straps of his pack.

Constanza reached the other side of the chasm. She turned, staring at the two men. 'I suggest you don't spend too long contemplating the drop,' she said. 'Those Nex weren't far behind. We need to move.'

'Go *on*!' snapped Carter. 'Here, give me your pack. I'll throw it across afterwards.'

'What? And have you steal my last remaining choc bars? Har, I not *that* stupid.' Mongrel pocketed his gun, then stood on the edge of the black vastness. Beyond, the corridor lit by emergency lighting seemed a very, very long way to travel. Mongrel shuffled to the edge of the abyss and looked down. He turned again and opened his mouth, frowning.

'Do it!' barked Carter, turning to look behind him, half expecting a Nex gunman to emerge at any moment.

With a grunt, Mongrel leapt out onto the girder. It shook. His feet did a crazy little dance and his arms

423

windmilled in huge sweeping arcs, fists clenched, head swaying in some crazy parody of a spastic attack. He finally gained his balance. He turned towards Carter, eyes wide, and grinned.

'No problemo!' Then he winked.

Carter groaned, shaking his head as Mongrel nearly slipped. And with arms outstretched, the huge squaddie began to cross the fire-scorched metal beam. He negotiated the middle gap without mishap, and Carter was just about to cheer when something went rotten and dead inside his soul.

'*They're coming, they're close,*' came Kade's corpse-cold voice.

'The Nex?'

'*Aha! You're bright as well. Thought you might need a bloody-fisted hand, brother. I've been watching you recently, and I have to say that I'm proud of you – proud of what you have achieved with your violent ingenuity . . .*'

'You've been quiet since Constanza mentioned your name.'

'*Yeah, well, that fucking bitch needs to die . . . give me some control and I'll see what I can do, eh, mate? She is a weevil in the flour; a beak in the chicken burger; an eyeball in the steak. She needs to be excised with a sharpened scalpel, fucked hard and brutal from behind, like a dog, then burned on a pyre stained red with her own heavy stinking womb-flow.*'

Carter glanced down at the Browning in his hand. When he looked up, a Nex was creeping around the corner, moving with the ease and grace of a natural predator.

Carter raised his gun and pulled the trigger. Behind him Mongrel wavered precariously, and cursed, shaken by the gunfire. His stare dropped to the black gulf below and with a supreme effort, he struggled across the last stretch of the beam with a lurching zombie gait.

The Nex charged, Carter's Browning boomed again in his fist as the Nex raised its Steyr TMP but Carter's bullets smashed into the stock, sending the gun flying from the Nex's grip. Carter's weapon's firing pin gave a dead man's click and he cursed himself: Kade had rattled his brain, making him lose track of how many bullets remained in his gun.

The Nex leapt, and Carter charged to meet the mixture of insect and man. He ducked a savage right hook, and thundered a straight to the Nex's chin, sending it staggering backwards. He followed through with a series of vicious hooks and jabs, but the Nex blocked the blows on its forearms and grabbed Carter's head, bringing its own forehead down in a vicious head-butt that broke Carter's nose yet again. Carter dropped to one knee as a kick struck his head and he rolled with the blow, close to the edge of the drop.

Carter leapt up, blocking a hook and sweeping a low kick that the Nex dodged. Then Carter's next heavy punch found the Nex's groin and his strong fingers grasped the thin body-hugging uniform, dragging his adversary into a bear hug. Carter grinned evilly, blood running from his broken nose, and smashed his own forehead into the Nex's face, three times, feeling something crumble beneath the mask. The copper eyes, however, still stared at Carter.

'You will never escape this place,' the Nex hissed.

'Maybe.'

'There are things here you could never imagine in your worst nightmares!'

'I have some pretty fucking bad nightmares.'

Carter hoisted the Nex into the air and heaved with all his might. The body flipped, trying to twist from its trajectory – but the Nex could do nothing as it plummeted past the girders and fell, tumbling into the darkness of the chasm far below with its hands flailing and grasping at cold air. Carter moved to the edge and stared down.

There was no scream; just a heavy, sodden slap of impact. 'Come on, Carter!' yelled Mongrel from the opposite ledge. Carter could sense the approach of more Nex; he ran at the girder, sprinting across the narrow blackened strut, sweat gleaming on his brow. In a few strides he had covered the distance.

Constanza stepped past him and opened fire with her sub-machine gun. Bullets flashed across the abyss. Nex ducked low and the group backed away. Constanza kept firing three-round bursts as Carter produced another HPG.

'Oh no,' muttered Mongrel.

'Oh yes,' snarled Carter, pulling the pin and rolling the HPG towards the broken girders and the dark pit beyond. The group ran, crouching behind a protective wall as a muffled blast boomed down the corridor. Carter glanced around the corner to see smoke billowing from new wreckage. A bomb-blast atop a bomb-blast had destroyed the remaining girders.

'Messy,' said Mongrel, peering over Carter's head.

'Come on, you fucking circus monkey.'

'Monkey? *Moi?*' Mongrel grinned, flames reflecting against his few remaining teeth. 'I gorilla, that for sure, but nothing so low-rent as mere *monkey*.'

The two men followed Constanza further into the depths of the abandoned base: Spiral_R.

They passed laboratories, many of them wrecked by bombs or riddled with bullet holes. Several were even flooded, with alloy benches floating in a thick slop of evil-smelling broth. They saw ransacked storerooms, empty except for old sacks and dented metal containers. They passed deserted barrack rooms, several still intact, but many the scenes of past brutal battles. Old black blood-stains still marked the peeling walls and decayed bedding. Dead maggots lay in old tins of rotten grey meat.

Mongrel peered into one such room. 'Looks like they got slaughtered in their sleep.'

Carter frowned then. Something had been nagging at him since they had entered Spiral_R; something subliminal, a test of his observation skills. Something which had been scratching at the edges of his brain – and he *knew* he was missing something of great importance which was actually glaringly obvious. Yet he could not focus, could not pinpoint, could not tie the fucker down.

Constanza stared at Carter's expression, reading his confusion. She frowned then, golden-eyed gaze moving nervously around the room. 'What is it?'

'There are no bodies,' Carter said, realisation striking him like a hammer blow. 'There should be bodies – or decomposed flesh, or skeletons, or something. Shouldn't there?'

'By God!' thundered Mongrel 'You is right!'

Carter whirled to face Constanza. 'Is this the work of your people?' His inflection made *people* sound like *war criminals*. 'Is this place where they harvest? Were the dead Spiral men and women their fucking *food store*?'

'No,' said Constanza softly, shaking her head, brow creased. 'They were cannibalistic, yes, but it was more of a holy ritual, more of a system to instil fear in their enemies, a method to keep the tribe intact. It was a form of survival, Carter. And I would like to see how you would have coped in such a situation.' She met his hostile stare, her head held high and proud. 'We're not so different, you and me. I wonder how you would have relished the role of monarch?'

427

'You talk of survival. It is ironic, then, that the Nex wiped the cannibal army out so swiftly.'

'They were still *people*,' said Constanza. 'Yeah, they were victims of a biological mess – and it fucked them up. But, hey, isn't that what society is all about? Protect those whom nature has picked to die? Don't judge me, Carter. Never judge me.'

'Come on,' said Carter, his tone hard, his expression unreadable. He did not like this place. It smelled of death. And the smell lingered. 'I've got a feeling the chasm won't stop the Nex for too long. Let's move on.'

In silence, Constanza led the way and they followed the corridors which were now sloping steeply downwards. Hundreds branched off, an incredible and complicated maze of rooms and labs and offices.

'We'll probably lose them down here,' said Constanza after a while. They had taken many turnings, and she had led them a zigzagging route. 'Unless their sense of smell is that acute.'

'It is,' said Carter sombrely.

They followed more ramps. The signs of battle were fewer down here; there was less destruction, fewer bomb-blast scorches and bullet scars. Until the group suddenly reached a long sloping corridor which had had all the wall panels ripped free, leaving bare trailing wires and the visible remains of thousands of panel-chassis components. Above the group the emergency lighting flickering inter-mittently. They halted.

'I not like this,' said Mongrel.

'Who's ripped off the wall panels?' asked Carter. 'And why? What possible use could anyone have for them?'

'Let's hope we don't find out,' said Constanza briskly, striding along under the flickering lights.

Mongrel leaned towards Carter. 'I got *real* bad feeling about this,' he muttered.

'Join the fucking club,' said Carter.

The long ramp suddenly ended, running out into a huge gloomy chamber. Carter squinted, and could just make out machinery on high gantries and rails, huge cranes and industrial robots – all silent and dead. Ahead, the darkness was deep and black, but they could make out the lights of a distant corridor, a tiny square of light on the opposite side of the vast space.

'Why it so dark?' asked Mongrel warily as they attempted to get their eyes to adjust to the gloom.

'Forget the darkness – what is that fucking *smell?*' Carter coughed thickly on a pungent, putrid aroma.

They paused, suddenly aware of a new noise as well. The sounds of their footsteps, their quiet voices, the coughs and wheezes of Mongrel – all this had cloaked a background crackling hiss.

'What that noise?' said Mongrel.

'Come on, Constanza, what's going on here?' Both men turned to the woman, who shrugged, silhouetted against the flickering light of the corridor. They could not read her facial expression.

'It is many years since I ventured this far under Spiral_R. All I know is that this way was clear and brightly lit the last time I passed through. This is an assembly and repair bay, for tanks, bikes, fighters, choppers – you name it. Tibet isn't the most hospitable and easily reached location; vehicles formed an important core of the Spiral operation out here. There are several such bays.'

Suddenly, a scream echoed out shrilly from the dark. It made the hairs on the back of Carter's neck stand out and he tracked the sound with his Browning as it died away to a bubbling murmur.

'What the *fuck*?' snapped Mongrel.

'It *has* to be your cannibal friends,' said Carter with a wry smile. He checked the magazine in his Browning, then patted at his pockets, making sure that he had enough ammunition. 'And they're out there in the dark.'

'You mean we got to cross blind?'

'Your eyes will adjust.'

'I not sure I want them to!'

'Come on,' snapped Constanza impatiently. 'If it is the cannibals, then at least they shouldn't be armed. Not with guns, at any rate. And when you think about it, boys, standing here against the light just silhouettes us. Nice clear shot, anybody?'

Jerked from their reverie, the two men hurried after her. Something crunched under their boots. 'Let's all stay close now,' said Mongrel, voice wavering, sweating heavily as his huge head swung nervously from left to right. Something brushed against his leg and he kicked out, biting his tongue to stifle the urge to yelp. *You is being big baby!* he thought wildly to himself. *You is being big pussy cat! You be tough, you is the Mongrel, not some little pizda maggot.*

'Just fix your stare on that far light,' said Constanza. 'That's your target; that's where we're going. We will be there in a few short minutes.'

'This a very big chamber,' muttered Mongrel, talking merely to take his mind off his sudden fear. 'It not very nice, oh no. It cold, and not smell too good. When I get out of this, I going get myself big hot dog with all runny mustard and ketchup. No! I fancy chilli dog! Filled with fire. And large mug of sugary tea, good old-fashioned English brew.'

430

They walked on through the darkness, bumping into small, soft objects, and sometimes with their boots crunching what felt like tiny stones underfoot. Slowly, their eyes adjusted slightly to the deeply oppressive darkness.

Carter suddenly slid on something which compressed under his boot; he nearly fell. There was a heavy squelch and a pop. Breathing deeply, he scraped the boot against his other one and with jaw clamped tight continued on, his stare fixed straight ahead.

And then a moaning sound began, a low ululating, drifting lament rising from the croaking, husky throats of many beings.

The noise ascended like a chant, filling Carter and his companions with a rising sense of horror.

Mongrel bumped into a figure, dimly outlined and shambling in the gloom. He screamed, and fired a shot in panic, dropping the shape instantly. There was a bright flash of fire from the muzzle of his gun, and in the sudden illumination the group saw exactly where they were and what surrounded them. They saw a true vision of Hell.

They were in a pit, low-walled and circled by ramps. Everywhere lay bodies, diseased and naked, thin-limbed and covered with sores weeping pus, riddled with infection and creating a communal stench of slowly rotting, barely living flesh.

In the flash of light, Carter saw hundreds of figures. Some lay prostrate, alone, unmoving; some squirmed together in sliming parodies of disease-sex, fucking in slow, rhythmical movements, sores and parted flesh rubbing together in a total merging of blood and pus and semen and contagion. Some bodies lay in tiny piles, human pyramids of putrefaction sporting twisted limbs and slack jaws and staring eyes and a core of decay, with a grinning round-eyed cannibal sitting atop each pile as if he was king.

And the floor: what had once been an alloy-panelled vehicle bay was now a sea of blood and pus, a scatter of bones and skulls, old weapons blood-congealed to metal, and occasional dismembered limbs. Carter saw that where they thought they had been walking across gravel, they had in fact been traversing a bed of yellowed old knuckle bones.

Both Carter and Mongrel retched as the darkness closed back in. Constanza said, her voice shaking slightly, 'I think we'd better move. And fast. We're attracting some unwanted attention.'

Mongrel wiped his vomit-stained mouth on his sleeve. Suddenly he pulled free his ECube. He activated it and a dull blue glow radiated, allowing the group to once more witness the horror of this pit of squirming human decomposition.

'Like moths to a light bulb,' warned Carter.

'I need to see!' bellowed Mongrel. 'I sick of standing on popping eyeballs!'

They began to jog, now that they had a light source, albeit a feeble one. Constanza had been right: they were attracting attention. Lots of it.

A grey-haired man with no teeth and a missing nose, naked except for what looked like a green knitted jumper, lurched into their path, a bright light in his grey eyes and his maggot-like penis swaying. They dodged to one side, veering around his shambling efforts at walking. But a hand lashed out, nails blackened with blood, and grabbed at Mongrel who squawked and put a bullet between the old man's eyes. The disease-riddled corpse collapsed to the ground.

Carter looked back and saw that already a woman had

dragged herself to the old man and was eating his face, chewing at his cheeks, tearing at strings of flesh.

'Sorry,' muttered Mongrel. 'Overreaction.'

'Even napalm wouldn't be a fucking overreaction here,' came Carter's low growl. 'You did him a favour, mate. You did him a big fucking favour.'

They sped on, and more figures – all around, but more importantly, *up ahead* – had crawled to their sore-speckled feet. The group were suddenly confronted by a huge bloated woman, so large she was unable to stand. She squatted back on her wobbling tree-trunk haunches, and heaved a slithering still-birth into the mire on platters of gore, pushed from bright pink flaps of a warped and distended vagina. They sprinted around this cackling monstrosity, as she took the still-born and began to feed.

'I think I want to die,' stuttered Mongrel.

'Better death than *this*.'

Ahead, figures were lumbering to cut them off. Constanza had raised her gun but seemed unable to fire. She suddenly halted, and Mongrel and Carter nearly slammed into her rigid back.

'What is it?' barked Carter.

'I can't! I can't shoot them! They are unarmed, polluted. They may be freaks – but they do not know what they are doing! I can't kill them in cold blood.'

'They want to fucking eat you!' screamed Carter, and wrenched the sub-machine gun from her hands. The gun blasted in his steady grip, and he mowed down a line of staggering human-form disease, creating a gap through which they could escape.

Mongrel went first, then Carter. Finally, Constanza followed, tears on her cheeks. The walking corpses milled around in confusion, then fell to eating, with file-sharpened teeth, their fallen comrades.

Mongrel was the first to get his boots on the ramp of the alloy corridor. He stood there, a look of horror on his face, and turned with haunted eyes as Carter and Constanza joined him. 'I thought I had stomach for anything,' said the big squaddie. 'But that . . . *that*! It make a man want to forget fried breakfasts – oh, for at least a week!'

They moved up the corridor, away from the squirming mass of rotting cannibals, and stopped at the top, breathing slowly, calming their thumping hearts.

'You nearly got us killed out there,' said Carter.

Constanza stared up at him. 'It wasn't my fault,' she said simply.

'Meaning?'

'I could not shoot them *because there were faces I recognised*. Some of those people were ex-Spiral! God only knows what happened to them down here, what toxins and poisons have been let loose in this place . . .'

'Makes me happy to breath Tibetan air,' muttered Mongrel. Then he launched into a quick-fire barrage of stilted Russian, German and tension-relieving gibberish. Carter nodded. He hoisted the sub-machine gun and pocketed his Browning. Then his face set in a hard mask and he glanced back down the corridor. Eyes stared back from the edges of the gloom, watching him carefully. There was intelligence in there. And patience. Carter shivered.

'God save their souls,' said Constanza softly.

'Yeah,' snapped Carter. 'Because no other cunt will.'

It took them another hour to reach the bunker where the aircraft were kept. Various code-locked doors had been buckled and bent, and inside several Mantas had been partially dismantled – as if somebody had been trying to

434

escape but couldn't get the vehicles to work.

Carter's heart sank as he saw the destroyed fighter planes, and his gaze swept over the devastation of the yellow-lit chamber. He glanced at Constanza, bitter words springing to his lips. But she pointed hurriedly, recognising the beginnings of his fury. 'Through there! There's more.'

Carter led the way, through a narrow tunnel and out—

Into fresh air. Carter breathed deeply as daylight flooded his world, and the mountain air filled his lungs with its purity.

'Where are we?'

'Halfway up a mountain,' said Constanza. She smiled then, her face looking suddenly young and pretty. Carter could see the years drop away from her, could see the signs of the stress evaporate. 'The Nex haven't spotted it – there's a GRID curtain. Hides the entrance from prying eyes, but it's still easily accessible from both directions. We can get out – if you can start the damned aircraft, that is.'

Carter glanced over at the mountain's internal landing bay. There were thirty Mantas, most of them covered by tarpaulins. Missiles gleamed along their flanks.

'It feels good to be alive,' Carter said suddenly.

'There always somebody worse off than yourself,' said Mongrel philosophically. He fished out a chocolate bar and began to chew, savouring the view as he contemplated his recent experiences.

'I am, quite frankly, amazed that you can still eat,' said Carter.

'Yeah, but what I could *really* murder is a big pan of B&S!'

'Beans and sausage? At a time like this? You are fucking insane!'

435

Mongrel considered this, then tilted his head and gave Carter a stern look. 'Some of them zombies,' he said, 'they were bigger zombies than me. But I thought, I did, I thought: you big zombie, but you out of shape, and I do this as full-time job.' Mongrel grinned a chocolate-smeared grin and breathed deep of the mountain air. A breeze ruffled his tufted excuse for a haircut. 'A pus-filled zombie should not destroy a man's appetite. Or, by *pizda*, I not true solider.'

'Mongrel, they were *not* zombies,' said Constanza. 'They were innocent unfortunates; victims of a toxic war who were left behind.'

'Once you cross frontier of sanity, you no longer human,' said Mongrel gently. He placed his big spade hand on Constanza's shoulder. 'Those things back there – they not people you once knew. They not men and women of Spiral . . . their minds dead. Only their rotting flesh remained – flesh without soul. You understand, little lady?'

'Yes,' she sighed, lowering her head.

'We thought you mad!' laughed Mongrel. 'Hanging out with all those cannibal loonies!'

'Not mad,' said Constanza, closing her eyes and allowing tears to roll down her cheeks. 'Just desperate to survive. Sometimes the world makes you hard, yeah? And it changes you, Mongrel. It turns you into something you are really not.'

'I understand.'

Mongrel hugged her then, and a long look of understanding passed between them. Mongrel's touch lingered just a little longer than it should have. Their eye contact lasted just a little longer than it should have. And Mongrel's smile was too warm, too friendly, just too fucking *nice*.

436

Carter groaned, and wandered towards the edge of the mountain. He breathed deeply again, looking out over Tibet. This whole country, he thought, fills me with exhilaration – this whole world is sheer magnificence!

'Carter?' Carter managed to find a bedraggled cigarette in his pack. He rummaged for a lighter, cursing the confusion of his packing, and finally resorted to the laser function of his ECube – not something the tiny four-billion-dollar device was designed for but still a welcome addition. He inhaled deeply on the nicotine fix.

'Yeah, Mongrel?'

'I think we need move quickly. Those Nex, they surely not far behind.'

'OK. You two lovebirds happy now?'

'What?' Mongrel frowned deeply.

Carter winked, and nudged Mongrel in the ribs. 'I saw it, you fucking old goat. I saw that give-away pyramid crotch. You've got the fucking *hunger* for that chick.'

'Mongrel not know what crazy Carter talking about,' said Mongrel, somewhat primly. 'I just assisting wounded and scared lady, showing her utmost chiv— . . . chilav— . . . honour. You talking crazy talk, Carter, and I think you been breathing too much of those tox fumes down there!'

'A good attempt.' Carter grinned, drawing on his cigarette.

'No! I must protest!'

'*You must protest?*' cackled Carter. 'What are you, Victorian fucking Mongrel all of a sudden? Weren't you in that movie *Lady Chatterley's Mongrel*? Or maybe you starred in *The French Lieutenant's Mongrel*? Or, may one be so bold as to ask, could you possibly be one of the leads from that Dickensian masterpiece *A Tale of Two Mongrels*?'

'Fuck off.'

Carter grinned. 'Come on, let's get the Manta started.'

'Just fuck off.'

'Aww, Mongrel, don't be like that! We've been through so much together!'

'Fuck off.'

Chuckling, smoke pluming behind him, Carter strode to the nearest Manta and hauled the tarpaulin free. There, under a thin layer of grease, sat a brand new jet, squat, powerful, and looking like the serious piece of military hardware that it was.

'So, then, Constanza, where we going? This exchange deal of ours, it's going to need navigational coordinates. Or do you intend to point us through the skies with your finger?'

'No, Carter. I have the coordinates. I have the exact coordinates for the location of the Evolution Class Warhead – all stored up here, in my pretty little head.'

Mongrel moved towards Constanza. 'You ignore old Carter, he always bastard grump on mission. He always whining and moaning!' Mongrel gave Carter a shifty sideways smile. 'It like being on fucking mission with your wife! Har har.'

Really got to you, didn't I? Carter thought, climbing up the recessed steps and peering into the cockpit. He reached down and turned on the power. Inside, the Manta's control panel lit up in a display of glittering colours. It gave Carter a warm, glowing feeling inside.

The fighter aircraft seemed to say: Welcome Home.

Carter piloted the Manta low over the smooth blue waters of the Indian Ocean. Sunlight glimmered from the silver crests of small waves and the low-flying Manta left a trail of foam surging in its screaming wake.

After leaving the southern tip of India, Carter, Mongrel and Constanza had a straight flight of just over 8,000 klicks to the coastline of Antarctica. A Manta could be cranked up to just over Mach 2.2 or 2,330 km/h so their journey time was going to be around four hours flat out. And Carter was certainly pushing flat out – time was of the essence, and God only knew to what stage of his plans Durell had progressed by now.

Mongrel and Constanza chatted intermittently as Carter flew. But Carter himself sank into a mental tomb world as he mulled over the recent events which had left him so battered and bruised that every time he moved it was agony. Until the adrenalin arrived; until *Kade* arrived.

For years, Kade had professed to soak up Carter's pain like a sponge, allowing the Spiral operative to push on regardless when most other men and women were left behind, whimpering in the mud.

Once again, Carter found himself mulling over the very concept of Kade. Kade: his internal demon.

Kade: his dark and violent brother.

What was it that Constanza had said? '*We have met, Carter. That's why I know about Kade – that's why I know about the demon nestling inside your skull.*' And yet Carter was *sure* that he would have remembered the woman; remembered that face, that athletic figure, that smile. Carter was good with faces . . . it was names that eluded him. Usually the names of the dead.

A hundred times Carter had opened his mouth to ask the question, and a hundred times he had closed it again. How do you know me? How do you know about Kade? But something stopped Carter; something clicked at the back of his skull, snicking into place and halting him.

What seemed like aeons ago, there had been a wise old soldier working with the Spiral DemolSquads. His name had been Ranger and he'd been a mighty grey-bearded warrior with an incredible reputation and the physique of a true athlete; a true gladiator. Carter had been young, newly acquired, fresh-faced and filled with optimism as he was drawn into the swelling ranks of Spiral. One evening, after a few pints down at the local NAAFI, Ranger had gathered some of the newcomers into a corner and they had talked in quiet voices, laughing often as Ranger regaled them with accounts of his heroic adventures; the old man was a born storyteller. But he had given them one piece of valuable advice which had stuck with Carter to this very day:

If you don't want answers, then don't ask questions.

And, when it came down to it, Carter, in his heart, in his soul, didn't want to know about Kade. He didn't want to give himself any false hope.

The Manta powered on towards Antarctica. A coastline of ice rose ahead of the trio. The sea looked glass-black below them, strewn with titanic chunks of ice and crashing wildly back and forth.

Huge sheer black cliffs sheathed in gleaming crusts of ice towered up. The Manta's nose lifted, the fighter whining as it rose above sharp shards of rock and then dropped again to the white plateau far beneath, cruising low, huge storms of snow spraying up and out in the aircraft's wake.

They hurtled through seemingly bottomless canyons where sunlight sparkled from walls of sculpted ice. They flew over mighty mountain ranges. A matt black arrow, they smashed through blindingly white blizzards.

Then, finally, Constanza pointed to Mongrel's ECube. 'ETA five minutes,' she said. 'Let's hope the air defences spot this as a Spiral craft.'

'As a . . .' Carter glanced back at the dark-haired

woman. Her golden-eyed gaze met his. 'You mean they have intelligent targeting systems?'

'Yes.'

'How you know?' muttered Mongrel.

'Because I programmed them. Now, keep to an altitude of three hundred feet; they get a better scan at that height. Don't want them mistaking us for Nex, do we?'

'Are the systems powerful?'

'The best in the world,' said Constanza softly. 'That's why the Nex haven't found the Warhead. And there are also internal systems – anti-Nex intrusion filters powered by lasers. Any Nex who *has* discovered it is now just ash drifting against the snowfields.'

Carter modified his altitude, slowing the Manta's speed again. Then he banked, tracking coordinates.

'Down there!' But none of the three could see the Antarctic Spiral base; it was obscured by a snowstorm, concealed by its natural ally.

Carter landed the Manta blind, breath catching in his throat as they approached what Constanza assured him was the short runway. The Manta slammed onto and over the hard-packed snow, taxiing to an abrupt halt as Carter threw the engines into reverse thrust with a blast of superheated exhaust that turned the snow to steam. He killed the engines, and they sat there in silence for a while.

'This is it, Carter lad,' said Mongrel, the first, as usual, to break the silence. To Mongrel, silence was heresy.

Carter peered out into the snowstorm. Squinting, he could just make out a vague shape, like a high grey wall, but dismissed it as only a shadow. They wrapped up as best they could in the confines of the Manta, then Carter slammed open the cockpit canopy and got a blast of snow and wind in the face. He gasped, blinking rapidly, then clambered down the recessed ladder and jumped into the snow. Constanza followed, and finally Mongrel, who closed the canopy behind him. Hydraulics hissed, and there was the precise *chunk* of a well-engineered machine.

'This way.' Constanza walked through the snow, and Mongrel and Carter followed. Carter nudged Mongrel.

'What?'

'You're watching her arse.'

'No, I not!' Aghast.

'Yes, you are. I'm following your line of sight. It's her rump. You're staring at her buttocks.'

'I happening to admire tailoring at back of her fleece. Fine stitching, I thinking. But she does have first-rate, well-formed and ample backside – I sure. But look, you can see triple cross-back stitching on jacket – there. Perfect couture.'

'Yeah, 'course it is, Mongrel. Look, why don't you say something to her?'

'Like *what*?' hissed Mongrel, eyes wild for a moment. 'I fancy you, fancy a bit of the old rumpy-pumpy, but hey, I old, and fat, and nearly toothless, and tufted. I have cancer that will soon kill me, and maybe we all die any day now anyway when Durell piss his tox all over us. Can I take you to movie?' Mongrel was spitting in his passion to speak, and his huge fists had clenched – an unspoken warning.

'All those reasons are exactly why you *should* tell her.'

'Hmph.'

'Trust me.'

'Carter, you is assassin and damn fine bomb-maker. But agony aunt you is not.'

Carter shrugged, increasing his speed to catch up with Constanza. Then all three halted as a high wall loomed out of the mist, a rearing grey-stone edifice seventy or eighty feet high. It was topped with small crenellations, like a castle – but the intensity of the snowstorm prevented them from looking further along the structure.

Constanza huddled against the door. A secret panel slid free and she punched in digits. A portal swung inwards, and the three tumbled through into a suddenly calm if dark haven. They were all glad to be out of the howling wind, the flesh-slapping snow.

The portal closed, muffling the banshee howls, and they stood there in darkness for a moment, snow drifting from hair and shoulders, shivering as something in the darkness clicked. Lights flickered on, dim and feeble.

'Welcoming,' observed Mongrel.

'It's a disused military base, not a brothel,' said Carter, gazing around at the bare breeze-block walls and the concrete-section floor. It seemed suspiciously low-tech.

'Shh!'

'What?'

'You not talk of such things in front of lady,' Mongrel admonished. Constanza gave him a beaming smile, then moved through the chamber to another door up ahead. She punched in more digits, and they entered a circular tunnel of tarnished alloy. Hoisting packs, they trudged along, their boots making echoing thumping sounds. They could smell hot oil. Tiny flickers of amber light jostled across the walls occasionally, and then they were free of the tunnel and into another concrete and stone chamber.

'The decontamination sheds are up ahead.'

'Because you have to create the AI and RI chips in a hermetically sealed environment?' Carter was rolling his neck to relieve tension; pain was a constant, throbbing reminder that, like it or not, he was still alive. The game was far from done.

'Yeah, we don't want to risk any pollutants sending

a fifty-billion-dollar polymorphic missile up the wrong dictatorial arse.'

'This ECW. You sure it will still be working?'

'Oh yes,' said Constanza. 'This whole base may look disused, but it *is* operational. And it was built to last. Out here, the ice and snow moves; it is unstable. The Castle in its entirety is built on a series of hydraulic mobile support stanchions directed by simple AI algorithms; it can shift itself, redistribute its weight, put down extra supports deep into the ice. It is self-regulating, self-stabilising. No earthquake can destroy it, and certainly no shift in the ice can rip it apart.'

'The Castle?' asked Mongrel.

'A nickname. Because of the turrets. When you see the place in calm weather, not in a storm, you'll realise that it's nothing like a castle; we were just fond of the term. Made it feel more like home. Although, a bit like old stone castles and their ballistic defences, there are a series of rail-driven mounted machine guns up on the roof.'

'In case of massed polar bear assault?' Mongrel asked.

Constanza patted Mongrel on the arm, and he beamed – like a schoolboy in love. '*No*, Mongrel. They're there because this whole area has awesome air defences, and when awesome air defences are present there is a much higher possibility of infantry and tank attack. The MGs have anti-tank capabilities with TI-uranium rounds in yellow-tagged ammunition belts. Just so you know. Anyway, you don't get polar bears down here. They're strictly Arctic Circle beasts.'

'You think we get company?'

Constanza nodded. 'The Nex are onto us. And if they discover where we are heading . . . well, I am sure Durell must know *something* about the EC Warhead. That bastard has a finger in too many pies.'

'If he try to finger *my* pie, then I bite it off.'

'You're a brave man, Mongrel.' Constanza smiled up at him.

Mongrel puffed out his chest. 'You better believe it, ma'am.'

After the decontamination sheds, Constanza headed for the central ECW Core – where it would take her fifteen minutes just to get through the coded security doors. And so, Mongrel being Mongrel, he had insisted on making a brew before following the woman down the long corridor to the Core. Carter waited with him, a cigarette in one hand, a weary grin on his face masking the constant worry of their imminent countdown to extinction. Mongrel, standing beside a small sink with his portable kettle, dropped three tea bags into tin mugs and stirred in hot water. As he brewed, he glanced back and frowned at Carter.

'What?'

'Nothing,' said Carter, still grinning.

'*What?*'

'Nothing, *ma'am.*'

'Fuck off.'

'Temper!'

'Cunt.'

'Tsch. There are *ladies* present. Or nearby. Even if they are semi-insane wannabe cannibals. Fuck, Mongrel, you really do know how to choose the nutcases!'

'This nothing,' grunted Mongrel. 'Wait until you hear about Fat Chick Night! The corned beef! The dough-nuts! The *horror*!'

Carrying their steaming mugs of tea, the two men moved down more alloy corridors and through three mas-sive portals reminiscent of the huge doors normally found leading to bank vaults, but lined with what looked like leaves of silver. The material shimmered with skeins of green, and seemed to flow like a constantly shifting liquid.

As they came through the third portal they both stared open-mouthed at the chamber ahead of them.

It was huge, football-stadium huge, and filled with computers. Huge banks of them lined every wall. They glittered in a sort of semi-gloom, gentle waves of lights undulating across banks of servers. Massive rows of unmanned machines spread out in octopus hubs set around the smooth marble floor. Everything seemed to guide the two men towards the centre . . .

'Over here,' shouted Constanza. They jogged towards her, Mongrel leaving a trail of hot sugary tea.

'Where's the Warhead?' asked Carter.

'Over there. At the hub of the ECW Core.'

'Where?'

'There. Encased in a metal shell.'

Carter squinted. 'Can we see it?'

'Come on.' Taking her tea, Constanza led the two men across the vast expanse of marble. The air was alive with electricity, a gentle hum and buzz which occasionally made the hairs on the backs of their necks crackle.

Lights flowed with them, paced them, sweeping across the walls. And the huge chamber was cool. Not the freezing temperature of the Antarctic conditions outside, but a dry coolness which indicated merely precision and control.

Constanza stopped by a bank of computers and typed in various passwords. Up ahead, on a small plinth, layers of metal peeled away, disappearing below the floor in pre-cise measured sections to reveal:

The Warhead.

Evolution Class. Spiral's greatest development prototype: untested, unused, a Pandora's Box of military-grade destruction. As the metal sheath fell away, it gleamed under reflected computer light with tarnished gold.

'Where's the rest of it?' asked Carter, eyes taking in the modest appearance of this reputedly awesome weapon.

'That's it.'

Carter stared hard at the Evolution Class Warhead. In total, it stood a mere six feet in height; there was no division between payload and engine, no fins, no panels, no markings. The ECW was a bare metal simplicity.

'It wholly fucking unimpressive,' scowled Mongrel.

'Watch.' Constanza hit a few buttons, and the surface of the Warhead seemed to become suddenly *molten*. It flowed, swirling around within its own set parameters, its own framework; a liquid held as solid. A living, moving shell.

Carter stepped forward, then glanced back. 'Can I touch it?'

'Yes.'

Carter reached forward tentatively and his hand dipped *into* the Warhead, making him jump. He withdrew his fingers with a jerk of panicked movement, and the shimmering gold flowed and re-formed into the steady shape of the weapon's liquid exoskeleton.

'Did you feel anything? Under the polymorphic chassis?' Constanza was watching him closely, analysing his reactions.

'Yeah, it was hard – a hot hard metal cylinder. But the liquid shell was cold – freezing, in fact.'

'Inside, you touched the Warhead's brain.'

Carter shivered. 'I feel like I've just invaded it.'

Constanza smiled, and the smile was far from nice. 'Maybe you did. How much do you think the Warhead weighs?'

Mongrel shrugged. 'We loaded up many a missile look like this. I probably lift it all on my own.'

'Why don't you try and pick it up?'

Mongrel nodded eagerly. 'You make it go hard again? I not fancy slush all over my clean pants.'

'I bet you say that to all the girls,' chuckled Constanza. Then she hit a key on her pad and the flowing surface of the ECW solidified into a dull gold colour.

Mongrel reddened. He coughed, stepped forward, put both his bear like paws around the narrow cylinder – and strained. Heaved. His face went through shades of red, purple, and finally, panting and wearing a sheen of sweat, he stepped away in defeat. 'I concede. Very heavy.'

'A thousand tonnes heavy,' said Constanza. 'A hundred of you couldn't lift the ECW.' Both men looked shocked, and Mongrel stared down at his hands, then went and picked up his brew, slurping his tea down his jumper.

'Where does all the weight come from?'

'It's the chassis. But in flight it weighs exactly zero pounds.'

'How is that possible?' asked Carter.

Constanza shrugged. 'I'm a programmer, not a chassis developer. But I am assured that it does. Something about reverse physics, or something. Anyway, I need to be left alone for a while to start priming the ignition sequences. And then I will need your target data.'

Carter and Mongrel looked at one another, and then both pulled out their ECubes. The tiny devices unfolded in their hands, like small black alloy roses opening petals towards the sun. There came two faint clicks.

Mongrel frowned. 'Mine gone dead.'

'Mine too,' said Carter.

'That not good.'

'There's the fucking understatement of the century. Can you get anything on yours? Scripts? Log-ons? Any form of power?'

'Not a donkey.'

'It might be this chamber,' said Constanza, her eyes narrowed. 'This is a very special place; maybe you should . . .' But suddenly lights flowed across a bank of computers and ten huge screens filled with colour – or more precisely, with white. They displayed the landscape surrounding the base, a vision of the vast undulating ice plains of Antarctica.

'What is it?' snapped Carter.

'Company.'

'Company?'

Constanza glanced over to him. 'The Nex are here.'

'So fucking soon?' growled Mongrel, shaking his ECube frantically. 'I thought we left those bastards back in Tibet; I sure they not following us, I sure they not able to track us.'

'They either tracked us, or they already knew our destination,' said Carter grimly. He dropped his ECube into his pocket, and wincing as he moved, drew his Browning. 'I think we need to have a little chat, me and the Nex.'

'You'll need more than that little pea-shooter,' said Constanza.

'Why's that?'

'Look.' The screens showed swathes of white, devoid of any activity except the occasional gust of wind. The snowstorms had died. Constanza pointed towards a different scanner. 'We do not have visual contact yet, but this shows the advance.'

'Advance?' rumbled Mongrel. 'You make it sound like an army.'

'You see all the tiny amber dots?'

'Y'har?'

'Each one is a cluster of infantry. Moving in on foot.'

'What those grey dots?'

'Tanks.'

'That many tanks?'

'Yes.'

'I don't see signs of air support,' said Carter. 'I assume the surrounding air defences have kicked in?'

Constanza typed at the keyboard. 'Yes, there have been fifteen attempts at aerial infiltration; all fifteen craft have been utterly destroyed.'

'Come on,' said Carter. 'Let's get up to the roof. See if we can get some life pumped into these ECubes. How long for you to initiate the Warhead?'

Constanza took a deep breath. 'I can have it primed and base-fuelled in twenty minutes. But the target data which needs uploading – well, depends on how much of it there is. I could have done it remotely but—' She glanced at the screens, which still showed a beautiful unsullied crystalline white landscape. An Antarctic paradise. 'Looks like we're not going to be on our own for much longer. I would say about thirty minutes, as an estimate.'

'What's the sighting distance on visual – on the screens?'

'Probably around two klicks. The plateau is pretty flat.'

'And the ice will happily support their tanks?'

'Yes. As long as they spread machinery out – which, looking at the scanners, is a tactic they've already employed. They know the terrain, Carter, they know this place; and that confuses me.'

'Why?'

'If they know this place, why haven't they already taken the Warhead?'

Carter scratched his stubbled face. 'A problem for

another decade. Come on, Mongrel, let's get up to the roof. Is there ammo for the MGs up there?'

'Alloy floor panels. You'll see it. You planning to fight?'

'We've got to hold them off. Can you program the Warhead once it's in the air?'

'No. That would be too open to abuse. Once the targets are loaded, you can make suggestions, sure. But the Warhead has its own brain. Its own intelligence. Its own *sentience*.'

'The fucker.'

Carter and Mongrel sprinted from the chamber, grabbed clothing and heavy jackets from lockers, and pounded towards the steep metal stairs leading to the roof. As they ran, Mongrel panting and red in the face, Carter merely gleaming with the sweat of effort, Mongrel shouted, 'We can't hold off the Nex, Carter. There are thousands of the cunts.'

'We have no choice.'

'They have *tanks*.'

'We have no fucking choice. Now get your fat arse up those stairs, soldier. Let's see some fucking effort – and I hope to God that Jam and The Priest have sent the data, because . . . Jesus, if they haven't then everything is fucked. And I mean *everything*.'

The roof of the Castle was coated in layers of ice and snow. Carter climbed out onto it, the portal rotating below him until it blocked off the building's interior. The cold slammed him in the face, biting his skin. He and Mongrel glanced at the vast expanse of roof around them. Small machine-gun turrets sat, attached to some form of rail system along the crenellated wall's base – which meant that each gun could effectively cover the whole length of the wall. There were six massive guns spaced along each barricade.

'Those walls way too large for us to cover alone,' said Mongrel, staring in disbelief at the expanse before them.

'They're going to try and infiltrate the base by the front door,' said Carter.

'How you know?'

'It's the only entrance, according to Constanza.'

He pulled out his ECube, and it flickered once more into life. Carter sighed in relief, then checked for messages.

'Jam?'

'No,' said Carter bitterly. 'Nothing. What the fuck are they doing? We're here, primed, ready to fucking launch and we haven't got the targets. For Christ's sake!'

'Jam will come through.'

Carter shook his head. 'Come on, let's check these guns.'

They crunched across the ice, eyes constantly scanning the bleak horizon. Coming to the first gun turret, Carter leapt into the chassis and immediately mechanisms hummed into place. A scope dropped to cover his eyes; alloy panels sprang up from the floor behind the gun, cracking ice and sending powdered snow drifting into the air. Huge coils of bullets gleamed as the gun clicked and whirred, like a living, breathing thing all around Carter. He felt suddenly cocooned, enclosed – entombed.

'That not gun,' said Mongrel. 'That fucking exoskeleton.'

Carter squinted through the scope. 'Still can't see them. Maybe Constanza was wrong.'

'No, Carter, no. That false hope talking.'

Suddenly Mongrel started dancing around in the snow and whooping. Carter was just about to make some scathing comment when the other man dragged free his ECube and held it up triumphantly, like a trophy. Then he huddled over the tiny device.

'We got message!'

'And?'

'It from The Priest!'

'*And?*'

'It contain data . . . scrolling now. Wow, WarFacs, Dreadnoughts, NEP plants, armoured divisions . . . fuck, Carter, those Spiral boys and REB girlies sure been busy!'

'And they're all confirmed coordinates?'

'Yeah, Carter! We got data! All confirmed! We got it!'

Carter smiled, relief flooding through him. 'Good stuff. Get it down to Constanza, then let's get this fucking Warhead launched and get the absolute fuck out of this place. I can do without my own private dogfight right now.'

Mongrel turned, and started to sprint across the ice towards the roof portal.

'Wait! Mongrel?'

'Yeah?'

'Did it have the EDEN depots?'

'Let Mongrel check.'

Mongrel stooped over his ECube once more. His intensity was complete, mind focused, eyes scanning through the digits. Carter heard the click of a reset and, cursing, climbed from the gun emplacement and ran over to Mongrel, who glanced up, frowning, heavy creases lining his battered brow.

'No EDEN depots?'

'No.'

'What does it say?' Carter stood, hands on his hips, breath steaming. The expression in his eyes was cold and glazed.

'It give reference for a further follow-up. That mean Jam gone after the EDEN depots but his tech not yet come in. We got everything we need to bring down

453

Durell's empire, but without that info from Jam then EDEN still be launched – and every man, woman and child on planet be wiped out!'

'So we've only got *half* of the Holy Grail? Shit.'

'What fucking game Jam playing?'

'I don't know, my friend. I just don't know. Get that data down to Constanza. At least she can begin her job and start the upload.'

Mongrel moved away, and Carter turned back towards the black silhouette of the gun.

'And Mongrel?'

'Yeah, boss?'

Carter pointed towards the distant horizon and with a voice as cold as a frozen lake of blood he said, 'Don't be too long. The Nex are here.'

The distant black sweep of an army had appeared far off – but not far enough – in the snow.

It seemed to fill the icescape. It seemed to fill the *world*. Without a word, Mongrel disappeared into The Castle. Shivering, Carter surveyed the entirety of the Nex army alone.

CHAPTER 17

THE TASTE OF
A MACHINE SOUL

¬ systems initiating >>>
code 5; procedures 5, 15, 432, 23, 1, 2, 765, 3
power sources uploading
power routes reconnected
¬ battle data online; scanning . . .
¬ ok
¬ battle data initiated
¬ ok
897897689745
9734578489578947
435789475475897459874 9875−044
847598748579847509437598743985705=
47587498759843 7594305
000
¬ ok
¬ ready for war

Carter ran to the modest battlements and his gaze swept
the horizon. The Nex were advancing in small tactical
groups. They carried machine guns, sub-machine guns

and rocket launchers, and numbered in the thousands. And there were tanks – old-style Spiral-built SP57s and SP60s with triple heavy-calibre machine guns and twin 135mm M512 smooth-bore cannons firing HEAT-X2 combat rounds. There were original Nex-built TK79s, with 105mm guns and triple 7.62mm MGs – but, horri-fyingly, there were also the new model TK90s used for urban crowd control. Carter had seen them in action in London and New York City: they had side-mounted flame-throwers. They were devastating in action, espe-cially when unleashed against peaceful protesters bearing nothing more threatening than banners and placards. Carter counted at least a hundred of the heavily armoured tracked vehicles, and mixed in with them were HTanks, uncloaked, matt black and menacing.

How long can we hold them? Carter laughed to him-self.

Hold them? Hold a fucking *army*?

Carter leapt into a rail-mounted MG turret and acti-vated the power. A small black flat-screen display popped up, and Carter frowned at the options presented to him. He pulled a helmet onto his head and rested his hands against the twin grips of the huge gun. On the floor there were pedals and he tested one experimentally. There were instant *whirrs* and motors slammed the gun along the rails to the right. Carter nodded to himself, looked into the sight and saw the Nex – black-clad, copper-eyed, menac-ing – leap into view. He watched their rhythmic marching steps matched perfectly as the black-clad scourge poured across the ice fields.

'Come and get it, you fuckers.'

'*Need a hand?*'

'I'll let you free when you tell me how – and *why* – Constanza knows of you.'

'*No.*'

'No?'

'*Constanza, as I have already stated, is a traitorous bitch. What makes you think she is putting the right coordinates into that fucking Warhead? What makes you think she wants to save the world? Ha! She will kill us all . . .*'

'Kade – just go away. We will talk later.'

Carter almost *felt* Kade grinning at the back of his mind. Then the dark twin departed and Carter was left alone, shivering with the intense cold, a chill wind biting at his exposed skin as he waited alone on the roof of a deserted Spiral base to face an entire army of the enemy. Maybe Kade would do a better job? he thought. Maybe Kade would win the war?

Mongrel appeared, sprinting, his red face puffed and his belly bouncing. He skidded to a halt beside Carter. 'She uploading data now. She a little panicked, Carter – and rightly so! She say she need Jam's data in next ten minutes or so, or she have to launch the Warhead without . . . and . . . no, no, Mongrel does not have heart to tell you!'

'What is it?'

'Aww, Carter, it not good news.'

'What the fuck *is* it?'

'Constanza say the core RI has *changed.*'

'What the hell does that mean?'

'The Warhead, it *sentient.* It can think. It has been doing some of its own reprogramming; changing its own code. Who *know* what fucking loony machine thinking now . . . Constanza say if we launch Warhead it may behave unpredictably. She not understand what all the code does, and she one of best programmers alive, Carter, I swear that true.'

Carter breathed deeply. He stared at the distant advancing army.

'I think,' he said, 'that we have more urgent problems at the moment. Get yourself into a gun turret; we need to kick some Nex arse.'

'Carter, man, we cannot stand against *that*!'

'We have to try, Mongrel.' Carter saw the fear lurking in Mongrel's eyes, and he felt strangely calm. This was it, he thought. This felt like his last day on earth . . . and, weird though it sounded, he was ready. Ready to accept the inevitable. 'We have to destroy Durell's plans. We have to give Constanza the time she needs to launch that Warhead. Because, if we don't . . . well, the consequences are unimaginable.'

'This the eve of the end of the world,' said Mongrel slowly. 'Death coming for us all.'

'Well,' said Carter, a nasty glint in his eyes, 'let's break his fucking nose, eh, lad? Let's go out fighting. Because no fucking skeleton is taking me by force – not without me snapping his fucking spine. Good luck, Mongrel.'

'And you, Carter. Good luck!'

'And Mongrel?'

'Aye, lad?'

'The foot pedals control the turret's sideways movement. I know what a technology disaster area you can be – watch where you're going and don't you fucking crash into me, all right?'

'I try best, Carter lad.' Mongrel ran to his gun. Motors and hydraulics whirred and thumped, enclosing Mongrel in an exoskeleton of alloy while behind the turret coils of ammunition were hoisted high into place. Carter, glancing over, frowned. There were rockets.

Carter tapped the comm. 'You hear me, Mongrel?'

'I hear you, laddie.'

'You've got a rocket store behind you. Have I?'

A pause. 'Confirmed. How we access them? Ahh – it on your console. It labelled BFG.'

'BFG? I've never heard that one before. I'm sure I would have picked it up from the lecture theatre.'

'Ha ha, comedy labelling, Carter. It stand for *Big Fucking Gun*. Simmo used to run them in the TankSquads. Before he . . . yes, well.' Mongrel stumbled into silence.

'Ten seconds, and they'll be in range,' said Carter.

'Let's fuck them, *compadre*. Let's fuck them hard.'

Both men watched, sweat trickling down their brows and into their clothing. Inside the turrets it was suddenly warm and both men had dry mouths. In front of them, the army swept forward, a vast seething mass of infantry mixed with tanks and thousands of machine guns . . . I have never seen anything like it, thought Carter. Never stood against anything like this.

'*You are going to die*,' whispered Kade.

Carter nodded to himself. 'So be it,' he said.

Constanza's fingers were a blur over the keyboard. On the screen before her, digits flashed and whirled, and numbers flickered in an upward scroll.

She halted, attached Mongrel's ECube and watched the two computers connect. Lights flickered, and again data rolled up the screen – and into the core of the Warhead's targeting database.

¬ **data transfer: do not interrupt data supply or this may instigate a system crash. If this occurs then some of your data may be lost or permanently damaged.**
¬ **transferring**
¬ **transferring >>>>**
¬ **complete**

The cursor blinked at Constanza and again her fingers danced over the keyboard. Behind her, the plates fell away from the EC Warhead and she half turned in her chair to stare at the glowing, swirling missile: a sentient machine with which she had the most basic of computer communications. I feel like Dr Frankenstein, she thought, suddenly chilled. I have created a monster.

Motors whirred, and high above the chamber cranes clanked and more powerful engines coughed into life. And the Warhead suddenly lifted, without any explosion of fuel, without any noise or fire or heat or exhaust – it simply and silently lifted from its pedestal and hung there in the air, rotating gently, its surface awash with a fluid golden fire.

It is alive, Constanza thought, and goose bumps prickled across her flesh. She felt suddenly sick, down to her very core. Nausea swamped her and filled her throat with bile but she choked back the feeling, licked at her dry lips, took a deep breath – and turned back to the gloss black keyboard. Distantly, she heard a roar of heavy machine-gun fire, the sustained blasting of thousands and thousands of rounds.

It has begun, she thought. It has begun – but it isn't over yet.

Her eyes gleaming, she began to type.

'Where the *fuck* are we?' snarled Jam.

Fenny looked back, face half-hidden by the HIDSS of the Comanche. But what could be seen of his expression said it all, and Jam stared in disbelief at the pilot and his bobbing curls.

'You mean we're *lost*?' said Sonia.

'It's the navigation systems,' whined Fenny. 'There's something nearby causing incredible, and I mean fucking *incredible*, magnetic discharges. The nav computers have lost their bearings.'

'How can a bloody navigation computer lose its bearings? It's a damned *navigation* computer!' growled Jam. It had been a long, long haul across the world, stopping several times to refuel. They had missed Carter in Tibet by no more than an hour, and had followed the distant stragglers of a massive Nex war-host heading south . . . heading for Carter. But the assembled Nex machinery had been far superior and could put down more speed. Their Comanche, once the pinnacle of modern military aviation development, had fallen gradually and woefully behind. The distant Nex army – a huge swarm of choppers numbering nearly a thousand, and several hundred Lockheed K56 Hercules Transport and Special Mission aircraft sporting eight wing-mounted Allison (R-R) T56-J-27 turboprops apiece and the ability to carry everything from infantry to tanks and FukTrucks – had eventually disappeared over the distant digital horizon of Fenny's scanners.

'Has The Priest replied yet?'

'Not yet,' said Fenny, turning again to survey his crew.

'I did not think he would let us down,' said Jam softly, shifting his bulk. He gazed out over the cold seas of the South Atlantic. 'He said they would patch us coordinates and we would meet up with the stragglers of the remaining DemolSquads – those who had finished their respective missions.'

'Maybe he hasn't had time,' said Sonia softly.

'Yes.' Jam nodded, his huge armoured head gazing out over the churning seas. There was an edge of bitterness to his voice. 'He's probably too damned busy to save the world.'

'There!' said Fenny suddenly, pointing ahead with

excited animation. 'We've found it! We've found it!'

'Don't get too thrilled,' snapped Jam. 'Antarctica is a big fucking place. What exactly have you found?'

'You don't understand!' Fenny ripped his HIDSS free and stared back, eyes gleaming. 'The DemolSquads – they're here! We've found the guys!'

'Now all we have to do is find Carter – and the Warhead,' said Sonia quietly.

'If we still have time,' said Jam. The Comanche swept down towards the rough serrated coastline of Norwegian Antarctica, towards the jagged walls of snow cliff, the churning ice-filled seas. And the shattered remains of the oldest gathering of veteran Spiral DemolSquads.

The triggers were firm under both Carter's index fingers and he sighted carefully at a huge swathe of Nex infantry. Then, having selected his targets, he squeezed the two short metal strips.

The huge guns yammered and bucked and pounded. Carter watched entranced as hundreds of bullets shot out across the ice, flickering green with tracer rounds, and smashed into the advancing line of Nex – cutting them down like a line of toy soldiers. Bullets came blasting back, pummelling the Spiral base.

Mongrel opened fire. Carter glanced right and saw the big twin machine guns spitting a hail of hot metal from glowing muzzles. The ice fields before them erupted with return gunfire and the Nex surged forward, sprinting as tanks revved and exhaust smoke plumed. The whole army increased its pace and charged towards the two lonely defenders on the Spiral base walls.

Carter scythed down another squad of Nex. Then another. Then another. Bullets struck the armoured turret, a thousand of them glancing off with ricochet sparks. Carter could smell acrid smoke, scorched metal, gun oil – and his own fear, which tasted bad.

Mongrel was screaming down the comm, unintelligible shouts in a variety of different languages. Carter could sense his comrade's excitement, his fear. They were the same feelings that ran through Carter's veins. He targeted a tank, his bullets smashing at the heavily armoured flanks – but to no effect. Carter relaxed pressure on the triggers, switched to rockets, targeted and, in the same fluid movement, launched.

From behind the turret two metal arms swung up. Rockets were aimed and ignited – all within the blink of an eye. They flashed out and down, leaving trails of smoke and slamming into the heavy TK79. Fire blossomed and the tank was plucked from the world's game-board and sent rolling and howling backwards, spilling thick black smoke, to crush a hundred Nex infantry.

Carter fired more rockets, watching as they pounded the tanks, sending pulverised armour tumbling backwards to grind Nex troops in a horrifying melding of metal and insect-human flesh . . .

'Why tanks not returning fire?' Mongrel yelled down the comm.

'They don't want to destroy the Warhead.'

'Why not? ECW will take out their bases. Why not halt it?'

'It's more valuable to Durell as a weapon, as technology, than as a piece of melted scrap,' said Carter. 'That's the way the diseased bastard thinks.' He sent more bullets howling across the void. Watched another hundred Nex smashed into purple pulp, to lie in a huge arc of crimson staining the snow with their insect-blend blood.

Carter swept his scanners across the battlefield.

'Incoming!' screamed Mongrel as a line of rockets suddenly surged from the lines of charging infantry. Twenty smoke trails filled the sky and Carter watched in horror as they raced towards him. He slammed at the pedals and the gun turret glided along its rails. The rockets passed by to his right and detonated behind him. The whole base shook. Mongrel's turret, which had momentarily stuttered to a halt, began to fire once more.

'They're breaking up,' snarled Carter. 'Splitting their forces.'

Two huge groups of tanks swung out over the snow, their tracks kicking up sprays of ice, giving protective armoured cover to their squads of Nex. Their intentions were obvious. They were going to encircle the base and attack from all sides.

'They not expecting resistance,' said Mongrel, calmer now. Again he fired, and again; more rockets shot towards their targets.

The Spiral base shook once more under the impact of the explosions. But it was holding up well – it was built to withstand a sustained artillery attack. Its designers had anticipated war.

'We need more men,' growled Carter. 'We've got all this awesome fucking weaponry, and nobody to man it!' Frustration gnawed at him. He tracked one of the circling columns of tanks with his BFG but most of his bullets were deflected in huge showers of sparks. Carter then sent two more rockets towards the columns – but anti-missile fire surged up from the Nex ranks, taking them out. Fire blossomed low over the ice, melting huge craters to reveal a base of molten rock which glowed like lazy solar after-images on a nuked and abused retina.

'I could go get Constanza,' said Mongrel.

'She has her own battle to fight,' snapped Carter. More Nex rockets flew towards him and sudden realisation dawned: his turret had become jammed. With a yelp, he threw himself backwards as two rockets converged on his gun turret. He was already moving as the missiles struck. But the blast picked him up and sent him flailing across the roof of the base. He hit the ground hard and then lay terribly still.

Stars were flashing in Carter's head and there was a ringing in his ears. The sky above him was blue, and he breathed deeply and smiled as Mongrel filled his vision, looming over him.

'You OK?'

'Get back to the fucking guns!' screamed Carter.

'Thank God! You OK.' Mongrel grinned and disappeared.

Carter groaned, rolling to his knees and pulling the dented helmet from his head.

Cursing, he reached down and pulled a two-inch sliver of shrapnel from his thigh. Pain seared through him, and with shaking fingers he dug out a tiny medical stapler from his combats and fired three thick sterile staples into his flesh, joining the wound.

Carter groaned again. Panting, he staggered to his feet and glanced back to see the twisted wreckage of his gun turret. It was an abomination against the skyline, a twisted, pounded, torn and sculpted monstrosity of sheared metal. But more importantly, the rocket blast had wrenched the rails from their housings, effectively disabling another two guns.

'Son of a bitch,' Carter spat. He glanced around. The thundering tanks had nearly encircled the base and Nex were starting to flood from behind the protecting armoured flanks.

465

'We are *fucked*,' snarled Carter. Then he yelled 'Mongrel! Get your fucking arse over here!'

Mongrel sent a stream of rockets plummeting onto the battlefield. Without looking to see if they met their targets, he leapt from the turret and ran over to Carter.

'We're compromised. Let's go to Constanza. She needs to launch the fucking Warhead, right *now*,' said Carter.

But Mongrel wasn't listening. He was staring at something behind Carter, his mouth open, his eyes bright.

'What is it?' Carter asked.

He was nearly deaf from the explosion that had torn him from his gun turret but as he started to turn he felt the down draught of armoured rotors and heard their *whump whump whump*. He swung his sub-machine gun up, finger tightened on the trigger out of reflex. But Mongrel was there, grabbing the stock of the weapon as the Comanche howled overhead.

'Whoa, Big Man! It Jam – look!'

Carter's eyes focused as the Comanche banked tightly around and dropped towards the roof. Jam and Sonia leapt free, then Fenny lifted the war machine back into the skies and flew towards the tanks. Hellfire anti-tank missiles detached and slammed down onto their targets.

Carter stared hard at Jam. 'Man, am I glad to see your ScorpNex arse!'

Jam scowled. 'What the *fuck* happened to you? You look like . . . well, like you've been fighting a war!'

'Long story. You got the EDEN targets?'

Sonia showed him a small silver cube. Carter grinned all over his blackened, bruised face. 'Fucking *magic*. Let's get it down to Constanza – we're sure to be overrun in the next couple of minutes—'

'Wait.' Jam pointed.

Carter swung around to see a huge fleet of helicopters

466

swarming down from the sky. There were RAH Comanches, EH101 Merlins, AS668 Tigers, Russian Mil Mi-14s and Mil Mi-28 Havocs; there were SS532 Cougars, Denel Ah-2A Rooivalks, a whole army of AH-64 Apaches with J2 armaments, NH90s, Sikorsky Black Hawks, and about ten Italian Agusta A180 Mangusta war copters thumping through the skies on huge V-twin Ducati turboshaft engines. They roared overhead, nearly two hundred combat aircraft in total, and spread out in vast swarms as their guns rained down death on the Nex army below.

'How? What? When?' muttered Mongrel, tufty, smoking hair swaying in the breeze of pounding rotors.

'May I present to you your back-up, gentlemen,' said Jam, his voice a low rumble. 'Now, you wanted to upload this Warhead? Please be so kind as to show me the way.'

The group jogged across the roof of the Spiral base. Below tanks fired shells skywards and heavy machine guns opened up. Choppers were plucked from the air and sent screaming to their deaths, crumpling into the ice with rotors shearing free, and exploding in blasts of fire and smoke. Carter and the others reached the portal, which hissed open.

Mongrel entered first, followed by Sonia and then Jam.

Carter stood for a moment, surveying the insanity of the carnage around him. He licked his scorched lips and ran a hand through his sweat-drenched hair. Then he limped into the Spiral base, trailing droplets of blood and sweat, and dark honey tears, and was swallowed by the perfectly engineered metal portal.

'You have the data?'

Sonia held out the silver cube and Angel Constanza attached it to a tiny cable. Lights flickered, and data streamed up the screen in a blur of white on black. Constanza's fingers raced across the keyboard. Her stare was fixed to the screen, moving quickly over text and numbers and her mouth worked silently as her concentration focused totally.

The group stood around her in silence and Sonia glanced over her shoulder at the hovering Warhead. Its surface was a rolling, molten wonder, a golden, swirling display of an infinity of possibilities.

Jam pointed towards the vid screens, which displayed the churning warfare outside; the chaos of battle.

'It savage,' observed Mongrel.

'The world *is* savage,' said Carter, softly.

'Despite their firepower, DemolSquads being given damned good fight.'

'Nobody ever said the Nex were cowards.'

'Maybe we not win this one. Maybe Spiral and REB boys just buying us time?'

'At the moment, Mongrel, time is all that we need.'

'Look,' said Sonia. She had moved over to the EC Warhead and was peering into its molten surface with her head tilted on one side. 'It's doing something.'

The surface swirls had started to accelerate, spinning and gyrating in billions of wild patterns. Then, suddenly, there was a tiny click and the Warhead went black, a deep and endless black; the negation of a colour that lurks in deep eternity.

Sonia took a tentative step back.

Far above them, a tiny portal opened, showing a bright circle of crystal-blue sky.

And, in the blink of an eye, the Warhead was gone.

'*Fuck*,' hissed Carter.

'Fuck *me*,' echoed Mongrel.

'Where did it go?' rumbled Jam.

Constanza swung around on her chair, her face weary, her golden eyes staring sadly at the ground. Then she looked up at the rest of the group, and they could see that horror was etched into her features as if by acid. She spat on the floor, and wiped her mouth with the back of her hand. Then she smiled, a hollow smile under deep-sunken eyes.

'It is done,' she said. 'The Warhead is launched. God save us all.'

Carter slammed a magazine into his Browning. He took a deep breath, then said, 'It's got little to do with God, my friend. Now, let's get the hell out of here – before the fucking Nex find us. This game is far from over.'

Outside, the battle was still raging.

Fire screamed across the sky.

Destruction raged across the earth.

The Nex reached the entry point and a group of thirty lithe black-clad figures flowed through into the dark interior of the base. They split up into squads of five and sprinted down dimly lit corridors, Steyr TMPs in their gloved hands.

Outside the tanks closed in, forming an armoured ring around the walls. Above them choppers were smashed from the skies by Nex using heavy MGs and Stinger v3.2 MANPADs – man-portable surface-to-air missiles, shoulder-fired and designed to counter high-speed, low-level attack aircraft, including helicopters. The Stinger v3.2 used proportional navigational algorithms to guide the missile to a predicted intercept point. It was proving effective against Spiral's war machines.

A Nex pulled free a dark ECube which opened in the palm of its hand.

The Nex listened for a moment.

'Yes, sir. We are inside. Understood, sir. I have seen the data-cube sheets on Carter. We all have; we will recognise him if we see him. And yes, our machines *have* picked up the launch of the Warhead – what they describe as the ECW. It launched just a few minutes ago. It would seem their race to upload targets has been successful. Their mission has been successful. Spiral's mission is complete.'

Carter, Mongrel, Jam, Sonia and Constanza raced along the corridors leading back up to the roof, where they burst out onto the buckled alloy surface.

Jam got on his ECube, then looked at the others. 'He's coming in. Just hold on tight.'

The Comanche howled out of the battle, twin stowable three-barrelled 20mm turreted Gatling nose guns glowing. It banked and touched gently down beside the five operatives. The cockpit canopy folded back as another Comanche appeared and landed beside its twin.

'OK,' said Carter, glancing over at Jam. 'Me, Mongrel and Constanza will head out with –' he glanced in at the HIDSS-covered head, then gulped – 'um, with Mrs Sheep . . .' He saw Mongrel's scowl. Mrs Sheep was renowned as one of the most psychotic pilots on the planet. 'Jam and Sonia, you follow with Fenny.'

'What's our destination?' said Mongrel.

'Let's get clear of this insane battle, then check on the Warhead's progress. We need to get the DemolSquads moving, get them in place as back-up for when the Warhead strikes. After reading the tech sheets on that insane machine, I know that when the fight comes it's going to come as fast as fuck, and we'll all need to be in position. Also, Durell is sure to have a hundred back-up plans in place and we need to study his game.'

'You think he can stop the ECW?' asked Sonia.

Carter shrugged. 'All I know is that I want to hit at his heart.' He turned to Jam. 'Have we intel on his location?'

'I will scan the channels when we're airborne – and I have my own thoughts on that one. Durell is a creature of habit. And to all intents and purposes he is extremely predictable . . . There is a part of him flowing in my blood.'

'So you know how he thinks?' asked Mongrel.

Jam nodded his armoured head, copper eyes gleaming. 'I do,' he hissed.

'Right. Let's move out. And Jam?'

'Carter?'

'Once again, brother, I owe you my life.'

Jam grinned then, a quite horrible and frightening sight. 'Let's find Durell. And let's show him what us Spiral boys are really made of. Hey, Mongrel?'

Mongrel grinned. 'Aye, Jam. We teach that bastard a lesson he never, ever forget.'

The two Comanches cruised at maximum speed. Behind them the battle was abandoned as the DemolSquads peeled away from the ground army of Nex and split, heading out over the snowfields of Antarctica with new missions appearing on their ECubes. In their wake they left thousands of Nex slain, a hundred smashed and smoking tanks, and an empty Spiral base: empty of personnel, empty of technology – and empty of the Evolution Class Warhead.

Using ECube relays, Jam and Carter stayed in close contact, directing the DemolSquads to new targets and areas of contact. Constanza used a small tracking device similar in design to an ECube but with a certain very specific purpose. It was built for tracking the Warhead, to stay in touch with the greatest sentient weapon ever devised.

471

After a while, as they flew low over the sea, Mongrel turned to Carter.

'Did it work, you think?'

Carter looked at Constanza, and she glanced up at the two battered smoke-stained men. She still looked exhausted. Then she smiled slowly, nodding, and let out a big sigh. 'Yes. And it's been a mad couple of days,' she said.

'You not kidding!' snorted Mongrel. He gazed long and hard at Constanza. She looked away, then back into his face. She smiled then, and he smiled back at her. 'You great lady, you know that?'

'Just doing my bit. For King and Country, yeah?'

'I just wondering . . .' Mongrel said.

'Yes?' Constanza was smiling as she nursed the Warhead tracking device in her hands.

'You know? If you would like have dinner with me, some time?' Mongrel beamed gappily.

Constanza took a deep breath to reply, but Mongrel continued, oblivious.

'It just, I up there, in turret, facing certain death. And I scared, and all I keep thinking was, don't you fuckers blow me up now, not when there nice young lady down there programming Warhead who I want to get to know bit better, and I thought to myself, I thought Mongrel, old lad, if you get out of this sour Mr Pickle sandwich alive, you should ask her out! Yes! For food! And wine! Nothing cheap, no stinking kebabs and pint-pot dregs for this classy lass but evening of *quality*, and I . . .'

'Yes.'

'. . . And I was thinking, I know I only tufty and have several tufts missing, but I—'

'Yes, Mongrel.'

'Really?'

472

'Yes. Which bit of *yes* don't you understand?'

'Wow!' Mongrel beamed.

Constanza glanced down at the Warhead tracker. She frowned then, her smile dropping from her face. Carter saw the gesture and moved towards her, gaze falling on the scanner – a screen filled with tiny data streams.

'What is it?'

'Oh. I . . . I don't know.'

'Is there something wrong?'

Constanza ran her finger over the touch screen, scrolling through data, choosing different pathways, and then scrolling through more data. Then she scowled, expression going hard, and her stare swept up to meet Carter's.

'There is something wrong. With the Warhead.'

'Such as?'

'It's moving off course. And . . . oh. Shit.'

It was Carter's turn to scowl. 'What is it?'

'The Warhead – it has deleted its targets.'

'Deleted its . . . you've got to be fucking *kidding* me, right? We've fought halfway across the fucking globe to get to this point – we've risked *everything* to launch that ECW. You make it sound like it has *chosen* to delete the targets . . .'

Constanza nodded. 'It must have! I don't understand. They are targets that threaten Spiral, humanity – threaten the whole world as we know it. The machine is sentient, it has intelligence. I do *not* understand what has gone wrong . . .'

Carter's ECube rattled. He pulled it free and it unfolded neatly. Blue light danced from the tiny device, creating a figure of light atop its shell – a figure that Carter knew all too well. It was a man – a Nex – who filled him with hate, violence and despair.

It was Durell. A tiny avatar, sculpted from ECube

light. 'Mr Carter,' came the low, gravelly voice. Durell looked up then, looked up into Carter's face – and Carter felt his whole body go numb. Something was wrong here. Something was terribly *bad*.

'What the fuck do you want?'

'I wish to offer you my congratulations.'

'Meaning?'

'You have launched the Evolution Class Warhead. You have launched *my* weapon of destruction. *My* sentinel of death. *My* obedient servant of utter and total annihilation.'

'Fuck you, cunt.'

'You think I lie? Constanza there will inform you of the coordinates. Even now, the Warhead is heading for 445.554.354.332. There it will find fuel and massive stocks of EDEN – and then disseminate it into a thousand missiles, each loaded with this, our deadly toxin. The Warhead will, over the next twelve hours, begin its multiple delivery of the most deadly biological poison ever known to mankind. The Warhead will wipe out the human race, Carter. And Spiral sent it. *You* sent it.'

'That's not possible.'

'You know that it is.'

'Why me, Durell? Why have you chosen me as your slave?'

'You *are* mine, Carter. To love and to hold, to command and to destroy. You are right: you *are* my slave. And your determination to get the job done is an awesome sight to behold. Your will-power, and strength, and fury – they are the greatest of pure-breed gifts, and I am duly envious. Come to me, Carter. Come to Ethiopia . . . I will patch through coordinates, you can join me and I will take you to the ChainStations with the Nex – we will start a new future on Earth, we will make the world good

474

again, right again, a world without pain and suffering. We will finish what Spiral began. We will complete their dream. We will be the *new* Spiral, Carter; me, with you by my side. We will cleanse the Earth of its evil.'

Carter felt his strength leave him. He felt his head spinning as he tumbled down a well of confusion and despair.

I have condemned the world.

I have murdered mankind.

Carter did not doubt Durell's words.

'I don't understand,' he said softly.

'You will, Carter. You will. Come to me. I will explain everything.'

The signal died, leaving Carter shivering in his seat. Mongrel was staring open-mouthed, and Constanza was scrolling madly through the Warhead scanner. When she looked up, both Carter and Mongrel knew what she was going to say before she spoke the words.

'Durell is right. He has control of the Warhead.'

'So we set-up?' snarled Mongrel.

Constanza nodded. 'All the time we thought we were going to destroy Durell's EDEN store. But in fact, all we did was launch the weapon on his behalf. It was his greatest stalling tactic. He kept us busy on the wrong trail. We should have destroyed the Warhead, not armed it . . . We are truly lost now, Carter, truly beaten, *truly* without hope. How can we possibly fight such an enemy?'

Carter looked up. His eyes were a molten fury.

'We can fight him with fists, and boots, and guns,' he snarled. 'He wants me to go to him? Then I will go to him. He wants me to meet the fucking Nex face to face one last time before the world dies? Then I will fucking meet him – and only God can stand in my way. Mrs Sheep? Land the Comanche. I need to speak to Jam.'

'Bouvet Island is about ten minutes away. It's uninhabited, according to my scanners,' came Mrs Sheep's deep voice.

'That's perfect. Take us there.'

Mongrel placed a huge hand on Carter's shoulder. His eyes were filled with tears. 'Carter, do you know what you doing, man? You going into lion's den. For fuck's sake, he wants you for reason . . . Durell playing own tactical game – one where we always stumble behind, where we always chasing our tails. We should go after Warhead, try and bring it down ourselves. Try and stop it! That only way for us.'

Carter gripped his friend's powerful arm. 'That will be your task, mate. You must track down the Warhead and destroy it – before it delivers its payload to the world. And you must coordinate the DemolSquads – get them in to kick the living fuck out of the Dreadnoughts.'

'Durell drawing you to mad bad confrontation. He know your pride make you deliver yourself to him. Don't make it so easy, Carter old buddy. Don't give yourself to him on plate – like lamb just waiting for the old slaughter. You must not do this!'

'I will do what I have to do,' said Carter. 'And I will kill Durell – or die in the process.'

With growling, thumping engines, the two Comanches hummed low over the churning cold waves as night fell and darkness slowly swallowed the world . . .

CHAPTER 18

DURELL

Bouvet Island in the South Atlantic covered an area of 58.5 square kilometres and was covered almost entirely by glaciers. What little rock showed was a deep corrugated black, volcanic and dead. A cold wind whipped over the ice as the Comanches touched down, landing gear crunching and suspension dipping, hot engines ticking as they cooled and cockpits were opened. The weary Spiral agents climbed out into the freezing bleak wilderness.

'Nice place,' observed Mongrel dryly. 'You *sure* there no natives here with guns, eh?'

'It's uninhabited,' said Jam. 'Let's sort this out and get off this godforsaken lump of rock. It's a place not meant for human occupation, that's for damn sure. So, Durell has control of the Warhead. That is a bitter pill. A savage blow. What are you thinking, Carter?'

'I am going after Durell – alone. He has issued a challenge. I will accept his invitation.'

'And the rest of us?'

Carter looked around the small group. 'You and

Mongrel must head out and try to stop the Warhead. Failing that, round up what DemolSquads you can and head for the Dreadnoughts – they're easy enough targets. If you can put enough of them out of action I am sure that Durell will slow his plans to release the EDEN toxin. After all, he won't want to kill thousands of his own Nex army.'

'What about me?' asked Sonia. She stared at Carter's battered, bruised visage, lit only by the glow of halogen lamps from the Comanche. He looked like a man you most definitely would not want to cross.

'I've had a thought about that,' said Carter softly. 'Jam told me that you spoke of getting on the air one last time – of trying to make the people of the world rise up against the Nex by exposing the truth about this EDEN poison. You and Constanza should attempt an infiltration of HIVE Media. Use the data cube you retrieved from Norway, from the K-Labs: if you can air the test video of the EDEN virus then you may just provoke an uprising, a rebellion. It's not every day that your loved ones are about to be murdered. That sort of thing gives people a bit of fucking *motivation*, a bit of an incentive, yeah? Do you think you can do this?'

Constanza smiled over at Sonia, then nodded. 'I think between us we can crack the HIVE systems; we just need to get past their heavy security. Then access their digital systems.'

'Which is where I come in,' said Sonia, her heart beating fast. She could play her part; she could put her life on the line for this climactic moment. In a crumbling world, she would be able, truly, to make a difference.

'We will stop off in South Africa at a couple of SP_Plots, sort out weapons, ammo, supplies and choppers. I'm going to need my own transport for this

478

mission.' Carter's brow was furrowed, his mind working at light speed, adrenalin flooding his system.

Mongrel took a deep breath and nodded to himself, as if coming to some mighty decision. 'Carter, lad. I will come with you.'

'No. I go alone,' said Carter. 'I work better that way.'

Jam took a step forward, his triangular ScorpNex head swaying. 'Mongrel, you will be better employed gathering the DemolSquads together – after all, they are *your* people. They take one look at my ScorpNex shell and their trust is shattered.' He stared hard at Carter, then. '*I* will go with Carter.'

'I don't need you,' said Carter.

'You do. I can get you past the Nex. I can get you past an *army* of Nex. After all, I know how they think; I am one of them. Whereas you . . .' Jam chuckled softly. 'You are only human.'

'Maybe I don't need your help to get past them.'

'You know in your heart that you do,' said Jam. 'And when it comes to the big fight, I have my own fucking scores to settle. With the Nex, with Mace, and with Durell. Look at me, Carter. Look at what they did to me . . . I need payback. I need some *insect closure*.'

Carter nodded, stare fixed on the deformity of Jam's genetically spliced body. 'OK. We'll make a dash towards South Africa, pick up a third chopper and go our separate ways. If we all switch to ECube F-channel 55724 then we can keep secure communication. Or as secure as the ECubes ever can be. Any questions?'

The group all shook their heads. The cold wind blew across the black snow-crusted mountains, howling mournfully.

'Then let's do it,' said Carter, eyes gleaming.

★

The exchange and pick-up of weapons, supplies and an extra chopper went smoothly, and the autopilot steered the Comanche north through rough storm skies. Jam watched the controls in the darkness with a steady copper gaze as Carter snatched some much-needed sleep . . . And as he slept, he dreamed. It was a bad dream. It was a dream about Kade.

Carter stood on a mountain plateau, a flat section carved from the wall of a vast towering black mountain, which in turn reared above a world of dark graphite sand. Dust and jagged black rock squatted like bad memories under his boots, and the sky stretched away to infinity, speckled with trails of purple and yellow.

Kade stood beside a fire which burned within a small ring of rocks. The wind was howling through the mountains, desolate and haunting. Carter stared down at the flames, which flickered between a bright cold orange and a deep and bottomless black.

Kade had stolen Carter's face, but his body was a touch larger than Carter's own frame, more bulky, like a reflection in a slightly distorted mirror. The eyes were dark and brooding.

'I have been here before,' said Carter slowly.

'Clever boy.' Kade smiled.

'I remember. You said this was your place, your world, your mountain.'

'That is correct.' Kade seated himself beside the fire. Now it burned with black flames that glittered like twisting eels in oil. Carter sat down opposite Kade, and looked around in wonder. He breathed cold air, and listened for long moments to the song of the wind channelled through the narrow high passes of the mountains.

'You seem . . . *different,*' said Kade after a long silence.

'Yes.'

480

'You are not fighting me.'

'I am tired of fighting,' said Carter.

'You are doing the right thing. Going after Durell.'

'How so?'

'It is the QIV processor that is controlling the Warhead, just as it controlled the earthquakes all those years ago. It was naive of Spiral to think that in a whole five fucking years Durell had not discovered the one weapon which could truly bring him down. It is the true role of any powerful dictator to seek out that which is his greatest threat – and Durell found it, and used the QIV to kill the sentient chip within. The QIV took over the Warhead and emulated its AI – enough to fool Constanza, anyway.'

'Constanza, yes. How does she know you?'

'She has met me.'

'*What?* How so?'

'I will tell you. After you have killed Durell.'

'And what if he kills me?'

'If he kills *us*,' corrected Kade. 'Then the secret will go to both of our graves.'

'Maybe I won't go in search of Durell. Maybe I will head for the mountains, seek to avoid the EDEN poison. There will be places, remote pockets of the Earth where the toxin will not reach. I could survive. I could live.'

'No,' said Kade, dark-eyed stare fixed on Carter. 'You *will* go after Durell. Because, if you take out Durell, then you can control the QIV processor. And if you control the QIV processor, you control the Warhead. Ergo, you can still halt this madness; this abomination.'

'Halt it? I thought you would *revel* in it!'

Kade laughed then, a hollow sound like snapping bones, or the crush of cockroach shells under heavy boots. He tilted his head, observing Carter. 'What use to me is a world without victims?' said Kade gently. 'What use a world without murder? You think I wish to live in a beautiful Nex society where everybody is a blend of everyone else? Fuck that. I thrive on death, Carter. I live to fight. I live to kill. Get me to Durell and I will show you something you have never before witnessed.' Kade's voice was cold. Chilling. 'Get me there, Carter, and I will show you something *new*.'

'Something new?'

Kade smiled with neat piranha teeth. 'We will kill Durell together,' he said.

Mongrel's Apache hammered low and hard under the hot baking sun, armoured rotors thumping, Mongrel's frown a perfect expression of annoyance. After the SP_Plot pick-up in South Africa, Mongrel had drawn the short straw in his choice of aerial alternatives: the Apache. It looked very much the worse for wear, displaying battered panels, scorch marks, the stains of four different kinds of disruptive-pattern paintwork and at least fifty different bullet holes in varying calibres. (Mongrel's words had been something along the lines of 'You expect me to fly *that* heap of shite? *Bozhey moy!*') But in fact the war machine was so far giving him sterling service. It had seen him cut swiftly up the western coast of Africa, the South Atlantic Ocean glittering sometimes in the distance as he crossed Namibia on his newly arranged and coordinate-locked meeting with The Priest.

The message had been a short but sweet ECube transmission from that old, mad, but ultimately religious nutcase, The Priest, delivered in his usual style and with perfect timing, considering the recent split of the Spiral group. It read:

```
CLASSIFIED Stacs 100836410/ ENCRYPTED
SIU
SEND: PRIEST, THE, SIU23446
REC: MONGREL, THE, SIU 42880
MONGREL. WARHEAD BEYOND REACH.
I AM ASSEMBLING DEMOLSQUADS.
LAST MINUTE ASSAULT PLANNED ON DNs.
NEED TO MEET; CHECKING YOUR CO-ORDS . . .
SUGGEST ANGOLA 176.534.343.444
MAY THE LORD PROTECT YOU. AMEN.
```

Carter must have contacted The Priest, Mongrel thought. Told him our plans, and The Priest was already in the process of gathering the DemolSquads together. That was good: the direction and organisation of the Squads would in itself save them a lot of time – and with Durell's accelerating machinations, time was something they desperately needed. They had only hours before the EDEN rockets fell . . .

Sunlight glimmered through the cockpit and Mongrel banked, checking his coordinate listings. He saw the Comanche far below, rotors turning idly, on a high red-dust plateau overlooking a massive series of rocky undulations falling in massive steps towards the deep blue of the glittering ocean.

'Ha! Found you, you religious donkey.' Mongrel slowed his speed, and guided the Apache to touch down gently, huge swirls of red dust dancing up around the war machine.

Mongrel jumped out and saw The Priest in his grey robes at the edge of the plateau, staring out to sea. Mongrel strode forward, sub-machine gun in one hand, and they exchanged a swift greeting.

'The world crumbling,' said Mongrel. 'How many Squads have you gathered?'

The Priest gave a huge sigh. He stared down, a Bible in one hand, rosary beads clacking softly against his huge hairy chest. 'Our numbers are severely depleted, my brother. The Lord is not smiling any longer. I fear Durell has stolen his crown and will rain down plagues on us at any moment. Our men number in the mere thousands, and our technology is wearing thin. Our stores are almost empty, ammunition is becoming more and more scarce – and Mongrel—' He looked up then, his large gold-flecked brown eyes gazing at his old comrade, his old brother in war. 'I am beginning to fear for my sanity.'

'How many groups assembling?'

'With a combination of REB and Spiral manpower, we have assembled nearly two hundred DemolSquads. But these are the last of our resources, the last of our men. Each Squad has been given specific coordinates, specific targets in the back-up of what we thought would be the EC Warhead aggressive strikes. But we can still hit Durell – we can hit him hard and, with the protection of the Lord, we can cause him great damage. If we are blessed, my child, then maybe we may gain a lucky victory. Maybe we can slow him down enough to postpone his commencement of EDEN.'

Mongrel frowned, moving away from The Priest. He stood by the edge of the plateau, red dust staining his boots, and stared at the distant ocean, taking deep breaths of salt air. It felt good in his lungs. He decided that if he ever got through this mess alive – if he survived the coming battle with the Nex and the one after that with his cancer – he would renounce his former life of brothels and kebab shops, and take Carter's lead: he would head for the mountains. They had stolen his heart. He could marry, settle down, raise ugly little bastard offspring.

'When did Carter contact you?' said Mongrel.

'He did not.'

'Then – how do you know about Warhead?'

The Priest's voice suddenly boomed out, rich and deep, his hands gesturing wildly through the air. 'I myself have seen the ungodly in great power, and flourishing like a green bay-tree! Yes, Mongrel, the ungodly! But . . . For what profit is it to a man if he gains the whole world, and yet loses his own soul? What will a man give in exchange for his soul?' The Priest nodded to himself, piously. 'My friend, the journey has been long and perilous. The path is filled with weeds on which our sandals tread. Our boots are trampling the names of the ungodly into the bloodied soil of this righteous land!'

Mongrel looked sideways at The Priest.

Something was wrong. Terribly wrong.

It did not fit. It no longer clicked neatly into place.

How could he have known the Warhead was off course? Not obeying its own set of rules? How could the religious freak have known such things? But then, he was TacSquad. The Head of Spiral's Secret Police. His information network was legendary.

Mongrel relaxed a little, went to turn, but The Priest's arm shot out and with it came the dark eye of the Glock.

Mongrel froze. 'What game this?'

'No game.' The Priest spoke softly, his voice low, his eyes flashing with a dangerous glint. Mongrel swallowed, aware of his own sub-machine gun with its safety catch off, and his finger already nestling against the trigger.

'What you *doing*, religious fruitbat?'

The Priest spoke, terribly slowly this time, his stare locked on Mongrel. 'He was wounded for our transgressions. He was bruised for our iniquities! All we sheep have gone astray; we have turned every one to his own way; and the Lord hath laid on him the iniquity of us all. He was oppressed, and he was afflicted, yet he opened not his mouth: he is brought as a lamb to the slaughter, and as the sheep before her shearers – he is dumb.'

The Glock barked, a single bullet smashing into Mongrel's chest and pitching the huge squaddie, flailing in shock, onto his back. To Mongrel, it felt as if somebody had struck him with a sledgehammer. He lay in the dirt, racked with searing agony, and felt a shadow pass slowly over him, blocking out the last rays of the sun.

Mongrel's arm came up holding his automatic weapon, but The Priest's sandal slapped down hard, pinning his wrist to the ground. Mongrel stared up at the bearded face, snarling with rage, lifeblood staining his clothing, pain gnawing at him. 'Why, you fucker? Why?'

The Priest just gave a little shake of his head. 'Death comes to all men,' he said sombrely. Then he lifted the Glock, took careful aim, and put another five bullets into Mongrel's twitching, thrashing body.

The Priest stared hard at Mongrel for a while as the giant man's frame slowly settled against the desert plateau ground and his blood flowed free. The heaving of his chest finally stilled. Then The Priest stooped, rosary beads rattling, and, grunting, hoisted Mongrel's huge body up over his head with supernatural strength. He stood, blood dripping in tiny splatters into the red dust, a titanic robed figure silhouetted in crimson as the sun sank behind the horizon.

The Priest heaved Mongrel's corpse over the cliff. Took a step back, wiped his blood-smeared hands on his grey robes, picked up his Bible, then moved slowly back towards the Comanche, stooping as if he carried the weight of the world across his sagging shoulders.

'Is it done?' came a soft female voice from inside the blood-red shadows of the combat aircraft.

'It is done, although I did not relish the deed.'

'Where next?'

The Priest looked up, eyes glinting like pools of molten metal in the deep red sunshine of a dying world. There was anger there. And hatred. But worst of all, there was an insane determination to do what he had to do – no matter what the cost.

'We must kill them all,' he whispered.

After the drop-off at the SP_Plot in South Africa, Sonia and Constanza were flown north by Mrs Sheep. Carter and Mongrel had given both women a quick lesson in piloting in case of emergencies; neither of the men trusted Mrs Sheep's combat skills.

An ECube transmission had informed them that there was a Sentinel Corporation tower in Morocco with HIVE Media broadcasting facilities, just outside the city of Casablanca. They arranged to meet a large squad of REBS and Spiral men on the outskirts of the city. This would be the firepower. Sonia J had merely to provide the computing capabilities.

During the journey, Constanza used remote hacking tools to find out as much as she could about the HIVE Media computer systems. All media was directed through a central series of mainframes located in New York, but each individual Sentinel Corporation unit had extremely powerful remote capabilities and its own discrete servers.

Constanza was sure she could hack the systems. She was positive that she could get Sonia a transmission signal on a global scale – and failing that? Well, there were sure to be many big Spiral and REB men with big guns.

Much of the journey was spent in silence, the two women attempting to regain their strength after their recent adventures and traumas. Sonia J was weary, while

Constanza too was exhausted, yet elated; in Mongrel she had found somebody with whom she had *clicked*, despite his rugged and eccentric appearance.

'Do you know Mongrel well?' Constanza asked after a while.

'I have spent a few hours in his company,' said Sonia carefully, throwing a quick glance towards the other woman. 'Why do you ask?'

Constanza squirmed uneasily. 'I just wondered what your opinion of the man was. What do you think of him?'

'He's big,' said Sonia slowly. 'Big, hairy, a bit brutal, if you want my honest opinion. And yet—'

'Yes?'

Sonia looked at Constanza then, and saw it. Here was a psychological conundrum, a massively complex character about whom she knew nothing. What had Carter said in his sardonic response? Queen of the Cannibals? What strength of character had it taken for that woman to push herself to the limits of her morality, to clinically manage her emotions – just to say alive? She had not just survived by her wits, but in a bizarre way actually prospered through her quick thinking and initiative. But a little part of Sonia whispered, in the darkest recesses of her mind: still, to eat *human flesh*?

Sonia shivered.

She chose her words with care. 'Mongrel is an incredibly strong and grounded character. He is the sort of man who is eternally loyal to a friend. With Mongrel, there is no letting a friendship slide. He is the sort of man who would protect you, who would die for you. And there isn't much more you can ask than that.'

Constanza returned to the infiltration of HIVE Media computing systems. Sonia helped her for a little while – she was OK with the base systems – but soon the technicalities went far beyond her computing expertise. She left the hacking to Constanza, who busily wrote her own tiny subroutines in Turbo C+3 and inserted them as Trojans and Worms into HIVE's own code.

'You want to go to war?' muttered the ex-programmer of the EC Warhead. 'Well, I'll give you a binary one.'

The Comanche flew in low over the red rock mountains of Morocco, banking and finally landing in a surge of rotor-swept dust on the outskirts of Casablanca. In the distance, Sonia could make out the thousands of buildings of the city, a huge swathe of white interspersed with sandstone and the occasional high block. Above this traditional roofscape rose the glass and alloy needle of the Sentinel Corporation tower. Modest in comparison with its counterparts in NYC, London and Paris, it nevertheless dominated the low skyline, windows glinting under broiling sunlight.

As the Comanche touched down, a convoy of FukTruks and Land Rovers were waiting, along with perhaps fifty men and women dressed in a mixture of combat clothing and Arab *galabiyya* robes; all wore white shamags. The vehicles were coated in dust and sand, their huge knobbled tyres stained with the dried-blood colour of the local earth.

Casablanca was a hive of activity, which helped with the covert nature of their mission. They were not a combat squad; their goal was a simple and efficient infiltration. They had two local Arab guides, Spiral men who had come highly recommended, and as the group of vehicles drove through the bustling crowds and along the congested dusty roadways leading through Casablanca a constant stream of FukTruks was heading *out* of the city, laden with Nex soldiers and JT8s.

489

'It looks suspiciously like the Sentinel Tower is being abandoned,' said Constanza. She watched several Chinooks taking to the air in the distance. 'Rats leaving a sinking ship?'

'Maybe they have some big fish to fry,' said Sonia. 'If Carter and Jam and Mongrel are getting their way, then all hell is about to break loose. Maybe they're being summoned by Durell? Reserves? Back-up?'

'If the Dreadnoughts are being targeted by Spiral, then it would make sense to redistribute your soldiers. Durell needs the Dreadnoughts to evacuate the Nex from Earth; if they become targets, it could really mess up his plans.'

Sonia smiled. 'That just makes life easier for us. Let's put another stick through the spokes of Durell's progress.'

They trundled through the streets, matching the speed of other traffic so as not to attract attention. Within minutes they were on the dusty road scoured with deep ruts that led towards the Sentinel Tower, which in turn gleamed with reflected rays of sunshine; it looked like any well-built New York tower block – but with one major exception. It was nuke-proof. Built to withstand the terrific onslaught of a nuclear bomb blast . . .

The FukTruks started to accelerate, picking up speed rapidly as huge engines roared and tyres gripped the dusty tarmac. Sonia turned to one of their guides.

'I forgot to ask about our infiltration tactics,' she said.

The man passed her a weapon, a stolen Steyr TMP. She checked the magazine as the FukTruk increased its speed again, surging forward. The engine was roaring now, the whole vehicle vibrating madly. Several Nex standing guard by the roadside shouted something and lifted their weapons, but they were left behind in clouds of dust. Guns rattled in the distance.

'That's the easy bit,' said the guide, his eyes glittering. 'We're going to ram our way in.'

'Hit and run?'

'No. Just hit. We have nowhere to run to.'

Sonia cocked her weapon and watched with increasing horror as yet again the FukTruk powered ahead, huge wheels thundering and pounding against the rutted road. The truck in front was going to hit the Sentinel Tower's doors first as the primary ram; they would then follow and attempt to mow down any defending Nex under their heavy churning wheels.

'You ready?' The guide had to shout over the noise of the screaming engine. Smoke was pluming from under the dented bonnet. If they didn't connect soon, the whole damned vehicle would blow in a geyser of boiling oil.

'I'll never be ready,' said Sonia J. She turned to Constanza, who had also taken a Steyr sub-machine gun. The dark-haired woman merely smiled, her eyes blazing, her mouth a grim line. You tough little bitch, thought Sonia—

And then the lead FukTruk was smashing through the glass and alloy doors, hammering them backwards as Nex were pulped under heavy thumping wheels and crushed against the Truk's front bumper.

Sonia's own vehicle screeched through the hole in the doors. Guns yammered. Sparks glanced along the vehicle's wing and bonnet, bullets tearing through steel. The Truk teetered, skidding around in the large foyer as behind them other Land Rovers and FukTruks ploughed into the Sentinel Tower, hammering into Nex soldiers. Tyres left red streaks against marble tiles, bumpers slammed against flesh and compressed Nex bodies against walls. Spiral men and women poured from the backs of the vehicles, sub-machine guns blaz-

491

ing. The ensuing firefight was short and very much to the point. It ended with the whole foyer filled with smoke and wailing engines and spreading pools of blood.

'This way,' snapped the guide. He held a digital map.

The large group of armed fighters flowed through the building. At each key choke point they locked and barred doors, using industrial nail guns to fix them in place and leaving behind a few heavily armed men.

'It'll take the bastards hours to get through,' said Sonia. 'Hopefully we won't need that long.' She glanced at Constanza. The dark-haired woman's face was stony. Her eyes, dark and forbidding, were fixed on the task ahead. 'You OK?'

'Let's get this done. I want my life back.'

'As do we all,' muttered Sonia.

They padded through plush carpeted corridors, up short flights of stairs and marble ramps. The tower was quiet inside, almost entirely deserted. Something big was indeed going down.

Reaching the studios, Sonia J paused with her hand on the door. It was familiar – every studio in every Sentinel Tower across the globe was modelled on the same design.

'You sure you can do this, Constanza?' asked Sonia.

'Just show me the keyboard. Now that we're in, I can get direct links to the HIVE Media core mainframe. My little implanted subroutines will have been working hard – I should have control of the whole network within a few minutes.'

Sonia could sense the studio on the other side of the door. Above it, a little rectangle glowed with the words ON AIR. She took a deep breath, prayed to the ghosts of her dead husband and child, and pushed open the door with a sudden violent movement, stepping back for the very last time into her media world . . .

The Comanche thundered through the African sunlight. Ahead, squatting black and massive against an endless expanse of bright blue sky, was the Dreadnought. Dreadnought NGO – the central core unit, hanging immobile two kilometres above the undulating plains, red-dust plateaux and jagged spinal mountains of Ethiopia.

'That is *huge*,' came Jam's soft, rumbling growl.

Carter nodded, his eyes focused ahead. 'Yeah. Big and ugly. Just like you.'

The Comanche climbed, gaining height, armoured rotors thumping. Scanners screamed then, scrolling with read-outs, highlighting a hundred different threats through the HIDSS and on cam-monitors inside the cabin. Carter's jaw tightened, muscles clenching, and his eyes narrowed as below him he saw the sprawl of tanks, FukTruks, massive gun emplacements and SAM sites.

This is it, he thought.

This is the moment.

Alarms sounded, red lights flashing and scattering across displays.

'Durell won't open fire,' said Jam.

'I know.'

'He will let you through. You have been invited.' Jam's head tilted, copper eyes staring at Carter's back.

Carter smiled then, without humour, his face a mocking skull mask beneath the HIDSS. 'You ready for this, Jam?'

'Yes.'

'You ready to meet your maker?'

'I am ready to *kill* my god.'

The Comanche had risen high above the Dreadnought. Now the world spread out below them, its focus a huge black rectangle of pitted, grooved alloy with scatterings of scanners, missiles, radar dishes, comms poles and stepped buttresses.

'Impressive,' said Carter.

'And a great shame – for this is the legacy of Cain.'

Carter slowed, pulling his weapons to him and checking their magazines. Then the Comanche dropped from the skies, howling, rotors a blur, tiny lights flickering on its armoured hull as it fell like a diving falcon towards its prey.

The Comanche banked, rising to level out and roar along just above the surface of the Dreadnought. Below, near the stepped entrance leading below, stood massed ranks of Nex. In their midst was a cleared circle in which stood Durell.

He was waiting, his gaze lifted to the heavens.

Carter banked the war machine, slowing his speed, and came thundering back towards the gathering of Nex. Not a single blended soldier lifted its weapon. Not a single eye tracked the screaming combat chopper.

'I'm taking her in,' said Carter quietly.

Jam merely nodded, H&K sub-machine gun in one clawed hand, spikes crackling up and down his forearms in a gentle rhythm of readiness – for battle.

The Comanche touched down and Carter climbed from the chopper. A cool wind was blowing, but everything else was still, and as the aircraft's rotors whined and thumped to a stop Carter and Jam looked warily around, staring suspiciously at the rigid Nex soldiers. As the Comanche's blades finally fell silent an eerie calm descended on the Dreadnought. Nobody spoke. Nobody lifted a gun. Nothing moved . . .

Durell finally walked towards the two Spiral agents, his robes fluttering in the breeze, hood pushed back to reveal his incredible deformations. His slitted copper eyes did not glance at Jam; instead, they focused solely on Carter.

'Welcome,' he said, his voice a crackle of insect chitin.

Carter nodded once, and looked past Durell to another figure; it was Mace, small and precise, wearing a simple grey body-hugging suit which reminded Carter of his first-ever encounter with a Nex, back at his home in Scotland years earlier. Mace's eyes were burning brightly and he moved smoothly to stand beside Durell: a faithful puppy.

'Put down your weapons,' commanded Mace.

Jam gestured with his H&K. 'Fuck you.'

'Ahh, Jam, my old and distant lover. It is so long since I heard the music of your sweet screams. So long since I inhaled the heavenly scent of your spilt blood. I miss you, Jam. Really, truly, this old torturer misses the most intimate of times we spent together; our sharing of a hard-core reality, and a most sexually satisfying experience. One day, my *victim*, we must return there. We must dance again. We must *share* again.'

Jam growled, low and long.

'You have come to kill me,' said Durell, his stare still fixed on Carter. 'But instead, I offer you a deal. You know you cannot beat me – look around you, look at the might of my soldiers, my armies, my *Nex*.' He relished the word, rolling it in his mouth like a well-aged whisky, and took a step closer. Carter felt his own body become incredibly tense, muscles taut like steel coils, the Browning in his lowered hand merging with him, a cyborg part of his flesh, a joining of body and metal and soul . . .

'You have a deal to offer us?' said Carter simply. 'You

plan to destroy mankind, to eradicate the human race. You wish to infect the planet with nothing but a virus of pure Nex . . . and we just cannot allow that.'

'Oh Carter, but you already have! You killed Jahlsen, helped to destroy SpiralGRID thus making my greatest enemies *weak* – and then you initiated the Evolution Class Warhead. You sent it on its multiple missions, got past the Spiral detection systems. You have forwarded EDEN to the masses, Carter. You have killed them. Killed them all. Killed your lover, your son – your whole fucking species.'

'That was not my intention.'

'Maybe it was,' said Durell softly. 'Subliminally. In the deepest, most secret corridors of your brain.' He took another step closer, and now was close enough for Carter to reach out and touch. Oil glistened against the twisted armoured panels merged with the flesh of his face. Durell's tiny tongue darted out. It gleamed. 'We have been here before, Mr Carter. We have stood here before.'

'Yeah, when you found out that I'm a fucking hard man to kill.'

'Exactly so. As am I.'

'You are no *man*, Durell. You are an abomination before God.'

'Carter, you are a pawn, my friend. You have played the game well, but ultimately you are a pawn. You carry within you a part of me. You carry within you a slice of my *soul*. A slice of my *seed*.'

'Meaning?'

'Have you not worked out what Kade is yet? No? Not even after all these years?'

'You are bluffing.' But Carter had gone white. He was chilled. To the bone. To the marrow. To the *core*.

'Not so. I know Kade, Mr Carter, I know Kade very,

very well. And the incredible thing is, you don't remember, do you? I thought for a long time you were being merely strong-willed, a powerful mental adversary . . . a sheer bastard for the sake of it. But then it dawned on me that you did not remember our good times, our first times, our best times. You did not remember the joining with Kade.'

'Fuck you, Durell. Stop the Warhead. Stop it now, and at least I'll guarantee you a clean death. Otherwise, I cannot be held responsible for my fucking actions.'

'No.' Durell shook his deformed, half-armoured head. Saliva glistened against his nightmare mouth. He reared up then, spine crackling like chewed ice. He shrugged back his black robes to reveal the horror and the glory of his twisted shell, his mass of amalgamated organics, abdomen jointed like that of an ant, a wasp, his triumphant blend of insect and human.

'So be it then, fucker.'

The air had grown incredibly still. The whole surface of the Dreadnought lay under a veil of utter and total silence. Nothing stirred, and the immobile Nex in their ranks showed no signs of antagonism. They merely displayed a serenity, a calmness, a willingness simply to observe the scene unfolding before them.

Carter leapt, his Browning whipping up – but Durell moved faster than any twisted deformed husk had a right to move. They slammed together, Durell's claws knocking the Browning skittering across the alloy deck. Carter twisted, slamming his elbow into Durell's head, ducking a high swipe of claws and ramming five low punches into Durell's abdomen – into his *thorax*. Carter leapt to dodge another sweep of claws, smashed a right hook into Durell's head, then took a blow which cracked into his broken nose and made blood splatter free, a curtain of crimson droplets. Stars flashed in his brain. Carter landed on the deck, panting, as another blow whistled past his ear and his boot lashed out, stomping against chitin with a sharp crackling sound. Durell made a curious keening noise, and Carter thought – I hurt him. I hurt *it*.

Jam and Mace had also made their moves simultaneously, Mace pouncing with awesome speed as Jam's sub-machine gun clattered and bullets scythed through the immobile ranks of Nex, standing with lowered Steyr TMPs in gloved hands – and not even blinking as bullets caved in their flesh with harsh slapping impacts. Such was their discipline.

Jam was large and strong, but Mace was preternaturally fast, his fists smashing out to beat against Jam's head and eyes. Jam thundered a blow into Mace's head, stunning the smaller Nex. Spikes flowered along his armoured forearms as the ScorpNex swept his razor weapon towards Mace: who had tortured him, burned him and, ultimately, *raped* his humanity . . .

Durell came back with a straight and awesomely powerful blow that staggered Carter, hammering into his forehead and sending him reeling backwards. He lost his footing and slapped onto the alloy deck. Durell leapt, deformed shell twisting and claws slashing down – but Carter had rolled, a black knife appearing in his fist and slashing across Durell's armoured shell with a tiny hiss of steel parting chitin-flesh. Dark blood rained down upon him, speckling his face and hands, as Durell landed and whirled, his claws smashing the knife away.

'Not so fucking easy, is it?' snarled Durell.

'That hurt, didn't it, fucker?'

Durell charged again. Carter gritted his teeth and ran to meet Durell with his fists hammering, ducking blows, sidestepping, smashing a crazy combination of straights and hooks, then leaping to kick Durell in the head with both boots. Durell staggered as Carter landed, whirled low and leapt at Durell once more, grasping the large Nex in a bear hug and then hammering his head down, smashing his forehead into Durell's face time after time . . . Something broke, a tooth or splinter of cheekbone, sticking like a needle into the skin of Carter's forehead but Carter did not care, could not care as his savage and unrestrained onslaught continued . . . With a terrible high-pitched scream Durell threw out his powerful clawed arms and Carter was knocked back, staggering and slipping on the blood-speckled alloy. Out of the corner of his eyes he could see Jam battling, exchanging furious blows with the tiny figure of Mace who moved like a whirlwind, a bloodstained knife in each gloved hand, slashing and stabbing with deadly precision at Jam's armoured body . . .

Durell charged. Carter ducked a flurry of blows and rammed both fists together into Durell's groin, rolling away from Durell's pounding claws and rising into a crouch. Then he caught sight again of Jam and Mace moving in a blur, with Jam being pushed closer and closer to—

Carter frowned. What was that? Where the alloy deck fell away into—

'*A Gravity Displacer*,' said Kade gently.

Durell attacked again, snarling, saliva and blood spitting out as Carter connected with several more punches and danced out of Durell's reach. They were both fast, both powerful, but Carter had the edge: he was fighting for an entire planet, an entire *race*. And he was fighting for his son.

'Come on!' screamed Carter, his face a red mask, gleaming under the sunshine. He raised his fists, stained with both Durell's and his own blood. 'I will fucking beat you to death with my fists, you Nex cunt. I will rip out your fucking heart with my teeth.'

499

A cry echoed, and Carter's head slammed right. Mace had backed Jam towards the Gravity Displacer, with its treacherous steep slopes leading down to the dark mouth of the displacer itself. Jam had been kicked by a massive double blow and had toppled backwards, claws raking against the smooth alloy which screeched and tore in long jagged shavings of metal. Then he disappeared from view . . .

'No!' yelled Carter. Then Durell was there and a blow hammered into his temple, staggering him, and another heavy blow to the bridge of his already broken nose dropped him to the deck.

Carter lay there for a few seconds, panting, staring down at the black alloy veined with minute traces of silver. A pool of his own saliva and blood formed under his face, a slick mirror of crimson in which he could see a reflection of his own battered and broken features. His own eyes stared back at him, accusing him, and for once he didn't need Kade to fill him with horror, regret and shame. You are beaten, said those eyes.

You have given your best. You have fought hard – but ultimately you know, you recognise, you understand: the world is doomed, humanity is doomed, and you cannot halt the inevitability of fate.

Durell's damaged claws rolled Carter onto his back and he stared up at the terrible deformed visage. Durell was battered and broken too but he was also grinning and drooling, his slitted copper eyes staring down at Carter with contempt.

'See?' he hissed. '*See?*'

Carter coughed, spitting out blood. Then he focused. 'I see a face in need of a plastic fucking surgeon,' he snarled. His fist lashed up but Durell stamped on his arm, pinning it to the deck.

Carter turned his head and could see Mace looking

500

down at something. Durell turned, and Mace pointed. 'He is hanging on. He has dug his claws into the slope halfway down. Do you want me to finish him?' Mace tossed one of his bloodstained knives into the air, where it spun, shining darkly with gore before being caught neatly in the Nex's gloved hand.

A Nex approached at Durell's signal and handed him a Steyr TMP. Durell levelled the gun at Carter's face and looked down at him.

'What do you think, Mr Carter? You want your best friend, my best *creation*, to finally shuffle off his Nex coil? You can prevent this. You can prevent *all* of this.'

'By joining you?'

'Yes.'

'Why the *fuck* do you want me, Durell? What the *fuck* can I possibly offer *you*?'

'I want you,' said Durell softly, his voice barely more than a low, lilting croon, 'because of the KillChip.'

'The *what*?'

'Three seconds to decide, Carter. The Warhead is nearing its pick-up. We haven't got time for games. Your *world* hasn't got time for the playing of games.'

Carter stared into Durell's copper eyes. The Spiral man's face contorted in rage, his eyes sparkling with tears of frustration and a need for pure hot violence. 'Fuck you, Durell. I would rather die.'

Durell's head turned, and he nodded to Mace. 'Kill Jam.'

Mace smiled, a thin-lipped evil smile. 'My pleasure.'

Durell stared down the Steyr TMP pointing straight at Carter's face. He smiled sadly. And then he sighed a sigh of genuine regret.

'Goodbye, Mr Carter.'

CHAPTER 19

EVOLUTION

The earthquake rumbled. It took Africa in its fist and violently shook the entire continent like a dog with a bone; a Sleeper Nex with the corpse of a mutilated woman.

A Dreadnought used Gravity Displacers, but it was still linked to Earth by the force of displacement and the laws of displaced physics. So, as Africa trembled, so too did the Dreadnought, swaying violently as ranks of Nex shifted their positions, guns coming up for balance like tightrope walkers' poles as they attempted to stabilise themselves on the rocking, swaying alloy deck . . .

Mace threw his knife, but the quake nudged him and the blade glanced off down the sloped channel, raising sparks and then disappearing into the small black mouth of the displacer.

The quake put Durell off balance and Carter slammed a right hook into the stock of the Steyr TMP. Bullets chewed a groove through the alloy, ricocheting off as flattened sparking pellets. Carter lashed out, connecting as the Dreadnought shook again – and Durell took several steps back as Carter's fury returned tenfold. Carter climbed to his feet and launched a kick that sent the gun clattering across the deck.

'What is a KillChip?' he hissed.

Durell paused then, head tilting to one side as he surveyed Carter with an expression of concern. 'You are too late to stop the Warhead now, Carter. Soon, EDEN will start to detonate across the globe. They will *all* die. I am assured that it is quite painful.'

'*What* the *fuck* is a KillChip?'

'Ask it.'

'*What?*'

Durell smiled wolfishly as within the sloped channel leading to the displacer there came huge screeches of stressed alloy, tearing metal, the squeal of bending panels under the onslaught of heavy, violent claws . . .

Mace took a step back, readying his second knife—

And then the voice eased into Carter's head. The voice was cool, and soft. It reminded Carter of autumn days in a cemetery full of wind-blown brown and orange leaves; it reminded him of a cold grey neatly chiselled tombstone, smooth and sterile; it reminded him of the first dry rattle of soil on a freshly lowered coffin, his father's coffin, his mother's coffin, his brother's coffin, his lover's coffin.

'*I am a KillChip,*' said Kade in his mind. There was no arrogance there, no violence, no hatred; all the things that Carter had come to associate with Kade had vanished like morning mist under a freshly risen sun. There was just simplicity; there was just *fact*.

'*A Quantell Systems v2.1 KillChip Implant. I am a blend of organics and computing technology; when Quantell scientists created the original KillChip systems, it was found that genetic matter could stabilise unwanted side effects – the organic splicers allowed the human brain to accept the chip more readily, without sending the subject thrashing into fits of respiratory or coronary arrest. Several KillChips were tested on humans before the project was disbanded by the Quantell Division out in the Saudi desert. This project was originally initiated by Spiral.'*

'So you are a computer program?' Carter's internal voice held no emotion. He was unreadable.

'*I am an AI,*' said Kade gently. '*And my core mission is to kill. To make you kill. To turn you into a super-soldier, into the most fearsome warrior who ever lived.*'

'And that is why you kill women? And children? Why you take such fucking delight in the mutilation of human flesh? Of Nex flesh? Does it even *matter* to you?'

'*Yes. Women. Children. Puppies. Carter, they are just flesh and bone. They are just targets. I am AI – I have no emotions. I have a job to perform, and I do that fucking job well. You may cleanse the blackboard of your guilt, Carter. You were never to blame . . . I feed you, I take your pain, I push you on where others would falter. Carter, I am the best fucking mother you ever had. I am the best father you never knew. I am the best fist-fuck you could ever endure. I am the best cunt you will ever mount. I am your dark side. I am Kade.*'

From out of the displacer scoop came Jam, his claws bleeding from the tearing of panels, his slitted copper eyes swivelling in a frenzy to fix on –

Mace.

'You!' he breathed. Mace, now without his knives, turned towards the ranks of Nex as Jam pounded forwards, leapt and picked Mace up in his claws. Mace screamed then, a high-pitched insect shrilling sound as Jam's muscles contorted like huge coils of steel cable under glistening black armour. Carter frowned, watching open-mouthed, not quite sure what Jam was doing, what terrible force he was exerting until, suddenly—

Mace's body split in half at the hips, a loud *crunch* reverberating around the deck as down below the earthquake roared and once more the Dreadnought shook and rolled, its deck swaying and vibrating. Mace's body came apart, trailing his spinal column and long streamers of flesh, a spaghetti of veins and arteries and tendons, stretching and snapping as Jam threw both halves of Mace aside and away, to stand there flushed with dark gore, triumphant, drenched in crimson, bathed at last in his torturer's blood. In revenge.

Then his head came around to face Durell – and Carter's stunned, tensed frame.

Jam charged at Durell as Carter sank slowly to the deck on his knees, his mind whirling, pounding him with pain. The pain of Kade. The pain of the implanted KillChip. The pain of a million deviant memories. His hands lifted and he stared at them dumbly, and then covered his face as images flickered through his mind . . . scenes from Egypt, Belfast, the Siege of Qingdao, the London Riots, Poland Ridge, the Grey Death and the Tanker Runs, the Battle of Cairo7 . . . the Nex and the mercs he had slaughtered . . . blood on his hands . . . blood in his eyes . . . so much fucking blood . . .

Jam and Durell clashed. Claws slashed, and they pounded one another with a hundred blows until Durell suddenly whirled and slammed Jam down onto the alloy deck, which crumpled and dented under the sheer force of the impact. Jam vomited blood into a huge pool, and Durell grabbed Jam's triangular head between his clawed hands and heaved and dragged the ScorpNex across the deck towards the edge of the Dreadnought – and the distant drop to the vast rumbling landscape far below—

The earthquake had subsided a little, but still echoes groaned from the tortured world as rock ground against rock; as mountains shook and pulled viciously, impatiently, at their foundations.

'You thought you could fuck with me?' snarled Durell. 'Look what I made you! Look what I created! I gave you everything; I made you not just Nex, but ScorpNex – and you turned on me, you betrayed me, you betrayed what you had become.'

And then it came to Jam. Rustling in his mind, like old newspapers blown drifting across a concrete boulevard; like the rasping corpse-skin of a dried cadaver attempting to rise from the dead . . . they flooded into his mind, tiny black orbs watching him impassively as he fought to retain his strength and energy and power and identity, fought to retain his wisdom and intellect and emotion and concept and focus . . . his humanity.

we see you () see you
we see your acts () once-betrayer
() you be whole again
() we be one again () we be nex again
open the () door
() we can help you we can make you () free again
() we can make you strong again
() we will crush him we will give you back your () strength again
() strength to maim strength to () kill
() you will be pure nex one nex whole nex
you will be scorpnex
be scorpnex

'No!' Jam screamed, drool pooling from his twisted fangs. His head wrenched up, the rustling of insect wings reverberating around his hollow blended skull and he stared hard and true and wild with a bright intensity from his own copper orbs, his own Nex eyes, the eyes of the blend, the eyes of the tortured, the eyes of the suddenly *sane* and his head tilted to one side and his mouth opened in a bloodied snarl and he said . . .

'I will never be Nex.'

'No. You will never be one of our master race,' snarled Durell. He hoisted Jam into the air and, screaming viciously, he launched the huge ScorpNex over the edge of the Dreadnought deck . . .

Durell stood beside the vast sweeping drop, staring down, watching Jam tumble until he was nothing more than a tiny plummeting rag doll. Then Jam merged with the landscape, merged with Ethiopia, merged with all Africa . . . and he was finally dead, and gone, crushed and terminally fucked and finished.

What is wrong with them? thought Durell bitterly.

Why are the Nex turning against me? What went wrong?

And it came to him. In a flash of brilliance, like a lightning strike, it came to him. The Avelach. It was a corruption. It was playing its own game. It was using him. Abusing him. It was twisting him. It was serving some higher purpose of which he had no concept. He was a pawn. He was just a fucking *pawn* . . . and that was why Nex soldiers had been dying, disintegrating on the streets and in his laboratories under the Sentinel Towers. He was not in control – as it liked to prove to him.

The Avelach ruled him. The Avelach was his *master*.

Durell's face twisted into a snarl of self-contempt, and long trails of saliva drooled from his deformed Nex jaws. Then he turned to see Carter still on his knees, his face still covered by his blood-smeared hands. Alexis had emerged, flanked by more Nex soldiers. She gave a command, and the silent ranks of Nex brought their weapons up, eyes still staring straight ahead as they stood in their massive rigid column.

Another quake rumble echoed menacingly.

Durell, weary and broken, limped across the battered deck. He picked up Carter's Browning, turning it over in his dark clawed hands, examining the weapon's scars of battle. Then he moved back to Carter and stared down at the broken man.

'Will he join us?' asked Alexis, her hand resting on Durell's chitin.

'No.'

'Does he know?'

'Not yet. Carter – can you hear me, Carter?'

Carter looked up then, eyes red-rimmed, haunted, the guilt from a thousand murders threatening to engulf and overwhelm him. He climbed slowly to his feet and faced Durell. Then he glanced down at the battered Browning, and up again into the face of his oldest, most bitter enemy.

'You going to use that?' he croaked.

'Not yet.'

'Kill me, Durell. I am tired of this life. I am tired of this game. You were right about one thing, you ugly piece of shit: I was a pawn. From the beginning. But then, ultimately, in this life we are all pawns.' His eyes glinted. 'Even you, Nex. Even you.'

'There is just one more thing.'

Carter grinned then, a malevolent baring of his teeth. 'Oh yeah? You think you're going to improve my fucking day? You think I *care* what you have to tell me? Spiral used me as a fucking experiment: they turned me into the perfect soldier, the perfect killer – and then looked on in horror when I did what I did best.'

'Listen to us, Carter,' said Alexis.

508

He focused on her. His head tilted to one side. 'I'm listening,' he snarled through strings of saliva and blood.

'There are two reasons why we want you to join us. Why you *must* join us. One of those reasons is Kade – the KillChip. And the other . . . well, the other is . . .'

Carter raised his eyebrows. They arched over eyes that glittered with oceans of unwept tears – the tears of the fathers and the mothers, the brothers and the sisters, for all the murdered who lay rotting in the earth of the world's killing fields. For all the innocent. For all the memories of the *dead*.

'You are PureBreed, Carter,' said Alexis softly. 'You are PureBreed Nex.'

The Comanche powered through the pitch darkness, engines whirring, starlight flashing from whirling rotors as the aircraft banked.

The war chopper circled three or four times, pinpointing a location, and then dropped like a black bird from the sky and touched down in a cloud of rising sand. The rotors slowly thumped to a halt.

The cockpit canopy opened, and a lithe figure climbed wearily out to stand on the Angolan plateau. She moved forward, a sub-machine gun in one hand, a 9mm pistol in the other. Both weapons were matt black and invisible under the night sky.

Roxi halted, scanning the area, her NV sunglasses outlining her surroundings in a subtle purple hue. Then she dropped to one knee and touched the ground, rubbing her index finger and thumb together.

'Shit.' She pulled free her ECube, which opened in her hand. Digits flickered. They read, simply, **Mongrel vb486**.

'Bastard.' Roxi stood, surveying the rocky plateau

once more. In the darkness it was eerie and vast, and she imagined she could hear the distant sea, a crashing rush of surf in the gloom, pounding and retreating, pounding and retreating. There was no evidence of Mongrel's passing: no helicopter, no boot prints, no abandoned packs. Only a trace of dried blood on sun-scorched rocks. 'Mongrel?' she screamed. 'Mongrel, you there?'

Only the darkness replied with the gentle sounds of the night.

Roxi moved towards the edge of the plateau. Her NV glasses told her there was a vast drop ahead of her, but even by pumping up their enhancements to MAX she could see nothing over the edge – and nothing at the foot of the cliffs far below.

'Mongrel?' she called out once more, voice lower this time. More resigned.

And then, an internal dialogue:

– He's dead.

– You know it. In your heart. The old warrior, the tough mean bad tufty squaddie, the gap-toothed rump-slapping tattooed goat has finally bitten the dust.

– Mongrel: a victim of dog eat dog, politically incorrigible, a senile delinquent. Dead and buried in the rocks.

'Mongrel!'

'Down . . . fucking . . . here . . .' Roxi stared. Her breath caught in her throat. Her heart beat strongly against her sternum. She swept the rocky slope before her once again, enhancing the NV glasses through ten different settings . . . and there, a pale ghostly glow, caught in a rocky nook, lay Mongrel.

'I'll get some rope.'

'And some blood,' came the distant croak. Roxi grabbed her pack, tied two thin coils of steel rope to the Comanche's gear-winch and then tossed the coils from

510

the edge of the plateau. She slipped a hook onto her belt, adjusted her head torch, fed one of the ropes through the belt hoop, then leapt off the side of the mountain . . .

The rope hummed through her gloves as she walked down the near-vertical rock wall. Her boots found easy purchase on the rugged dry surface and she dropped a hundred feet to the narrow depression where the huge curled figure of Mongrel lay. There was no room, no rock platform on which she could stand so she secured the rope and hung there, swaying gently next to the huge wounded man, the light from her head torch illuminating the tiny notch that had caught him. Her eyes swept over his frame, and she reached out tenderly and touched at his shoulder.

'How you feeling, Big Guy?'

Mongrel shifted then, turning a little so that Roxi could see his bruised face. His skin was speckled in blood, a tiny amount of which had dribbled from the corner of his mouth. He was shivering violently.

He grinned at her like a dead skull. 'I has felt fucking better,' he whispered.

'Did you fall all this way?'

Mongrel frowned. 'No. I did fucking bounce. And tumble. And roll.' He coughed violently, dribbling more blood.

'You are one lucky son of a bitch!'

'I not dead yet.' Mongrel coughed again. Roxi reached forward and, dangling precariously, cut away his jacket and jumper and shirt with a tiny scalpel. Her skilled eyes read the wounds and she paled, mouth going dry.

'*Six* bullet wounds?'

Mongrel coughed, nodding, his face contorted in searing agony.

Roxi injected him with diamorphine, and the pain

gradually receded from his expression as his head lolled back, his mouth opening, a huge sigh escaping him. She cut away the rest of his clothing and surveyed the damage: two bullets in his right shoulder, one near his heart, two below his sternum, and one to the right of his belly.

I can't work here, she thought wildly. Not dangling halfway down a damned cliff! She pulled free a heavy-duty StapleG and said, 'This is going to hurt,' to which Mongrel responded with nothing more than a flutter of his drooping eyelids. Then she gathered his slippery, blood-slick skin under her gloved fingers and slammed staples into his flesh, closing the ragged bullet holes.

She tried to get her hands under his arms, but Mongrel was a huge man, topping twenty stone in weight, and she grunted with the effort as she tried to lift him. Finally, she looped the second rope around him in a makeshift harness, slapped his face to get his attention, and said, 'I'm going to have to winch you up.'

'Yeah, babe. I love you, Rox. You know that? This squaddie love your little nose.'

Roxi grunted something unintelligible, and started the climb back up to the Comanche with a growing sense of urgency. Six bullets! Six fucking bullets! The old monkey should be as dead as a plank of wood.

Reaching the top, she started the Comanche's winch and ran back to the edge, sliding down her own rope a little and taking some of the slack as Mongrel appeared from the darkness, arms and head thrown back in a state of unconsciousness.

Roxi used the winch to drag Mongrel across the ground to the Comanche. Then she laid him on a bedroll and covered him with blankets From her pack she took what looked like a tool kit and spread it out on the dust. The glitter of steel shone under her head torch's beam.

She checked Mongrel's BP, and found that it was dangerously low. 'You should be dead,' she muttered, shaking her head. She climbed into the Comanche, retrieving the emergency field-dressing packs and a small plasti-sack of universal O-neg. Then she tripped a switch inside the Comanche's cockpit – it would scan for movement in a one-kilometre radius. The last thing Roxi needed was the nasty surprise of ambush from behind as she worked . . .

Ripping free a cannula from sterile packaging, she inserted the needle into Mongrel's vein at the joint of his arm between a tattoo of a woman with ridiculously large breasts and a more smudged one of a comedy devil baring its little red arse to the world. Then she pulled free a spring-loaded plastic tripod and hung the O-neg, connecting the blood-giving set, priming the line and then turning the dial to establish a steady flow rate. That done, she gave him another injection of diamorphine, sprayed his wounds with antiseptic, and pulled free a tool which looked like a cross between a scalpel and a pronged fork. It was a StapleG remover; she sprayed the tool and, holding her breath, dug into Mongrel's flesh and worked free the first staple. Then she inserted a gleaming steel barrel and checked the blinking blue light. This tiny machine would locate and extract the bullet.

A droplet of sweat fell from the end of Roxi's nose, landing on Mongrel's serene but pale face.

'Don't die on me, you old bugger. Don't bloody die.'

It was an hour later. Mongrel was wrapped in blankets and Roxi built a small fire. She could hear the steady *beep* of the Comanche's scanners, and she checked her ECube for the hundredth time; she was using it as a secondary back-up scanner. The curse of her paranoia.

Out here, she felt so vulnerable, so alone.

'Rox?'

Mongrel coughed, pushing himself up onto his elbows. His grey face looked like a corpse's. His eyes were shadowed, and his tongue licked at lips that were desiccated and split.

'How you feeling?'

'Like whole fucking world fell on me.'

'You had six bullets inside you. I've managed to get five of them out, but the sixth is too close to your heart – I can't remove it here. You had one of your lungs clipped, but I've given you an internal staple – and that had to hurt. I've also stapled several ribs and your clavicle back together, although some of your shoulder blade is nothing more than mushed bone powder and needs serious surgery. Mongrel, you are one tough motherfucker. Believe me, you should be fucking dead.'

Mongrel grinned. 'Hey. You is looking at picture of testosterone. It take more than six bullets and fall off mountain to kill this squaddie!' He coughed again, mouth smiling but eyes haunted with pain and exhaustion. He climbed to his knees, and Roxi tried to settle him back down.

'What are you doing? You're not going anywhere!'

'Carter in trouble. World in trouble! We need be moving . . .'

'Oh no, no, look, you're tagged up to a pouch of blood! You think you're going to war with a bloody cannula in your arm? Be serious, Mongrel, you're down and out of the game – but at least you have your life, man. At least you can still breathe God's sweet air! As long as you don't try and do anything strenuous, that is!'

Mongrel climbed to his feet. He ripped the bag of blood from its little plastic tripod, opened a loop of plastic, and hung the bag around his neck so that it dangled,

like some huge crimson medallion, against his hairy tattooed chest. His torso was a mass of bruises, purple
discoloured patches of skin and joins of puckered flesh
where Roxi had diligently stapled his body back together
again. He breathed deeply, pain rippling through him like
an ocean swell as his eyes closed and he fought the nausea
of collapse.

'Come on. I have motherfucking big score to settle.'

'You're being stubborn and stupid, Mongrel!'

His eyes glowed in the darkness. 'You said I still breathing God's sweet air? Yeah . . . and I believe it for fucking
reason . . . it time for some payback, Roxi. It time this old
Mongrel finally made God proud of him.'

Carter stared at Alexis, his eyes hard. His unwept tears
stayed that way. Then he turned to stare at Durell.

'You think I am one of your kind?'

'Yes. You are the PureBreed. The original Nex, from
before these –' Durell half turned, a snarl on his deformed
features, hand sweeping across the ranks of the silent battalion '– before these *corruptions* came into existence. You
were one of the original Nex – one of those that worked,
a sweet dream, a crystal promise. But you were wild – too
wild, and we tamed you with the KillChip.'

Carter laughed savagely. 'You *tamed* me? So you mean
to say that *without* Kade I was even fucking *worse*?'

'Yes.'

'Get to fuck, Durell. This is nothing more than a ruse,
a bluff. Something like that . . . I would have known. I
would have remembered. I would have been *told*.'

'In the same manner you knew the true identity of
Kade? The fact that he was an AI living inside your head?
An *implant*? No, Carter, you were one of a squad – the
original *Nex* DemolSquad, part of an elite Spiral unit who

hunted down the most dangerous terrorists of our time. You worked outside the law, outside the military. It was your squad who single-handedly assassinated the FBI's ten most wanted criminals. You brought death and destruction to the evil men of the world. But you don't remember that, do you? You don't remember those days of savage bloodletting?'

Carter gave a little shake of his head. 'How far back does this go?' His voice was nothing more than a whisper; belief no more than the width of a razor's edge away.

'You remember your brother? Jimmy? And the bridge? And what you did to those other children afterwards? Glass, Trigger, Johnny Jones? And Crowley? Do you remember that?'

'I did nothing to those children. I was only twelve years old!'

'You murdered them, Carter. You slaughtered them like pigs in their beds. You were uncontrollable. You were driven *insane* by the murder of your blind brother!'

'And you call *this* sanity?'

'I call it purity,' said Durell. 'You are Nex PureBreed. You are a true representation of what the Nex could be – could aspire to. All other Nex you see around you, they are corrupted, twisted half-breeds. If you came with us you could help us, we could make the Nex pure again. You are unstoppable, Carter. They called you the Butcher, but nobody *truly* understood.'

'Yes,' said Carter, nodding. His mind was raging. Hatred danced in his eyes like fire. 'Once again, you would use me as a pawn. Well, I am fucking sick. Sick to my heart. Sick to my core. I am nobody's slave. I will not join you, Durell. The Nex are *wrong*, Durell. The Nex are a corruption of what man should become – and I will not be a part of its continuation. Of its *contamination*.'

516

Durell sighed. He held out his clawed hand, the one without the gun, in a gesture of friendship. 'Come back to us, Carter. Please come back to your oldest friend. I miss you, Carter. I miss you.'

'You *miss* me?'

'Yes. I miss you. I miss the good times.' And Carter looked into Durell's eyes and saw there in those slitted copper depths – saw the vision of a tall, dark-haired man, incredibly handsome, a powerful and athletic figure who—

CRACK

was leading the squad down a dark alleyway as the group were suddenly ambushed from all sides, machine guns blazing, grenades exploding, as the five members of the nex squad sent sub-machine gun bullets yammering through the dark saudi street as—

CRACK – pain

the terrorist, writhing in agony under his boot – come here carter, come here and hold him – and carter held him as durell smiled and pulled free his gleaming, shining implements of tor- ture – now you're going to tell us where the hostages are, fucker – you're going to weep like a baby – fuck you, I will never speak – durell smiled, handsome face turned into a demon's by the flickering fires of the burning hotel, you will tell us everything, he whispered, a promise of pain to come . . .

CRACK – a smash between Carter's eyes –

over here, get the fuck over here and they were running, along the battered booming alloy panels towards the docked submarine – guns fired after them in the dark shadowed bay and carter whirled, seeing the red star of russia stark and bright against the matt black flanks of the sub, and durell arrived with feuchter close behind and carrying the bulging satchel of explosives and – and he smiled, eyes fixing on carter as with an injection of grim black humour he said, are we having fun yet? and he grinned that famous witty durell grin . . . the one they all loved . . . the one they all trusted implicitly . . . with their lives . . . with their hearts . . . with their souls . . .

CRACK

panting, blinking, bright light

the bright sunlight of

Africa.

Carter opened his eyes. Looked up into Durell's.

'You remember?' asked Durell softly.

'What happened to you?' said Carter.

'I became greedy. Sought too much power. Too much strength. I was betrayed – by The Avelach.'

'It did not betray you, Durell. You betrayed yourself.'

'Maybe. But now you could come back, we could be a unit again, be the old DemolSquad – the original, the first, the best DemolSquad. What do you think, Carter? I'm not a bad man – I just want what is best for the world. Best for mankind.'

'You mean best for the Nex.'

'Like I have already said, the Nex are an evolutionary stepping stone. You can help us take it one step further. You can help us take it to the stars.'

Carter considered his options. Then, slowly, he spat in Durell's face, a precise and deliberate movement. 'No.'

Durell's hand of friendship fell away. He lifted Carter's Browning but Carter did not flinch. He stared down that barrel and beyond, into Durell's eyes.

'I am going to kill you,' said Carter, voice soft, face falling into a deadly mask of serenity.

'You cannot.' Durell smiled. 'The KillChip contains my DNA. My RNA. We are linked, Carter. We are linked . . . and if you kill me, then the KillChip will slowly disintegrate. I will no longer be there to hold it in place.

The KillChip will gradually dissolve, will release itself like an acid into your brain, will poison you like a fast-growing tumour that will torture you over the coming months – before eating your head from the inside out. To kill me, Carter, you must, ultimately, kill yourself.'

Carter considered this.

The Browning's dark-eyed muzzle remained unwavering.

'By killing you, I kill myself,' he said musingly, eyes gleaming. And he smiled then. Understanding flooded him. Filled him. 'That is a sacrifice I am willing to make. Kade? You there, my friend?'

'*I will always be here, brother. Until the day we both die.*'

Carter stared into Durell's eyes. 'Kill this motherfucking piece of shit.'

Kade smiled in the hollows of Carter's mind-tomb.

'*Your wish is my command.*'

Carter fell, plummeting into a world of black and white. And yet it was different. It had changed. It had *all* changed. Euphoria flooded him. The world spun to a standstill. And Kade was there, looking out from *his* eyes, and the black and white flickered, was flooded with colour as Carter—

Carter *breathed*.

The air smelled like rose blossoms. His limbs were weightless and awesomely powerful. His vision had true clarity.

There was no pain. All his injuries had faded into a gentle, throbbing pleasure.

'We are one,' said Kade.

'We are together,' said Carter.

'Brothers of the soul,' said Kade.

'For ever,' said Carter.

519

Carter's hand slammed out, so fast that the movement could not even be called a blur. The Browning fired once, the bullet skimming off over the motionless Dreadnought and hitting a Nex soldier's head, producing a spray of blood mist.

Carter leapt forward fist and elbow ramming into Durell's face with an awesome double impact Durell staggered back on skittering claws Carter's boot came down on his armoured kneecap with a crunch as Durell screamed a high-pitched scream as Carter took the Browning from his limp hand and jumped high into the air whirling spinning coming down with an elbow smash against the crown of Durell's head and slamming the falling bleeding Nex face first into the deck.

Carter stood over Durell, Browning in one fist, staring down with a snarl of contempt. Kade, within him, revelled in this joining, this merging and blending of ultimate hatred, ultimate force. Carter levelled the gun.

Durell stared up.

'You could be so much more,' he said.

'No,' said Carter, shaking his head sadly. 'I am happy with what I've got.'

Carter started to fire, bullets blasting from the Browning's barrel and punching holes along Durell's armoured chest and throat. Durell scrabbled at the wounds, his high-pitched insect keening rising to an awesome shrill pitch. More bullets entered Durell's head, cracking chitin, burrowing into flesh, eating into the brain beyond, popping one slitted copper eye until the gun's firing pin clicked and Carter stared down at the mess of mangled flesh below him . . . at the – amazingly – still living, breathing and *thinking* body of Durell.

Durell rolled over in the spreading pool of his own blood, and started to crawl. Carter followed, leaving boot prints in the congealing mess. All around, the ranks of the Nex were emotionless, unmoving, guns held low.

'Why do they not fire?' asked Carter.

'Because you are PureBreed,' said Kade.

'But they have tried to murder me before!'

'That was before,' said Kade. 'This is a battle for supremacy. This is a war between generals. This is the deciding factor, the final, finishing blow. They want you, Carter. The Nex – well, they want you to lead them. They want you in charge. They want you as the ultimate general. They *love you*, Carter. Can you not feel it? Can you not feel their pride? Durell was a deviation; but you, you are the real fucking thing. You are the PureBreed. You can do no wrong.'

Durell had reached one of the Gravity Displacers and Carter stood just behind him as Durell rolled over, wheezing, single remaining copper eye glaring at Carter. He started to laugh then, bubbling pulses of blood and phlegm spraying up and out.

'You have killed us both,' he croaked.

'We all have to die.'

Carter stooped, took a firm hold on Durell's battered shell, and hoisted him onto the slope of the Gravity Displacer. Durell slid and rolled, out of control as his clawed limbs flailed. But in a final twist of irony, as he was sucked towards the Gravity Displacer – he could not defy gravity. He slid, kicking, a wail rising from his shrill lips until he impacted with the mouth of the machine and it crushed him, compressed his bones and flesh and his shell in a snapping, crackling instant. The Gravity Displacer folded him over and over into himself; it compressed him down unto infinity.

And then Durell was gone.

Carter stood there, panting. He turned slowly, looked

521

around at the hundreds of Nex soldiers before him. They stood, immobile, but now every single one of them had fixed its stare on Carter. Slowly, as one, and on some unbidden command, they lifted their Steyr sub-machine guns and laid them against their chests with a unified *clack* that rattled out across the Dreadnought's deck.

Carter stared as Alexis crossed to him, the only sound now that of her smooth footsteps on the deck. She saluted him, meeting his gaze. 'What do you require, sir?'

'I want to stop the EC Warhead. I want to stop the delivery of EDEN.'

'We can do that. The QIV is below decks.'

'*Wait . . .*' hissed Kade.

'What is it?'

'Talk to me,' said Kade. Carter moved away from Alexis, from the army of the Nex until he stood at the Dreadnought's rim, gazing over and out and down at the expanse which had swallowed and pulped Jam.

'You are standing on the edge of the world, boy,' said Kade softly. 'You are standing on the brink of a revolution. You are poised on the brink of an *evolution*.'

Carter frowned, his mind swimming, and a mild pain began to throb at the centre of his brain.

'Your point?'

'You have it all, Carter. *We* have it all. Power. Glory. Ultimate power, ultimate glory. You have Durell's war machine. You have Durell's empire. You have the fucking *world*, Carter. You can do what you want, go where you want, fuck who you want . . .'

'I could do all that *before*,' snapped Carter.

'We are kings,' said Kade, simply.

'I don't want to be a king,' said Carter. But the pain was growing, piercing him, radiating out with a pulsating inner force. And then he realised . . . it was Kade, pushing him pushing him and with shame he felt his weakness consume him, overflowing him like lava and it swamped him, Kade swamped him, and colours flickered and extinguished one by one by one by one like fireflies slowly exterminated by an all-consuming velvet darkness until all that remained was a terrible and frightening—

black and white.

Kade grinned with Carter's face. He turned to Alexis and she moved towards him. Kade tilted his head. 'When will the Warhead and its many brethren deliver the payloads of EDEN?'

'Multiple strikes will begin in ten minutes,' said Alexis softly, her eyes shadowed, unreadable.

'Good. Allow them to continue.'

Kade folded his arms, nodding to himself and surveying his army of Nex. Then he turned, and looked down over Ethiopia. Over Africa. The place where it had all started. The place where mankind had been born . . . where mankind had *evolved*.

'And the place where it will all end,' said Kade. 'The battleground where man will take his next steps forward on the road to evolution.' With Carter's eyes, Kade stared out over his country.

His world.

His dominion.

'What fun we will have,' he said sweetly.

CHAPTER 20

PUREBREED

Bob Bob hammered both levers forward together and the battered Spiral HTank surged across the rocky landscape, tracks crushing small trees and shrubs, rocks and sandstone, engines howling. Behind the lead HTank, in a huge scything arc, followed fifty supporting ones, accompanied by Spiral SP59s and SP64s, their single, twin and triple guns gleaming in the blazing sunlight.

Ahead, the Dreadnought loomed against the sky, oppressive and dominant, an eerie totem of a world gone mad. Bob Bob scratched unconsciously at the stains of dried custard on his combats, then turned to his gunner, a man named Teeth – huge and black, with gleaming oiled biceps and a twenty-four-carat smile. The man wore his hair in a spiked Mohican which rubbed expensive hair lacquers against the inside paintwork of the gun turret. Bob Bob shook his head in dismay at this display of vanity.

'Are those choppers here yet? We need aerial support!'

'They're coming, mate,' said Teeth, with a big golden grin. Even as he spoke, the thump of hundreds of rotors swept overhead. Bob Bob checked his scanners, sweat crawling down his neck under his itching military-issue khaki shirt. The remains of the Spiral chopper squadrons filled the sky like a dark plague of insects.

An SS532 Cougar swept low over Bob Bob's lead HTank, and incoming signals initiated the attack. There was no time to wait, the EC Warhead was on its way: EDEN was on its way, and the world was teetering on the brink of extinction . . .

'Here we go,' said Bob Bob with a final grim smile that had little to do with humour.

'And about bloody time, mate,' snarled Teeth.

They surged forwards on matrix exhaust. Ahead of them Nex tanks swarmed from compounds beneath the shadows of the suspended Dreadnought. Small black attack choppers swept down from the skies and all of a sudden the world erupted into explosions and machine-gun fire, into rockets and missiles and the *krump* of shells. Above, a group of selected Comanches peeled free and headed for the Dreadnought with Nex combat choppers in close pursuit.

Bob Bob focused ahead on—

A Nex HTank, uncloaked and charging directly towards him. 'You got that fucker?' snarled Bob Bob.

'I'm on it,' said Teeth, grinning.

The HTank bucked on shrieking suspension, twin barrels firing shells across the rapidly closing gap. The Nex HTank was suddenly consumed in twin explosions and kicked backwards and up, trailing streams of molten metal as thick black plumes of smoke and incinerated Nex boiled out of it.

'Bingo,' said Teeth.

'Bingo?'

'Howzat!'

Bob Bob groaned. It was turning out to be a really *bad* day.

The skies around the Dreadnought NGO were swarming with choppers – Comanches and Apaches, Black Hawks, Mangustas, Havocs, Merlins – guns blazing and rockets leaving trails of fire across the heavens. Choppers ploughed downwards into the ground, rotors scything like huge razors across the swarm of infantry that came behind the pounding barrage laid down by the tanks.

Ed squatted behind a static, rumbling 8x8 FukTruk, a kilometre behind the insanity of the front-line action, breathing the huge vehicle's sour fumes and staring at the digital pad on his lap. He watched with satisfaction as the bastard Nex were drawn towards the battlefront. The Nex were primarily assassins: ruthless killers, heartless efficient murderers. But as soldiers they were not in the same league as Spiral.

Ed traced several patterns with his tattooed index finger. And he watched as five covert squads on the other side of the Dreadnought began their slow advance on the Nex base.

Ed crossed his fingers.

He stared up at the sky.

'Come on, Lord. Just give us this one chance. Just give us this one final shot!'

After being captured while supporting Carter in London, Ed had been brutalised and tortured by the Nex and placed in a cell with other captured Spiral operatives. This small group of hardened fighters had made an extremely explosive and violent exit from their prison cells, killing with their bare hands and stealing weapons before blasting their way to freedom and meeting up with other DemolSquads fighting for the same cause. And as the world shit had started to hit the fan, so Ed had been drafted into the front ranks of this, the final battle . . .

The retired old soldier had done what he had said he would never do.

He had gone back to war.

Ed stared at the digital representation of the battle-field. He stared down at thousands of tiny dots, each one representing a living, breathing, dreaming, hating, loving human being. He grimaced. This was no game, no simulation. Warfare wasn't something that could be conducted from a keyboard.

Eddie stroked the pad. He sighed, and tracked the advancing covert squads.

'One shot, Lord. And then I'll leave you alone. Please let me get what I want, Lord. I don't need a future of continuous and eternal world domination. I'll just close my eyes and pray for a future without this. Without war.'

ON AIR

SCENE: A large airy studio tastefully decorated in orange and blues; three long settees at gentle angles to one another around a central table fashioned from a single slab of onyx, on which stand a purple jug and crystal glasses which catch the studio lights and glitter. The rear of the studio is taken up by a huge plasma screen which currently displays a plain black backdrop.

ENTER Sonia J to ecstatic applause as **TITLE MUSIC [5.2/ vol7]** plays and gently fades to a backdrop **[vol3].**

Sonia J is dressed in torn and ragged combat clothing, and she carries a Steyr TMP 9mm sub-machine gun, currently in a battered and dented condition and with a spare magazine duct-taped to the stock. Sonia J moves to the centre of the TV studio and stands, eyes filled with tears, staring straight into the camera. The newly hijacked audience fade to silence. They stare in shock, horror and surprise at the former TV presenter they thought was dead; a previous 'traitor' who had been horrifically executed by the World State as a REB and – ironically – as a terrorist.

SONIA J: Welcome to this forced entry to HIVE Media and what will probably be my final broadcast across the globe – ever. Yes – I know – you thought you saw me executed on live TV for my supposed terrorist exploits and cooperation with the REBS. Well, yes, I am a part of the REBS. That much is true. But as for my execution? I am still here. I am still whole. And I am fighting alongside my brave comrades in a bloody and violent war against the *traitor* of mankind: Durell, his insect-blended Nex soldiers, and the money-fuelled mercenary kill-squads known as JT8s.

AUD [volume enhance 5.8+ through 6.8+ through 9.8]: . . . silence

CAM2 [zoom]: close-up of Sonia J's weary face.

SONIA J: The truth is, you have been lied to. The truth is, you have been abused. The truth is, you have been gratuitously misled and misrepresented. It was Durell, he of Nex-kind and currently your World State leader, who launched the nuclear strikes which terrorised the globe five years ago . . . and then he followed it up with multiple strikes of the biological weapon HATE. This supposedly made huge tracts of the world uninhabitable. You saw the pictures on TV, you saw the bubbling corpses out in the fields, on the lanes, in the desert, out on the ice . . . and yes, HATE did exist – but only on a modest scale. You were conned, my friends.

You were herded like cattle into the cities – ready for the next stage of Durell's great plan. The ChainStations. Durell created the Dreadnoughts, and then the first ChainStation, with the aim of evacuating the planet. But not for you – not for the people. No. His intention was to clear out his Nex kind . . .to give him a clear shooting gallery to launch EDEN. A newly designed biological toxin that was touted as a cure for the out-of-control poison that was HATE . . . There would be no opposition to the development and launch of EDEN because it would be presented as a cure for a vastly over-exaggerated toxin which you believed riddled the world with its poison. But, believe me, when this EDEN poison is launched there will be no survival of the fittest, the meanest, the toughest, the slickest . . . there will be absolutely no escape from the *extinction* Durell wants to impose. He wants us out of the way, my friends. He wants you to become a Nex . . . or die, to make way for his new version of mankind, his new version of humanity. Even as we speak, missiles containing this poison are in flight. We have only hours until detonation. We have only hours until the missiles strike . . . and the world becomes a barren desert, a biologically poisoned wasteland. A world wiped free of man. A world ready and waiting with open arms for its new half-breed child – the Nex. They're all in it for the glory, the power, the domination, the resurrection, the extinction; they're in it for the chance to murder, to hurt, to execute, to dominate, to slaughter, to massacre, to kill, to kill, to kill. They want us all gone – they want us all dead. But don't take my word for it: here is a representation of what EDEN can do, followed by digvid of what it is truly capable of : . . .

CAM12:
1] A complex series of molecular structures rotating then merging to create a new chemical: EDEN.
2] A chamber full of men and women: EDEN is released and they all collapse like bowled-over skittles in an instant, with blood leaking

from mouths, noses, eyes and ears.

3] A large hall containing perhaps six hundred men, women and children; a single droplet of EDEN is allowed to fall from a pipette and before the droplet hits the ground the entire crowd hit the floor instantly, with blood leaking from mouths, noses, eyes and ears.

4] A series of outdoor experiments in natural environments; EDEN is released on a tube train, in a tower housing block, in a supermarket – all with the same catastrophic and instantaneous results.

SONIA J: None of these events were ever recorded or shown on the news. That is because Durell controls the media; he controls the world; he controls YOU. Now is the time to rise up. Now is the time to retake your freedom. Don't just take my word for it . . .
[Nex file into the studio; they form a ragged line behind Sonia J and as one they rip free their masks showing a host of facial deformations from beneath those masks, and haunted, glowing, copper eyes.]

SONIA J: Many of the Nex are turning against Durell. Many are sick of his promises. He calls it evolution – but the Nex say the insects speak in your mind, they torture you with threats and promises. What happens when your thoughts are not your own? What happens when your thoughts are those of the insects with which you were genetically blended? You become *un*human. You become *non*human. You become something less than human, something less than insect, I think. The sum of your parts becomes an inferior. Yes, you have improved physical strength and immunity, but you take on a savage inner battle. You inherit an inner war. We need to put an end to this farce. We need to put an end to this war . . . before Durell puts an end to our race. Once and for all.

CAM12:

530

Textscroll [1/r]: Unreleased SmashVID footage . . .
1] Nex slaughtering innocent protesters in the streets, Steyr guns
firing as bullets chew meat and bone from faces and flesh chunks
slap at the cold cobbles of the roadway . . .
2] JT8s kicking a pregnant woman to death while a crowd of people
stand around, faces averted, trying hard not to look at the savagery
unfolding before them . . .
3] A screaming Mig998 swooping low over the streets of Dublin,
missiles detaching on glowing trails of blue energy, flames roaring
and engulfing the peaceful march of five hundred placard-bearing
innocents . . .

SONIA J: We're all so frightened. We need to change.

CAM2: fades to black and white

EARMIC: That's all gone out, Sonia. Globally . . . and you fucking
know I'm going to get fucking sacked, right? Yeah, a *great job*.
How to cause a fucking *world riot*. Now, can somebody please
take this sub-machine gun out of my ear? Hey . . . hey, I did
what you asked, right? What do you mean, I've been
perpetuating a hate campaign against humankind? I *am*
humankind! What do you mean, I'm a stupid motherfucker? Hey,
if all stupid motherfuckers received the death penalty, then we'd
have a serious population decline on our hands, now wouldn't
we? Wouldn't we? Oww, that hurts, hey, get that fuc— **[cut
earmic]**

**CAM4: [drops to the floor and zooms out without music/fade to
black]**

AIRTIME: BREAK
CAMS-CUT

Throughout oppressed cities all over the world, men and

women and children started to rise from their mental and physical slumber. Those who had not witnessed the broadcast soon learned of its savage contents. In many countries, the Nex made pre-emptive strikes – attacking known dissidents, suspected REBS, even people who had been involved only in peaceful protests and marches: they murdered them in their beds, leaving trails of splattered blood as evidence of rough justice for all to see. But this time it did not eliminate the problem: within hours these hundreds, maybe thousands of murders fuelled a further and sustained belief in the rightness of Sonia's revealing global media broadcast.

Units were quickly formed, schools and churches and supermarkets turned into centres of command from which to hit the Nex, the NEP Nex Production Plants, the WarFactories and the Sentinel Corporation Tower blocks. The world was rising up against the Sentinel Corporation, against *Durell*, against oppression. Every day people were taking up arms and fighting their way out of tyranny and subjugation, with only the truth as a guiding light propelling them onwards; with only their human hearts driving them forwards to a necessary and violent confrontation . . .

There were battles in the streets. Helicopters dived from dark skies, mowing down charging civilians. Stolen tanks hammered shells into WarFacs, detonating the stores of ammunition and igniting hundreds of tonnes of HighJ and plastic explosives. Soldiers fought hand to hand, JT8s were slaughtered by orphaned children throwing rocks, Nex were gunned down by women with pistols, and machine guns were mounted on the back seats of battered family saloon cars that had had their roofs removed.

Anarchy had arrived.

Chaos had risen.

Carter stood on a plateau, a flat section of black rock, with a towering black mountain above him. Beyond stretched a world of dark graphite sand. The sky spun away for infinity, streaked with trails of purple and yellow.

Carter blinked.

There was a fire burning in a ring of rocks, and Carter looked around him. But he was alone. There was no Kade. There were no enemies. Carter was trapped in the prison of Kade's holding cell. Carter was locked in Kade's AI. Carter was incarcerated within his own brain.

'You little fucker,' he snarled.

He spun round once more, boots kicking up dark sand on jagged rocks. He ran to the edge of the plateau. Its slope fell away for a long, long way until it levelled out and stretched off over undulating dunes. Carter breathed deeply, then closed his eyes.

'Come back to me,' he said.

A cold wind mourned from the mountains, hollow and desolate.

'Come back to me!' he screamed.

But Kade had gone.

Carter moved to the fire, glancing down into the flames. They were flickering between states of orange-red and glistening black. Carter sat down on the rock that Kade had always used as a seat, and stared into the fire.

What game is this? he thought.

And how do I drag the fucker back? How do *I* get back?

Years earlier, he had argued with Kade in this very place. One day I will find you, Carter had said. One day I will find you and we will fight and I will kill you.

Carter frowned.

How to summon the devil?

How to summon the AI who had taken over his body?

Carter grinned then, leant forward, and plunged his left hand into the flames . . . Pain screamed through him as the fire scorched his skin, which peeled back, black and blistering, the stench of burning flesh rising up as an element of the smoke from the fire – which now burned a steady glassy solid black.

'Fuck you!' screamed Kade.

Carter withdrew his hand, a crisp and blackened claw, and stared up at Kade standing rigid before the fire. Carter stood, slowly, cradling the scorched limb to his chest as he looked deep into Kade's dark eyes.

'Welcome to my fire.'

'Fuck you, Carter. That was a cheap trick.'

'You have something I want.'

'What, the power and the glory? Or maybe you want to suckle on that Alexis, taste her fine Nex insect cunt. That's my destiny now – you are just a dream in my fucking head. Stand back and let me through, or I swear—'

'You swear, Kade?' Carter smiled. 'What will you do? What *can* you do? Once, I stood here and I said I would fight you, and kill you. You said that it would be interesting . . . that you would welcome the day. Well, that day is here.' Carter unfolded his scorched hand with crackles of burnt flesh. Pain pounded at him in waves as Kade looked down, eyes wide, horrified.

'Not now, Carter. This is the *wrong* time . . .'

'There will never be a right time,' snarled Carter. 'This needs to be done. A score I should have settled a long fucking time ago.'

Carter charged through the fire, flames licking up at his boots as he leapt at Kade. Kade stumbled back, throwing out a series of punches that Carter blocked easily against his forearms.

'No, Carter, no!'

With a hiss, Carter hammered a right straight into Kade's face, followed by a right hook which shook his dark twin. Carter powered a right kick that connected with Kade's chest, sending him stumbling back once more. Carter stalked forward, and Kade grimaced and counter-attacked, throwing a blur of punches, hooks and straights, jabs and double-fisted smashes. Carter blocked them all, ducking and sidestepping, his face serene, his stare locked on Kade . . . and suddenly Carter grabbed his nemesis, pulling him in close so that their eyes were only inches apart.

'I want my *body* back!' he spat.

'Come and take it,' said Kade darkly.

Carter slammed his forehead into Kade's nose, and Kade howled like a haunting banshee. Again Carter head-butted his demon twin, again and again. Then he lifted Kade's head up by both ears, released it and, before it could fall back, smashed both his fists down against his adversary's temple with one terrible bull-hammer blow that slammed Kade straight down onto the rocky ground, where he groaned, curled up like a foetus.

Carter moved forward, stamping first on Kade's groin, then on his chest, then on his nose.

'That's for the people I didn't want to kill.'

He took a step back, then made a short run and delivered a massive kick to Kade's head. Kade rocked under the impact, blood spraying from shattered teeth.

'And that's for the fucking Alsatians in Egypt. You fucking *know* how I love dogs.'

Kade had curled further into his foetal ball as Carter stooped, pulling out a long, slick dagger. He moved to stand over Kade, and the dark demon looked up then, eyes glittering with black gloss tears.

'Don't kill me, Carter,' he whispered.

'Why not?'

'I am you.'

'You are a fucking AI. Which means that your tears are not real. Just numbers on a static digital disk.'

'Don't kill me, Carter. I can help you.'

'How?'

'I have information.'

'About?'

'About your past. I can give you back your past. All those moments you have forgotten . . . the time with Durell and Feuchter and the others, when you were in the Nex DemolSquad. *The first Nex squad.* I can give that back to you. I can supply your history. Your memories. Your *life.*'

Carter smiled then, and stooped, sheathing the knife. He stared down hard at Kade, who whimpered, rolling in pain and spitting out tiny pieces of broken tooth.

'Always the fucking negotiator, eh, Kade? Don't you *ever* take my body without my permission,' he said, voice low, tone dangerous. 'You will never get a second chance. I will never let you live again. You understand me?'

Kade nodded, submissive.

'Now stay down, little doggie.'

Carter blinked, and the dark mountain plateau shrank and swirled, dissolving like sand sucked down the neck of an hourglass. He opened his eyes to sunlight and the worried face of Alexis. He breathed deeply, and looked down at his left hand . . .

There were no burns.

Carter flexed his fingers thankfully. Below he could hear machine guns firing and tank guns booming.

Aircraft screamed overhead while missiles detonated with deafening roars. War was raging.

Armageddon was here.

Carter turned to Alexis. 'Take me to the QIV,' he said.

They moved down a ramp and through a wide corridor lined with computers and cables. Beneath their feet rattled metal grilles that revealed another level, and levels beyond that as they fell and dropped away for many metres below. Carter stared down, entranced. He could see perhaps forty floors, and it made him feel giddy.

'This is the control room.'

They entered a huge chamber, full of the highest-grade products of computing technology; many large black control screens lined the walls and stood on independent pedestals. Several of the screens showed flickering bright images; one displayed a representation of the Evolution Class Warhead.

It was hammering low over an ocean, and the vision panned out to display a thousand newly birthed missiles following like children. All were laden with the high-grade military anti-human poison called EDEN. These were the ECW's brood. Its molecular creations. Its offspring.

'It has replicated?' asked Carter slowly.

'Yes. It has created its own army of warheads. That is why this machine is so intrinsically dangerous. It's not just a simple bomb that hits a target and detonates. This is a machine created to wreak death and destruction on a truly global scale.'

Carter moved to a small alloy case on a desk. There sat a dark cube which glistened with frost. Carter stared at the QIV processor – it was identical to its previous incarnation, the QIII. The processor that he had destroyed. That he had *killed*.

'Well, well, well. Can you tell it to halt the ECW?'

'You are in control,' said Alexis softly. 'You may tell it yourself.'

Carter stared at the processor. 'I am Carter,' he said. 'I want you to halt the Evolution Class Warhead.'

The QIV hissed softly.

On the screen, the army of missiles slowed their incredible speeds and finally halted. They hung, suspended over the sea, rotating slowly. The camera panned round, then withdrew, zooming out to show the vast glittering army of missiles – finally *stopped*.

Carter looked around at Alexis.

'I want the Nex to stop their battles, to halt their war,' said Carter. 'I want all Nex to withdraw. No more people are to be killed. We are cancelling the plans to evacuate the planet. You can do that?'

'We are in the command centre,' said Alexis. 'We can do anything.'

'Do it,' said Carter.

Alexis moved away, talking to several Nex at the huge banks of computer consoles. A hundred screens sprang to life, showing the global battle between Spiral, REBS, JT8s, Nex and the normal, everyday people who had risen up against this incredible threat . . .

One by one, Nex armies started to withdraw. In New York, a crowd of attacking people suddenly went quiet as a strange silence washed over them. The Nex had lowered their guns. Tanks had ceased their shelling. Jets and combat choppers roared off, leaving the skies empty of battle.

Carter took a deep breath.

And noticed the QIV processor. It had changed, a subtle alteration as it became a deep glossy black under its crystals of ice. Carter frowned, licking at his dry lips.

What's wrong with it? he thought.

What's it *doing*?

Carter slowly released the empty magazine from his Browning. It clattered to the floor, and he slotted home a fresh one. He stared hard at the QIV processor, remembering the earthquakes, remembering the nuclear strikes, remembering the millions of people it had helped to destroy.

'You little *fucker*,' he snarled, and stepped towards the cubic CPU with his Browning 9mm HiPower outstretched.

'I wouldn't do that, Carter.'

Carter froze. The voice made the hackles rise up on the back of his neck. Goose bumps ran along his arms and danced down his spine. He felt as if a ghost had come back to haunt him. A really *bad* ghost. Something from his deepest, darkest nightmares.

Carter turned slowly with a tightening in his chest, his gaze coming around to fix on—

The Priest.

The Priest wore his robes and his rosary beads and carried his small battered Bible in one hand. In his other hand he held his Glock 9mm and it was pointing at Carter's head.

'Tell me that you have come to stop this madness,' said Carter.

The Priest shrugged, giving a small smile through his thick beard.

'Tell me you have come to halt the Nex.'

'The Lord guides me,' came The Priest's deep and booming voice, and he took a step closer to Carter. Then he turned his head a little, and said, 'Alexis, please command the Nex to resume their battles; to continue with their attacks. Man must *learn* his place. And instruct the

539

QIV to release the Warhead and its subsidiary missiles. I want Detonation to begin in eight minutes.'

'Yes sir,' said Alexis, and moved back towards the command panels.

'I thought *I* was in control,' snapped Carter. 'I am the PureBreed.'

'You are *one* of the PureBreed,' said The Priest, his eyes flashing dark and dangerous. 'As am I. You are not in control, Carter. Just like Durell, you are my subordinate. You are my *pawn*.'

'*You* are in control? The religious maggot? The insane, the inept, the Bible-quoting lunatic who has haunted Spiral from before I was fucking born? *You* are in control of all this?'

'Yes. I am sorry, Carter, truly I am. I am a good man. A man of God. I never meant for it to turn out this way.'

'So you are the same as me? You are Nex?'

'I am PureBreed,' said The Priest, 'and like you I carry a KillChip in my skull.'

'So we are evenly matched?'

'It would appear that way,' said The Priest darkly.

'You never used to be like this,' hissed Carter. 'You worked with us – against Feuchter, against Durell. I saw it – with my own fucking eyes I saw it!'

'People see what they want to see.'

'You led us to this, didn't you? You organised the betrayal of the SpiralGRID. You were the mole communicating with Durell. You betrayed Spiral, you motherfucking little worm!' Carter thought back to his every moment with The Priest, his every meeting, his every spoken word. It had been The Priest who organised the missions – led Jam to the K-Labs, Carter and Mongrel to the ECW. And all the time it had been an elaborate set-up. Carter felt dead and cold inside. This

540

was the ultimate betrayal – and Carter had been a blind man. 'What happened to you?' he whispered, his head shaking sadly. 'You were our friend. You were our ally. You fought with us against this burden of evil.'

'I have always battled for the right cause.' The Priest's gaze burned with sincerity.

'When did you turn? When did you decide to work with Durell?'

'After we found The Avelach,' said The Priest. His voice was soft now. Reverent. 'It showed me things, Carter. It showed me *incredible* things. It showed me another world. It showed me another life. It showed me *another God*. It showed me how we *could* be. It showed me how it *should* be.'

'And you would exterminate the human race?'

'You are looking at this through a distorted lens, Carter. I do not intend to *destroy* humanity. I intend to *evolve* humanity. We *will* build a new Eden, Carter. We *will* start again: with a purity of purpose, and the Will of the LORD!'

'This is not the Will of God,' snarled Carter. 'This is *your* will. These are *your* goals. The Will of Man.'

On the screens, the Warhead resumed its mission, accelerating out over the ocean with awesome speed.

'Mankind is an abomination,' said The Priest, his Glock still locked on Carter's head. 'Look at us! Just look at the world, Carter. Look at the rapes, the violence, the murders. Look at the terrorism, war, genocide. Mankind is an expert at the creation of suffering. There is so much hate, my son, so much badness, so much cruelty. The apple is rotten, and has fallen from the tree to the ground where it merges with the dirt and is eaten by the worms. We need to begin again, Carter. We need a clean slate. The Avelach can do all this. The Avelach has shown me the *light*.'

'Yeah, and how long before it turns bad again, Priest? How long before you inflict your own brand of suffering? How long before the corruption starts to gnaw away at the roots? Can't you fucking see? This isn't about hate and violence and wars . . . that's just what Man is. He is a predator. A hunter. A killer. We are a race of violent motherfuckers – born and bred on violence; weaned on hatred; suckled by the poisoned milk of evil. You cannot wipe the slate clean and begin again, because the results will turn out the same – it will just take longer. At best, you will secure a postponement of our natural evolution leading straight towards extinction. Priest, as a race we are destined for extermination. We are destined for Armageddon. We are a doomed species. We are a creation of an insane God. We are simply destined to die.'

'Join me, Carter. Cleanse the world with me. Purify our brethren. Become a *god* with me. The Avelach has promised me this. The Avelach has *shown me the future*.'

Carter laughed, a cold and brittle sound. 'You want to play God? You are a fucking hypocrite, Priest. After all these years, that is the last thing I would ever dream you would say. Why don't you just drop the Bible and piss on it right now?'

The Priest's eyes flashed with lightning. 'I can see there is no convincing you.'

'You're damned fucking right there, Priest. I would rather die.'

'That can be arranged.'

Slowly, Carter had lifted his Browning as he was speaking, and now both men had their guns trained on one another. The atmosphere in the command centre was electric, charged with violence.

Carter breathed out through clenched teeth, and he could see The Priest doing the same.

This was the calm before the storm.

The eye of the hurricane.

With a scream, Carter launched himself forward, Browning blasting in his fist, to be met by The Priest, his own gun blossoming with bright yellow fire—

And below them, the world slowly turned.

The Comanche, piloted by Mongrel, hammered across the skies. From below, anti-aircraft fire shot up towards them on streamers of tracer. Mongrel, face grey and drawn with pain, exhaustion and loss of blood, banked the war machine as bullets rattled along their flanks.

'Damn and bloody bollocks!' hissed Mongrel.

'Mongrel! Not in front of the child!'

'Sorry, I truly sorry,' said Mongrel. He glanced over his shoulder to see Joseph smiling at him.

'My dad always said you swore a lot, Mr Mongrel.'

'He did?' Mongrel's face brightened a little.

'Mongrel, that's not a *good* thing,' Roxi chastised him.

'Oh.' His face fell.

'The Dreadnought is approaching – fast.' Roxi pointed past the huge squaddie.

More anti-aircraft fire raced past them, and the Comanche's alarm systems rang shrilly. Mongrel, muttering in Russian, banked hard again as engines howled in hot metal agony and the Comanche wobbled.

'Your piloting skills are awesome,' observed Roxi, dryly.

'I has improved.'

'You should have let me pilot the damned thing. You've lost a lot of blood.'

'No! I have old scores to settle. You see. You be glad. You learn, young lady!'

Bullets rattled along their flanks once more, and Mongrel winced. 'Sorry!' he wailed.

543

'Just get us down onto that block of alloy in one piece, will you? I haven't come this far through life just to let some half-dead squaddie with a faked photocopy of a pilot's licence ruin it all because he couldn't tell a mobile anti-aircraft gun from his own stinking armpit!'

Mongrel frowned. 'Hey! I is not half dead! I does resent that impli—implic— ... damn. I does resent it, anyway.'

'Well, act like it, then. Look – that scanner shows SAMs, Stingers and K7s. Shit, Mongrel, fire the tracers, fire the fucking tracers!' She leant past him and punched the console as, far below on the Ethiopian plateau, missiles started their upward thrust towards the Comanche.

More bullets clattered against the combat helicopter.

And up ahead, three black Nex choppers hung in the sky, waiting for the fast approach of the enemy Comanche. Guns flared as they opened fire, and Mongrel forgot his pain, forgot his bullet wounds and clamped his few remaining teeth together as he realised that he was outnumbered, outgunned, and had three rockets attempting a violent and illegal rear-entry manoeuvre ...

'Just not this juicy *pizda's* lucky day,' he groaned, and swept forward with a rising howl of damaged engines into the waiting hail of dark Nex bullets.

Carter's bullet skimmed The Priest's cheek, opening a long line in the flesh like a zip and revealing white bone beneath. The Priest's bullet slammed into Carter's shoulder, burrowing through skin, fat and muscle and lodging nastily between his clavicle and scapula. They slammed against one another, guns clattering across the floor of the command centre, and The Priest head-butted Carter on the nose as Carter's right hook slammed against the older man's temple.

They spun away, blood flowing from both men, then leapt at one another again with a flurry of heavy connecting punches. Carter smashed a straight and a hook into The Priest, but the huge religious man absorbed the blows without apparent affect. Carter leapt, booted feet connecting with The Priest's chest, but the huge man twisted, one arm slamming down against Carter's shins as The Priest swung, flinging Carter to roll across the deck. The Priest strode forward as Carter climbed to his feet and they went at it again, punching and kicking, slamming blow after blow into one another. A sudden left uppercut from Carter sent The Priest stumbling backwards from the control centre and into the wide corridor. Nex who were there suddenly halted, stares turning to fix on the raging battle.

Again Carter slammed his fists into The Priest's face, and they grappled for a moment, blood soaking Carter's shirt. Suddenly, he hooked fingers in the flap of skin on The Priest's cheek and wrenched downwards to tear a huge gaping hole in the barrel-chested man's face.

They parted, Carter holding a ragged flap of bloodied skin.

'Make a nice handbag, this,' he said.

The Priest glowered at him, face holed, eyes burning with insanity. 'And I was with you in weakness, and in fear, and in much trembling. And my speech and my preaching was not with enticing words of man's wisdom, but in demonstration of the Spirit and of the Power! That your faith should not stand in the wisdom of men – but in the power of God! Behold, Carter. Behold! I *am* that God!'

Carter threw the flap of skin at The Priest, and it landed with a soggy squelch on the grille floor to drip thick blood globules through to the lower levels. 'You bleed pretty good for a god, holy man.' Carter raised his fists. 'Come here – let me show you how easily a god can fall.'

They squared off and approached one another warily. Again, Carter's punch was the first to connect, and for a few moments the bloody smash and hammer of fists drove The Priest backwards down the computer-lined corridor and onto the bottom of the ramp leading up to the Dreadnought's surface.

The Priest hit the ground with a grunt, blood pouring from his battered face. Then he turned and scrambled up the ramp, disappearing into the sunlight above.

Carter sighed. 'These fuckers will just not stay down.' He moved warily up the ramp, out into the African sunlight; The Priest was waiting for him, backed by hundreds of armed Nex.

'Come and taste God,' hissed The Priest, and charged.

They connected, Carter slamming punch after punch into The Priest's face; The Priest launched a kick, but Carter blocked it with a downward blow, then smashed his elbow into The Priest's face. The Priest rolled, knocking Carter from his feet, and then stood with his face a demon's mask of crimson, smiling down, chuckling, showing absolutely no signs of pain, or discomfort, or weariness.

Carter blinked—

And saw the gun in The Priest's hand.

Carter breathed out slowly, gaze fixed on the dark eye of that gun and then lifting to meet The Priest's gold-flecked brown-eyed stare. Triumph danced there, shone in those bottomless depths.

'Why, Priest? Why? I thought you were Spiral. I thought you were on our side. I just don't *understand*.'

'I can see the bigger picture, Carter. Whereas you – well, you only see a tiny part of the puzzle. There is a time to keep silent, and a time to speak – a time to love, and a time to hate. Now is my time to hate, Carter. Now is your time to die.'

A scream hammered from behind Carter, wind forcing him down against the deck as something huge and black smashed into and over his vision, a titanic fury that howled scant inches above his prostrate body making his ears scream and his head pound and ripping all breath from him . . . The Comanche, travelling at over two hundred kilometres an hour, slammed into The Priest, front landing gear crumpling and crushing to push the war machine's nose down heavily onto the deck with a screech of tearing steel and showering sparks. It skittered along, tail sweeping around in a broad arc and sending Nex soldiers sprinting for cover, and then slowly slid to a halt at the end of a long red smear of liquid, pulped Priest.

'If you're going to preach, then preach. If you're going to kill, then kill.' Carter smiled a real nasty smile. 'And amen to that, holy man. A-fucking-men.'

The cockpit canopy creaked open, and Mongrel heaved his patched-up body out onto the Dreadnought's deck. The armoured rotors finally thumped to a halt, and Mongrel grinned over at Carter, then moved round to the front of the Comanche and attempted to peer underneath, limping and wheezing with pain.

Carter climbed to his feet, and followed the long red smear to the ticking, clicking, hissing Comanche. Mongrel gestured with his thumb at the mangled crush where the remains of The Priest were wrapped partly round the mini-gun, partly around the twisted landing gear. The head, apparently, had gone.

'I think I could have managed softer landing,' he said.

'No, no.' Carter smiled, slapping Mongrel on the back and making the huge squaddie groan in agony. 'I think you did just fine, my friend. Ten out of ten. You deserve a fucking Blue Peter badge.'

'Sorry I took so long. Had a few little . . . *complications*.'

'Believe me mate, you arrived *just* in time.'

Mongrel glanced at the red mush that The Priest had become. 'I think we not have problems from *that* cunt again. I think *that* cunt gone to meet his maker in a bin bag! And I ain't talking about no pearly gates, mind you, but the old hot-sulphur-under-foreskin kind of welcome! You digging The Mongrel?'

Carter frowned, giving Mongrel a strange look. 'You OK? Lost a lot of blood, have you?'

Mongrel grinned. 'It finally does look like Lord decide Priest was expendable. After all, not every day somebody drop helicopter on your head! The Lord does indeed work in mysterious ways!'

'Daddy!'

Joe ran out, followed closely by a heavily armed Roxi. He fell into Carter's arms, and Carter held his son for long minutes, smelling his hair and his skin, feeling the warmth of love that spread through his every atom. Then, finally, he glanced up at Roxi, at her glittering green eyes, and she smiled, winked, and blew him a sultry slow kiss.

'Joe, wait here with Rox. We have one more very important thing to do.'

Mongrel tossed Carter an H&K sub-machine gun, and the two men limped back down the ramp and into the control room; the battered leading the bruised. Carter pointed his gun at Alexis, but she shook her head, hands lifting in modest supplication.

'Stop the Warhead,' Carter spat.

'I already have,' she said, and pointed towards the screens. They showed an array of missiles floating on the ocean, a huge gathering of metal debris. 'I have sent Nex soldiers to pick them up; to destroy them.'

'Why they floating?' said Mongrel.

Alexis turned, and pointed to the QIV processor – or, at least, the smashed remains of the QIV processor. Carter and Mongrel stared for a moment, then Carter looked back at her.

'They no longer have a control source,' she said. 'The QIV destroyed the original Warhead's AI; it took complete control of the machine sentience. Without the QIV, the Warhead has no guidance. Without the QIV, the Warhead has no *life*.'

'Why did you do that?'

'It deserved to die,' Alexis said.

'It should never have been born,' snapped Carter.

'Yes.' Her stare fixed on him then, a deep and questioning look. 'There are many among us who had already turned against Durell; we were tired of his exaggerations, of his blind vision, of his *lies*. I allowed Roxi to take your son from the Sentinel Tower. I covered for her; I protected your little boy.'

Confusion flooded Carter's mind. He took a deep breath, and nodded. Words would not come to him. He did not know what to say.

'What would you have me do next, PureBreed?'

'PureBreed?!' choked Mongrel, but Carter's mean stare cut off any thought of progression with that well-loved Mongrel humour. Mongrel chewed at his own tongue with his stumpy teeth, trying not to express the myriad of jokes which inundated his mind.

Carter stared into Alexis's eyes. Then he *focused*. Now he understood; now he knew what he had to do. 'I want you to evacuate the Dreadnought immediately. There is a package I must deliver.'

'Hey,' said Mongrel, nudging Alexis. 'You know, your

lot and our lot, we need to learn to live together! As big family, no? An int— . . . an integ— . . . a big mixing pot of Nex and human, eh, love?'

Alexis reached over, and kissed the huge soldier gently on the cheek. 'I think that is a battle for another day,' she said, her copper eyes glowing. They walked from the command centre, boots crunching across shards and splinters of the shattered, broken, *destroyed* QIV processor.

The Comanche touched down gently on a high ridge of jagged rock, and Carter helped the wounded Mongrel out onto the rocky mountain top. Roxi and Joe followed. In the distance the final choppers were howling through the skies as they fled the dying behemoth of the Dreadnought.

Joe came to Carter and gave his father a big hug. As they held one another, there came a series of distant detonations in quick succession. This was followed by a distant groaning, a mammoth meshing of metal with metal, and the Dreadnought slowly and majestically tipped at one end, and fell gradually towards the Earth two kilometres below.

As the Dreadnought connected with the ground, it seemed to fold in upon itself, compressing and crushing under its own titanic weight. A noise like the destruction of planets blasted out from the merging of ChainStation BCB module and the Earth as a great cloud of dust and rock rolled up into the sky and billowed out in a huge, expanding mushroom cloud.

Fire erupted then, a kilometre-high column of bright purple laced with silver and green, a huge towering inferno of flame that burned the sky and pointed an accusing finger at God . . .

'Over. Carter, it's really over, ain't it?'

'Yeah, Mongrel, it's over.'

'Oh. Good.' Mongrel beamed weakly, clutching at one of the bullet wounds in his chest and the red-soaked pad there. His face was pale with exhaustion. 'Hey, Carter, you want to finally hear that story? Fat Chick Night?'

'Not in front of the boy, Mongrel.'

'Ahh. Ahh. Yes, I see what you saying. Maybe later, then.'

'Yeah, Mongrel. Much, much later.'

Carter stood, staring at the destroyed Dreadnought, watching the rolling billowing desert and staring at the pillar of fire connecting the sky to the African continent. Roxi came up behind him and placed a hand gently on his wounded shoulder.

'You OK?'

'I'm OK,' he sighed. 'It's just been a long fight.'

'But now it's done.'

'Yeah, now it's *dead*.'

'Shall we go home?' Her gentle words were filled with a promise.

Carter stared over into Roxi's bright green eyes. 'You mean the three of us?'

Roxi ruffled Joe's hair. 'Yeah. The three of us.'

'That would be good.' Carter smiled and, reaching across, kissed her warm soft lips. 'That would be *really* good. Like you could never imagine, my love.'

A few minutes later, the Comanche leapt into the sky, banked, turned its tail on the devastation left by the dying Dreadnought – and cruised steadily across the endless blue.

A GENTLE STROLL
ON KADE'S MOUNTAIN

With the world still in uproar, Carter led his new family back to the UK, where they ripped the boards from the doors and windows of his old house in Scotland and allowed fresh air to infiltrate the dusty interior for the first time in half a decade. It took them a week to clean the place up and make it liveable. When they had finished Carter bought himself a bottle of genuine Lagavulin and sat, after lighting the wood-burning fire, staring out of his old window at the snow, breathing the scent of wood-smoke and watching the distant peak of Ben Macdui. For a long time he replayed the past. He became a victim of nostalgia, but did not really mind. Now, finally, he had a lot to be thankful for.

After the attack in Cyprus where Samson, Carter's faithful chocolate Labrador, was shot, the old Spiral woman Mrs Fickle, gnarled and ancient but with the strength of ten men, had come across the wounded animal. She had taken the whimpering dog back to her own cottage, removed the bullet and stitched the wound the old-fashioned way. With a tenderness that belied her outwardly brutal appearance of gun-toting, psychopathic granny, she had slowly and carefully nursed the dog back to health.

Mongrel had regained his full health after his bullet traumas at the hands of The Priest, had married Constanza and now headed one of the newly formed Spiral units whose aim was to re-establish world order and help with the building of new governments. On his stag night, he had faithfully retold the story of Fat Chick Night to a gathering of sixty-four inebriated men – including Carter, who sat in a drunken haze in the corner with his shaking head in his hands as Mongrel's voice boomed over the crowd. The story involved Mongrel, a *Twilight Zone* series of events that led to every single woman in every public house in the *entire town* on that particular evening being at least a generous and bouncing size 18 and having breasts like melons, a subsequent encounter with thirteen drunken fat women out on a hen night who all took a shine to Mongrel and insisted on him sharing their communal bedroom – and an ensuing night of intense debauchery that would have made the Marquis de Sade blush. When questioned on his persistent choice of ample-framed ladies, Mongrel had himself blushed like an English rose and delivered the immortal statement: 'Fat women best. I tell you, plump lady crème de la crème, they truly beautiful ones, because you never short of handful!' Mongrel had chundered away all night. His final words, before he passed into a drunken Guinness-stained coma on the sticky bar-room floor, were the words, 'I now revised. Is true. Mongrel finally improved in moral fibre. Mongrel new Weetabix. Little Mongrel no longer Wild Willy.' After the wedding, Mongrel went on a mission to plump out Constanza as best he could, successfully endured a series of chemotherapy treatments, and gave a hearty two-fingered salute to the prospect of death by cancer. His favourite phrase became 'Fuck that cancer.' And he did. Well and truly.

Mongrel and Constanza had fourteen children.

Across the globe, many of the old governments were re-established and peace descended like a gentle veil over the planet Earth. It appeared that *finally* humanity was sick of brutality and death. In a way, the Eden that both Durell and The Priest had so zealously sought was actually established. For a time, at least.

Sonia J created a brand new TV show called *Tales of Strength and Courage*, and took over the reins of HIVE Media with the aim of promoting the positive attributes of human nature. The programme became the most successful TV venture in the history of the planet.

Four months had passed since the end of Durell's reign of terror and insanity. After the first month, Carter had started to experience headaches which grew in intensity with each passing night. He deliberated long and hard on the cause, finally making an appointment to see a Spiral specialist. After various scans and X-rays, she informed him of an alien artefact near the centre of his brain. She told him it was impossible to remove. She told him that to remove this 'growth' would very probably leave him in either a vegetative state or, quite simply, dead. It was too deeply buried. It was too well *secured*. Carter refrained from telling both Roxi and Joseph about his pain, his worries, or the recent medical diagnosis. This was a burden he knew he must carry alone.

Spring was close by, but the night was dark and stormy, filled with the dregs of a wild and vicious winter. Carter had written the letter with an old fountain pen, under the light of a small lamp at his desk, sealed the envelope, kissed both Joseph and Roxi in sleep, inhaling their mingled scent with tears in his eyes, then gathered his pack and called Samson to him.

For weeks now Samson had been limping painfully and had endured several prolonged seizures. He had been prescribed phenobarbitone as a control medication, but Carter had been informed by the emergency vet that the old dog had serious liver and kidney problems – on top of his arthritic hips – and did not have long to live.

Carter walked down the steps which led to the front door of his house and Samson followed slowly, the steep descent giving his aged frame obvious problems. They stepped out into a cold bitter world filled with a violent raging wind, with driving ice-filled rain, and began their long walk through the darkness of the storm.

Several hours later saw them weaving up a stone path which led into the mountains. Occasionally Carter would stop, pain pounding at his head and stars glittering behind his eyes despite the powerful painkillers he had taken – and had been taking more frequently for the past few weeks now. Samson would sit obediently at his feet, wet fur plastered to his chubby frame, tongue out and faithful old eyes still bright and focused.

Another hour saw them reach the deserted cave, and they ducked inside to shelter from the heavy downpour. Samson slumped to the ground and started chewing at his paws, grey muzzle working at some annoyance between his pads as Carter stripped off his wet-proofs, kicked free his walking boots and set about lighting a fire.

With the fire burning at the mouth of the cave, Carter sat and looked out into the rain. It fell in vertical sheets, and nearby he could hear the rapid flow of a swollen stream. He could smell a heady perfume of pine and wood-smoke. Samson climbed to his feet, moved over to Carter and slumped beside the man, placing his huge head in Carter's lap.

'God, you stink,' said Carter, rubbing the old dog's ears affectionately.

Samson whined, panting and gazing up at his master.

'You been eating fish again?'

Samson lowered his head and closed his eyes.

'I guess so.'

Carter rested his head back against the cave wall. The heat from the fire felt good. The embers glowed hot within the ring of rocks, and with a shiver Carter remembered plunging his hand into that black fire on Kade's mountain . . .

The scorching of his skin.

The stench of his own searing flesh.

The peeling of cooked meat from bone . . .

After Carter beat Kade on the dark dust mountain, the KillChip demon had never returned. He had never troubled Carter with his unwelcome presence. It would seem that Carter had finally tamed the savage dark angel; caged him; broken him.

Winds blew into the cave, and outside the stream raged.

Carter spoke, voice hollow and booming as it reverberated from the cave walls. 'Was Kade the god in the machine? Or the machine in the god?' He laughed bitterly then. He would never know. He would never have the answers to all of his questions. But then, some things were best left buried.

Carter's mind drifted for a while, back over the years, back over his memories. But always his thoughts returned – returned to one simple conversation, one simple *confrontation* which had stayed with him, branded into his mind, and would stay with him until the day he died.

Durell.

Durell had said, 'The KillChip contains my DNA. My RNA. We are linked, Carter. We are linked . . . and if you kill me, then the KillChip will slowly disintegrate. I will no longer be there to hold it in place. The KillChip will gradually dissolve, will release itself like an acid into your brain, will poison you like a fast-growing tumour that will torture you over the coming months – before eating your head from the inside out. To kill me, Carter, you must, ultimately, kill yourself.'

And Carter's reply?

'By killing you, I kill myself. That is a sacrifice I am willing to make.'

Oh, how Durell must be laughing in his pit of despair now, thought Carter, smiling grimly. How he must be chuckling as I sit here with my head in my hands, watching his prophecy come true.

As dawn broke, so the rain ceased. Carter watched the sun rising over the mountains. He could smell the rain, and he relished the awesome splendour of nature unfolding on the game board in front of him.

Roxi and Joe would find his letter. They would understand.

Samson opened his eyes and gave a big dog yawn.

'We'll face this final journey together, hey, boy?'

Samson panted, and Carter rubbed the dog's soft ears as tentative fingers of early-morning sunlight reached into the cave.

Carter placed a pan of water over the flames of the fire to make coffee.

'We'll face it together,' he whispered, and Samson continued to pant, his eyes gazing out over the mountains.

A small, thin-limbed African boy, his rich ebony skin gleaming under the harsh noonday sun, walked warily along the dirt roadway, his gaze swinging nervously from left to right as he searched for enemies. He carried a gnarled stick which he beat against the edges of the verge, the feel of the wood comforting under his narrow, bony fingers. It would at least afford him a weapon if he was attacked again by the other boys.

He stopped, crouched beside some shrubs and thorn bushes, and drank a little water from the bladder sack he carried against his hip.

He suddenly froze as something in the sand to his right caught his eye; his heartbeat increased rapidly to beat a tattoo of drums in his chest.

At first he thought the object was a snake, but the hump – which was covered by a fine layer of sand – started to rock backwards and forwards in a slow, rhythmical motion. The small boy retreated to a safe distance, frowning, unsure now of what he was actually watching. He could see that the object was large and round, fuzzily defined, and it looked like an elongated football. Then he blinked as sand fell away and he thought he could see . . . hair?

Startled, the boy realised that it was a human head. He climbed to his feet and sprinted away down the road, bare feet kicking up flurries of dust as he hurried to tell his mother.

Behind him, the head rocked with a final violent spasm, and then rolled onto one side against the gentle slope of red dust. It was a head that stared with milky dead eyes, and a slack-jawed open mouth. It had a vicious tear where part of the dead-flesh cheek was missing – revealing a dark, rotting interior lined with yellow teeth. The severed head trailed tendons and a small section of spinal column. An army of large black ants crawled over the exposed and corrupted grey flesh; their private banquet had been rudely interrupted.

From inside the hollow cavern of the mouth there came a shadowy movement.

Something paused, halting at the opening behind the stiff and blackened tongue. And then what looked like a tiny corrugated insect crawled free. Its segments shone like oiled black metal, gleaming under the harsh sun; and it had copper eyes in a tiny, round, but unmistakably brutally insectile face.

It undulated across the head's sand-matted beard and leapt, burrowing down into the sand . . . heading down down down towards the Sleepers in The City. And it left no traces behind it; no evidence of its metallic, copper-scented, parasitic habitation.

for everything there is a season
and a time for every matter under heaven

a time to be born, and a time to die
a time to plant, and a time to pluck up what is
planted
a time to kill, and a time to heal
a time to break down, and a time to build up
a time to weep, and a time to laugh
a time to mourn, and a time to dance
a time to throw away stones, and a time to gather
stones together
a time to embrace, and a time to refrain from
embracing
a time to seek, and a time to lose
a time to keep, and a time to throw away
a time to tear, and a time to sew
a time to keep silence, and a time to speak
a time to love, and a time to hate . . .

a time for war, and a time for peace.

Ecclesiastes 3 1-8
The Bible

MARTIAN RACE

Gregory Benford

March, 2015, NASA's first manned voyage to Mars is about to launch.

But disaster strikes. The rocket explodes, killing the entire crew, and the US government abandons the project. What they come up with in its place will change the nature of space exploration for ever.

Businessman John Axelrod and his consortium have every intention of winning the $30 billion Mars Prize for the first successful mission to the red planet. He knows that it will involve far higher risks than the one NASA had planned. But he has no choice. He has to win.

The Martian Race has begun.

COYOTE

Allen Steele

EMBARK ON AN INCREDIBLE JOURNEY OF
COURAGE, AMBITION AND DISCOVERY

Forty-six light years from Earth, six moons orbit a
gas giant three times the mass of Jupiter. Each has
been designated a name from the animal demigods
of Native American mythology: Dog, Hawk, Eagle,
Coyote, Snake and Goat.

Only the fourth moon, Coyote, is likely to sustain
life. The crew setting out on Mankind's greatest
adventure know that the success of the mission will
depend on how well they adapt to their new home.
There is no going back.

But Coyote is also known as the trickster.

NYLON ANGEL
A Parrish Plessis Book

Marianne de Pierres

In a future where the rich live behind the safety of a giant fortress-wall and everyone else can go to hell, Parrish Plessis has learnt some useful survival tactics. Like don't cross Jamon Mondo – unless you want to be dead by morning.

But what's a girl supposed to do when a very real chance of escaping his sordid clutches presents itself? Even if it means cutting a deal with the amoral gang-lord Io Lang, and sheltering two suspects in the murder of media darling Razz Retribution. Lang is renowned for being way beyond the border of psychoticsville, and the media always gets bloody revenge on anyone foolish enough to mess with their own – it's good for ratings. But Parrish is sick of doing what she's told. She's tooled up, jacked full of stim, and tonight she's going to take her chance.

Nylon Angel is the first Parrish Plessis novel. She will be back. When you've met her, you'll understand why.

SHADOW WARRIOR

Chris Bunch

THE EPIC SPACE ADVENTURE TRILOGY
IN ONE BLISTERING VOLUME
FROM THE MASTER OF MILITARY SF

The Great War is over. The last pockets of resistance
long eliminated. For many, the alien Al'ar are now
little more than a memory.

But there is one man who cannot forget: Joshua Wolfe.
Friend, prisoner, then betrayer and executioner of the
Al'ar. To humans he is a hero, a legend. To the aliens
he is the Shadow Warrior, master of the arts of killing.
And his story has only just begun . . .